A Study in Cloud Formations

CLARK GUIRE

First edition
Paperback ISBN: 978-1-7358648-0-8
Ebook ISBN: 978-1-7358648-1-5
Library of Congress Number: 2020918759

Illustrations by Ashley Santoro
Cover art by Ashley Santoro
Published by Jessica Clark

I'm dedicating this book to those who have been hurt, lost and afraid. 1017

Acknowledgement

If you or someone you know needs help with grief, abuse or suicide never hesitate to reach out. Thousands of people suffer everyday, please know that you have a choice. You deserve the world.

National Domestic Hotline
Hotline: 1 (800) 799 – 7233
Available 24 hours a day, 7 days a week via phone and online chat. The National Domestic Violence Hotline (The Hotline) is available for anyone experiencing domestic violence, seeking resources or information, or questioning unhealthy aspects of their relationship.

Pathways to Safety International
Hotline: 1 (833) 723 – 3833
Email: crisis@pathwaystosafety.org
Available 24 hours a day, 7 days a week via phone, email, and online chat.
Pathways to Safety International assists Americans experiencing interpersonal and gender based violence abroad.

Gay, Lesbian, Bisexual and Transgender National Hotline
Hotline: 1 (888) 843 – 4564
Youth Talkline: 1 (800) 246 – 7743
Senior Helpline: 1 (888) 234 – 7243
Email: help@LGBThotline.org
Hours vary, available via phone and online chat.
The LGBT National Help Center serves gay, lesbian, bisexual, transgender, and questioning people by providing free and confidential peer support and local resources.

Womens Law
Email hotline: https://hotline.womenslaw.org/
The WomensLaw online helpline provides basic legal information, referrals, and emotional support for victims of abuse.

Rape, Abuse, and Incest National Network (RAINN) – National Sexual Assault Hotline

Hotline: 1 (800) 656-4673
Available 24 hours a day, 7 days a week via phone and online chat.
RAINN (Rape, Abuse & Incest National Network) is the nation's largest anti-sexual violence organization. RAINN created and operates the National Sexual Assault Hotline (800.656.HOPE, online. rainn.org y rainn.org/es) in partnership with more than 1,000 local sexual assault service providers across the country and operates the DoD Safe Helpline for the Department of Defense. RAINN also carries out programs to prevent sexual violence, help survivors, and ensure that perpetrators are brought to justice.

National Human Trafficking Hotline
Hotline: 1-888-373-7888
Text: 233733
The National Human Trafficking Hotline is a national anti-trafficking hotline serving victims and survivors of human trafficking and the anti-trafficking community in the United States. The toll-free hotline is available to answer calls from anywhere in the country, 24 hours a day, 7 days a week, every day of the year in more than 200 languages.

National Runaway Safeline
Hotline: 1 (800) 786 – 2929
Email: info@1800runaway.org
Available 24 hours a day, 7 days a week via phone, email, forum, and online chat.
The National Runaway Safeline provides crisis and support services for homeless and runaway youth in the United States.

National Center for Missing and Exploited Children (NCMEC)
Hotline: 1 (800) 843 – 5678
Cyber Tipline: http://www.missingkids.com/gethelpnow/cybertipline
NCMEC serves as a clearinghouse and comprehensive reporting center for all issues related to the prevention of and recovery from child victimization.

ChildHelp National Child Abuse Hotline
Hotline: 1 (800) 422 – 4453
Available 24 hours a day, 7 days a week via phone and text.
The Childhelp National Child Abuse Hotline is dedicated to the
prevention of child abuse. Serving the U.S. and Canada, the hotline
is staffed 24 hours a day, 7 days a week with professional crisis
counselors who—through interpreters—provide assistance in over
170 languages. The hotline offers crisis intervention, information,
and referrals to thousands of emergency, social service, and support resources. All calls are confidential.

National Suicide Prevention Lifeline
Hotline: 1-800-273-8255
Available 24 hours a day, 7 days a week via phone and online chat.
The National Suicide Prevention Lifeline provides free and confi-
dential support for people in distress, prevention and crisis resourc-
es for you or your loved ones, and best practices for professionals.

National Alliance on Mental Illness (NAMI) Helpline
Hotline: 1 (800) 950 – 6264
Email: info@nami.org
Available Monday through Friday, 10:00am to 6:00pm Eastern
Standard Time.
The NAMI Helpline assists individuals and families who have
questions about mental health disorders, treatment, and support
services.

Substance Abuse and Mental Health Services Administration
(SAMHSA) Helpline
Hotline: 1 (800) 662 – 4357
Available 24 hours a day, 7 days a week via phone in English and
Spanish
SAMHSA's National Helpline provides free and confidential treat-
ment referral and information service for individuals and families
facing mental and/or substance abuse disorders.
https://www.thetrevorproject.org/
Hotline: 1-866-488-7386

Trained counselors are here to support you 24/7. If you are a young person in crisis, feeling suicidal, or in need of a safe and judgment-free place to talk.

TrevorText is a confidential and secure resource that provides live help for LGBTQ youth with a trained specialist, over text messages. Text START to 678-678.

Chapter 1 Sawyer
April 4th 8:47 P.M.

Incoming call: YaYa

Sawyer watched the phone vibrate, unable to get himself to answer it. Carter would whine at him to answer so she could talk to Wyatt, luckily for him, she was sleeping across two chairs, curled up with his sweatshirt draped over her. The phone stopped vibrating and it showed him the 7 missed calls from Wyatt. It wasn't long before the screen went black, showing the bright reflection of the fluorescent lights. The room had a sterile scent and it was surprisingly quiet for a Friday night, though his experience with ER's was limited. If he went by what he saw on T.V. then the place should have been packed with a bus accident and a possible but impossible victim that caused high-stress situations and made everyone scramble around. There were only 4 other people in the room, one group of 3 and a single person, who really didn't look like they needed urgent care. Maybe they were also waiting for news, the same way he, Carter and Lio were. There was a sick pull in his gut at the thought that they were waiting for the same news on the same accident. That his parents were the high-stress situation that had everyone scrambling around.

Sawyer gripped his knee tightly to stop it from bouncing, he heard the emergency door open but didn't look up. He tightened his grip, squeezing his eyes shut.

"Mr. Losada?" His head shot up with his eyes open. A woman in scrubs stood in front of him, giving him a weak smile that wasn't worth the effort. "I'm so sorry to tell you this, your father is still in surgery and we're doing everything we can to save him. There is a lot of internal damage and his skull was fractured-" She paused looking at him and then down to Carter and Lio in his car seat asleep next to him. "Is there an adult I can speak to?" she asked.

Sawyer's tone was less than polite when he spoke next. "I am an adult, just tell me."

"I'm sorry, your mother was unable to survive the surgery."

Sawyer stared at the woman. He hoped she wasn't as shitty of a doctor as she was at speaking to patient's families. He wanted to throw the adult question back in her face considering she only looked twelve. He was so focused on her that he barely registered the words she had told him until she was walking away. His phone vibrated again, this time he answered.

Wyatt's voice was annoyed when he spoke. "Dude, where are you? I'm at your house and the door was open, what's going on?"

Sawyer forced his voice into normalcy though it came off more strained than anything. "Oh, sorry I had them both in my hands and I tried shutting the door but it was hard and then I meant to go back but I just forgot once I got them in the car and-" Sawyer rambled. His voice suddenly cut off, his grip tightened on the phone. He squeezed his eyes shut and forced them open, he almost missed Wyatt speaking.

"Where are you?" His voice was a solid presence and Sawyer answered.

"The emergency room," Sawyer said in a breath.

Wyatt was quiet barely a second before he asked, "Why?" Sawyer struggled to answer dropping the phone to his lap, he looked back to Carter then to Lio. They were sleeping through his struggle, unknowing of the danger their parents were in. He lifted the phone to his ear again, it was silent on the other end, Sawyer spoke with a crack in his voice.

"My parents got into a car accident." He blinked at the bright lights, causing his eyes to burn.

He heard Wyatt's harsh intake of breath and when he exhaled he said, "Fuck, I'll be right there." Sawyer let his arm fall into his lap, not caring if Wyatt spoke again or if he hung up. He leaned back in his chair harshly, his body felt like it was being dragged down by cement blocks.

He couldn't even think of it as a nightmare, no dream to wake up from. He was too aware of the situation, the strange quietness of the room, the hard chair under him. The burning in his eyes from the lights, the slight burn in his nose from the sterile smell. Everything almost felt tangible and it was all coming down, crushing him into the hard white tiled floor.

Time was something that went far too slow and too fast for him to comprehend, the only thing that let him know time had passed was when Wyatt was finally standing in front of him. Sawyer slowly raised his head to look up at him, it was the only time that Sawyer had felt Wyatt was tall, too tall. He felt miles away and yet he was also too close, his knees were almost touching Sawyer's from where he stood. Sawyer was unsure if he needed space or comfort, he felt as if he was being pulled one way and pushed the other.

"Sawyer," Wyatt spoke and everything felt like it dropped. One word, his name, that voice. Sawyer stood from his rigid position on the chair, wrapping Wyatt into a tight hug. He ignored Wyatt's grunt when he squeezed tighter. It was in those few seconds that Sawyer felt like he could breathe. Then a nurse was walking

towards him. He was just barely shaking his head, hoping to anything that was holy that she wasn't coming to speak to him.

"Mr. Losada?" Sawyer pulled away from Wyatt, looking at a
different woman this time, similar scrubs. "We're moving your
father to the ICU, that's the-"

"I know what it is," he cut her off, his father had made it. He
was alive.

"I'm sorry, if you would like to move to the waiting room
there, we can inform you of any changes." She waited and then
with a nod from Wyatt, she was walking away, her steps like an
echo in a cave. Wyatt moved first, stepping away from Sawyer.
Sawyer shifted at the loss, Wyatt was carefully lifting Carter into
his arms, she shifted and whined until she was settled. Sawyer bent
down, gripping Lio's car seat handle tightly as he followed Wyatt
to the elevator.

Sawyer couldn't bring himself to ask about seeing his dad, a
nurse brought him papers to fill out about his mother. He did it almost mechanically, never really taking in the information on any of
the sheets. His handwriting was foreign to him when he skimmed
over the information. Wyatt was a silent presence next to him, every so often he would touch him or say something that would pull
him out of his spiraling thoughts.

"I think you should see him," Wyatt said. Sawyer shifted away
from him, no more than an inch but it felt like a mile.

Sawyer sighed,."Yeah," he replied. His limbs felt heavy when
he stood, carrying himself out of the room to the nurse's desk outside to ask about his dad. They told him the room number, allowing him to go past the metal doors. He moved through the hallway
slowly, stepping outside his father's door. It opened, shocking him
a few steps back.

"Oh, I apologize, I'm Dr. Menzel." Sawyer shifted his gaze back to the door and the doctor. It was barely a second, he had just opened his mouth to ask, when there was a flurry of beeps and movement of people and shouted words. He was pushed back as he heard and watched them try to bring his dad back.

His father had made it, his dad had been alive. Just one more second and he would have seen him. One more second and maybe… Sawyer clutched at his shirt, tears streaming down his face as he watched his dad's body lift off of the bed. As much as he didn't want to see, he couldn't look away.

Then the doctor was in front of him again, this time there was no surprise, no thoughts of hope. He had just lost his father and mother, hours apart on different days. He heard them call out the time, 12:04 A.M.

Sawyer didn't move, he didn't breathe. It was like he was watching an intense T.V. show that no matter how hard he pressed the button, it refused to change channels. Even if he closed his eyes, he opened them to the horror scene that had become his life. Death scenes were ways to make viewers feel something, it was to get them to care. Maybe it was even to get rid of an actor. Sawyer couldn't describe what he felt; as if he had pressed pause. Nothing moved, no one breathed, and it was fast-forwarding. There was no time to pause, no time to stop, everything rushed by too quick and too slow. Emotions were numbed and too strong. He felt as if he couldn't breathe but he had too much air. Like he was a concept of a person instead of actually being a person.

Chapter 2 Wyatt
Friday April 4th 5:48 P.M.

Wyatt glared at Zeke. He was already late and his parents wanted them to have dinner together tonight, so he was already going to be extremely late going to Sawyer's.

Zeke gave him a shrug from his wide shoulders, looking down at him, he said, "Don't get mad at me, you were late to practice this morning. You're lucky I'm helping you."

Wyatt didn't drop his glare, "Morning practices are bullshit, who has soccer that early anyway?"

"That's because you sleep like the dead, pretty sure you've been late to first period every day since school started, except when we have morning practices. Coach is probably trying to help your attendance records."

Wyatt dropped the glare, picking up another ball, he added it to the near-full bag. "School is over in a month, who gives a shit about that?"

"Two months. Why are you so pissed? Oh, do you have a date?" Zeke's face transformed into a grin.

"Fuck off," Wyatt muttered, leaning down to grab another ball.

"Wyatt has a date tonight!" Zeke yelled. Wyatt ran towards him, dodging a ball Zeke threw to stop him. When the ball fell to the ground, Zeke took off.

6:58 P.M.

Wyatt walked into his house, his parents were already at the dinner table. Their meals untouched, each of them on their phones. Wyatt took his place, where a plate was already full of food. They simultaneously set their phones down, they were always in sync with each other.

"Ji seok, perhaps you should shower before you eat," his mother said. It wasn't worth fighting her when she had that tone. He stood back up, heading to his room, he showered.

When he made it back to dinner, his steak was cold, his green beans were cold and his mashed potatoes were lukewarm. He ate without a comment, his parents looked at each other and his mother set down her fork after one bite of her steak.

"Your letters of acceptance have arrived, a list has been made of what you need to do with each of the choices," she said, as if reading off of a stilted script.

"A list of what?" Wyatt asked, continuing to eat because he knew she wouldn't let him get a word in once she got going.

"For admissions, the best apartments near campus, whether you should take your car or not, and so on. You can check them yourself. Now, your graduation is coming, which means the family will be coming. I need you prepared to help me. Moving on, we need to talk about your choice of majors. Finally, Ji seok, are you listening to me?" she asked. He looked up from his phone. He had been texting Sawyer, he sent the message off.

"Yes, I was listening. I'll look at it later."

"Ji Seok, don't give me that tone."

"I will happily look at it later," he said. She looked at him, it was how she always looked at him, her own face of disappointment and annoyance. No one else would be able to tell but he knew. "I will, I'll even take it with me tonight," he offered. Though he would just throw it in his backseat and forget all about it.

"And where are you going?"

"To Sawyer's," he told her, she turned away picking up her knife and fork and started eating. He quickly finished eating and left the table, grabbing the packet off of the kitchen counter.

8:19 P.M.

Wyatt parked on the curb outside of Sawyer's house and stared at the empty driveway for two seconds before he got out of his car, realizing the front door of the house was cracked open. Wyatt opened his messages calling Sawyer. He pushed open the door, looking around, the house was quiet. Sawyer's house was never quiet this early. Wyatt called him over and over and over. No answer, he called Sawyer's parents, with no answer.

"What the fuck," he swore. He looked all around the house making sure it wasn't a stupid plan to make him worry by playing hide and seek. The house was empty. For thirty minutes Wyatt tried to call Sawyer, he paced the house unsure what he should do. Sawyer never disappeared like this.

Wyatt called again, this time Sawyer picked up. "Dude, where are you? I'm at your house and the door was open, what's going on?"

From the shakiness of Sawyer's response, Wyatt could tell something was wrong. "Where are you?"

Wyatt looked around the house like that would give him the answer, Sawyer told him.

"Why?" Wyatt was already shutting the front door and jogging to his car as he got the answer. He stood at his car door. "Fuck, I'll be right there." Wyatt yanked open his door. He had to force himself not to speed all the way there.

Chapter 3 Hae Na
Friday April 4th 7:29 P.M.

Hae Na laid across the couch with her head in Sam's lap as her fingers carded through her dark hair. Hae Na twisted from the show to look up at Sam. Sam smiled down at her, dropping a kiss on her forehead before pulling away and putting her attention on the show. Hae Na watched her for a little while longer, enjoying the moment. It would end soon, when Sam's best friend would come crashing into their apartment ready to go out to clubs.

"I love you," Hae Na said, smiling up at Sam though she didn't look down.

"Love you too," Sam said, her focus stayed on the T.V. Hae Na sat up, leaning her head on Sam's shoulder. She had just a bit longer to enjoy it. This moment was rare and she was soaking it up as much as she could.

Chapter 4 Rye
Friday April 4th 7:04 P.M.

Rye stared at the mess of a vase his mom set on the table in front of him. "New hobby?" he asked.

"Yeah, I think I'm starting to get better too," she said. "The teacher said that I'm pretty good for a beginner," she added, holding the vase up to the light as if that would make it better.

"And the vase is your masterpiece?" he asked, earning a quick glare from her.

"Vase? It's a cup," she said, setting it back down on the table.

His eyes darted between her and the vase. "Really?"

"Yes," she said, he rolled his eyes. "Kidding, but we could use it as a cup. If we had nothing else."

"Why wouldn't we have anything else?"

She shrugged, "Who knows? But if it did happen, we would have the vase." She lifted the vase, dangling it back and forth.

"Yay, the vase," he said. She knocked her knuckles against his head.

"Do you want to join my next adventure?"

He looked at her, shaking his head. "No."

"It'll be fun, you're going to miss out," she said, moving her shoulders back and forth in a slow shimmy.

He picked up his plate setting it in the sink, "No," he said.

"You're really going to be mad you missed this one."

"That's what you said about the cat hair knitting class."

She leaned forward, her arms supporting her on the table. "When are you going to get over that?"

"Never, I'm going to bring it up at every opportunity, even at your funeral."

"It wasn't that bad. Okay fine it was a little bad."

Rye still had nightmares where he was drowning in cat hair, and cats were pulling him down deeper.

"Decide on college?" she asked, her tone more serious.

"No," Rye said as he made his escape out of the kitchen to his room. Shutting the door behind him.

Chapter 5 Sawyer
Saturday April 5th 2:36 A.M.

Sawyer was finally able to get Lio to sleep, he didn't even want to attempt to look at the time. Instead, he crawled into bed, Wyatt shifting to give him more room. Sawyer was ready for sleep. He would welcome it like a large homemade pizza.

Except he couldn't. His mind was filled with a thousand different things and all he wanted was to shut it off. He groaned and flipped around facing towards Wyatt, watching him sleep peacefully. Sawyer closed his eyes, trying to think of nothing so he could fall asleep. He wasn't sure how much time had passed but no matter what, he couldn't sleep.

Sawyer opened his eyes and poked Wyatt in the side. Wyatt didn't react so he poked him again and again. Wyatt shifted his body away from Sawyer. Sawyer kicked and pushed Wyatt to the edge of the bed, watching him drop off of it before he turned back and feigned sleep.

"The fuck," Wyatt groaned. Sawyer heard Wyatt pull himself off of the floor, dragging his body back onto the bed. Sawyer let Wyatt shift him, his breath tickling his neck as he buried his nose into Sawyers' neck, easily falling back asleep.

Sawyer sighed, the blanket was at their knees. He tried to move his arm out to grab it but Wyatt tightened his grip. Sawyer pushed back on him and was able to pull the blanket up, Wyatt muttering unintelligibly as he did.

"I don't know how to take care of kids. How am I supposed to survive without my parents? I can't do adult things. What the fuck are taxes? I can't do this, I know I can't," Sawyer spoke quietly, he watched the shadows outside of the window change when certain street lights would flicker on and off. He ignored the tears, ignored the gaping hole he felt ripping his chest open.

"I shouldn't have said I would watch the kids, I wanted to hang out with you and maybe get high or drunk. But I offered to watch them. My parents were happy, they didn't need the break, but Lio had been cranky the last few days so I just thought-" Sawyer bit his lip leaning back into Wyatt as he pressed closer, shifting his face a few times.

"I'm not ready to take care of them." His voice broke and he wiped the tears away. He lay there a few more minutes in the quiet, he heard a car passing by.

"But I would never be able to live with myself if I gave them away. I would hate it. I would hate not seeing them every day or reading them stories at night. I love them and if they were gone it wouldn't be worth having just a little bit of an easier life."

Sawyer pressed his face into the pillow. He slowly fell asleep with tears drying on the pillow.

April 9th 1:43 P.M.

"Carter?" Sawyer looked in all of her hiding places and still nothing. He picked up an irritated Lio and continued his search. "Carter where are you?" He went down to the kitchen looking on his way. He made Lio a bottle and settled him down in his arms before he checked the laundry room, the empty study, and all around the living room.

He looked in her room again then Lio's before he stepped up to his parents' slightly opened door. He pushed it fully open, finding

Carter curled up with her frog in the middle of the bed sleeping.

Sawyer climbed on the bed sitting cross-legged, his eyes flickering between Lio and Carter. He set his hand on her forehead sighing in relief when he couldn't feel a fever.

"I'm so sorry," he apologized. "We should have just had a dumb family night with dumb movies and dad's over-seasoned popcorn." Lio was falling asleep so Sawyer burped him and laid him down next to Carter. Sawyer laid down on his back, staring at the ceiling.

His voice was barely above a whisper. "I remember when we first moved in here. It was still a couple of years before you guys came along. I wanted this room, I even challenged them to games and bets hoping to win it. So they slept in your room, Carter, and I slept in mine until we could decide on who would get this room." Sawyer sniffed before he continued.

"I lost 15 games of rock paper scissors, 7 games of Uno, 3 games of poker, 2 games of Jenga and one game of life. Dad won most of them, so he got the room and then I argued that because he had won he couldn't share with mom and she would have to stay in her room." He paused, smiling at the memory, he slightly shifted on the bed as he continued. "Then dad told me it wasn't fair of me to keep him from the love of his life. I told him it wasn't fair to keep me from the love of a room."

Sawyer ran his fingers through Carter's hair, pulling some of it out of her face. She was going to need a haircut soon. His voice was softer when he spoke. "Then he asked me what was more important: love of an object or love of a person, I told him it was of an object. His face told me that we were going to end up having a huge talk so I added that objects can't hurt you and they can't die like people can." His fingers stilled in her soft hair, tears welling in his eyes, he took a deep breath to stop them. When he didn't feel like crying anymore he spoke again.

"Then he said that since people die he needed to spend as much time loving mom before she died. I gave in after that." Sawyer pulled his hand away from Carter, curling around his siblings.

Sunday April 13th 3:24 P.M.

Sawyer was six the last time he went to a funeral, his last living grandmother. He never knew the work that went into arranging a time, a date, services, food, guests, cremation or burial. It took over a week to get everything arranged, to accept everyone's condolences, to finish paperwork, to realize they weren't coming home. The only family he had left was his 4-year-old sister and 8-month-old brother.

Tomorrow he had to go back to school, back to his life, back to some idea of normalcy. He was standing next to the couch, his brother was napping on the floor on a blanket. His sister was staring intently at a children's movie that was playing. People had been in and out of the house with food or to help babysit and now they were alone. Everyone had their own lives to go back to. His life was now sitting in the living room, one asleep, the other content. Neither had really known what happened, he couldn't explain it to a baby and Carter didn't understand why their parents couldn't simply come home. She had asked him multiple times if they forgot where they lived, like the one time she got lost in the neighbor's garden.

"Sawyer." Sawyer turned his head to Wyatt. Wyatt was a whole different situation he was avoiding. Wyatt had pulled him out of the haze when he got too close to getting lost. He was constantly pulling him back into focus. Wyatt handed him a turkey sandwich.

"Eat it." Sawyer nodded, making no move for it. He had no appetite, which was strange for him. Weeks ago, he and Wyatt ate two large pizzas and three servings of Ramen. "I can make it into a smoothie if you don't want to chew it." Sawyer couldn't help but smile.

Wyatt had made him a food smoothie before when he had accidentally got knocked in the jaw at a party and didn't want to chew anything. He didn't realize what it was until he was already drinking and then spitting it all over Wyatt. He thought they both learned something that day. Wyatt had said that he just needed to wear a poncho or get out of spit range and Sawyer learned never to drink smoothies from Wyatt. Sawyer took a bite of the sandwich earning a slight smile from Wyatt before he was turning back to the kitchen. Sawyer dropped the sandwich back on the plate. Carter was watching him now.

"What?" he asked her when she pointed to him.

"You better eat it," she said, pulling her hand back into her lap and turning back towards the T.V. as a song began, she happily started singing it. He took another bite, sticking his tongue out at her with it full of food. He pulled it back in when he heard Wyatt walk back towards the living room.

"I'm not sure if you're listening to me or her," Wyatt said, standing next to him, Sawyer was hyper-aware of the small distance between them.

"Both," he replied, taking another bite until it was finished. He handed the plate back to Wyatt who stared at it.

"You have feet," he said. Sawyer attempted a more genuine smile, taking the plate to the kitchen himself.

The kitchen was a strange mess, it was clean but it wasn't. He couldn't pick out what was wrong or dirty, just that it didn't have the meticulous cleaning his mom always strived for. It was like his house was in a different universe, even if he had been in there for breakfast. It was easier to focus on the kitchen than on the man standing in the living room. Easier than to focus on the two missing people who should be in the house. The full facts and weight of what happened had yet to hit him, he knew that when it did, it would hit him like a punch to the face. For now, he was getting through it by focusing on everything but the accident.

He set the plate in the sink with a few cups and forks and turned to find Wyatt standing in the open doorway.

"What are you going to do tomorrow?"

Sawyer shrugged, shaking his head a bit. Tomorrow was a different start, it was different than any other start he'd had in his life. He was now the guardian of his siblings and a high school student. It was a less than ideal situation, one he was going to struggle with. He could already imagine all of the disasters. His parents had been young when they had him, too young. They had his siblings when they had gotten secure jobs and paid off the house.

Sawyer watched as Wyatt moved in front of him. Unlike at the hospital, Wyatt was no longer tall, he was shorter by just a few inches, enough that Wyatt was standing a step away.

He needed to figure out daycare and get the kids back to their schedule. He had to give them a semblance of normalcy. It was also the only way that he could make it to school. Eventually, Wyatt was going to go back to his life and then he would be alone. For now, he wouldn't think about it, he would think about this hour right now with Wyatt in his kitchen and the growing sounds of Lio waking up. His voice getting louder every second he waited to check on him.

Monday April 14th 6:01 A.M.

Sawyer was too warm when he woke up. Even stranger was that he could just see the light coming in from the window. He had slept through the night, which meant Lio had slept through the night. He was pressed close to Wyatt, the blanket was pulled up high and if he wasn't mistaken about the little heater behind him, Carter had snuck into his bed. It was getting to the point that the heat was stifling, but he couldn't move. He couldn't bring himself to disturb either of them. Though he had no control over the alarm going off, Wyatt moved to stop it. Sawyer watched him get up, his dark hair stuck out on one side. Sawyer sat up, Carter slid into his side.

Wyatt moved to the bathroom, turning on the light before coming back in the room. It gave them enough light to see but not enough to bother Carter. "I wasn't going to say this yesterday, but you need to shower."

"I showered yesterday," Sawyer half whined, squinting at the bathroom.

Wyatt threw a clean towel at him, "When?"

"I- I don't know." Sawyer pulled the towel away from his face.

"Because you haven't showered since Friday and you smell."

Sawyer stared at him, had it really been that long? The days were blurring together, it was hard for him to pick out what events happened on any single day. He shrugged, climbing out of his bed heading right into the bathroom. He didn't have time to waste figuring it out. When he came out of the shower, a towel wrapped around his waist, his room was empty. He could hear Wyatt on the baby monitor talking to Lio, the slamming of a drawer told him Carter was dressing herself for the day. That alone was a small disaster. He quickly dressed, his shirt and jeans sticking to his still wet skin.

Carter had dresses and shirts scattered around her room, she was rummaging in her closet for more. "What are you looking for?"

She jumped, bumping her head on the low shelf, she stepped out of her closet rubbing the bump. "I want my cloud dress." Carter demanded.

Sawyer moved forward looking over the mess in case she missed it, none of them had clouds. He stepped over the clothes to the closet but it held no more dresses. "It might be in the laundry," he said, stepping back over the clothes, he picked up his pace once he got out of her room. He was quick on the stairs and slid towards the kitchen. When he made it to the laundry room he found a new disaster. He searched through the piles of mixed clothes, unsure which ones were dirty or clean. In the end, he found no dress with clouds on it. He sighed, kicking the fallen clothes closer to the washer. He headed back up the stairs to find Carter making her own cloud dress. The dress was a light blue with white lace on the bottom, now it had blocky shapes he assumed were clouds. He plucked the marker out of her hand, she started to whine and hit his arm until he made his own clouds on the dress. When he finished he helped her pull it on. She grinned brightly at him when she did a twirl in the dress like it was brand new.

She clapped her hands as she ran out of the room yelling, Yaya, Wyatt's nickname. Sawyer followed her at a slower pace. Wyatt was in the hallway, Lio fussing in his arms. Wyatt handed over Lio.

"I'm making breakfast," Wyatt said, Sawyer nodded. Carter was already naming off everything she wanted.

"Want craps!"

"I can't make them today, maybe a different day," he said, Sawyer watched them head down the stairs, Carter trailing after Wyatt like a puppy. Lio quickly took his attention with a slobbery hand to his face. Sawyer looked down at him, "Hi, Lio," he said. Lio grinned up at him, giggling as his small fingers tightened in a fist hit his face again. "Thank you for sleeping through the night." Lio leaned away from him as if asking to fall. Sawyer shifted him closer, earning a few more slaps to his face.

Wyatt had Carter at the table eating heated up waffles, while he was leaning against the counter. "I already fed him," Wyatt said. "When you were in the shower." Sawyer nodded, opening his mouth to respond. Lio shoved his hand into his mouth, stopping him. Sawyer grinned, pretending to bite on it, making Lio laugh. It was so easy to make him laugh, he could laugh at anything. He didn't understand that their parents were gone, or that their lives were going to completely change. Lio would live the rest of his life not knowing them. Everything they wanted to teach him, wanted him to know, was gone. His parents were young and healthy, they had never talked about what would happen if they died.

Sawyer jerked back when he thought Lio was falling, then he saw Wyatt in front of him. "I'll take him so you can eat." Sawyer let him go, he looked over to Carter who was pushing her plate away with sticky fingers, her long hair just barely missing the syrup covered plate.

"Sticky fingers!" Carter yelled. Holding her hands up she kept separating and putting them together showing how they stuck together. She hopped off of her chair grabbing at Wyatt's shirt, laughing when they stuck to it. Normally Sawyer would be laughing, Wyatt had a way of charming children even though he had zero experience with them.

His sister had clutched onto him the moment he walked into their house. When he had been babysitting for a friend, Wyatt had come over and the kid fawned over him like he was a superhero. There were multiple times when they would be out somewhere and a kid would stare at him or reach out to him. It was made funnier because Wyatt had expressed more than once his dislike of children.

Seeing him take care of Lio and Carter would show that he was lying. Sawyer ate cereal as quick as he could, he couldn't keep burdening Wyatt. They were his siblings, they were his family and responsibility. Sawyer put his bowl in the sink, heading into the living room where Carter was swinging around a purple play purse and Wyatt was putting more diapers in the diaper bag. "I'll drop the kids off at daycare," Sawyer said.

Wyatt stood up, staring at him. "Don't be an idiot," he said. Carter's voice rang out as if she had been waiting for someone to swear, though he would hardly call the word 'idiot' a swear word.

"Alright, Carter, we get it," he said. She pouted crossing her arms tightly across her body before she stuck her tongue out at him. He rolled his eyes, focusing on Wyatt who scooped up Lio while he tried to make a break for the front door, crawling as quick as he could.

"Come on Carter, we're *both* taking you to daycare."

"Yay!" she yelled, running circles around both of them, weaving around them. Sawyer grabbed his backpack off the floor, following Wyatt and Carter to his car. He watched Wyatt strap in Lio and help Carter to her booster seat. He did it so easy like he had been doing it for years. When he shut the back door, he pushed Sawyer away from the driver's door. Sawyer let him, moving to the passenger side.

Sawyer slid in the passenger seat, leaning his head against the window. The ride was filled with Disney songs and Carter singing most of them.

"Sawyer stop pouting, I'll sing along this time," his dad said.

29

Sawyer turned his head away from him. "A new fantastic point of view," his dad sang off key.

Sawyer shifted forward, changing the song. Carter protested loudly until the next song started and she thankfully liked it more. Sawyer shifted to look at Wyatt who was focusing on the road. His dad hated driving, his mom loved it. Sawyer had gained his father's distaste for it, he had never had anything bad happen while he was driving. There was no traumatic event to cause him to dislike it. Now when he drove he couldn't help but think of all the ways it could go wrong, how his mother who drove them everywhere was cautious in the city and crazy on the highway. She was a great driver, there was no rain, no ice, no other reason than a human mistake to take their lives.

Wyatt loved driving. When they first started hanging out, Wyatt insisted on driving them everywhere, even if it was two blocks away and easier to walk than to find parking. Sawyer had on more than one occasion hidden his keys. The only times Wyatt had driven his car was when he had drank too much at a party when he promised to be the sober driver. Wyatt held his alcohol better and he always knew when Sawyer hit the point of no return, stopping his own drinking. It caused Wyatt to crash at his house more times than not.

Sawyer remained quiet, the twenty minutes it took to drive them to daycare and then to school was close to torture for him. He needed to get through the rest of the school year and make sure he could afford the bills to make it to summer. Summer presented a whole different set of problems that he would deal with when they arrived.

The people were the same, the teacher, the classroom, everything felt the same. He was the only one who felt different, though that was wrong. A couple of people had gotten tans, someone was probably wearing a new outfit, someone probably got laid for the first time or got a significant other. Everyone in this room was different and yet still the same. If he had bothered to really get to know anyone from this class, he would probably know what was different about at least one person.

Instead, he was focused on Wyatt. Liking Wyatt was a drunken dream he had 3 months ago. From that point on he saw Wyatt completely different. He was no longer just his best friend, he was a crush too. He could deal with people having crushes on him, except Wyatt. He couldn't brush off Wyatt, he liked Wyatt, he wanted Wyatt to like him. He wanted Wyatt, so why was he being an idiot trying to push him away? Sawyer stared at the board, missing half the notes for class.

Friday April 18th 6:04 P.M.

Sawyer woke up on the couch when his phone started ringing, still tired from lack of sleep and he barely heard what the woman was saying. "It's after 6 and I'm waiting as long as I can but someone needs to pick them up."

"What? Pick who up?"

"I'm sorry this is the number for Sawyer Losada correct?"

"Yeah," he yawned, his mouth slamming shut when she spoke again.

"Your siblings, Carter and Helios are still at daycare and I'm wondering when you're going to pick them up."

Sawyer scrambled off the couch, cursing when he stepped on one of Carter's toy trucks. "Right now, I'm on my way, 10 minutes I promise." Sawyer hated himself, he had forgotten his siblings.

"All right, I'll be here." He shoved his phone in his pocket as he looked for the keys in the bowl by the door, the bowl was empty. He looked all over the floor, couch, kitchen, his room, they were nowhere. He paused, shoving his hand in his pocket, he found the keys. He raced down the stairs, tripping at the bottom he kept going until he was in the car. He didn't allow himself to race the yellow lights but it was close. He pulled up to the daycare with a slightly annoyed teacher. She was nice enough but he could tell that if he ever did it again he would pay for it.

"Sah why were you late? Mommy never late."

"I had some stuff to do," he said, putting Lio in his seat as Carter climbed into her own. He watched her buckle the seatbelt after a few tugs, then pulled away, shutting Lio's door and going to the other side to shut Carter's. He drove them home, getting them settled. He started dinner cursing himself the whole time. He shouldn't be taking care of them, he was barely an adult. He knew how to play with his siblings, he didn't know how to raise children.

Monday April 21st 6:58 A.M.

When Carter was finally dressed and fed, he loaded her and Lio in the car. He sat in the driver's seat just staring at the gages.

"Sah, go to daycare," Carter said in the back.

"We're going," he said, starting up the car and gripping the steering wheel tightly before he changed gears and headed out of the driveway.

"Sah, did Yaya die?" Sawyer quickly looked at her in the rear-view mirror, Carter's face was scrunched in confusion.

"No, he didn't."

"But Yaya did not come back."

"He's only been gone a day or two."

"Yaya die," she said, starting to cry. Sawyer stopped at the stop sign, banging his head against the steering wheel. Pulling out his phone he called Wyatt.

"Hey, could you talk to Carter?" Sawyer asked, putting him on speaker.

"Carter?" Wyatt's voice filled the car.

"Yaya?" Carter sniffled as she blinked the tears out of her eyes.

"Why are you crying?"

"Yaya die," she yelled. Sawyer winced at her pitch.

"I didn't die, I just had to go home."

"No no no this home," she said, crossing her arms angrily.

"What's home?" he asked.

"This Yaya home."

"Ok, I'll be there later I promise."

"Pinky," she said, sticking her pinky out. Even though he wasn't there to see it.

"Pinky," he replied as Sawyer hung up.

"See he's fine, he's not dead."

"Fine." She nodded, uncrossing her arms.

Sawyer continued through the stop sign. "We will be fine," he told himself over and over until he pulled into the daycare. When he stepped in, one of the younger workers looked over Carter's dress then to him and back to her dress. She was wearing the cloud dress she had made before.

Sawyer ignored her, saying his goodbye he dropped Lio off and headed to school. Wyatt threw an arm over his shoulder the second he entered the school doors.

"Why did she think I died?" he asked.

"Because you were gone. I've been trying to read up on how kids grieve and I think she's clinging onto you."

Wyatt shrugged. "Fine by me."

Sawyer pushed against him. "No, it will crush her when you leave."

"Then I won't leave."

"Wyatt."

"Sawyer." Wyatt just grinned so Sawyer dropped it, taking comfort in Wyatt's warmth.

Wyatt pulled away before his classroom, saluting, he headed off to his own.

3:11 P.M.

"May I help you?" Sawyer looked up to the teacher. Her long black hair was wrapped in a bun with four paint brushes sticking out of the top of it.

"I was wondering if you had those huge rolls of blank paper."

"I do, is there a specific reason why you're asking?" the teacher asked, heading around her desk and towards the back of the room. Her dress looked as if she painted it at home. It was artistic, with shapes and colors.

"I was reading that drawing is good for a grieving kid and my sister was drawing on her dress and then on the wall, so I was thinking if I took a long piece of paper and placed it over the wall she could draw on it. That probably sounds dumb."

"No, it sounds wonderful." She unlocked a closet, and stepped inside. "I have black, blue and white. We use it for school banners."

"Blue and white would be awesome."

Sawyer helped her take the large rolls out and started cutting large pieces off. Rolling them up he placed a rubbed band around each smaller roll. He now had four of each, at least five feet in length with all of them.

"This is really awesome, thank you so much," he said, smiling at her.

"Of course, I have some other old art stuff, do you think you'd like to take some?"

"Really? That would be great."

She moved to a closet, opening the door. "You'd be doing me a favor, I've been meaning to give it away but I've been busy with all these school events and projects."

"Well then it works out for both of us. Thank you."

She handed him a box, he took it gratefully, heading out to the car. Wyatt was leaning against it when he arrived.

"What is all that?" Wyatt asked, taking the rolls of paper from his left arm. Sawyer opened his back door setting the box inside, Wyatt handed him the paper.

"Some art things for Carter. Where's your car?" Sawyer pulled out of the car after putting the paper in.

"At your house, Garrett followed me and drove me back here."

"Why?" Sawyer asked, looking at Wyatt.

"So we can pick up the kids together," he said, taking the keys out of Sawyers' hand.

Sawyer opened the passenger door, relieved that Wyatt was driving. "Oh, ok," Sawyer said.

Tuesday April 22nd 1:54 A.M.

Sawyer looked down in the crib where Lio was wailing, again. Sawyer blinked his burning eyes, sighing as he leaned down and picked up his brother. He rocked him, tried to sing, put him in a rocking chair, fed him, changed his diaper. Nothing worked, Lio continued to be fussy, he refused to sleep.

Sawyer swayed around the room, sighing when Lio finally fell asleep. He swayed a while longer before carefully laying him down. Once out of his arms, Lio bunched up his face and began crying again.

Defeated, he picked him back up and rocked him till he fell asleep again. He carefully sat down in the worn rocking chair, slowly drifting to sleep. He woke up when his alarm went off in his pocket. He carefully slid it out, turning it off. He pushed out of the chair relieved that Lio continued to sleep. He moved around the room gathering clean clothes and socks and a new diaper and wipes. Sawyer carefully laid him down, and quickly changed his diaper. He smiled and yawned as he woke up, stretching his arms and legs. "You, good sir, are adorable, even if you are a sleep stealing monster," Sawyer said. Lifting him up he got him dressed, carrying him to Carter's room to wake her up.

"Come on Carter, up up." Carter dragged herself out of bed yawning. Sawyer was not going to like her during her teenage years. She stood in her room looking around, before looking up at him. "I want doughnuts," she said.

Sawyer looked at her, "Well, maybe tomorrow we can have them."

She scrunched up her nose, "Is Yaya home?"

Sawyer rolled his eyes. "Yes, at his own home," he replied.

"No, this home." She glared up at him.

"We can talk about it later, right now I need you to get dressed and then we can eat breakfast."

"I want a doughnut," she said again. Dragging her body to her drawers, she pulled out her clothes dramatically.

"You are so dramatic," he muttered loudly.

"What does that mean?" Her face scrunched in confusion.

"Nothing," he said. When she was finally dressed he followed her down the stairs, Lio biting on his shirt as he did.

The doorbell rang as they ate. "I want to see," Carter said as she sprung up from her chair and ran towards the front door.

"Hey, no answering the door," Sawyer yelled as he followed her, picking Lio up out of his chair. Lio happily smeared his peaches all over Sawyer's shirt.

Carter stood at the door waiting until he nodded before she pulled it open.

"Hi! I'm Marina, do you remember me?" she asked, looking between the three of them.

"Of course," Sawyer said. She was a mom from the daycare that his mom had been friends with.

"I want to apologize and say how sorry I am. I was honestly shocked when I heard the news. We've been out of town on vacation. If you need anything at all you just call me. Oh and if you'd like on Tuesdays and Thursdays, I would love to pick up the kids."

"Oh, uh thank you that would be great actually," Sawyer said looking around at the kids

"Perfect, are they ready now?" Marina asked, her dark blue flowy dress blew in the door from the wind.

"Oh right, it's Tuesday, um. Yeah, just one second. Carter put your shoes on for me."

"Okay," she said, sitting on the floor as she shoved her shoes on her feet.

Sawyer took off Lio's bib and headed into the kitchen, washing his hands and face. He got everything ready and took them out to her car.

"I still have a car seat from when Piper was little so I brought that in case you said yes," she said. Piper was bouncing her seat excitedly as Carter climbed in. Her eldest son nodded from the front seat. Sawyer strapped Lio in and stepped back.

"Thank you again for this," he said.

"Oh don't you worry about it, now you call me if you need anything."

"Alright I will." He didn't think he would end up calling her but it was nice to have the option.

"Bye Sah! Tell Yaya to come home," Carter yelled before he shut the door.

"I will." Sawyer waved them off and texted Wyatt to pick him up for school.

Chapter 6 Wyatt
Saturday April 5th 3:49 P.M.

Wyatt cleaned up the kitchen, starting on the counters and rounding up the dishes.

"This fucking sucks," Sawyer said, knocking his head against the doorway.

Wyatt half turned towards him, continuing to clean. "Brain damage might help though."

"Shut up," Sawyer muttered, banging his head again. "I don't know what to do." He left his forehead against the frame.

"It'd probably be more twisted if you did," Wyatt said. Sawyer huffed a ghost of a laugh. He turned his head to look at Wyatt who was still standing by the sink.

"What do I do?" he whispered so quietly that Wyatt had to guess what he said. Wyatt moved forward until he was standing in front of Sawyer. He was just as lost as Sawyer. Wyatt tugged him towards him pulling him into a hug.

The first time Wyatt had met Sawyer's mother had been two weeks after they had become friends, it was her birthday and he had been invited to a small party. She had pulled him into a hug before he could even say hello. He had frozen, and she tightened her hold telling him how she was happy to have another son. He was easily accepted in the family, without them knowing him, he was thought of as their son. She always treated him like family and now she was gone. Two days Wyatt hadn't seen her and now he would never see her again, no one would.

"What do I do?" Sawyer asked, pulling his face away from Wyatt's chest until he could rest his forehead on Wyatt's shoulder. Wyatt didn't have an answer for him, instead, he held him promising to be there for him. It was all he could do and he would do anything for him. Sawyer lost his parents, his amazing loving parents, and Wyatt couldn't fix it.

He could spend all of his own parent's money, he could give up his own life but none of that would change anything. Sawyer would never give them up to foster care but Sawyer wasn't ready to be a parent. "I'm here," Wyatt said, though he doubted it was any comfort. He had even less to offer as a friend. "Whatever you need I'll get okay?"

"I need my parents." Sawyer clung onto him tighter, his fingers pinching his shirt and skin.

"We could get an Ouija board," Wyatt offered.

"Hah, hilarious. Let's do it," Sawyer said, though his voice was far from the joking mood.

"Fine, I'll buy one tomorrow," Wyatt told him, his hand was a slow movement on Sawyer's back.

"Great," Sawyer whispered.

"Sah! The door knocking again," Sawyer pulled himself away. Wyatt let him go, stopping himself from reaching out again.

Wednesday April 9th 2:21 P.M.

Wyatt set down several bags of groceries, listening around the house before he quickly put the food away. When he finished, he went upstairs to find Sawyer and Carter's rooms were empty. When he got to Lio's he was really confused. Looking around he found Sawyer's parent's door opened.

He paused at the doorway as all three siblings were sleeping in the middle of the bed. Going to the hall closet he grabbed a blanket, carefully laying it across them. He took a few pictures with his phone and headed back to Sawyer's room.

Grabbing Sawyer's notebook off of his desk he scanned through the to-do list, very few things were crossed off. Opening Sawyer's laptop he got to work.

Thursday April 17th 7:41 A.M.

Sawyer rushed outside before Wyatt could get out of the car. "Come on we're going to be late," Sawyer said, pulling open the passenger door, dropping into the seat. Wyatt began backing out and then hit the break startling Sawyer. "What's wrong?"

Wyatt pushed the gear into park and half turned to Sawyer, "When was the last time you showered?"

"Uh, yester- no two days wait what's today?"

Wyatt looked over Sawyer's clothes. "Thursday."

"These are clean," Sawyer protested, Wyatt gave him a blank stare. "I'm serious," Sawyer said, pulling his shirt up to smell it himself.

Wyatt pushed him, "Get out of my car before it smells like a garbage dump."

"We're going to be late to school," Sawyer whined.

"I don't give a shit, you reek." Wyatt shut the car off, opening his door he headed into Sawyer's house with Sawyer whining his name behind him.

Wyatt laid on Sawyer's bed while he showered. He turned his head to see the massive pile of dirty clothes, it even had a couple of Lio and Carter's clothes mixed in. Wyatt pushed himself off of the bed, gathering up the piles into the basket. He carried it downstairs to the laundry room and cursed Sawyer. A load was already in the washer, and from the smell, it had been there for at least a few days. He started that wash again, leaving the basket next to the washer.

He cleaned up the dishes, counters, and the table in the kitchen, then straightened up the living room. He looked up at the stairs when he still heard the water running. Wyatt headed back upstairs, opening the bathroom door. Sawyer was sitting on the shower floor, sleeping against the shower wall.

Wyatt shut the water off, grabbing a towel he threw it over his shoulder before yanking Sawyer to his feet. Sawyer stumbled by the action falling into Wyatt.

"What the fuck?" Sawyer cursed, holding onto Wyatt as he shook the drowsiness away. "Dude, give me that." Sawyer grabbed the towel quickly covering himself up. Wyatt watched Sawyer's neck flare red in embarrassment as he walked in his room.

Sawyer pulled on a shirt and moved to find underwear. "Shit," he muttered before he looked for a pair of jeans or shorts.

"I thought you had clean clothes," Wyatt said. Sawyer glared at him, looking back at the bathroom. "No, those clothes are dirty. We're skipping school today."

"I can't! I have to go to as many classes as I can before daycare stops. I have to do a shit ton of random projects too. And another fucking cloud on top of my rainstorm there's no gas in the fucking car," Sawyer said, opening all of his dresser drawers. He slammed a few of them shut when he only found socks and shirts.

"Here," Wyatt said. Sawyer turned his eyes shifting from the shorts to Wyatt's black and gray boxers. "Take them, take my car and go to school."

"No, you've already skipped a lot this year. I know you got reprimanded by the vice principal."

"My grades are good, he can't do shit. Go to school." Wyatt shoved the shorts into his chest.

Sawyer looked back to the bathroom "My other shorts are fine."

Wyatt grabbed onto the towel, threatening him. "Take them before I kick your ass and put you in them."

"Always so violent," Sawyer muttered, pulling them on. "Oh, I didn't know we were the same size."

"We aren't," Wyatt said. Sawyer frowned at him and tugged on the shorts. "Go to school, you already missed first period."

"Oh shit, I need the study guide from that class."

Wyatt shook his head, pushing him towards the door. "Go

during lunch."

"I'm going to Mrs. Robbins at lunch."

Wyatt pulled away, shrugging. "Personal problem."

Sawyer pulled the keys out of the shorts pocket. "Fine I'm going," he said with one last look at Wyatt before he headed down the stairs and out of the house.

Wyatt cleaned up all of the rooms except Sawyer's parents. He finished several loads of laundry and cleaned out the fridge. Wyatt went to the front door, everyone else on the block had their trash cans out. Wyatt quickly pulled the trash cans out when he heard the garbage truck. He grabbed at least 8 days worth of mail from the mailbox, dropping it on the kitchen table. He shifted through all of it, getting rid of the junk mail and opening the important ones. He grabbed Sawyer's laptop and got to work on all of the things Sawyer neglected. He searched google, wrote a list and texted his dad about the legal choices with the car accident.

Wyatt created a budget on Sawyer's computer, he found old bills and added them in, estimating the new bills. He added everything he could think of that cost Sawyer money. There was no way Sawyer could afford everything, even if he worked full time, it was impossible. There was a lot he was going to have to cut down on to survive. It wasn't going to be easy and there was no way he could do it alone. Wyatt tapped his fingers against the table. A slow grin took over Wyatt's face. If he couldn't do it alone then Wyatt was going to help him.

When he finished the laundry, he pulled on a pair of Sawyer's sweatpants. He had to roll the bottoms up to avoid tripping. He didn't understand why they were so long; Sawyer was at most two inches taller than him. He tightened the drawstring, dropping onto Sawyer's bed for a nap. He woke up to his phone vibrating against his face.

"What?" Wyatt answered, his eyes still closed to the afternoon light.

Sawyer's light laughter rang on the other side. "Were you sleeping?"

"Hm," Wyatt hummed.

"I'm letting you know that I'm coming home for lunch, you can at least make the last of your classes."

"Whatever," Wyatt said, hanging up the phone. He pushed it away from his face, burying his face into the pillow.

Wyatt startled awake when he felt Sawyer pull him off of the bed. "Get up," Sawyer said. Wyatt kicked him with his other foot. "Ow fucker, your kicks are worse than your punches."

"Soccer," Wyatt said, grinning. Sawyer threw a pillow at his face. Wyatt hit it back towards him. Sawyer was already out of his room, Wyatt jumped up to follow him.

He found Sawyer in the kitchen searching for food. "There isn't any food," Wyatt said.

Sayer sighed, shutting the fridge. "I know, I have to go shopping."

"Wait, I thought you were seeing Mrs. Robbins," Wyatt said.

"I had enough time left of first period to see her and Mr. Finch," Sawyer explained, still going through the cabinets. "Why do we have so much canned food? We never eat any of it."

Wyatt didn't answer him, his eyes roamed over Sawyer. When Sawyer turned to look at him, Wyatt flicked his eyes back to his face.

"I should have eaten at school," Sawyer said, leaning against the counter. Wyatt soaked up the view before he spoke, breaking Sawyer's light mood.

"Take a casserole out of the freezer. Also I talked to my dad about the accident," Wyatt said. Sawyer crossed his arms, his face closing off. "It needs to be handled."

Sawyer shook his head. "I can't, I can't do it," he said. Wyatt knew he wasn't talking about the casserole, he bit his tongue to not make a joke about it.

"I'll do it, I'm just letting you know it needs to be done."

"I don't think I can do this." Sawyer said, waving his arms around. "I was stupid to think I could, I haven't even graduated high school yet."

Wyatt lost the humor as he watched Sawyer break down in front of him. "Sawyer, knock it off. Do you want your siblings to be in foster care? Do you want to let someone else live in this house?"

"No," Sawyer said.

Wyatt leaned on the chair. "Then shut the fuck up and find some food."

"What's wrong with you?" Sawyer's face scrunched up. Wyatt thought it was adorable.

Wyatt shook his head. "You're pissing me off."

Sawyer lifted his arms. "What did I do?"

Wyatt stared at Sawyer who was looking at him, lost. "Nothing, just hurry up you're going to be late getting back."

Sawyer crossed his arms, rolling his eyes. "You're coming with me."

Wyatt didn't want to fight him. "Fine, let's go."

"I still haven't eaten," Sawyer whined.

"You won't starve," Wyatt said, already heading out of the kitchen. Sawyer followed him out to the car, handing over the keys. The ride to school was silent, each in their own small misery.

5:35 P.M.

Wyatt stopped right inside of the house, he was still halfway out the door when he heard the yelling. He heard his dad try to interject in Korean, though even after years of trying his pronunciation was off. His grandmother yelled at him before continuing the argument with his mother who was silent. She only yelled because she couldn't hear properly and she loved to be heard. Wyatt waited for another second, knowing they were fighting about him. She wanted him to go to South Korea, marry a nice Korean girl, go to college and work in a Korean company.

Wyatt slowly backed out, pulling the door shut. He looked out at the street, going back to his car and to Sawyer's house. He opened the door with his key and heard yelling, though this yelling was different than the one at his house.

Carter's voice was loud, she had lowered her voice as far as she could, which was still high. "I am a magical unicorn, I will have my avenge!" she yelled. As he climbed the stairs he could hear Sawyer laughing, Lio was making his own sounds.

"I love unicorn stew," Wyatt said as he stood in the bathroom doorway. Carter was startled at first and then grinned brightly, splashing the soapy water around. Her hair was full of bubbles, sitting atop her head like a limpy horn. Wyatt casually slid out his phone to take a picture of the three of them. Sawyer was mostly soaked with bubbles in his hair and on his face. Lio was in a bath seat happily splashing and making gurgling sounds.

"Oh god, don't take pictures," Sawyer moaned.

"Eww, water is going yellow. Bad Lio, no peeing in the bath," Carter said, hopping out. Carter ran out of the room and past Wyatt, laughing maniacally.

"Wait wait, you still need to rinse off, hey Carter!" Sawyer yelled, shaking his head. "I'm never having kids," he told Wyatt as he stood. "Watch Lio, yeah?"

"Sure," Sawyer smiled at him as he passed. Wyatt stepped into the bathroom, Lio was blinking up at him with a nearly toothless grin. "Let's get you cleaned up." Wyatt drained the water, pulling the hose and turning the water back on, he carefully rinsed off Lio and wrapped him in a duck towel. He pulled the hood so it sat on his head. Then he took a picture of the two of them.

Sawyer laughed, catching him taking a few more pictures. He was carrying Carter at his waist with his arms wrapped around her abdomen. Wyatt headed into Lio's room, grabbing a onesie and a new diaper. Wyatt played with his feet after he was finished, Lio laughed reaching out for him. Wyatt put out his index fingers, Lio latched on. "Ah ah, a monster has my fingers," he said, tilting his head down touching foreheads with Lio.

"I'm a unicorn, I'll save Yaya from the monster!" Carter said. She crashed into his legs, hugging them tightly. He looked down at her and then up at Sawyer who was grinning behind his phone.

"Fair is fair," he said, talking more as he walked closer.

Wyatt smiled, "Yeah," he said softly, his eyes tracing over Sawyer's face. Sawyer avoided his eyes, reaching down to pull a now dressed Carter off of Wyatt. He swung her up onto his hip, she swung her hand out as if it were a sword, pointing it to Lio.

"Bad monster," she said. Wyatt lifted Lio up, holding him mirror to Sawyer and Carter's positions.

"I think he's a good monster," Wyatt said. Lio reached out for Carter who pulled back into Sawyer.

"Wait wait, I want Yaya, Lio go with Sah," Carter said. Scrambling to get down, she stood at Wyatt's feet staring up at him until he handed Lio to Sawyer and lifted her up.

Carter play fought Lio, as Lio just reached out for her, giggling when Carter touched his fingers or tickled him under his chin. Finally, Sawyer called it off and carried Lio down to the kitchen for dinner. Wyatt followed, carrying Carter down. She told him about her day at daycare and how the dinosaurs drove cars. Wyatt nodded, oohing and aahing over the story.

"What's for dinner?" he asked when they entered the kitchen and he set Carter on a chair.

"Mac and cheese?" Sawyer asked.

Wyatt lifted an eyebrow, "Seriously?"

Sawyer rolled his eyes, lifting the box and setting it on the counter "Fine what do you want?"

"Not cheddar cancer noodles."

"Are you serious? You eat ramen like they're shutting down the factories."

"They could be, however, that's a totally different type of cancer that I'm willing to endure."

Sawyer nodded as he opened several cupboards and then the fridge, then shut all of them. "I need to go shopping. Wait, aren't you supposed to be at your house tonight, isn't your grandma coming over?" Sawyer asked, leaning against the counter. Wyatt stared at him and then at the box and back to him. Wyatt shrugged. "You staying the night?" Sawyer asked.

"Forever," Wyatt said. Sawyer shook his head grinning.

"I'm making mac and cheese, if you want real food then go home."

"One box won't feed us," Wyatt pointed out.

Sawyer started opening the cabinet again. "I only have one box, I'll add peas or something."

"No!" Carter and Wyatt said, Carter with more heart and Wyatt with disgust.

He shut the cabinet, mock glaring at them. "It's so hard to please you guys."

Wyatt smirked. "I think you could please me easily."

Sawyer sighed. "Wyatt, there are children."

Carter began chanting, her fists lightly banging against the table. "No peas no peas."

"Fine, no peas," Sawyer said, getting Carter to calm down. After the cancer cheese and pasta, they headed into the living room. Carter sat in her special chair in front of the couch watching a cartoon show. Lio crawled around slamming blocks on the floor. Wyatt leaned towards Sawyer on the couch as he messed around on his phone. As soon as Sawyer noticed the attention he put it down, half turning towards him.

"She still wants me to go to Korea, I half think that my mom might send me just to stop hearing about it."

Sawyer nudged his shoulder towards Wyatt. "You did tell me that you liked it."

"I was 10 and it was a vacation, of course, I liked it. I don't want to live there though."

Sawyer shifted until he was comfortable. "Really?"

"Okay, when I was younger I did, but I don't anymore. Maybe in the future, but I want to be here now."

"Good, I would hate it if you left now," Sawyer said, he looked to his siblings.

"Would you miss me enough to fly to Korea and kidnap me?" Wyatt asked, his hand reaching out to Sawyer's hand.

Sawyer smiled away from him, then shifted to him "I would kidnap you before you even got on the plane," Sawyer said.

Wyatt didn't say anything, his eyes roamed Sawyer's face before landing and staying on his eyes. "Don't move," Wyatt said.

Sawyer huffed a laugh, "Why? Are you going to kiss me or something?"

"Yeah, I am." Wyatt leaned forward, Sawyer was very still. Wyatt stopped inches away. Sawyer groaned and pushed forward just barely touching, immediately pulling back when Carter yelled for her own kisses.

"Well I can wait till after bedtime then," Wyatt whispered, pushing himself off of the couch quickly. He swooped up Lio and quickly headed up the stairs, he paused halfway when Carter called for kisses from him.

"When you're in bed," he said, continuing up. It was barely a kiss but even the idea that Sawyer was interested in him was enough. He hadn't been joking when he said it, but he expected Sawyer to take it like one. After putting Lio to bed, he headed into Carter's room. Sawyer was reading her a book, Wyatt walked in giving her a kiss on her forehead. He pulled away, looking at Sawyer who stuttered his words, and headed to Sawyer's room.

He dropped onto the bed, grabbing Sawyer's laptop. Sawyer joined him not much later and sat on the edge of the bed closest to the door.

"Knock it off," Wyatt said, grabbing a pillow, he smashed it against Sawyer's head.

Sawyer grabbed it, yanking it out of Wyatt's grip. "I'm not doing anything."

"Sure, whatever."

"What- where- I mean does anything change?" he asked, holding onto the pillow for a second before smashing it back at Wyatt.

"Fuck you," he said.

Wyatt let the pillow smash against his face before he snatched it from Sawyer's hand. Wyatt laughed, throwing the pillow to the floor. "Everything and nothing changes."

"Don't try and be wise with a dumb motivational phrase."

Wyatt shook his head, grabbing onto Sawyer's arm, pulling him closer. "Nothing changes for me, everything changes for you."

"What the hell does that mean? How doesn't it change oh-oh, wait back up what?"

"Calm down molasses, nothing has to change if you don't want it to."

"Funny," Sawyer said, leaning his forehead against Wyatt's shoulder. Wyatt didn't move. He gave Sawyer the time he needed. "So much is changing, it's always changing, constantly."

"Sawyer, if it's too much-"

"No, no it's not that, I want you, I just, I don't know."

"Then don't know, I like you molasses, that's it, simple, no other changes."

Sawyer shook his head. "Don't start calling me that."

"Molasses molasses." Sawyer pushed him off of the bed, Wyatt sprawled out on the floor, looking at the ceiling before shifting his eyes to Sawyer.

"Let's watch a movie or something, actually, we can finish our show. We haven't been able to watch it for weeks," Sawyer said.

"Only if you make popcorn," Wyatt told him.

"Fine, you set it up, I'll go make some." Wyatt mock saluted him from the floor. He didn't get up until a few minutes passed. He dragged himself off the floor to set up the show. He saw his phone light up with a text at the end of the bed, his mother asking where he was. He reached for it and began to type back that he was home, before deleting it and telling her he had a test to study for and he would be home tomorrow.

Tuesday April 22nd 3:21 P.M.

"Ji Seok." Wyatt stopped shoving groceries in the bag and shut the fridge. His mother always used his Korean name and not the American one he normally went by. Her tone told him she was questioning what he was doing and she was not happy about it. It's one she used when she thought her clients were guilty and got them off anyway.

He turned to her, her expression said pissed off. He had no idea why she was there.

"Your school has called me several times to tell me that you have been missing classes, care to explain about that and about this?" She didn't move to gesture what she meant., She was very still in her movements, his father was the opposite.

"Food drive at school," he lied and she didn't believe him for a second. Nothing on his face gave him away, it was the lie itself.

She moved around the island, it was blocking the rest of the bags he had been planning on taking. "Why would a food drive need paper towels, paper plates, and toilet paper?"

"Well you need plates to eat on, paper towels to clean up and toilet paper is pretty obvious." He shrugged, his arms crossed at his chest and he leaned against the fridge in a feigned casual manner.

She huffed quietly, nudging the bag with a black high heel. "I see, and how many of these *food drives* have been going on at your school? Your father has had to go shopping twice as much recently."

Wyatt shifted, shrugging. "Maybe he just likes it."

"He does, however, I find it strange that you can drink a whole gallon of milk in a day and eat massive amounts of food as well."

Wyatt tapped his fingers against his stomach. "I've been practicing cooking, I burn a lot of things so I have to throw it out."

"Doubtful, you've been cooking since you were eight and now ten years later you're burning things? How many lies are you going to rack up?"

He leaned back against the counter. "At least two more."

Her eyes shifted to the stove clock, then back to him. "Alright, let me hear them then, I have to get back to my office. I don't have time to fight you."

"I'm done, that last one was a lie. Fine, I'll take less food. Are you happy with that?"

"I'm more concerned about where you're taking it," she said.

"To a friend's."

"Sawyer."

"Yeah."

It was quiet in the kitchen, as she assessed him and the food, her eyes calculating every inch of him. All he could think about was that she knew. "His insurance check should be coming in, he won't need you to steal food anymore."

Wyatt looked at the stove clock. "He doesn't know about this."

"Doesn't he though? Where does he think the food comes from?"

"I didn't tell him I was taking it from here."

"How noble of you, but let me tell you now, that your obsession with that boy will ruin your future. If I thought that I could stop you then I would. You will go to college and you will have a great career; what you do with him should not affect that and if it does I will destroy what's left of his family." His mother was ruthless and he knew she would go through with it, she had been sweet to him a long time ago and even that faded away. She had worked with too many criminals and liars to treat him that way again. She was also deeply protective of her family, as long as they kept in their lines. If he didn't go to college then he would be nothing to her.

"You won't touch him. If you touch him I'll ruin our family."

"Then be sure to keep your promise. Decide on a college soon, your grandparents have been asking about it, also you know better than to let them find out about him. I fought tooth and nail to marry your father because he wasn't Korean. If you don't want the same issue then do as I tell you to." With that, she was done, it was her closing argument and she had nothing left to say. She left the kitchen, her heels clicking on the floor. He could hear her steps until the door opened and closed behind her. He waited until he heard her car leave and another minute to make sure she was down the street before grabbing all of the bags and taking them to the car.

Wednesday April 23rd 6:52 A.M.

Wyatt woke up minutes before his alarm, he lay in bed staring at his phone until the alarm went off. He dragged himself out of bed, quickly getting dressed he looked for his backpack before remembering where it was. He quickly brushed his teeth and ignored his parents as they got coffee and headed out to his car.

Sawyer was just pulling into the driveway when he arrived. Wyatt glared at him, Sawyer smiled tiredly. Wyatt waited in his car while Sawyer ran inside. He came out a minute later with both of their backpacks. He dropped them on the floorboard next to his feet. Slumping back into the seat, he rolled his head towards Wyatt. "I'm so tired, " he said, yawning towards the end. "Lio refuses to sleep and Carter has been asking for you non-stop."

Wyatt leaned over, pulling the passenger seat seat-belt across Sawyer's body. "I can see that, why don't you just stay home today?"

"Can't, I have another meeting with the counselor and then she's going to talk to the social worker. She wants me to talk to all of my teachers about what I can do to make sure I finish, maybe even a bit early."

"There's only a month left," Wyatt said, backing out of the driveway to the street.

"Yeah, but I can't stay in school and take care of the kids. Do you know how much daycare costs? It's insane. And I need to get a job because my parents' savings aren't going to last forever."

Wyatt took the chance to look at Sawyer, Sawyer was slowly leaning over to the door.

Sawyer fully leaned against the door, shifting to get comfortable. His eyes fell shut and Wyatt focused on the road.

"I'm staying at your place this weekend," Wyatt said when they were at the stop sign before the school parking lot. He shifted his eyes to look at Sawyer who was sleeping. Wyatt parked and waited for Sawyer to wake up.

Wyatt worked on his homework as he waited. He was just finishing his physics packet when Sawyer jumped awake next to him.

"Oh we're here," he said when he settled back in his seat. "What are you doing? We're going to be late." Sawyer grabbed his backpack, opening the door. Wyatt finished the last problem on his packet before joining him outside.

"Why is it so empty?" Sawyer asked, heading past cars to the school building.

Wyatt shrugged, even though Sawyer wasn't looking at him. "Probably because we're in the middle of 2nd period."

Sawyer whipped around stopping in front of Wyatt. "Are you serious? You're joking right? Wyatt! Dammit, I told you I needed to go to my classes," Sawyer yelled, pushing at Wyatt's chest. Wyatt remained solid against the attack.

"I wasn't the one sleeping."

"You could have woken me up!" Sawyer pushed him one last time before he pulled away, quickening his steps to the door. Wyatt kept his slow pace, watching Sawyer get further away.

"I could have," Wyatt called after him.

"What is with you lately?" Sawyer asked, though from the speed he was going, he was already at the door, not waiting for an answer.

Wyatt rolled his eyes, he wasn't even going to try and tell him that they were only halfway through 1st period.

He did grin at the text he received after 1st period calling him an asshole.

He finally saw Sawyer during 3rd period for PE, today they were running laps outside. "I hate running," Sawyer whined. Wyatt ignored him, he was always whining about running. "P.E. is unnecessary."

"It's pretty sad when Jeremy is in better shape than you and he's 50 pounds overweight," Lace said, coming up from behind them. Jeremy turned around at his name, grinning. Sawyer was struggling to breathe while Jeremy was happily moving along.

"That's because he works out," Sawyer protested, Jeremy affirming it with a hell yeah. "I have a high metabolism, give me ten years and we'll be in different situations."

"Yeah, Losada would probably snap if you shook his hand," Jeremy called out laughing. Wyatt bumped shoulders with Sawyer lightly, though he stumbled a few feet. Wyatt smiled at Sawyer's glare, it quickly twisted into a smile.

"You two need to stop being cute," Lace said before picking up her pace to reach Jeremy.

Sawyer reclaimed his spot next to Wyatt. "I really hate running."

"Tell the teacher you sprained your ankle."

"No, then it'll become a whole thing." Wyatt ignored the rest of his complaints, and when they went around for the third lap, he tripped him into the coach and continued on his way alone.

Sawyer beamed at him when P.E. finished and they changed back into their clothes in the locker room. "Stop looking at me like that," Wyatt said.

"But I love you so much," Sawyer said. Wyatt's heartbeat went into overdrive and he quickly pulled on his shirt. "Teach was a bit pissed but I didn't have to run anymore."

"Idiot," Wyatt said, grabbing his bag leaving the locker room before he became the idiot.

Wyatt stared down at the chicken he got for lunch; he was sure it wasn't real chicken. More than likely it was artificial chicken made from grass and wheat, he would never prove it but he wouldn't eat it either. He saw Sawyer already at their usual table talking with Rowan whom he could hear from four tables away.

"I can help with the kids," she offered. Wyatt wanted to scoff at that, she had practically killed the doll they had to take home. "I took child development with you," Sawyer replied, looking at his own meal like he didn't want to touch it.

"Oh right," she laughed. Her voice was quiet and if he was any further away or not paying attention he wouldn't have heard her offer. "I could help with sex."

"Wyatt already does that," Sawyer said. Wyatt isn't sure if Sawyer knew what he said or if he said it to just mess with Rowan. It worked of course before she was laughing. Wyatt set his food on the table.

Sawyer perked up when he saw him. "Can you do me a favor?"

"A sexual one or a regular one?" Wyatt asked. From the shocked embarrassed look he didn't think Wyatt had heard his earlier comment.

Sawyer pushed through. "I need you to pick up the kids. Carter has a fever and she puked in the toilet."

Wyatt looked down at his food, sliding it to Sawyer. "Eat it, share it. I'll see you at home," Wyatt said. Rowan commented but he didn't hear or care what it was.

Wyatt drove to Sawyer's house to change cars before heading to the daycare. He entered the brightly colored room where Carter was sitting in a small chair near a door. She saw him walking in. "Yaya!" she yelled, laughing happily, turning into coughing.

Wyatt picked up Carter, looking at the young woman working. "I'll get Lio," she announced heading down a short hallway. Carter yawned into his neck, smearing snot across his skin. Her forehead blazed against him, he shifted her higher getting a better grip. The woman was coming back, Lio was gnashing on a cracker. "I'll help you to the car," she offered. He thanked her and led her outside.

Carter and Lio were both sleeping by the time he got to their house. Carefully carrying them inside, he set Lio down, shutting the door with his foot and carried Carter to her room.

When he got back downstairs, Lio was still sleeping. He carried him into the living room, setting the car seat in the center of the room. He dropped on the couch texting Sawyer that the kids were home. He looked around the room for Sawyer's laptop. He groaned, pushing off of the couch he quickly ran upstairs to grab the laptop, dropping it off in the living room. Wyatt headed into the kitchen finding a dismal amount of food and pulled out his phone ordering pizza, sliding back on the couch as he called.

He grabbed Sawyer's laptop, he snooped around on his computer, grinning when he saw a folder named WWW. He clicked on it and frowned. The folder opened but it was photos of him. He scrolled through them; half of them were with Sawyer, others were when they were drunk. He clicked on a video. He looked completely trashed in the video, Sawyer didn't sound much better when he spoke.

"Wyatt, how much do you love me?" Sawyer asked. Wyatt had to replay it three times to actually catch all of the words.

"All of it," he replied. He was smiling brightly at Sawyer and then the video cut off. There were years of photos in the album, all of the recent videos were from the last few months and they were always wasted in them. One had Sawyer shoving his birthday cake in Wyatt's face and proceeding to lick off some of the frostings from his cheek and mouth. "This little shit," Wyatt cursed. He didn't remember any of these, he had blacked out. He closed out of the folder, closing the laptop. He tapped Lio's car seat with his foot, causing the car seat to rock back and forth. He watched it rock for a while until the doorbell rang. He quickly got off the couch, pulling open the door, grinning at the smell of pizza.

Carter came running down the stairs, as he shut the door. She hugged him around the legs. "Yaya stay home! I want pizza!" He smiled down at her as she smiled up at him.

"Okay but you have to let me go and be quiet because Lio is sleeping." She grinned and tiptoed slowly to the kitchen, Wyatt watching her in amusement following behind her. He set the two pizzas on the kitchen table, pulling out paper plates he opened the large first.

"Eww," Carter said loudly.

"Shh," Wyatt told her. She nodded seriously but frowned at the pizza, it was covered in black olives and pepperoni.

She pouted, crossing her arms. "I don't like the black dots."

"Olives, and that's why I got you this." she shifted towards the other pizza box, pulling it open to reveal pineapple pizza.

"Peeapples!" Carter yelled.

Wyatt lifted his index finger to his closed lips. "Shh."

"Sorry," she said, already trying to pull out a piece of pizza. Wyatt helped her, setting it on the plate. "Hot hot," Carter said, staring at the pizza as if it would cool at her gaze. He pulled two pieces out of the large pizza for himself.

"Yaya," Carter said. Wyatt set his pizza down, giving her his attention as he closed the pizza boxes. "Why do you keep leaving?"

"What do you mean?" he asked. She frowned at him.

She sighed like it was a struggle for her to explain it to him. "Cause this Yaya's home."

He smiled at her. "It is, isn't it?"

"It is!" she yelled.

"Shh," he whispered. It was too late Lio was already crying to get out of his car seat. "Wait don't eat that if you're sick," Wyatt said. Sawyer was going to kill him if Carter threw up because he fed her pizza.

"I'm not sick," she told him, her smile was gentle and her eyes were wide.

"Sawyer said you threw up," Wyatt said, though he didn't know why he was talking to a child about it. She shook her head, smiling.

"You little-" He didn't finish his sentence, heading to the living room to get Lio. When he came back with Lio in his arms he said, "Brat," to Carter who took a large bite out of her pizza, smearing grease across her chin and mouth. Wyatt leaned over checking her forehead, the heat from before was gone. Her cheeks were no longer red and her eyes were bright.

"Lio what do you want for lunch? Some bananas? Or maybe some bread?"

"He wants pizza!" Carter declared.

Wyatt shook his head. "No, he's still too young for pizza."

"Mine then," she stated. Hitting her hands on her chest, smearing grease on her shirt. Wyatt nodded to her and she continued to eat the rest of her pizza while he got Lio settled in his chair.

3:37 P.M.

Wyatt heard the front door open, turning his head he saw Sawyer and Rowan. He was sitting on the living floor with the kids. Carter perked up and then frowned at Rowan. Carter moved away from where she and Lio were playing with blocks together. Wyatt quickly moved the laptop out of his lap before Carter could sit on it. She snuggled into Wyatt, he set the laptop on the coffee table, using it above Carter's head.

"Hey Wyatt and kids. Aw they're so cute," Rowan cooed. Wyatt ignored her.

"Did you check her fever?" Sawyer asked.

"Yeah after lunch, it went down on its own and she said she doesn't feel sick anymore."

"Okay good," Sawyer said, slipping onto the couch behind Wyatt, his feet hitting Wyatt's tailbone. Wyatt turned to watch Rowan sit by Lio. Lio looked up at her and then for Sawyer, he crawled away from Rowan to Sawyer. Sawyer leaned down, lifting him up.

"Did you miss me?" he asked Lio, raising him above his head. Lio yelled out, reaching his hands for Sawyer's face. Sawyer grinned and looked down. Wyatt smiled at him, taking a few pictures on his phone. If Sawyer was going to have a secret file of him then he was going to have one of his own of Sawyer.

"Carter do you want to play with me?" Rowan asked. Wyatt leaned back a bit, feeling Sawyer's shins against his back. Carter shook her head.

"Oh, okay." Rowan shifted a few of the blocks, starting to build. Wyatt looked down to see Carter watching her. His attention was stolen away by Lio who yanked his hair. Wyatt leaned back, resting his head on Sawyer's knees. Sawyer forced Lio's hand open to drop his hair. Wyatt stared up at Sawyer with a bright smile. Sawyer stared back, his look of surprise suddenly turning to a grimace. "Fuck." he swore. Looking down, he saw a bite mark just above his elbow on the inside of his bicep from Carter. Carter got up, running to play with the blocks with Rowan.

"What did she do?" Wyatt held his arm up for Sawyer to see the mark.

"Carter! You can't bite people like that," Sawyer told her.

"Why not?" Carter asked.

Sawyer pushed up Wyatt's arm. "It's bad and it hurts."

"Okay," she said, starting to stack the blocks. Wyatt turned so his body faced Carter and Rowan but his head was facing Sawyer. Lio was squirming in his hands, Sawyer set him down, letting him crawl to Rowan and the blocks. Wyatt slid back towards the computer, opening the spreadsheet he created. Lifting it up he set it in Sawyer's lap.

"What's this?"

"Read it and fix the mistakes."

"Are you pawning your homework onto me?"

"No, this is your *home*work," Wyatt said. Sawyer spent a few minutes looking it over, typing and changing a few things. Wyatt watched him, only taking his eyes away when Carter called for him.

"Yaya, come play with us." He hesitated, looking over at Sawyer who was still looking at his computer. "Yaya," Carter called again, he crawled over to where they were building an uneven faulty castle. Lio was babbling and knocking over the blocks in front of him.

They spent the rest of the day playing different games with the kids. Rowan decided to stay for dinner.

Thursday April 24th 1:58 A.M.

Wyatt shifted around the bed; it felt too large, too empty. He stretched his body out, his room was dark and the house was silent. His parents had come home, though they went to bed hours ago. He lifted his phone up, it was already 2:00 A.M.. Pulling off his sheets, he got out of bed and moved through the hall quietly until he was in the kitchen. He flicked the light on, pulling open the fridge. The shelves were full of various foods and nothing interested him. He looked at his phone again, he texted Sawyer.

A second later his phone was vibrating with a call, he answered it.

Sawyer was talking before Wyatt got out a hello. "Lio is just staring at me, every time I put him down for bed he wakes up and freaks out. I've been in this rocking chair since like 7. After I put Carter to bed. I think he misses our mom."

Wyatt waited another second before answering, "Need me to come over?"

"Nah, we have school tomorrow. Also what are you doing awake?"

"Can't sleep."

"You're almost as bad as Lio. Normally you're out pretty quick and it's impossible to wake you up."

Wyatt rolled his eyes even though Sawyer couldn't see him. "You're not sleeping either."

"Because I'm watching Lio. I would love to be sleeping right now."

"I could watch him and you could sleep."

Sawyer was quiet and Wyatt enjoyed the seconds of just listening to him breathe. Wyatt wanted to bang his head against the fridge.

"Is something going on at home?" Sawyer asked.

"No." Wyatt shifted a few of the magnets on the fridge, thinking of the difference between his fridge and Sawyer's. Wyatt's fridge had uniformed magnets, all 1-inch squares.

"Are your parents fighting?"

"No idea, not my business." Wyatt leaned his head against the fridge.

"Wyatt," Sawyer started, pausing just a second before continuing. "Nevermind. Get some sleep okay?"

"Yeah, you too," Wyatt said, pulling away from the fridge.

"I'll try."

Wyatt waited until Sawyer hung up, letting his darkened phone drop onto the counter. "Idiot," Wyatt whispered, pulling open the fridge again.

Chapter 7 Hae Na

Saturday April 12th 11:56 P.M.

Hae Na let the doctor wrap her wrist as a nurse wrapped her abdomen where they were deeply bruised. She was trying to take slow light breaths because each movement spread pain to the tips of her fingers. Her fingers were scraped and bruised as well but none of them were broken so she counted it as a win.

"There are ways to stay safe, if you're being hurt-" Hae Na shook her head immediately, stopping the nurse from continuing.

"Stop, I know what it looks like and honestly the story is so embarrassing I wish I could say it was something so serious. I was coming down the stairs at school and I wasn't paying attention. I saw a cute guy and totally missed a step. I thought I was fine, I mean I knew it hurt but I thought it was just the initial fall but then it kept hurting so I thought I should come in."

"I'm glad, I was so worried. I've seen quite a few patients and it breaks my heart when I see young women being hurt by people they love. Here take this card anyway. Just in case you know someone who may need it." She pulled a light blue card out of her pocket, placing it in Hae Na's hand.

Hae Na shook her head slowly with a sad smile. "Thank you, I mean I can't understand it. Why someone would do that," she said quietly. She listened as the nurse spoke about her volunteer work at a women's shelter and a lot of the women just haven't realized what real love is but that she was working on showing them how to find it. Hae Na remained quiet, there was nothing she could say, she couldn't reach out and ask for help and she couldn't continue to lie.

When the nurse finally left and she was alone, she shoved the card in her pocket. She stared at her fingers. Making a fist with them, she ignored the shooting pain. Slowly she released them, she continued doing it until the nurse came back with discharge papers. Hae Na took the papers, signed, smiled at the nurse's joke about not being distracted by boys, and left.

Hae Na looked out at the parking lot, her car wasn't in it. It was to the left in a parking structure. As she stood there she saw several different types of people enter. A woman and her daughter, a young boy with a possible older brother holding his arm close. Some people were young and some were old. A coughing baby, a limping man, a drunk college student, a crying woman. The hospital was a place that anyone could need, whether rich or poor, young or old. A place where babies were born and people died. This could be a place of a miracle or a tragedy. It took her awhile for her to start moving again, she went slow, choosing to walk up the stairs instead of taking the elevator to the fourth floor. Each step was painful, each step a reminder of how easily she fell down the stairs. One tiny nudge and she was falling, she thought she was going to die. She thought it was the end and for that second she was relieved. It was over, she was free and now she wasn't.

The fourth-floor lot was mostly filled, the spots on either side of her were empty. Her parking job had been less than stellar and she was half surprised her car wasn't keyed. She carefully got in the driver's seat and pulled out. She pressed on the brake when the car was straightened out. Switching gears, she slowly let off the brake and the car rolled forward back in the spot. Putting it in park, she shut it off, pushing the seat back. She wanted to be free for just a while longer.

Sunday April 13th 3:03 A.M.

Hae Na came home, the lights were off and the front door was locked. It meant that Sam wasn't drunk anymore. Hae Na grimaced at the noise the front door made as she opened it. She tried to carefully shut it and all but tiptoe to the bedroom. She nearly thought she made it until she heard Sam's voice.

"Mm, Han, come snuggle with me," she said. Hae Na thought she hated this the most. The comfort, Hae Na slid into bed, careful with her wrist. Sam wrapped an arm around her, pulling her in tight. Hae Na held the tears in as her body ached as much as her heart did. She couldn't do it anymore, she couldn't let herself be hurt like this. She could be stronger than this, she was stronger than this. She didn't move the entire night, she barely slept.

When she finally got up, all of her confidence dwindled down to nothing. Her strength was zapped out of her as she ate waffles and eggs Sam made for breakfast. She smiled and nodded as Sam spoke about work and how she was going out that night. Hae Na stopped smiling when the door shut behind Sam as she left.

The small apartment was quiet, Hae Na shifted in her seat, the chair squeaked. Dropping her fork onto the paper plate, she watched syrup splash onto her sleeve and the table. She threw the fork in the sink and the plate in the trash. It needed to go out, it was already days overfilled. She pressed down on the back of the plate trying to push some of it down. When it was far enough she pulled it out and tightened the strings. She could easily pack up her things, carry them out of the apartment just like the trash. She could do it, instead, she took the trash to the dumpster and returned to do the dishes, struggling with her wrist as she did so. She headed into the messy living room, dropping onto the couch, she immediately sunk in. She lay across it, reaching her hand under the couch. Her hand stopped when it hit a plastic bottle, she pulled it out. Four pills left, she shook the bottle. She struggled to open the bottle with her wrist when it didn't open, she threw it across the room, not watching when it hit the wall.

She took a deep breath and stared at the ceiling, she hated the ceiling. It was a cream popcorn ceiling, she wanted to pick each piece off. She didn't move from the couch for a long time, this wasn't how she wanted to spend her time. She had a class that she was missing, she had been missing a lot lately. "This is what you've become Kwon Hae Na," she told herself, she used to have a goal, she used to want things and now she wanted nothing. She wanted to be alone, but then she was lonely. She was lonely now even though she was with someone. She lost her friends, her ambition, her family. She groaned as she lifted her wrist, this wasn't the beginning, this wasn't even the middle. Hae Na sat up, this was the end.

She grabbed a duffle bag and started shoving her clothes in it, her charger, her laptop. She gathered everything that was important and threw it all in her car. Her phone charged as she drove towards home, stopping at a rest stop along the way. Leaning her chin on the steering wheel, she jumped when she accidentally hit the horn. She laughed as she leaned back against her seat. She watched trucks come in, trucks leave, watched families park and run inside before coming back out and leaving. She sat there for hours watching people go about their lives.

"Make a choice," she told herself. Go back to Sam or go forward alone.

She headed home to Sam, she had nowhere else to go. Sam was home when she arrived, she was sitting on the couch watching a show she didn't recognize.

Sam spoke first, her tone telling Hae Na she was in danger. "I called you," Sam said, tilting her head back against the couch looking innocent.

"My phone was dead," Hae Na said, looking for her phone in her pockets. The duffle dropped from her shoulder to the ground. She left her phone in the car. Hae Na quickly lifted her head when Sam pushed off of the couch, setting a bottle of rum on the coffee table. Hae Na knew she should run, knew she should go before Sam was any closer.

"Where did you go?" Sam asked as if it was an innocent question. Hae Na knew it wasn't.

Hae Na answered truthfully when she spoke, "Nowhere." Sam laughed, it was a sweet-sounding thing, it was deceiving. Sam moved around the couch looking down at the bag at Hae Na's feet.

"Going nowhere with everything?" she asked."Hae Na, you know how much I love you. I was really hurt last night." She continued talking, not giving Hae Na a chance to speak or explain. Sam reached out to Hae Na, Hae Na took a step back. Sam grabbed onto Hae Na's hurt wrist, holding it tightly. "Where did you go Hae Na?"

"I really didn't go anywhere, Sam you're hurting me."

"You didn't go to class, you didn't have work today, so where could you have gone?"

Hae Na tried to pull away, Sam tightened her grip pulling her closer. "Sam please you're hurting me."

"I really don't understand it, I love you so much and then you do things like this and then I thought to myself, what really is the problem here?" Sam reached into her black jacket pocket. Hae Na knew what it was before she pulled it out, she could hear them knocking against each other. "You haven't been taking your pills." Sam smiled. "But I'm going to help you with that too," Sam was quick when she grabbed Hae Na pulling her to the floor. Hae Na struggled against her, trying to push the bottle away.

"Sam stop, please stop," Hae Na begged. She was 7 months sober besides her near slip, and she had no intention of going back. Sam opened up the bottle, Hae Na knocked her hand against it scattering the pills around them. She nearly screamed when Sam punched her face, grabbing onto it she shoved a few pills down her throat. Hae Na struggled against her, earning another punch to the face and gut. Sam sat on top of her holding her nose and mouth shut. Hae Na smashed the heel of her hand against Sam's nose, knocking her off. Hae Na pushed Sam over, grabbing her bag she ran out the door.

Hae Na drove as far as she could get, then she pulled over and puked as much as she could. She wiped at the tears on her face and drool on her mouth. She stared at the mess in the bushes, reaching into her jeans she pulled out the card the nurse gave her. Hae Na was more than the girl who acted as a puppet, allowing someone else to make her decisions. She was a person and no one was going to treat her like she wasn't.

Monday April 14th 6:13 P.M.

Hae Na stared up at the structure. It was an unassuming white normal farmhouse, just outside of the small town and it was where she was going to stay for the next month. She pulled her car to the back of the house where a few other cars were parked, parking next to a car just as beat up as her own. It used to be nice until Sam took a few different tools to it. Now it looked like a junker, not worth the 10,000 dollars she paid for it three years ago. She shut it off, another car pulled up on the other side of her. It was a woman with hair as bright as her smile, on the ends of her hair was a pastel lavender color. Hae Na got out of her car, pulling her duffle bag with her.

"Hae Na?" she spoke, her voice was as sweet as honey in tea and deeper than she expected.

Hae Na nodded. "Yeah."

"I'm Henny, normally this goes through different channels, but it sounds like you really needed somewhere to stay and Tali called in vouching for you."

"Tali?" Hae Na tried to remember who the name belonged to.

"She's a nurse," Henny said. Hae Na remembered her, remembered her kind words and smile.

"Oh, oh yeah I remember."

Henny nodded her head. "A sweet girl, have you seen a doctor?"

Hae Na tilted her head away then back to her again. "Yeah I'm okay." Henny didn't look like she believed her.

She lifted her arm, her hand open as she showed the way. "Alright honey, come on let's get you settled."

Hae Na nodded. "Okay," she said, following her up the stairs. The house had a wrap-around porch and a porch swing. It was all very moviesque until the door opened. The entrance had very little personality. It was almost clinical, white stairs that led up. A sitting room to the left with two chairs and a couch, and a side table with magazines. The walls held few pictures and the ones they did were of flowers. Henny leads her further in, the scenery slowly changed, another room that felt more lived in, even though it was a near copy of the first one. Knitted blankets were thrown over the back of the couch and chairs, books lay randomly on several surfaces, a T.V. sat on a stand.

"It's still quite early for anyone to be up," Henny said. "There's a schedule that is mostly followed. It's more like a guideline, however, there is a chore schedule that needs to be followed. You'll start on that tomorrow." Henny moved past the room, talking as she went a hand waving in the air. "The living room, no one uses, this sitting room everyone uses. The kitchen is just past here and that is a free-for-all, you want food? You cook it. Or you find someone who can cook and ask them, maybe trade a chore. We try and keep arguments and fights to a minimum of zero. There are a lot of traumatized people and fighting is a major trigger. Now if you really really need to do something take it up with me or Alise," she said. Hae Na followed her to the dining room. Henny fixed the display of flowers on the table before continuing into another room, this room had doors shut on the other side. There were a few chests open full of toys and mats on the ground. The shelves were filled with books, the bottom shelf was children's books, from there and up were books of different sizes and colors.

"Last room on the first floor, all of the bedrooms are upstairs. This is a playroom for the kids and a library. You really find an appreciation for books when there isn't much else to do, some people sew or knit." Henny said, she pushed a few books that stuck out back into place. "Let's get some tea before the others wake up."

Hae Na took the tea, it was an amber tinted liquid, the same color as Sam's eyes. Hae Na swirled the cup around like it was wine. Hae Na took the small cup of milk, pouring it in until the color changed and drank it down until there was only a drop left. She stared at the last bit in the cup; it was no longer recognizable as the tea it had originally been. When she looked up she realized Henny had been studying her. Hae Na set the cup on the kitchen island, stretching out her body awkwardly.

She winced at the pain in her side, she curled back down staring into the cup.

"I met a man once, who told me that the world was only as big as I could see. If I stood on the porch then the world was as far as I could see. He was wrong of course, it took me a long time to realize it. I left twelve times and each time I went back I felt like that world got smaller. I wish I could have left on my own. He died and my world got a lot bigger." Henny smiled, it was a gentle smile. She wasn't looking at Hae Na, instead she was staring into her own amber colored tea. Henny looked up at Hae Na. "I'm really proud of you. Even if it takes you twelve times. People don't always understand but in this house, everyone will. I know it's not much but we'll be here for every time that it takes you to see how big the world really is." Henny stared at her and Hae Na realized her eyes were the same as the tea she just looked into like it was a reflection. Hae Na shifted her eyes to the black toaster on the counter. She looked at all of the appliances and cabinets. In her peripheral she saw her move, Hae Na watched her pull the bread out and start toast for them.

At seven Hae Na met Alise, she had thick long dark hair that she wore around her like a coat, and thick, perfectly arched eyebrows. Her olive skin made her pale green eyes brighter. Her sculpted face and cotton shirt didn't hide her brawny figure. She smiled showing a gap between her two front teeth. "You must be Hae Na, I got a late-night call about you," she said, her voice didn't match her look. It was sweet, the voice you would get from someone working in customer service who was trying to appease you. "I'm Alise, I'm going to show you to your room, the girls in your room are already up and about." Hae Na followed her up the stairs. She continued to explain more rules. At the top of the stairs, Hae Na followed her two rooms down and to the left where a door was open, the first door they passed, she could hear a shower running.

"Pick a bunk, we have these two open." Hae Na looked across the bunk to another bunk, the top one was empty and the bottom one had a woman not much older than her sitting in it. She looked up, her eyes roamed over Hae Na and then went back to her lap where she was folding a piece of paper.

Hae Na took the empty bottom bunk opposite the woman, setting her bag in front of it.

Alise clapped three times. "Great, I have a few things I have to do. If you have any questions, ask one of the women or me and we'll get it answered okay?" Hae Na nodded, sitting on the edge of the bed, she stared down at her bag.

Hae Na jumped when a blue paper fish landed on top of her bag. She looked up, the woman nearly mirrored her position. "Might want to pick a hobby, it gets pretty boring in here without one," the woman said.

"How long have you been here?" Hae Na asked.

"Two weeks, though it feels like a year." She pulled open a drawer on the nightstand that sat next to her bed. She pulled out handfuls of paper origami and flicked a few at Hae Na; a crane, dog, frog. They were all different colors with patterns. "I still can't get the dragon right, but I've been trying," she said, flicking over a half-finished one.

"I'm not really good at these, even boats and hats I was terrible at," Hae Na said. She smiled at the pile in her lap. She looked up and took in the sight of her new roommate, she was nearly the opposite of the woman. She was brittle looking, Hae Na could see from her faded orange sweater how deep her ebony collarbones looked. Her hair was cut short, it fit the structure of her face.

"Yeah, I was okay at a few of them but youtube would be better. We don't get those luxuries here though." She sighed dramatically falling back onto her bed. She sat up throwing a lot of origami back into the drawer. "By the time I leave, I'll be able to take a bath in them."

"You'd have to be careful of papercuts," Hae Na commented.

"Oh, I didn't think of that," she said, staring at the drawer a second longer before shutting it. "You can keep those if you want." She stuck her hand out gesturing to the pile in Hae Na's lap.

"Thanks, I'm Hae Na by the way."

"Shay, and my bunkmate is Jordie, she takes a shower every day. Don't be surprised when she comes out looking like a lobster. She's working on it with a therapist."

Hae Na put away all of the origami into her bag, it didn't take long before Jordie joined them. She paused in the doorway as she stared at Hae Na, it took a few seconds before she moved. Jordie wasn't quite a lobster but she was very pink. Her light hair was tied up in a tight bun on the top of her head. She was broader than Shay and the light blue dress showed her wide shoulders.

12:19 P.M.

Hae Na sat in a chair in the sitting room, watching as people went about their days. Three women started lunch, offering it for the whole house. Hae Na sat until a plate was thrust under her nose. She sat back looking at the plate, then she lifted her head to a woman she hadn't met yet.

The woman smiled, reminding her of a mom from the '50s who makes snacks for her kids with a doting air about her. "It's delicious, I promise." Hae Na took the plate, it had a sandwich and a pile of chips on it.

"Thank you."

"The first day is the hardest," Hae Na knew that as an absolute. The first day anywhere was horrible. Fear, anxiety, and doubt sat heavy in her mind and stomach.

Hae Na ate slowly, smiling appreciatively to her. "My name is Sandy."

"I'm Hae Na," she responded, she looked around the room and a few people looked at her curiously.

"That's a lovely name," Sandy said. Hae Na returned her focus to her.

"Thank you, everyone pronounces it wrong like when they see it they say Hannah but it's Hae Na."

"How do you write it?" she asked. Hae Na looked around for a piece of paper. "Oh, let me get you a notebook." She stood up going to one of the bookshelves, she grabbed an empty notebook and pen handing it to Hae Na. "You can keep it, that shelf is full of empty and half-full notebooks people have left behind."

"Thank you," Hae Na said, she flipped open the first page, she wrote her name in English first and then Korean.

"That's beautiful, can you write more?" Sandy asked, leaning forward, staring down at the Hangul.

"Yeah, I actually learned when I was a kid, my grandmother was very strict on everyone learning Korean."

"That's good, too many people lose their culture and traditions, that's a real tragedy." Hae Na gave her a sad smile, she felt like she was already losing it. Her family had been a large part of her and now she was disconnected from them. She felt disconnected from everyone.

Thursday April 24th 1:23 P.M.

Hae Na leaned against the counter munching on a stolen cookie as people busily moved around the kitchen. Cassie stood on a chair to reach the counter as she stirred the dough for another batch of cookies. She was sticking her tongue out as she worked, she was about the size of a four-year-old at the age of seven. Her mom, Renee, was average height. She was sitting on the counter opposite of Hae Na reading off an ingredient and measurement list to Sandy who was making some other dessert that was French and supposedly fancy. The cookies and other pastries they had been making were placed in boxes on the kitchen table. Hae Na had been filling the boxes until they got to the point where she had to wait for them to finish baking. Cassie finished mixing. Grabbing a cookie scoop, she started filling up another pan of perfectly shaped cookie dough scoops.

Cassie stuck the scoop in her mouth as soon as the last one dropped on the pan. She grabbed the spoon she was stirring with and offered it to Hae Na.

"Thanks, girly," she said, taking the spoon from her and sticking it in her mouth.

"Maybe now you'll start gaining some weight," Sandy said.

"I've always been small, my whole family is pretty small, except maybe one of my uncles and cousins."

Sandy slid off of the counter. "The one you're seeing after you leave here?"

Hae Na huffed a laugh before replying, "No, he's about my height though he's built a lot better, he plays soccer."

"Do you think it'll be better with that side of your family?"

Sandy asked, her tone was gentle and mothering.

Hae Na shook her head. "No, my aunt hasn't been the warmest person. But my cousin will be, we've always been pretty close. Since I went to college, we haven't talked as much."

"Well it's good to have someone in your corner, you've got us too."

"Thanks," Hae Na said. She looked down at the flour-covered floor. These women, in the week that she had known them, had felt more like family than her real family. Her family didn't want her, they didn't want her sexuality, they didn't want her lifestyle, they didn't want her. These women, would they not want her if they knew too?

"I'm a lesbian," she blurted. Sandy cut off her laugh to stare at Hae Na. Hae Na was scared now, probably more fearful than when she told her own family.

"Oh dear, I know the perfect girl. She works down at the grocery store, blue hair, super cute."

Hae Na grinned. "Not ready for it yet but thanks."

Sandy nodded. "No worries, I'll get her number just in case."

Renee clapped her hands together, stealing their attention. "Oh no, what about the girl, oh you'll see her, she's picking up the boxes later. She is just the most precious thing. You'll love her, of course when you're ready," Renee said. And Hae Na fell just a bit in love with both of them.

Hae Na turned when Tanya walked in, she twisted her long black hair into a bun. "When I was in high school there was this beautiful girl, I hated her. Until I realized I hated her because I was in love with her. Let me tell you I was not the greatest bisexual woman, that was before I even knew being bisexual was a thing." She laughed. Hae Na smiled at her. Tanya pulled her into a quick hug. "Now where are my cookies?" She asked looking around the kitchen until she found a box of cookies that had been filling and emptying with cookies. Tanya nearly skipped over to it pulling out two cookies. She took a bite, moaning and grinning. "Delicious," she said, spitting a few crumbs.

"Tanya, get out, we don't need your spit in the cookies." Tanya stuck her tongue out at Renee, diva-walking out of the kitchen. She did a turn in the doorway, striking a pose before walking off.

Shay walked in, dropping her duffle bag at the door. Hae Na dropped off of the counter. Shay made the rounds giving everyone a hug in the kitchen. Stopping in front of Hae Na, she put a hand on her shoulder, squeezing lightly.

"Keep in touch," she whispered before pulling her into a hug. Hae Na hugged back, letting go when Shay pulled away. Hae Na nodded and Shay waved as she left the kitchen, and with the front door shutting, Shay was gone.

Saturday April 26th 9:49 P.M.

Hae Na was just finishing the fold on a dragon, leaning over the desk with the lamplight gleaming down when she heard the shout for lockdown. She stood up, leaving the finished dragon and opened her door. She was pushed back when Jordie came in locking the two locks on the door and moving to shut off all the lights. Hae Na stood near the door watching her flit around before she shoved Hae Na in between the bed and dresser. They both squeezed into the tight space together. Jordie's breathing was slowly returning to normal though her body was trembling. Hae Na felt the silence of the house, not a sound was made, even the children who were usually rambunctious were silent.

Hae Na startled when there was a bang at the front door. The banging continued, then shouting. He kept screaming for her to come out, for her to stop hiding. Hae Na wasn't sure who he wanted to come out. It was the shattering of glass that got her attention, that he could really break-in, that anyone could break in and hurt them. Fear settled in her body, she held so tight to Jordie's wrist she was afraid it would snap. Jordie didn't complain. Hae Na took a few breaths as more glass shattered, and more bangs echoed through the house. . It was the lights of police cars that filled her with a sense of relief. She heard more shouting as the officers got out of their cars, the man continued to yell that his wife was inside and she had no right taking his child. The voices slowly quieted and the silence slowly returned as the lights faded into the distance. Neither Hae Na nor Jordie moved, even as voices and footsteps returned outside of their locked door. When there was a knock at the door, the pair jumped. "Are you girls alright?" Henny asked, her voice calm and reassuring.

"We're fine," Hae Na responded automatically, not really believing her own words but Henny probably understood as she moved on down the hallway checking on the others.

Hae Na wasn't sure how long they stayed there until finally, she couldn't anymore. Her bones cracked as she stood. She didn't want to cower in the corner, she was tired of being scared. This is why she left Sam, this is why she was here. She wanted to be strong, she wanted to be stronger.

Chapter 8 Rye
Saturday April 19th 4:11 P.M.

Rye held Otis' right hand as his left was being wrapped in tape, Rye was trying not to laugh as Otis's face squeezed tight in pain. Rye always knew that Otis had a low pain tolerance but from the way his hand was being squeezed, he thought he was going to need them wrapped too. His fingers twitched and Otis loosened his grip.

"Sorry," he said. Rye just grinned at him and squeezed his hand. Otis smiled and turned his head away from Rye.

"You're all done now, I want you to wait at least a week before you even try to raise a weight lifting bar," the doctor said. Otis nodded his agreement, pulling his hand away from Rye. Rye poked him in the side causing him to jump off of the hospital bed. Otis glared as he followed the nurse out of the room. Rye followed behind, he didn't expect their Saturday night to turn into a hospital trip. Otis was clumsy and Rye had watched him trip over a chair and slam into the ground. It had been funny until Otis got up staring at Rye with tears racing down his face. Otis was tough when it came to everything but any type of pain to his body, which was strange since he used to beat up kids when they made fun of Rye. Rye had been too weak to stand up to them and Otis had stepped in. They had been friends ever since. Rye got in the driver's seat of Otis' car and waited for Otis to drop into his seat.

"Are we still hanging out at my place or did you want to go home?" Rye asked, waiting to reverse the car. The answer would dictate which direction he pulled out.

"Your place, my mom will freak if she sees this," he said lifting his arm, carefully setting it back down against his abdomen. Rye shook his head as he checked the back window and carefully backed out.

"Dude, she's going to see the insurance bill and she's gonna see it when you go home tomorrow."

"I'll deal with it tomorrow." Otis sat forward and then leaned back in the seat, moving around a few times before settling. He pulled a cord up from between the seat and console, placing his phone between his legs he easily plugged it in. Rye focused on the road and soon music played throughout the car. It was German pop, Otis had been listening to it since his parents decided to go to Germany for a month in the summer, four months ago. Rye had long ago gotten used to it, especially since Otis had the rule that his car meant his music. Since Rye didn't have a car, they always took Otis'. If he wasn't in Otis' car, he was on the city bus.

Otis lowered the volume on the music. "I want to switch seats," Otis said.

Rye huffed, checking his mirrors before switching lanes and taking a right. "I'm not that bad of a driver and you're injured, you would be worse than me."

Otis' laugh was more of a breath of air. "You're a good driver, it's just hard for me to hold your hand in this seat."

Rye laughed, "You idiot. If you were driving you still wouldn't be able to hold my hand."

"Why? My left was hurt, I could hold your hand with my right," Otis said as he waved his right hand to prove his point.

"And you would drive with what?" Rye asked. He glanced sideways to see a slight pout and furrowed brows.

"My legs," Otis finally said.

Rye rolled his eyes. Otis wasn't always like this but when he was, he always played it up. Especially when he was hurt. "I think you can survive the 15 minutes to my house," Rye said.

"And if I can't?" Otis leaned half his body towards Rye, his chin was down but his eyes were up.

Rye nudged his shoulder at him. "Then I'll mourn you deeply."

Otis grinned, he pulled away sitting properly in the seat. "You'll moan deeply? I can think of other ways to make you do that without my death."

Rye sided eyed him. "I thought the nurse just gave you some Tylenol."

"She did," Otis declared, he switched the song a few times before stopping on one Rye didn't recognize.

"Then why do you sound high?" Rye asked.

Otis lifted his right arm to his chest. "Because I'm high on just looking at your face."

"Oats," Rye warned. Otis simply grinned brightly at him, turning carefully in his seat to stare at him. Rye couldn't stop the grin on his face, even though he tried.

"Stop trying to act tough, it doesn't suit you. If you're happy, smile, if you're sad, cry. Stop trying to hide your smile," Otis said.

He leaned over grabbing Rye's right hand. Rye tightened his grip.

"I think you should be telling yourself that," Rye said, tilting his head towards him.

"Acting tough suits me better," Otis said, kissing Rye's hand before letting him take it back to drive.

"You're mashed potatoes, stop trying to act like a baked potato," Rye said. Otis laughed openly, his eyes shutting briefly before opening to stare at Rye. Rye was hopelessly in love with him, Otis was the type of person that was easy to love. Rye was not so easy or open, yet Otis loved him anyway. Otis' family hadn't been as easy to convince. Even though they had been friends for over ten years and boyfriends for nearly one.

"Is your mom home?" Otis asked, poking Rye in the neck.

Rye shrugged his hand off. "Nope, she's off to Zumba or yoga or whatever she's trying this week, she'll be back later."

"Could we-" Otis looked away, shaking his head. "We should start a new show and order some Chinese."

"Don't act like I don't know what you were going to say."

"Don't act like I don't know what you were going to respond with," Otis mimicked. Rye grinned, pulling into the driveway he shut the car off, facing Otis.

"Well, I'm right, you seriously just hurt your arm. I'm not making it worse. Also, you're going to Germany soon. You would hate to go in a cast."

"My right hand is perfectly fine," Otis stated.

"You are too clumsy to even try. Your second thought sounds even better."

"Ah, only to you," Otis laughed. Rye shrugged before leaning in giving Otis a quick kiss, pulling away and quickly getting out of the car before Otis could complain.

Rye turned the T.V. on in the living room, dropping onto the couch. Otis glared at him until he moved to the other side of the couch so he was on Otis' right side.

"So needy," Rye teased.

"One of us has to be."

"Is that how it works?" Rye asked.

Otis shrugged. "We'll find out." Otis had always been clingy when they were younger, their parents thought it was cute. As they got older, Otis's parents had tried to separate them more. They put Otis in weightlifting, they did more family outings. It worked for a while until Otis realized how little time they had hung out and decided to camp out at Rye's house for a week when they were thirteen. From there Otis still continued weightlifting but spent most of his free time with Rye. Otis leaned his head against his shoulder, turning and biting him.

"I thought you were going to stop biting me?"

"I can't help myself," Otis said. Stretching up and kissing Rye's cheek, then the side of his mouth. Rye turned towards him, allowing Otis to kiss his mouth. Otis pushed against him, Rye smiled into the kiss pulling back just slightly. Otis pulled back, standing up. Rye watched him head into the kitchen.

"Bring me a drink!" Rye yelled, focusing back on the T.V.. He jumped when Otis sat back down on the couch, handing him a can of flavored sparkling water. "I wish my mom bought real soda."

Otis shrugged, setting his on the side table. Rye stretched out on the couch, kicking Otis' leg. Otis lazily tilted his head towards him. "Hmm," Otis hummed.

"Why are you all the way over there?" Rye asked.

"Because someone thinks I'm going to hurt myself if we even kiss," Otis said, pouting.

"We did kiss," Rye said. Otis smiled, Rye rolled his eyes, turning to watch the show.

7:09 P.M.

A few episodes later Rye heard the front door open. "Hello boys," Rye didn't move, Otis twisted around to talk to his mom. Rye jumped when his mom poked his side of the neck, he groaned in annoyance.

"What have you boys been doing?" Her eyes shifted between the two of them as she wiggled her eyebrows.

Rye rolled his eyes at her antics. "Nothing," Rye replied.

"And what type of nothing is that?" his mom asked.

"Mom," Rye complained as Otis laughed.

"Well excuse me trying to be a supportive mom, interested in my child's well being." Rye dipped lower on the couch, wishing he could sink into it.

Sunday April 20th 7:41 P.M.

Rye laid his head on the kitchen table, his mom was shuffling through his acceptance and rejection letters from colleges. He had applied to a variety of schools, in multiple states.

"If you stay local it's cheaper; you won't have to pay out of state costs," his mom said, separating each letter into piles on the counter. "You could even stay at home. You could save a lot of money living here instead of getting a dorm or apartment." He knew exactly what she was saying and it was all true, however, he didn't want to. He didn't even want to go to college, though if he ever mentioned it to his mom he was sure she would beat him. Well, maybe she would just chain them together and she would take him to all his classes. Either way, to her, not going to college was not an option. To her, successful people went to college even if they never did anything with their degree. He could never explain to her why she was wrong because she would never listen. College wasn't the only option and he had already explored other things he wanted to do without her knowing.

He didn't really want to pursue them either, he simply wanted to travel. To see the world and learn about other cultures. College wasn't the only place to learn, he wanted real-world experience.

"Didn't you say Otis was also staying local?" she asked. Otis was an interesting topic. She was fine with them dating, she was afraid of the people who weren't okay with it. She told him countless times to be careful in public, to make sure to blend in. It wasn't exactly what he needed to hear but he knew she just wanted him to be safe. After the news of attacks, she was even more paranoid and terrified. He had tried to reassure her that the world wasn't that scary but she had stayed firm in her opinions.

"Yeah, he is," he said, "He's going to community college before university."

"That's a great idea, you should follow him. Take your generals and basic classes first then go to the university," she said, pulling two papers out of the stack. She sat them in front of him.

Rye rolled his eyes, mocking his mom's tone he said, "I thought you told me not to follow him too much, that high school relationships don't last and as soon as I see a cute boy in college I'll fall in love all over again."

"I did not say that and I certainly did not use that tone," she said, mocking his tone.

Rye scoffed. "You did."

She sighed. "Well then I was wrong, Otis is a great kid."

Rye narrowed his eyes, scrunching up his face. "What's with the change of heart?"

She rolled her eyes, waving her hand in front of his face. He dropped the look as she replied. "I've always liked Otis."

"Yeah, as my friend."

"Hey, I've always accepted your relationship, I just want you to be safe and if you have Otis with you, two is better than one," she explained, leaning forward on the table.

"Mom, I can handle myself."

"I know, I just worry."

Rye took it for what it was. "I love you too, now can we talk about dinner? Because I'm starving."

She nodded, pulling away from the table. Looking at him seriously. "Yes, but this discussion isn't over."

"It never is," he muttered.

"What? It can easily be solved."

"Mom, dinner," Rye whined.

"Alright, alright," she said, pulling out the envelope of takeout menus. She dropped it on the table, pushing it to Rye when her phone chimed with a text. Rye watched her open and read it. She grinned, responding to it before looking back at him. "What?"

"Who are you texting?"

"Your father, now pick something," she responded. Rye stared at the thick envelope. His mom started pulling out the menus, setting them in three separate piles. He was silent as he watched the piles grow. She pushed one towards him. "Pick from these," she said. Turning around she opened the cabinet pulling out her tin cans of tea.

Rye spread his hand through the menus, he pulled out an Italian one and went back to watching his mom. She swung her body back and forth to a silent song. "Here," he said, picking up the menu and waving it around. She turned around plucking it out of his fingers. She ignored his look, her phone sounded with another ping. She checked it, frowning as she responded. "What does he want?" Rye asked.

She gave him a quick glance. "He wants to see you."

"Why?"

"Perhaps because he shoved his di-"

"Mom!" Rye yelled like it was a complaint.

"Because he's your father and it's been a while since he's seen you."

"That was his choice," Rye said. His mom ignored him, calling their order in.

Rye's phone lit up in front of him, he stared at the message from his dad.

Hey, kiddo. Rye flipped his phone over. He set his elbows on the counter placing his chin in the palm of his left hand. When she finished, she stood across him, mirroring his position.

"I don't want you to think he left because he didn't love you. I was really upset when he left and *I* thought it would be better if you didn't see him. Then he had other things going on and we both agreed that leaving things how they were, was better for you."

"So I have no say in it?"

"No, as your mother, I made the decision that I thought was right. You may see it differently and if you ever have kids you'll understand but-"

He cut her off, knowing it was rude and not caring. "But until then I have to deal with the consequences of your actions?"

She stood up straight. "Rye, don't talk to me like that."

"You did what was better for you, not me." He pulled back, leaning against the back of the chair. She was quiet as she stared at him, he looked down at the still stacked piles of menus.

"If you want to think of it like that, then fine, yes. But I did think it was better for everyone that he keeps his life separate."

"Does he have some secret family? I already know he got married. Did he have a bunch of kids too?"

She shook her head. "No, it's nothing like that and how do you know he got married?"

"So he did get married. Why? Is his wife prettier and younger than you with a trust fund or something?"

She gave him that "mom look" like he was the only one who came up with crazy theories. "No, god no. Don't be ridiculous. That would almost be better, kidding. Listen, just talk to him, he'll explain everything."

He was the only one who could explain it to him, he was the one who left.

Friday April 25th 3:38 P.M.

Rye lay on one of the empty weight benches, he closed his eyes as he waited for Otis to finish lifting weights; He had been careful not to use his left hand. He could hear grunts, small chatter and the movement of weights. He threw his arm over his eyes to block out more of the light.

"So Otis you're coming with us right?" Rye listened in, not sure whose voice it was.

"To where?" Otis asked.

Rye slid his arm off as he blinked at the ceiling. Did he forget he was there or did he not care?

"To Corey's. It's our senior year and you've been spending it with... bread. Man you keep ditching us and you're gone this summer." It was a quick pause before he said the nickname, Rye wasn't sure if he debated because Rye was actually there or because of how Otis would react.

Rye heard something drop. "I told you to stop calling him that," Otis said.

Whoever it was, laughed. "Who cares what I call him? Are you coming or not?"

"I care, and no I'm not. C'mon Rye lets go."

Rye sat up. "Oh shit, you never said he was here." Rye didn't comment as Otis gathered his stuff, Rye following after him. When they made it to the parking lot Rye spoke up.

"I really don't mind the nickname."

"I do." Rye let it drop as he slid into the passenger seat of Otis' car. Rye pulled the seat belt over him, settling in. Otis played German pop as he backed out of the parking spot and parking lot. He really didn't mind, his mom called him stuff like that all the time. Though her nicknames were out of affection he had said it out of malice.

The drive to the store was quick. Otis grabbed his hand as they walked through the parking lot, it was loose and casual. Rye looked at the cars they passed, making sure none of them backed out. When they entered the store, Otis snatched up a basket. They headed to the freezer section, navigating around other customers. Rye let Otis lead them to the ice cream section. Otis let go of his hand, grabbing a large vanilla tub. Rye pulled open the freezer door, the chill of the freezer made him shiver as he grabbed a tub of chocolate, adding it to the basket. Letting the freezer door shut behind him, Rye followed him down the aisle to the cookie dough, where Otis grabbed chocolate chip and snickerdoodle. "Do we need more sprinkles?" Otis asked.

"Yeah, remember last time? The top came off and you spilled like half a bottle in the ice cream."

"Yeah it was so crunchy, should we skip the sprinkles?" Otis asked, tilting his head, his hair just falling into his eyes.

Rye shrugged. "You're the one who always wants them, if we don't get them then you'll complain we don't have any."

Otis grabbed his hand again pulling him to the baking section. "You're right, we need

sprinkles."

Rye shook his head. "You need sprinkles," Rye corrected. Otis smiled at him. Rye squeezed his hand, his smile turned into a laugh as Otis knocked their shoulders together.

"You should buy a plane ticket to Germany," Otis said.

Rye's forehead scrunched as he stared at Otis. "I'm sure your mom would love that."

Otis tightens his grip. "She loves you, sort of."

Rye snorted, tugging on Otis' hand. "She'd love me more if we were just friends."

"Probably, but that's her problem, not ours." That was what Otis always thought. "Alright, let's grab some strawberries and get out of here."

4:26 P.M.

Rye pulled out the large plastic mixing bowl, setting it on the counter next to Otis who was already scooping up vanilla ice cream, he dropped the large scoop into the bowl. Rye grabbed two large spoons, chocolate sauce, a knife to cut the strawberries and caramel sauce. Rye quickly cut the strawberries, tossing a few in the bowl as Otis added chocolate ice cream, then threw away the waste.

When he finished, they both added in the toppings. "Are the cookies ready?" Otis asked, Rye nearly forgot about them. He pulled open the oven. They were more cooked than he wanted but still not fully done. Rye pulled them out, setting them on the stove.

"Did you add more movies?" Otis asked. Rye sighed.

Rye stared at Otis. "Do I ever forget?"

"Yeah, remember a few months back." Otis smiled, his dimples standing out.

Rye pushed against him. "I was sick, you should remember because you got sick right

after I did."

"I do remember, you're the one who has a faulty memory."

"I'm just selective," Rye said. Otis simply smiled at him, finishing up the bowl with sprinkles. "Careful with that," Rye warned. Otis stared at him as he shook the container. "Fine but you're eating all of it if they spill again." Otis' hand stopped, setting it back on the counter. Rye smiled at him, grabbing the pan of cookies he led the way to his room. Rye made the nest on the floor last night for them. He would just leave it if his mom didn't nag him to clean it up every week. Otis set the bowl down, grabbing his laptop he hooked it up to the small projector. The wall across from them lit up in blue light until Otis changed the settings.

"Which one first?" Otis asked, tilting his head back towards Rye.

"Any of them," Rye said, pulling another pillow off of his bed for his back. Otis grabbed the bowl again, sitting next to Rye he set the bowl between them.

When the bowl was finished, melted ice cream and sprinkles settled on the bottom. The movie was halfway through. Rye shifted his eyes toward Otis as he moved, dipping his head to kiss Rye. Rye met him halfway, Otis was always gentle. Rye pulled him in closer with a hand on the back of his neck. Otis pulled away from his lips, "Can we?"

"Yeah," Rye responded, earning another kiss.

7:29 P.M.

Rye heard the front door open and his mom yelled, "Boys!" Rye moved backward so she could see him in the kitchen. "There you are, I brought home Chinese for dinner," she said making her way into the kitchen as he went back to the sink to finish the dishes. "You know one of these days you boys are going to get sick of that ice cream concoction you make every week."

"Never," Otis declared, from the kitchen table. Rye laughed putting the last dish in the drying rack.

"If we do then we'll switch to frozen yogurt," Rye said, grinning before he even heard Otis' reply.

"Take that back," Otis told him.

"You both showered," she commented. Rye paused opening the bag, he continued when Otis spoke. "Weightlifting after school, we had to work off all the ice cream we were going to eat. Though I guess we already ate it, and Rye can barely bench the bar."

His mom hummed. "I see. Well, I got your favorites. I'm going to change my clothes before dinner."

"Okay," Rye replied. Pulling containers out of the bag, he didn't look at Otis until he heard his mom's door shut. Then he looked at Otis who laughed. "Shut up, it's not funny," Rye muttered. He brought chopsticks, forks, and the food to the table. Otis shut his computer, setting it on the empty chair next to him. Rye grabbed the Sesame Chicken first, he didn't turn when his mom returned, more focused on shoving food in his mouth. He choked when next to the rice a small easter egg basket full of condoms dropped on the table. His mom slapped his back a few times as he reached for a drink he didn't have.

"Chew your food properly," she told him, grabbing a soda off of the counter for him. "And if you're going to have sex, I want you doing it safely. This has different sizes and styles."

"We're not-" Rye tried, still choking on the chicken.

She held up her hand. "Cut the bullshit, I'm not stupid. Now when two guys have sex they-"

Rye lifted his hands to his ears not caring that the chopsticks were now in his dark hair. "Stop stop please don't, please okay fine we are, we have been, are you happy?"

She smiled. "How long?" she asked, the focus of her dark brown eyes was on him.

Rye turned away. "I don't know, a while."

She didn't stop, she picked up a piece of broccoli, pointing it towards him. "How long is a while?"

"A year or so," he finally said, looking back to his chicken.

"How many times?" she asked.

"Mom!" Rye yelled he could feel the heat rising to the tips of his ears.

She laughed, dropping her broccoli. "What? I can't be interested in your life?"

His eyes pleaded as he looked at her. "Not this."

She rolled her eyes, picking up the dropped piece of broccoli. "Don't be so squeamish, I could tell you things you wouldn't even dream of."

"Someone please stab me," Rye muttered, shoving a piece of chicken in his mouth, hoping he would choke on it.

"Stop being so dramatic, have you been safe?"

"Yes," Otis spoke up. Rye wanted to bury himself in the backyard and never show his face ever again. "Every time, I promise."

"So then what posit-" she started, Rye cut her off before she could finish.

"Don't finish that question, mom please stop it's embarrassing."

She stilled her hand that held another piece of broccoli. "It shouldn't be embarrassing, you should be able to talk about these things."

Rye shook his head quickly. "Not with you."

She sighed. "Why? Would you talk to your father about these things?"

"NO! Mom please, we'll take the basket and promise to be safe and whatever you want but please stop asking questions," Rye begged.

She stared at him, he stared back. "Fine, I'm just trying to be a good mom."

"I know, just please stop."

The rest of their conversations remained mundane. Rye couldn't look at the Easter basket or Otis and when he finished his chicken he quickly stood from the table. "I'm full," he stated, turning to leave.

"Don't forget your condoms," his mom called after him. He walked faster, ignoring her cackling. She was evil.

Otis dropped the basket on his chest, Rye lifted the pillow to glare at him. Otis smiled down at him, Rye shoved the pillow back over his face.

"What? Now we don't have to buy any for a while. It wasn't that bad," Otis said. Rye threw the pillow at him.

Rye's eyebrows lifted. "You're only saying that because it's not your mom."

Otis laughed. "My mom wouldn't have reacted like that."

"No, whose mom would?"

Otis shrugged his broad shoulders. "Yeah it was cool, my mom would have freaked and it's not like she actually caught us. That would have been worse."

Rye smiled at him. "I really would never have sex again."

Otis laughed. "I'm not sure I would either, my mom would probably kill me." Otis lay across Rye, Rye started laughing. Wrapping his arms around Otis, he was not looking forward to half of the summer without him.

Chapter 9 Sawyer
Saturday May 10th 7:21 A.M.

Sawyer got everyone up an hour later than their normal schedule. "Carter, I have a surprise for today," he said. Carter blinked up at him before she sat up in excitement.

Her hands opened and closed in quick succession. "I want," she squealed.

"It's too early for that noise," Sawyer said. "We're going out today so I need you to get up. Wyatt has been practicing a special breakfast for you then you have to take a bath okay?"

"Okay," she said before heading downstairs. Sawyer headed to Lio's room lifting him out of his crib. He could already hear Carter's excitement before he made it out of Lio's room.

Carter was happily bouncing in her chair. "Yaya make craps craps!" she screamed. Sawyer winced as he set Lio in his high chair.

"Carter no yelling," Sawyer told her tiredly.

"Sorry," she said, not apologetic in the least. Sawyer left her to her bouncing happiness as he checked on Wyatt's progress.

"I want a banana Nutella one," Sawyer said standing with their shoulders touching.

"You get what I put on a plate for you," Wyatt said, sliding a strawberry one onto a plate and covering it in whipped cream.

"Someone's being snarky," Sawyer muttered.

"You had me catch up on all my homework for this week and part of next week and then you have me cooking these since 1:00 this morning practicing and then you wake me up at seven to make breakfast. After Carter's, you can make your own cause I'm going back to bed," Wyatt hissed quietly. Sawyer grinned even as Wyatt glared at him, dark circles under his eyes.

Wyatt grabbed the plate and set it in front of Carter. Kissing the top of her head he headed back to his room.

"Yaya not eating with us?" Carter asked, pouting as she waited for the answer.

"He's still tired, he's going to sleep a little more."

"Oh," Carter said before focusing on the plate in front of her. Taking a huge bite, Sawyer watched the whipped cream slide down her chin and throat to soak her pajamas.

Sawyer grabbed two baby food containers and set them in front of Lio. "Do you want gross peas or gross carrots?" Lio knocked the peas away giggling as he did. "Does that mean you want those or that those are out?" Lio knocked the carrots away. "We'll just go with the peas then."

9:41 A.M.

They all got into Wyatt's car. "Where are we going Sah?" Carter asked, poking the back of the chair with her toy wand.

"It's a secret," Sawyer said, leaning back in the passenger seat.

Carter pouted. "But I want to know." He wondered if someone taught her to pout or if she naturally knew it worked.

"It'll ruin the surprise," Sawyer replied, flipping through a few radio stations.

"Oh but I want to know."

"Carter just wait, we'll be there soon, what do you want for dinner?" he asked, easily distracting her.

"I want ice cream." Sawyer sighed, shaking his head. "Lots of ice cream."

Sawyer left Carter babbling to Lio about the importance and need to have ice cream at least once a day.

Sawyer watched Wyatt until he turned towards him then back to the road. "What?"

"Nothing," Sawyer said. Wyatt reached his hand over with his palm up. Sawyer happily took it into his own. Wyatt rolled his eyes but grinned anyway.

Wyatt parked the car, the zoo wasn't packed but it had a decent amount of cars in the lot.

"Where are we?" Carter asked lifting herself to see out the window.

"The zoo," Sawyer said, turning around. Carter frowned and sat back in her seat, crossing her arms.

"You don't want to go?" he asked, quickly looking to Wyatt then back to Carter.

She shook her head. "No."

"Why not? You love the zoo," he told her. Their parents had taken them at least once a month.

"No," she said, turning her head away from him. Sawyer sat back in his seat staring out the front window.

"What about the aquarium?" Wyatt suggested, looking at Sawyer for his opinion.

Carter perked up. "The fishies?"

"Yeah," Wyatt replied.

"Fishies fishies," Carter chanted.

Sawyer threw his hands up and leaned back in his seat, fastening his seat belt as Wyatt drove away from the zoo. Wyatt took his hand again rubbing his thumb soothingly.

Sawyer stared out the window trying not to feel hurt that Wyatt's suggestion was chosen over his. He squeezed Wyatt's hand and focused on the fact that Carter was going to have a good day no matter where they went.

Carter was finally excited as they walked up to the building holding each of their hands. Sawyer was pushing Lios's stroller with one hand. They walked through several different exhibits taking their time with each one, letting Carter soak up everything she could. Sawyer took several pictures of her and their small make-shift family together.

2:47 P.M.

By the time they were walking out Carter was beginning to droop. On their way home both kids had fallen asleep.

Sawyer didn't get out of his seat when they parked in the driveway, Wyatt opened his door before he looked back to Sawyer. "We're home, why aren't you getting out?"

Sawyer sighed, turning back in his seat to look at his siblings. "Because then we have to wake Carter up."

Wyatt leaned back in his seat turning to stare at Sawyer. "Okay," he replied.

Sawyer sat back in his own seat. "I'd say we could wait another five minutes," he said to Wyatt, looking at him.

"Why?" Wyatt asked.

"We now have 4 minutes and 45 seconds so if you don't kiss me I'm-" Sawyer smiled into the kiss before pulling Wyatt closer. When they finally pulled away they were breathless, leaning their foreheads together. Wyatt smiled, his near-black eyes bright as they stared into Sawyer's light brown ones.

"I-" Wyatt started unable to finish when someone knocked on the window.

They both pulled away, Wyatt turned around and Sawyer leaned around him.

"Wow, I haven't kissed anyone like that in a very long time," Marina commented. Fanning herself with her hand.

"Mom," Xander whined.

"Do you need help getting the kids out?" she asked, still grinning.

"No I uh, I got it," Sawyer ducked his head as he opened his door and then the back door to pick Lio out of his car seat. Wyatt did the same with Carter, waking her up.

"Carter it's time to wake up." Carter yawned, blinking awake.

"I want ice cream," Carter muttered, her voice still sleepy. Sawyer rolled his eyes at her request.

"I want ice cream too," Piper said as she bounced her pigtail curls bouncing with her.

Carter fully woke up at Piper's voice, pulling away from Wyatt to be put on the ground. Wyatt wordlessly complied and set her down.

"Piper!" Carter yelled, she was already bouncing around Piper.

Sawyer raced in front of them to unlock the door and let everyone into the house. The two girls headed up the stairs as soon as the door was opened, the rest following much slower in pace. As they were sitting in the living room, he headed up stairs putting Lio in his bed before joining the others downstairs.

"Wow, I'm very impressed with how well you keep the house clean," Marina said.

"Mom," Xander whined again.

Marina ruffled his hair. "Oh quit it."

"It's not hard with just the four of us," Sawyer explained with a shrug.

"Oh? So you're living here too?" Marina winked at Wyatt who grinned. "I'm glad that you're not doing it alone," her voice took a softer tone. "It's not always easy."

"If you ever need us to take the kids we can. Carter seems very happy to have a new friend," Sawyer offered. He swallowed ignoring the thought of when he last gave out that offer.

"I may just have to take you up on that offer, it's been a very long time since I've had a day to rest without pesky children." She grinned as she tried to pinch her son's cheek. He ducked away with ease, obviously used to her attention.

"Do you want anything to drink?" Sawyer offered.

"Water please," she said, moving around the room to take a seat in the living room.

"Do you have any juice?" Xander asked.

"I think we have lemonade and apple juice," Sawyer said.

"Lemonade," Xander said following Sawyer to the kitchen.

"You didn't have to follow me," Sawyer told him.

"I have a question for you," Xander said, watching Sawyer pull out two cups, filling one with water and the other with lemonade. "Tommy said that kissing other boys is bad."

"Oh? And do you believe Tommy?"

"I don't know, that's why I'm asking you. I didn't think Tommy was wrong but I've never thought about boys kissing boys or even kissing girls."

"Well do you think I'm a bad person?" Sawyer asked him. Xander shook his head. "Do you think it's bad if I kiss someone I love?" Sawyer asked.

"No, mom said it's hard to find someone you love and that you shouldn't," Xander paused biting his lip, "shouldn't let it go because you don't like that they leave the toilet seat up but I don't know what that means."

Sawyer nodded. "Since love is really hard to find and since anyone can love why would it be bad if two boys happened to feel it for each other? It would be good, wouldn't it? Every one should find love and if it happens to be your best friend who you may or may not have always loved and now you love in another way wouldn't that be okay? Because love is love no matter what," Sawyer said, mostly to Wyatt who was standing in the doorway. He looked back to Xander who nodded.

"I guess so. Then Tommy was wrong. I should tell him, mom says that when people are wrong it's not always bad to correct them."

"If you do it politely then yeah it should be fine."

"Thank you, I can take mom's water to her," Sawyer handed him both cups and he headed out of the kitchen.

Wyatt stepped in after the kid had left closing the gap between them. "Look at you giving advice to children. You could be the next Gandhi."

"Shut up." Sawyer pushed Wyatt out of his personal space and started to head back to the living room. Wyatt pulled him back into his chest hugging him.

"I love you too," Wyatt whispered into Sawyer's ear. Unwrapping his arms, Wyatt headed back into the living room first.

Sawyer put his hands to his heated cheeks taking a few deep breaths before he followed Wyatt. The girls had come down and Piper was happily talking about how Carter was able to draw on the walls.

"They have banner paper over them, I got some of that big banner paper from the art department at school."

Marina's green eyes were wide as she responded. "That's such a great idea."

"Thanks, she knows she can only draw on those pieces, right Carter?"

"Yes only blue and white pieces," she said, rolling her eyes.

"Oh, I can already imagine her teenage years. You're going to have so much fun." Sawyer shook his head. He didn't even want to imagine that far ahead in time.

"Sah want ice cream now," Carter demanded.

"When did I say we were having ice cream?" Sawyer asked, playing innocent.

"You did," Carter said, starting to glare.

"I don't think so, but on our way home I ordered pizza and

we're going to have a special cake for dinner."

"Yay," Carter clapped her hands. "Can we play?"

"Can we build a fort?" Piper asked Carter who frowned.

"Fort?" Carter whispered as if trying the word in her mouth she repeated it again. "Fort?"

"You haven't built one? Please mommy can we?" Piper asked, turning to her mom, her pigtails swinging around.

"This is not my house, those decisions are not up to me," Marina told her, obviously enjoying the moment of a little freedom. Her head tilted to Sawyer giving him the decision.

Both girls shifted their stares from Sawyer to Wyatt with big pouts and fluttering lashes.

"Yes, you can build a fort," Sawyer said. They jumped together in excitement.

"We need sheets and pillows and something to hold it and and," Piper said quickly, her chest pumped quickly and her breathing sped up.

"Piper sweetie, breathe ok? Breathe slowly." Piper stopped and did as she was told. "Better?" Piper nodded.

"I can get the sheets, Wyatt, go find some pillows," Sawyer said, giving Piper time to recover.

Carter sighed, folding her arms. "You have to ask. Right, Sah?"

"I'm sorry, Wyatt will you please go get some pillows?" Sawyer asked.

"Yes, of course, anything for my beloved," Wyatt said mockingly as he marched off.

"Be be- what that?" Carter asked as the two headed up the stairs.

"We don't have all day so none of those shenanigans like earlier," Marina called out to them. Both of them quickening their pace to gather things. Sawyer made it down the stairs in record time, Wyatt not far behind him.

"It's just a name to call someone you love," Marina said, answering Carter's question.

"I'll get some chairs from the kitchen," Sawyer said, dropping the clean sheets into the empty chair.

"You boys are so easy to tease," Marina said, getting up to help the kids. Wyatt started to help but stopped when the doorbell rang to answer the door.

Sawyer returned to the living room with a chair in each hand, turning around with them when Wyatt came in with the two pizzas and breadsticks.

"Let's eat and then build the fort," Sawyer said.

"But I wanted to eat in the fort," Piper said.

"Maybe another time," Sawyer offered. Wyatt set the pizza on the table while Sawyer put the chairs back in their places.

Marina lifted her brow at Piper. "Okay," Piper said dejectedly, following them into the kitchen.

After dinner, Sawyer set all of the plates into the sink before opening the freezer to pull out the cake. Wyatt put the candles on as the others were building the fort.

"She's going to die when she sees this, you got a birthday cake-flavored ice cream birthday cake with a birthday cake drawn on it," Wyatt commented, amusement in his voice.

"I thought it would be hilarious," Sawyer shrugged, "I also already took photos, but we need to take more," Sawyer said, taking his phone out. "Okay now head in there, no wait give me your phone." Wyatt pulled his phone out handing it to Sawyer. "Okay now go." Sawyer held out both phones, one was taking pictures, the other was taking a video.

They stepped into the living room. "Carter, come here for a second," Sawyer said. Carter spun around before pulling herself out of the sheet. When she saw the cake, she squealed. She ran over tripping on the sheet that was caught on her foot. She took a second to be stunned before she stood up and walked slower to the cake. Wyatt lowered it down.

"Happy birthday Carter!" Sawyer yelled quietly. "Now blow out the candles." She did with minimal spit.

"Yay!" She clapped. "I love love cake," she said to Piper who was looking at the cake with interest.

"Do you want to guess what kind it is?" Sawyer asked. Wyatt took the cake back into the kitchen, Piper trailing after him.

"Kind? Birthday cake is birthday cake," she said with a smile.

"I love birthday cake."

"Yeah, yeah it is," he finally responded. He shook his head shutting off the video on Wyatt's phone and pocketing it with his own.

"Are you ready for some?" he asked.

"Yes!" Carter yelled running into the kitchen.

"So what kind is it?" Marina asked.

"Birthday cake ice cream," Sawyer told her with a smile.

"How clever, you kids these days are getting a lot more creative," Marina said. Sawyer shrugged at the compliment. Marina pulled him into a hug.

"It'll get easier, more birthdays will pass and before you know it, she's going to be where you are. Not the exact same place but she'll grow up and have to find her own way and you'll be there to help her." Sawyer swallowed roughly, hugging her tighter before letting her go.

"Thank you." His voice was thick with emotion but he held it back as he entered the kitchen and smiled at the mess Carter had already made of her face and clothes. Sawyer pulled out his phone to take photos, taking a few of Piper and Xander as well as Wyatt and Marina. Lio was still sleeping and Sawyer was glad for it, and for the fact that he had been sleeping through the night recently.

"It's birthday ice cream cake cake," Carter sang, spitting some of her cake onto the table.

Sawyer grabbed a paper towel and wiped it up.

"You need to clean up before you can go back into the fort," Sawyer told her. Carter nodded, taking another bite of the cake.

"I'm gonna check on Lio," Sawyer said. Wyatt nodded.

When Sawyer came back down they were back to working on the fort. Sawyer headed into the kitchen where Wyatt was working on the dishes. "I wiped her up and gave her a clean shirt from the laundry room," Wyatt said, turning his head towards him.

"Thank you," Sawyer said, wrapping his arms around Wyatt's waist, resting his head between his shoulder blades.

"Hey, we're going to head out, both of the girls kind of crashed pretty fast." Sawyer let go of Wyatt and turned to Marina who was holding a sleeping Piper and a tired looking Xander at her side.

"Yeah it's been a long day," Sawyer said, following her out to the front door.

"Don't hesitate to call," she said. Sawyer nodded, shutting the door behind her. He looked at the mess in the living room and decided to deal with it tomorrow.

Sawyer moved the front sheet of the fort, he lifted Carter off of the ground and carried her up to her bed.

Monday May 12th 9:41 A.M.

Monday morning had Sawyer fidgeting in the counselor's office, the social worker next to him. She looked plain enough in a ponytail, t-shirt, and jeans. She could easily be mistaken for a high schooler.

"How are things at home?" she asked.

He didn't hesitate to answer. "Good, great, things are great."

"You look tired." Her tone wasn't accusing but it made him defensive anyway.

"I'm not tired," he told her.

She smiled at him and it put him on edge; this woman could ruin his life easily. It wouldn't even be hard for her. "It's normal to be tired, I would be worried if you weren't."

He frowned, playing with the end of his shirt. He didn't know what the right answer was, was he supposed to be handling everything perfectly? Or was he supposed to be a tired mess? He would say whatever he needed to keep them, he just didn't know what that was.

"I've been talking to Julian and she says you were asking about early graduation. I know we talked about it when I first spoke to you but it was so brief. She has informed me that it is a possible option for you. Are you still thinking of continuing that way?"

"No, it's only a few more weeks so I think I'm going to finish normally."

"Alright well I have a few more questions and then in the coming months there will be a home inspection."

Sawyer froze, he blinked at her. His throat was dry and he felt like he was stranded in a desert with no water "What? Why?" he finally croaked out.

"I'm not questioning your ability, you're quite young and you just lost both of your parents. It would be a hard time for anyone let alone someone who only has their younger siblings if you need any help-"

"I have Wyatt," he interrupted her. He knew it was a mistake, her face twisted and then smoothed back out to a smile.

She nodded, her voice changing as if she was talking to a child. "I just want to make sure it's a good environment for all three of you."

"It is," Sawyer said confidently.

Her legs straightened out and then she crossed them. She leaned forward. "I understand that you want what's best for your siblings but sometimes that means giving them up for a better home."

"There isn't a better home and I'm not giving them up! They're the only family I have left and I'm all they have. I'm not giving them to strangers who don't give two shits about them." Sawyer knew his voice was rising along with fear and panic, he couldn't lose his siblings.

"There are plenty of homes-" she started, stopping when Sawyer spoke up.

Sawyer shook his head. "No, I'm sorry but I'm not doing it. I told you before that I can take care of them. I don't care if you do five hundred home inspections or visit every week. I'm not giving them up."

She nodded. "Alright, do you have a job at this moment?"

Sawyer stared at her, he was irritated and wanted to leave. Would she take the kids if he didn't have a job? Would she think he was incompetent? She waited for his answer and he shook his head no.

"Taking care of children isn't easy or cheap," she told him like he didn't know.

He clenched his teeth, forcing himself, he responded. "I know, I'm getting one when I finish school."

She shifted her legs, she looked innocent as she spoke to him. "How are you managing your grief?"

He looked to his counselor, Julian, then back to the social worker. "What does that have to do with anything?" he asked.

She sat up straight. "Unfortunately grief and anger coincide and some people don't always handle it well."

"I'm fine," he told her, she was the only one pissing him off.

She fixed her bracelet that slid too far up her arm, she looked him in the eye as she spoke. "That isn't what I asked."

He shrugged. "I don't know."

"You don't know how to handle it or you don't know how you're handling it?"

"I..." Sawyer hesitated, he didn't know. He just wanted to give her the right answer and go back to class. He wanted to go home and see his parents, he wanted them to congratulate him on being able to graduate early. He wanted them to take the kids to daycare. He wanted his dad to make crepes for breakfast and his mom to make lasagna for dinner. He wanted his life back, he wanted to get drunk with Wyatt on the weekends and sit around playing video games for hours. He wanted to go off to college and come home for the holidays, he wanted things he couldn't have anymore.

She continued on without his answer. "I've left a list of therapists and coping mechanisms with Julian. I also have a packet of information and condolence cards from both of your parents' co-workers." She twisted in her seat to her large purse, pulling out the thick white opaque folder that had been sticking out. She handed it over to him, standing with her purse on her shoulder.

"Unfortunately I have another meeting so I must be leaving, do you still have my card?" He nodded. "Call me if you need anything," she said and then she was gone. His counselor was handing him two sheets of paper. He grabbed both, shoving them into his backpack, and left without another word.

12:33 P.M.

He met Wyatt in the locker room, he had already changed into his uniform. Sawyer quickly changed, following the others to the track. Sawyer stared ahead, ignoring Wyatt's questions. Wyatt nudged him and he bumped into someone else but he didn't care. He had fucked up the meeting and he didn't doubt that they would take his siblings away soon. When they were told to run, he ran. He gritted his teeth against the pain his body felt as he ran. He wanted to punch something, he wanted to cry. He ran until his legs gave out and he collapsed to the rough track, he closed his eyes against the blinding sun. The track was hot under his body but he refused to get up. He could hear the others still running, he had run past everyone and now they were lapping him. It was the last thing he cared about but the sound was strangely soothing. The idea that he wasn't alone was comforting, he didn't move when a foot nudged him in the ribs.

"I know you're not dead, your breathing is so heavy you could fill a hot air balloon," Wyatt said. Sawyer would know his voice even if he was deaf. He's not sure how that would work but he would. "Babo." Sawyer groaned at Wyatt's use of Korean, even though he knew it was an insult, he'd had too many dreams about him whispering Korean to him. One of his favorite drunk videos was of Wyatt saying something in Korean, he could never figure out what it was because his words were slurred, it was already hard enough trying to type it out in google.

"Come on get up," Wyatt said, effortlessly switching back to English, "Unless you want to be crisp bacon."

Sawyer threw an arm over his eyes, shutting out some of the sun. "I think I fucked up."

"What's new? Come on, we're playing soccer." Wyatt kicked him lightly, Sawyer shifted away from him.

"I don't like running," Sawyer said blandly.

Wyatt scoffed. "No one would know that with the way you ran off like a madman."

"How far did I get?"

"Not even around the whole track, now come on." Sawyer let Wyatt pull him up. Everyone was scattered between the field and track, some were playing soccer, others were playing with a frisbee and most were just walking the track. "Jeremy was impressed and then highly disappointed, he offered to help you out."

Sawyer brushed off his clothes stretching out a bit before he snorted. "Willingly exercise? I don't think so."

Wyatt jabbed his stomach with his fingers "When your metabolism drops you're going to start gaining weight."

Sawyer swatted at his hands, trying to push them away. "Will you still love me?"

"Only if you're fat and healthy," Wyatt said, letting Sawyer hold his hands before he dropped them.

Sawyer hummed, then asked, "Like Jeremy?"

"Yeah."

Sawyer grabbed Wyatt's hand again, swinging his arm in a large motion "Why don't you love Jeremy then?"

"Idiot." Wyatt shook his head, leaving Sawyer behind.

Thursday May 15th 5:03 P.M.

Sawyer pulled out the box of cake mix and a bowl, taking a deep breath and waiting just three seconds. One, two, three, he heard Carter's socked feet racing across the floor and watched as her small body slid into the kitchen.

She posed as her feet stopped, turning to him with wide eyes. "What Sah making?"

"A cake," he replied.

"I want to help!" she yelled.

"Shh, Lio's sleeping."

"Shh," she responded, already bouncing with excitement. Sawyer pulled a chair up to the counter. She climbed up, slapping her hands against the counter.

"Mix mix mix," she said quickly, reaching for the bowl.

Sawyer pulled it out of her reach. "Not yet, I need to fill it first."

"I want to mix," Carter pouted.

Sawyer rolled his eyes at her go-to face. "Just hold on, okay?"

"Okay!"

Sawyer nodded as he gathered the ingredients, he added each thing in one by one, letting Carter stir after each addition. He put away the eggs, turning back to see Carter dumping pepper into the cake. He shot forward pulling her hand up, stopping the downpour of pepper. He pulled it away, shutting the lid on it as Carter stirred it into the batter. He stared down at the ruined strawberry cake, the black pepper making it look like dead ants.

"Bake it, bake it," Carter chanted. He mechanically poured the batter in, scraping the sides, getting as much of it as he could. When he finished, he put the bowl under hot water before Carter could ask to lick it. He carefully set the pan in the oven, banging his head against the front of the stove. He stepped away from the stove, opening up several cabinets, pulling out a smooshed bag of marshmallows. He couldn't guess how old they were, definitely at least 4 years. He pulled out the last three marshmallows which were plastered together and set them on a plate, tossing the bag in the garbage and praying for Wyatt's safety. He grabbed the box of birthday candles and shoved two in the marshmallows.

"Sah, what's that?"

"My sanity," he muttered.

"Sanny?"

"Close enough," he responded.

6:47 P.M.

Wyatt stared at the slice of cake and marshmallows.

"Happy birthday!" Sawyer said, Carter imitating him.

"Did you make this?" Wyatt asked Carter who nodded happily. Wyatt glared at Sawyer, smiling at Carter before taking a bite of the cake. He paused his chewing for a second before he continued, grabbing the glass of milk quickly.

"What's with the marshmallow?" he choked out a few seconds later.

"I thought they might be a nice palate cleanser," Sawyer said. Wyatt stared at him.

"I want cake cake cake," Carter said, her voice changing from high pitched to demonic.

Sawyer turned away from the table cutting up a small piece of the cake for Carter.

"I don't think you do," he told her, plating the cake. He set it in front of Carter, stepping out of the frame of Wyatt's phone as he recorded. Carter happily used her fork to take a big bite of the cake. She chewed and paused. Opening her mouth, she let the mess in her mouth fall onto her plate. She let out a loud pitched whine. "Eww it bad." She spat the rest of it out reaching her hand out for the milk. Wyatt slid it forward for her as Sawyer struggled to breathe through his laughing, banging his hand on the table.

"Why is it bad?" she asked, her voice earnest and confused. Sawyer burst out with another fit of laughter. Tears streaming down his face, clutching at his stomach, he took deep breaths to calm down. "Bad cake bad," Carter scolded the cake, shaking her finger at it.

Saturday May 17th 6:53 P.M.

Sawyer stared at the road closed sign, it was creeping on 7 P.M. and this was not helping his headache. He took a left, following the road until he passed several 'road closed' signs blocking the streets. He took a right, following until he could take another right. When he finally reached home he was starving and exhausted. He opened the door to mostly darkness, some of the blinds were open letting in the fading sunset. "Wyatt?" he said, loud enough he would hear him from almost anywhere.

"Up here," came his reply. He headed up the stairs, pausing at the mess of pillows and blankets at the top of the stairs.

Carter came running out of her room with an arm full of stuffed animals. She dropped them on top of the pile before quickly running back into her room.

"What's going on?" he asked, stepping over the pile towards Lio's room. He could hear Wyatt groaning about a smelly diaper and Lio giggling back at him. He pushed the door fully open, Wyatt was lifting Lio up with a fresh diaper.

"Power went out, some idiot ran into a power line, I meant to text you about the road being closed."

Sawyer waved it off, taking Lio from Wyatt. "What's with the pile of shit?"

"Bad word! Sah, bad word," Carter said. Sawyer rolled his eyes as she continued on.

Wyatt answered, ignoring Carter's dramatic cries. "Campout in the living room, also dinner is on the table we already ate."

Sawyer smiled at him. "I love you, you know that right?"

"Not even a little bit," Wyatt told him.

Sawyer handed back Lio, shaking his head at Wyatt. "Liar."

He headed back downstairs for dinner before joining the others in the living room. They had pushed back the furniture creating a large nest of blankets, pillows, and stuffed animals. Wyatt had a couple of flashlights on and fake candles scattered near the nest.

"What about Lio?" Sawyer asked.

Carter turned towards him, sticking her arm and finger out. "Lio's bed is right there." Sawyer saw the pack-and-play laid out near the nest where Lio was already falling asleep. The house was mostly dark beside the glow of light. Carter jumped in the center of the pile, pulling one of her stuffed animals close to her chest. Sawyer lay down on one side of her, Wyatt taking the other. They stared at each other above Carter's head. "I want a story," Carter demanded. Sawyer grinned. "I'll tell you one," he said quietly. He weaved a tale of dragons and a fierce Princess who befriended them and how they showed her a new world and adventures they would go on. Sawyer tilted his head down, when he saw her sleeping he sighed, lying his head back down.

Chapter 10 Wyatt
Sunday May 11th 6:21 P.M.

Wyatt finished toweling off Lio who squirmed in his arms. Wyatt set him down, Lio stood for a second before dropping down to a crawl. Wyatt watched him crawl off to the stairs where Sawyer and Carter were coming down. "Wyatt, why is Lio crawling around without a diaper?" he asked. Carter began giggling.

Wyatt leaned back on the couch, throwing the towel over the arm of it. "He's airing out." He smiled when Sawyer groaned. "He's going to pee everywhere."

Wyatt pushed off of the couch, walking around it he met Sawyer at the bottom of the stairs. Sawyer reached down to grab Lio, Lio quickly crawled out of his reach. "It's fine, he just had a bath. After he dries off a bit, I'll put one back on." Sawyer stared at him, rolling his eyes. He was about to speak when Carter beat him to it

"Sah! Lio pooped on the ground!"

Wyatt and Sawyer turned to where Lio was crawling away from his mess on the floor chasing after a big plastic red ball. Sawyer pushed Wyatt. "You're cleaning it up," Sawyer told him.

Wyatt took a step back, shaking his head. He pushed Sawyer towards it. "It's not my kid."

Sawyer glared at him. "Wyatt, clean it the fuck up."

Wyatt grinned, moving another step back. "Fuck no."

"Dude you were the one who didn't put a diaper on him. Go clean it up, you dirty muffin," Sawyer said, changing his insult when Carter walked up to him holding her nose.

"Stinky," she said, her voice more high pitched than usual.

"I have that meeting with my parents, have fun," Wyatt said, running out the front door.

"You lying crusty corn cob," Sawyer called after him. Wyatt laughed on his way to the car. He drove around the block a few times before deciding to drive to the store. Wyatt absently walked around, he smiled as he thought of the mess Sawyer had to clean up. He stopped smiling when he ran into a friend from school.

"Wyatt," Jay waved. Wyatt nodded, trying to turn down a different aisle. Jay followed him, leaving his mom and sister behind. "Hey, are you going to Rand's party this weekend?" Wyatt turned towards him, he hated standing near Jay. Wyatt tilted his head nearly all the way back to look at his face.

"No," Wyatt responded. Jay pushed him lightly, though he still shifted several inches away.

"You haven't been hanging with any of us lately and you always leave right after soccer practice," Jay complained. Wyatt turned down another aisle, hoping Jay would realize that he needed to find his family again. "The guys have been joking about you playing house with Sawyer," Jay laughed. Wyatt stopped, it took a few seconds for Jay to realize this. When he did, he turned around to look at him. His head was tilted with confusion. "What's up?"

Wyatt looked to the side. An older woman had two different

types of tampons in her hand. Wyatt looked back to Jay. "Who's been talking about Sawyer?" Wyatt asked, glaring at Jay. Jay held his hands up.

"No one, I just meant- you know that you haven't been around," Jay hurriedly said. "I mean it's really terrible what happened. I didn't - I'm sorry," Jay said. Wyatt turned down the tampon aisle, passing by the woman and leaving Jay behind even as he kept apologizing. He was angry as he drove back to Sawyer's house. He parked in the driveway and sat there for a few minutes, setting his forehead against the steering wheel. That's what he wanted. He wanted to be with Sawyer, he wanted more than to "play house". They were at a weird place, they were together without being together. Sawyer wanted things to stay how they were, he wasn't ready for so much change. Wyatt wanted more, he wanted everything to change. His mother called him naive.

7:12 P.M.

Wyatt went into the house, everyone was upstairs when he opened the door. He could already see the mess was cleaned up. He quietly shut the door, locking it before heading up the stairs. Carter's door was halfway shut, only her night light was on. Wyatt headed into Lio's room. Sawyer was laying Lio down in the crib, he turned to see Wyatt. "You're dead," Sawyer mouthed to him. Wyatt sent a kiss towards him, stepping out and into Sawyer's room where he threw himself on the bed, spreading out.

He didn't move when he heard Sawyer come in, he grinned into the sheets when he heard him. "I'm really going to kill you," Sawyer said. Wyatt groaned when Sawyer pressed his knee into his back before sitting on him, lightly pounding his back.

"That feels good," Wyatt said, causing Sawyer to hit him harder. Wyatt pushed him up, flipping around, catching Sawyer's hands as he sat on his stomach. Sawyer leaned forward, Wyatt held him up. Sawyer pushed forward, smiling when Wyatt's arms shook before giving out dropping Sawyer inches above him.

"That scared me," Sawyer laughed trying to pull up. Wyatt stopped him, letting go of his hand, holding the back of his neck to keep him close. "Wyatt?"

"If this is your plan of killing me, then you can kill me whenever you like," Wyatt whispered.

"Why are you whispering?" Sawyer asked, dropping his face so their noses touched briefly before pulling back up, his eyes darting between each of Wyatt's eyes.

"Why are you?" Wyatt asked back. Wyatt lifted his head, kissing his nose then his lips. Wyatt let Sawyer's neck go. Sawyer sat up staring down at him. Wyatt held up his left hand that was still holding Sawyer's.

"I'm still going to kill you for leaving that mess."

"Then kill me," Sawyer poked him a few times, making Wyatt squirm below him. Wyatt tried to grab him. "Dammit Sawyer," Wyatt laughed. Sawyer stopped, his hands dropping to either side of Wyatt.

"I hate pretending to be an adult. School sucks, taking care of kids is hard and I have no idea what I'm doing," Sawyer said, hanging his head above Wyatt. "And I still have to pay the bills," Sawyer shifted back up, turning away from Wyatt. He ran a hand through his hair.

"You also need a shower," Wyatt said. Sawyer glared at him, jabbing him in the ribs as he rolled off the bed..

"I was planning on taking one tonight anyways," Sawyer said, sticking his tongue out.

"Sawyer wait." Sawyer turned from the bathroom door. Wyatt stood up. "I know I said things don't have to change but…" Wyatt paused, Sawyer took large strides to the bed.

"Is this about us?" Sawyer asked, a lot more serious than a few seconds before.

Wyatt nodded slowly.

"Are you breaking up with me?" Sawyer asked.

Wyatt's eyes widened. "No! Wait, are we going out?" Wyatt asked.

"Yes, I mean I thought we were. Aren't we?" Sawyer said, pulling away from Wyatt.

"I don't know, yes?" Wyatt said, reaching for Sawyer and missing as he got further from the bed.

Sawyer ran a hand through his hair. "Ah fuck, I'm terrible at this."

"No, I just. I wasn't sure where we stood."

Sawyer smiled, getting back on the bed, he sat on the edge. "I already told you I liked you, I thought I was the slow one. And how many times have we made out?"

"I don't want… I don't know." Wyatt responded he didn't want anyone to think badly of Sawyer.

"What happened when you were out? Did you have some kind of teen-life crisis?" Sawyer jokingly asked.

Wyatt grabbed a pillow from behind him, throwing it at Sawyer. Sawyer caught it, dropping it to the floor. "Fine don't tell me, I'm going to shower though." Sawyer waited a second, Wyatt staring at him. Sawyer finally got up, shutting the door behind him.

Wyatt lay back down on the bed, throwing an arm over his eyes.

Saturday May 31st 4:21 P.M.

Wyatt leaned on the door frame to the kitchen, his mother was pulling containers filled with food out of royal blue reusable bags. "Su Yeon needs a raise." His mother glared at him.

"She gets paid well enough," she said. Her voice was stilted, it was as close to frantic as he'll ever hear it. "Get in here and help," she told him.

Wyatt took the few steps into the kitchen and pulled out containers full of traditional Korean dishes. He wondered how his extended family would react if they knew she didn't cook and make these herself. It would waylay the conversation about which college he was going to choose. Especially if his grandmother had a heart attack from the news.

"If you're planning a murder be sure to do it properly, I have enough cases without adding yours to the pile," she told him.

"I'm not planning a murder," he told her, though his annoyed voice didn't help his stance.

She stared at him. "I've seen that look on enough faces to know that whatever is going on in your head is disturbing."

He sighed. "Do we have to do this bullshit? It's annoying."

She slid one of the bags across the counter for him to empty. "Yes we do, they are family."

Wyatt didn't understand the emphasis on family, or the importance she always put on it. The only time they ever saw family was for big occasions, then it was a huge family affair. After it was over everyone went back to their lives, if there was any information that needed to be shared then his aunt would be told and she would spread it to everyone. She was the aunt you could never tell a secret to because everyone would know within the hour. Most of his family sucked, the only ones he could stand were the kids, Hae Na, his cousin Gi Kwang, and a couple of the members that married into the family. His mother was even more strict because they were now hosting all of them in their house.

"I need you to pull out the comforters and move the desk in the office to create space. And don't think you're staying at that boy's house, your family expects you to be living here and they will hear no different. If Chin Sun hears about this I will be the one murdering someone."

"I understand, I don't talk to her anyway," Wyatt muttered, she was the last person he wanted to talk to.

"Watch the tone," she said.

Wyatt finished emptying the bags, then he started piling them up in the fridge. It was tedious work and he was annoyed it had to be done.

"I hired someone yesterday to clean but I need you to make sure it was done properly, if not, you need to clean it."

Wyatt shoved the rest of the containers in a little harder than necessary. When he finished he found his mom putting clean dishes in the drying rack. Everything she did was an act he thought fruitless, his family would still find faults. They found faults everywhere they went, like Chin Sun's toilet handle was loose. His uncle's house was too small and his wife never cooked enough dishes. No one ever spoke about his grandmother's house because she was living with his aunt Jae Hwa who never did anything to displease his grandmother. She had married properly, had several successful children and took care of the house properly. If clones were real his aunt was the clone of his grandmother, she was the eldest of the women and she had no issues handing out insults. She was the one Wyatt hated most, she was vicious and had no hesitation raising a hand to him or to any of the cousins she saw fit to hit. However, she never laid a hand on her own children when they were the ones who caused the issue.

There was also another rule, one he had watched his dad struggle with. Everyone only spoke Korean, his grandmother wasn't interested in learning English so she didn't accept when others spoke it around her. She didn't like not knowing every little thing that was happening. Wyatt had gotten a spoon to the hand when he spoke to his dad in English as a child. His father was furious but unable to do anything. It was the first time he had seen his dad's anger and he was almost tempted to push it again but the pain from the spoon was too much. It had left a bruise for two weeks.

He never understood why his father had decided to marry his mother. They had fought hard for it, went through unnecessary turmoil. He had never heard them whisper or speak lovingly to each other, not the way he saw Sawyer's parents dote on and adore each other. His parents were reserved, quiet and solitary. He had this idea that they have only ever had sex once and that was to make him, for no other reason than to get his grandmother to stop asking about grandchildren. His mother was the only one in the family to have one child.

His grandmother had 8 children, they were split between the US and South Korea. His grandmother, her second oldest son and 3 daughters were in the US, and his grandfather, her oldest son, third son and 2 middle daughters were in South Korea.

His mother was the youngest and the only one born in the US, for that reason his grandmother had stayed. He thought that she resented her for it, even though it had been his grandmother's choice.

"I wasn't joking about the face," his mother said again.

"You never joke."

"So drop it. We've been playing this game long enough, it'll be easier for you to miss events when you're in college and this is the last big one," she said. She made it sound like she was also going to start getting out of them. He doubted that though.

"If I tell her about Sawyer she may have a heart attack, then we can all hang out at the hospital."

She turned to him. "Ji Seok, that is not funny. Do not joke about such things." Wyatt shrugged, she never told him not to do it though.

5:17 P.M.

His family arrived in quick succession, conversations overflowed over everything, his aunts all went into the kitchen to check on all the food his mother had "made". The men stayed in the living room talking as if they hadn't spoken in years. His father was sitting in his chair, he didn't try to join in on the conversation, but he wasn't avoiding it either. Wyatt took a step back when the kids ran past him to get out to the back yard.

He didn't show his surprise when Hae Na nudged his shoulder. He turned to her; she was dressed in a nice dress, her hair was straight, with a small bow in it. The whole look gave her an innocence he didn't think she had possessed since she was 10.

"How excited are you for this?" Hae Na asked in English.

"Negative ten," he commented, surprised enough to respond in English.

"Oo that beats my negative eight, heads up," she said. He turned just slightly to his right and he could see his grandmother heading towards him. Hae Na was gone from his side and he put on a quick smile.

She tsked right away, her Korean was quick and precise when she talked. "Bad manners not greeting me. What has that mother of yours been teaching you?"

Wyatt swallowed his retort and answered in formal Korean, bowing slightly. "I'm sorry grandmother."

She tsked again, her gaze behind him so he was sure she was looking at Hae Na. "School is important, do not end up like that child. You finish school, do you understand me?"

"Of course," he replied and the answer appeased her and she turned her head up at Hae Na before heading back to the kitchen. He turned to Hae Na who was staring at her hands.

Hae Na's mother passed him without a word or glance, pulling Hae Na up the stairs. He leaned against the wall again and studied his dad. Wyatt went back and forth between the kitchen and the living room, starting up short conversations and leaving before they got too long. He did it for a grand total of ten minutes, then he was back in his same spot by the wall, watching Hae Na all but jump down the entire staircase and slam out the front door. He did another short round of conversations, then headed out back to the kids, did one short round, then he snuck out the side gate and followed after Hae Na.

Chapter 11 Hae Na

|Monday May 12th 10:56 A.M.

Hae Na packed up her car again, her stomach was twisted with anxiety. Her smile was bright as she said goodbye. Cassie reached up to her for a hug, Hae Na leaned down hugging her tight. "Your mom has my number," she said, pulling away. "You all do."

"Don't worry, we'll call you. Now go out there and be the strong woman we've all come to love."

"I will, just wait till you see me next." Hae Na waved another goodbye as she got in and drove away. She turned up the radio, her hands tight on the steering wheel. She took three deep breaths and unclenched her teeth. If Wyatt didn't accept her then she would move on, the world wouldn't end. It would just be a bit bleaker. She looked ahead of her, dark clouds and rain were in her forecast, strangely she found it comforting. She relaxed back in her seat, she had a few hours of a drive.

1:51 P.M.

Halfway she stopped for the gas station and food, she went through the drive-thru and parked in the parking lot. She set her bag of food on the passenger seat and called Wyatt.

"Hello?" he answered, though there was some noise in the background.

"Hey, what are you up to?" she asked, her voice casual.

"Hanging out with Sawyer."

"Still have a crush on that kid?" she asked. Wyatt had never told her he had a crush on him, but she loved to joke about it. She reached over to the passenger seat, opening the bag.

"Yeah," he responded.

"Wait, really?" she laughed, she knew Wyatt was her favorite for a reason. She grinned as she dug around to the bottom of the bag pulling out a few curly fries.

"Yeah, is something going on?"

She waved the fries around. "Sort of, but nothing really, just checking on my favorite cousin." She shoved the fries in her mouth.

"Exactly, so what's wrong?"

Hae Na took a large sip of her drink before responding. "You know life takes you on so many journeys. Well, cousin, my journey is leading me to you. So you think Auntie will let me stay?"

"No, also I'm not staying at home anyway."

"Did you move out? Have you already left for college? I missed your graduation!"

"No, it's next weekend. Your mom didn't tell you about the family reunion?"

"Well, we're not exactly talking right now. Wait where are you living then?" she asked, she pulled the bag in her lap pulling out her burger.

"At Sawyer's." She paused her movements.

"Did you knock him up and get married? Scratch that thought, it was more of a first instinct than anything else," she said taking a large bite of her burger.

"That one is going in the scrapbook," he said. She rolled her eyes.

She swallowed her bite, taking a drink before talking again. "I'm going to visit you for your birthday."

"Really? We're probably not going to do much but it'll be great to see you."

"Yeah, it will. I bet you haven't grown an inch. Well, I have to go but I'll see you soon, bye!"

"Bye," he responded.

She set her phone in the cup holder and looked down at drops of ketchup on her jeans. "How? How did you do that? You're wrapped up like a swaddled baby in the middle of a winter blizzard in a broken down car on the side of the road with no one in sight to save it," she said, glaring at her burger before biting into it again, ignoring the fact Sam wasn't next to her laughing; she always laughed when Hae Na came up with strange scenarios.

4:39 P.M.

Hae Na checked into the hotel. Dropping her bag at the end of the bed, she looked around the basic room. She promised herself she wouldn't stay long, just until she sorted out the group therapy sessions. She pulled out the sheet with information, looking over the different types of therapy. Three were highlighted for her, Hae Na felt a bit more of her confidence return, shaking off any lingering feelings of doubt. She pulled off her shirt, ready for a shower and maybe a new haircut.

Looking through her clothes she frowned at the repetitiveness of it. She had been wearing her limited outfits for a month. After pulling on a tired outfit of a t-shirt with a hot dog and hamburger shooting finger guns at each other and a pair of dark jean shorts, she looked up thrift stores in the area.

6:29 P.M.

Hae Na moved through the racks of clothes, her fingers quickly flicking through the hangers. She paused on a light grey shirt with a bright orange fox paw on it. She took it off the rack holding it up to herself and added it to her pile. This was her third store and she still hadn't found nearly enough clothes to make up for what she left behind. She paused at the end of the aisle. Taking a breath, she reminded herself that she had time to replace all of it.

After finding a few pairs of jeans and shorts she headed to the counter, looking through random trinkets and a bowl of buttons. She paused on a white button with *One step forward* written in a light purple that caught her attention. She hesitated before digging it out and adding it to her pile on the counter. She made a mistake before, she took two steps back when she should have taken one forward. She smiled politely at the cashier. After paying, she picked up the large bag of neatly folded clothes and started her walk forward.

Tuesday May 13th 5:22 P.M.

Hae Na walked into the meeting wearing her new button on her old shirt. It reminded her of the few NA meetings she went to. She found a seat in the medium-sized circle of chairs in the room. She picked at her nail polish, she stopped when she realized Cassie had been the one to carefully paint them. She lifted her head when she saw legs enter her vision.

"I'm JJ." Hae Na looked up to a chipper woman with a more chipper smile.

Hae Na gave a small smile and a nod back. She looked down again, her button catching her attention. Hae Na looked back up. "I'm Hae Na."

She turned around when someone said her name, she smiled with a wave before turning her attention back to Hae Na. "I'm sorry I have to set up a few things but I'm glad you joined us today."

Hae Na remained in her seat watching as more people arrived taking the chairs around her. A few other people said hello, Hae Na nodded back to them. She felt like a middle schooler going to a new school with no friends. Every move she made felt awkward, every time she shifted she felt like everyone put their attention on her. She picked at her nails again and then everyone was moving and leaving. She looked around as everyone broke off into smaller groups, some of them going out for pie others, leaving right away. Hae Na had missed it, she had missed everything she had come there for.

Hae Na stood up to leave. JJ walked up to her with another girl that Hae Na probably should have known the name of since she probably spoke during group but it escaped her.

"Do you want to get ice cream with us?" JJ asked, her tone was light and friendly.

Hae Na was shocked. She quickly recovered. "I.. Yeah. I love ice cream," Hae Na stumbled over her words, giving an awkward smile to make up for it.

"Awesome, I'm JJ if you forgot and this is Benji," JJ gestured to the woman next to her. Hae Na followed them out, instead of heading to the cars they went to the sidewalk. "We usually get ice cream or food after group," JJ explained. She and Benji walked in front of her, JJ turned around walking backwards to talk to Hae Na. "I know… I know after everything it can be really hard to adjust again, there's a few of us, we sort of started a-" JJ stopped speaking, she turned to Benji, "What did Rem call it?"

Benji shrugged, slowing her pace to walk next to Hae Na. "Something to do with the babysitters club, Rem likes code names," Benji explained. "You'll meet her eventually, there's 4 of us who hang out," Benji added.

JJ's head tilted as she squinted her eyes. "I thought it was a *Stand By Me* reference," she muttered loudly.

"I think she had a few of them, one time it was something about *Powerpuff Girls* so at this point who really cares?" Benji asked. Her tone is more curious than dismissive.

"Because it's fun," JJ said with a grin. Spinning around, she avoided a man and his dog as she turned the corner and then spun again to face them.

"Don't be impressed by that, she's naturally gifted," Benji told her. Rolling her eyes as JJ beamed at the compliment. JJ spun again though this time it was to a doorway that she held open for them. Hae Na went in first, one wall was brightly colored while the rest of the walls were white. Hae Na walked up to the counter, looking over the flavors they offered.

After they decided what they wanted and found a table to sit at, Hae Na decided that she liked them. "So are you from here or are you new here?" Benji asked with the same curious tone.

"New, I don't know if I'm going to stay but I'm going to try," Hae Na told her, she didn't really have a plan. She was living each day as it came. She wasn't living for the future.

Benji nodded like she somehow understood. "I think you should stay, not to be cocky or anything but you won't find a group as good as us anywhere else," Benji gave a bright grin.

JJ set her spoon back in her bowl of ice cream. "She's right we're awesome."

Hae Na smiled. "I have some family that lives here but I haven't talked to them in a while."

Benji moved her straw around her shake creating a squeaking sound. "Family isn't always worth the effort." She dropped the straw lifting the cup to her mouth and took a sip. JJ didn't comment on Benji, instead she pulled her phone out of her pocket. Hae Na didn't agree, family was worth it, but sometimes biology didn't have anything to do with it.

"Are you always this quiet?" JJ asked. It felt like her eyes were piercing through her.

"No, sorry. I'm just…" She had no idea what she was. Nervous? Scared? She looked down at her melting ice cream.

"No, no, we're sorry, we're kind of pushy. We should have learned from Dana." JJ rushed in, nearly knocking her ice cream over. She caught it, not even spilling a drop.

"She has this weird basic superpower that saves her from looking like an idiot," Benji said, looking down at the near mess. Hae Na laughed. It felt good for her to laugh at something so mundane.

"I think I could use that," Hae Na told them.

JJ leaned forward as if to tell her a secret. "You hang out with me enough and it'll rub off on you," JJ said.

"She's lying, it doesn't," Benji said. JJ rolled her eyes, nodding despite Benji vehemently shaking her head, mouthing the word no.

Hae Na smiled, this was exactly where she needed to be.

9:47 P.M.

Hae Na went back to the hotel room feeling more content than she had in awhile. Her phone vibrated with a text in her pocket, she shifted, pulling it out. A text from JJ and Benji that both said hey. Hae Na dropped the phone next to her, her smile fading away as doubt crept in. She closed her eyes wrapping her arms around herself. Hae Na lay there until her stomach growled in protest of the lack of food. She lifted her phone for the time and found her battery was almost dead. She crawled off of the bed, digging through her purse for the charger. Finally finding it in the side pocket, she plugged it in near the bed and looked at menus for delivery.

As she waited, she pulled out her new clothes, realizing they probably needed to be washed first. Shrugging at the thought, she stacked the piles together from the three different bags. Her phone lit up with a notification that she turned to look at; the food was on its way. She moved them to the dresser then paused and turned to set them near her bag. She wouldn't be here long enough to need the dresser, that's what she kept telling herself. Right now she was going to sort through her clothes, her emotions could wait.

She jumped when she heard the delivery person knocking on the door. She opened the door to a stocky man with a bright smile. Taking the bag, she handed him a five from her wallet and he left with a wave. She was glad she had paid online as her cash was running low. She looked at the 43 dollars she had left. She sighed, dropping her wallet next to the bag of food on the table.

She ate slowly, it had been a while since she'd eaten alone. She got up, set her fork down and grabbed the paper with information, looking through the other types of groups and activities that were on it. She ate as she skimmed through it, tapping her finger on the self-defense class. "One step forward," she told herself. Grabbing the pen from the table she circled the class.

Wednesday May 14th 5:21 P.M.

Hae Na was less shy at the next meeting, Rem greeted her when she arrived. "JJ told me about you, don't think I'm stalking you," Rem told her, giving her a pointed look.

"She texted me," Hae Na told her, a small crease in Rem's face disappeared.

Rem nodded, her top lip going over her bottom, pulling her lip ring in before releasing it. Rem's attention was across the room. "Dana should be here soon." She narrowed her hazel eyes before opening them brightly again as someone walked in looking like a K-drama killer. Hae Na blinked. The girl wore a black hoodie with the hood up over a black baseball cap and a black fabric mask over her mouth. The girl came right to them, sitting in the seat next to Rem, she pulled one side of the mask off.

"Are you Hae Na?" she asked.

"Yeah," Hae Na responded. Dana looked over her shoulder then back to Hae Na, her eyes scanning her. "I'm Dana."

"Dana is like a spy, so ignore her weird getups," Rem told her with a smirk

"Shut up," Dana said, quickly looking over her shoulder again before taking a breath and leaning back in her chair.

"Have you ever seen a Korean Drama?" Hae Na asked.

"A what?" Dana asked, leaning forward.

"A Korean show?" Hae Na tried again.

"No," Dana stated.

"Oh well, you kind of look like a killer from one," Hae Na said. She pulled her phone out searching for one, when several came up she showed it to them. Rem nearly fell off her chair laughing, Dana just rolled her eyes at Rem.

"I've never seen it, but it's actually a good resemblance," Dana said. "Are you going to the meeting tomorrow? The other girls will be there."

"Yeah I think so, I was planning on going to the self-defense class after it."

"Oh, Rem and JJ go to that," Dana said, unimpressed.

"You should go too, especially you," Rem said. Dana shifted the hat around, another glance behind her shoulder to the door.

"I'm fine," Dana said. Rem just shook her head, turning her attention back to Hae Na.

"You should go though, It's a good class," Rem told her.

Hae Na nodded before responding. "Yeah, I think I will."

Rem gave an approving gesture, her arm sat on her knee, her hand twisting around. "Good, maybe you can convince Benji."

Dana shifted her legs, huffing a little. "She doesn't have to if she doesn't want to."

Rem pushed a hand through her hair, leaning back into the chair. "I never said she did, I just think it'd be good for her."

"To lose weight," Dana said. Her tone had taken a colder edge to it.

"I never said that!" Rem nearly yelled.

Dana's eyes narrowed at Rem. "Yes you did, the first time you told her about it."

Rem's face scrunched, then smoothed out. "I just said it was one of the perks."

"Whatever, you know how she feels about that," Dana said.

Hae Na thought back on what Benji looked like. Hae Na's nose scrunched up, she didn't think Benji needed to lose weight and didn't think anyone should be talking about it. Though she wasn't small like Hae Na but that was mostly genetics, most of her family was small. Benji was like a teddy bear you would want to snuggle next to. She looked soft and squishy.

"Shut up, I never said anything against it. She can look however she wants. I just want her to be able to protect herself, that's it," Rem said. Dana rolled her eyes at Rem's comment, not bothering to respond to Rem as the group started.

They did not go out for ice cream or food, Dana replaced the mask on her face and she was out the door without a goodbye.

"Don't mind her," Rem said, "See you tomorrow." Rem headed out the door, Hae Na not far behind as she headed back to her hotel room.

Thursday May 15th 10:01 A.M.

Hae Na sat on the edge of the bed, her phone lit up with a message. She was almost afraid to look at it. Picking it up, she smiled as the doubt and fear left her instantly as she replied.

Shay: How does it feel to be free?

Me: bittersweet

Shay: Chin up, I'm here if you need me

Me: Thanks and me too!

Hae Na smiled at the phone, Shay hadn't stayed much longer at the shelter but Hae Na was glad to know they would still try to keep in touch. Hae Na felt like she learned something from everyone at the Shelter. Shay showed her how to fold origami. She taught her how to focus on something other than the pain.

Hae Na immediately checked when a new text came in.

JJ: Hey! Let's get some food, the others are joining us too! I can add you to the group chat if you want?

Me: sure

Another text came in, from Wyatt this time.

Wy Ji: Hey when are you coming?

Hae Na stared at the text, smiling at his name. When she had first got a phone she knew his name wouldn't be normal. She had come up with mixing the first parts of both his names and had kept it ever since. Anxiety rose in her, she bit at her nail then her lip. It had been a few years since she last saw Wyatt. Doubt trickled in like a broken faucet. She tried to remember when fear didn't grip her so tightly. It had been a long time but she was taking control again. She called Wyatt.

"Carter, careful with the milk. Hey Hae Na what's up?"

"I'm in town now at a hotel so…" her voice trailed off, she fidgeted with her clothes.

"You're already here?" he asked, surprise evident in his voice.

"Yeah, I didn't want to be a bother so I was going to wait but yeah. I was going to talk to auntie but…" Hae Na was starting to make a habit of not finishing her sentences. She hated it.

Wyatt spoke up when she didn't finish her sentence. "But she's a stone, you can stay here. Sawyer said he didn't mind."

"What about his parents?" she asked, Wyatt didn't answer right away. Instead it seemed as if he was focused on something else in the background.

"You're coming over for my birthday, right? I'll send you the address."

"Okay, sounds good," she said. He still hadn't answered her question.

"Bye," he said, hanging up quickly. Hae Na looked at the phone.

"Bye," she said to herself. Hae Na dropped her phone when a flood of texts came in. She hated group chats.

11:58 A.M.

Meeting the girls for lunch went nothing like she expected. JJ and Rem were sitting next to each other at a table for six. Hae Na took the seat across from JJ.

"Hey, Rem told me you were going to join the defense class," JJ said.

Hae Na nodded slowly. "Yeah I was thinking about it."

"It's a good class, I'm hoping to convince the other girls, especially Dana," JJ said, staring at the door as she said it. Hae Na didn't ask why they thought Dana was in more need of the class than the others. It wasn't her place and if Dana wanted her to know, she would tell her. Though that didn't mean she hadn't made her own observations. Hae Na looked over her shoulder when JJ waved, Hae Na barely recognized Dana. Her hair was cascading down in lavender waves and her makeup was an extension of that, with a black and purple smokey eye.

"Is that a new wig?" JJ asked. Dana pulled the chair out next to Hae Na.

"I got it yesterday, I didn't have time between work and the meeting to try it."

"Which is why she looked like a…" Rem paused before laughing, then adding. "A Korean killer."

"It was a drama killer," Dana said, squinting her eyes at Rem.

"A Korean drama killer," Hae Na clarified.

Hae Na watched JJ's eyes light up with amusement. "What is

that?" JJ asked.

"It's just... nothing," Hae Na laughed, shaking her head.

"Fine, have your inside jokes, but know that I'm the queen of them and after a week with me, you'll forget all about this one with them," JJ told her.

"You are so dramatic," Dana said, getting the attention of the waitress with a pointed smile and eye contact.

"Go look in a mirror and then tell me *I'm* dramatic," JJ said, lifting her glass of water up before taking a drink and setting it back down.

Dana leaned forward on the table, her arm bumping into Hae Na's. "You're dramatic," Dana said clearly with a sharp smile.

JJ sat back in her seat, before shooting forward. "There's Benji, she's always on my side."

Benji pulled the chair out next to Dana. "Sorry I'm late, oh Dana you look really pretty."

"Thank you," Dana said, her stiffened shoulders dropped a little.

"I got a new work schedule and I can't go to Thursday meetings anymore," JJ said.

"Seriously? Today is the only one we have with all of us," Dana said.

"It's for like two weeks, I don't want to do it either. Until they find someone else, I'm stuck with it. I can start going to the meetings on Wednesday with you and Rem which leaves Benji out."

"It's okay, plus now we have Hae Na," Benji said.

Hae Na smiled as all of them turned their attention to her. "Yeah," Hae Na added. Benji gave her a thumbs up.

"Does that mean individual meetups change?" Benji asked. Her fingers tapped a few things on the menu.

JJ rolled her eyes, "It's for two weeks, you guys act like it's the end of the world."

Dana scoffed. "No one said that. Now look who's being dramatic."

"Still you," JJ said, lifting a perfect arched brow

"So what are individual meetups?" Hae Na asked, avoiding what could have been a fight. JJ redirected her attention from Dana to Hae Na her face shifting to a smile.

"So we all have different ideas of comfort and safety. I mean everyone does, we all have boundaries that we respect. I'm not explaining this well. Basically we're each other's support systems, even if some of us are dramatic."

Dana scoffed at that, about to retort when JJ cut her off. "We meet up like this, or with someone who has a free day. So Rem has Monday and Thursday off so if I have a Monday free most of the time I hang out with Rem or with the group of us since we all usually have Thursday free. Benji usually has weekends free. Dana is kind of all over the place."

This time Dana didn't let herself be cut off. "I freelance, so I have time to work around my job."

Rem spoke up this time. "Yeah, she's smart whatever, so what days do you have free?"

Hae Na closed her menu, looking at Rem. "I don't have a job yet, so I have every day free."

Benji leaned over the table. "I can help with the job if you need it," she said.

"Thanks," Hae Na responded.

Rem nodded, lifting her menu. "Let's order because I'm starving."

Hae Na enjoyed listening to the girls, it had been too long since she had hung out with friends of her own. The women she met in the shelter felt different, they were like the aunts and cousins she was missing out on.

2:03 P.M.

When Hae Na went back to the hotel, it felt too quiet. Hae Na had never lived alone before. After she had left home, she had a few roommates before living with Sam. Then she stayed at the shelter, the past few days she was so wrapped up in her mind she hadn't noticed the silence. She grabbed the remote, turning the T.V. on, she flipped through the channels before leaving it on a cooking show. Her phone vibrated with two texts, she looked at them. JJ and Benji sent their open schedules.

Hae Na texted Wyatt for a time the following day, she set her phone down and picked up her dirty clothes as she waited. When she finished she sat on the bed, a new show starting. She could admit that she was bored and lonely.

Friday May 16th 8:02 A.M.

Hae Na started her day with a shower before she got dressed in a new outfit to see her cousin. She brushed her hair out, remembering that she needed a haircut. Wrapping it all into a bun, she headed out. She didn't give herself any time to think or second guess herself, she only focused on the directions to the house, repeating after the GPS until it gave her new instructions and then when she got to the door it opened to a child and her being yelled at.

The voice was far away but the more they spoke, the closer it got. "Carter I told you not to open the door! Stop opening the door for people, it could be a stranger or a kidnapper." The guy before her was not Wyatt, it was Sawyer Losada.

"Hae Na? I haven't seen you in forever," he said surprised, even though Wyatt had told her Sawyer had said it was okay.

"About five or six years, give or take," she said. Sawyer pulled Carter to the side as they let her in.

Carter stepped in front of her as soon as the door was closed. "I'm Carter."

Hae Na crouched down. "The last time I saw you, you were in your mom's tummy."

"Really?" she asked, looking up to Sawyer to confirm, he nodded. Carter looked her over again before shrugging and running into the living room.

She followed Sawyer to the living room as he spoke. "She's always like that, Wyatt's in the shower. We're just hanging out." He dropped onto the couch. A baby boy was crawling around chasing after a rolling ball. Hae Na sat on the floor near Carter who was smashing a Barbie car and a truck into each other. Hae Na messed with a few of the other toys spread out on the floor when a hand and then two pressed on her leg. She looked over at the baby, he was grinning up at her drool sliding out of his mouth, landing on her leg. "That's a lovely face you got their kid," she told him, he reached up for her face, his arms wobbly as he tipped. She caught him picking him up, she set him in front of her.

"I want to play a game!" Carter announced. Hae Na turned at the clattering sound of Carter dropping the truck and car. Carter moved around so she was in front of Hae Na. "Want to play a game?"

"Sure, what do you want to play?" Hae Na asked her. Carter looked at her then away.

Carter tilted her head as she thought about it, she twisted her body back and forth. "Sah, what do you want to play?"

"How about pay the bills?" he asked her.

"What's that?"

"It's where you find money around the house to pay the bills," he told her, no doubt hoping it would distract her.

She shook her head. "No, that's dumb."

Sawyer shrugged. "I thought it was pretty smart actually."

Hae Na smiled, turning when she heard feet on the stairs. "There's my favorite cousin," she said, Wyatt smiled as he made his way from the bottom step to her.

"I see the kids already have you wrapped in their madness," Wyatt said.

She shrugged. "It was inevitable."

"True," he replied.

"Invet table?" Carter asked, "Is that like vegtable? I only like corn and carrots."

Hae Na laughed, falling back onto the floor, not even caring that a block was pressing into her back until the boy crawled up onto her pressing it further in. The pain shocked her into moving, her hands nearly shaking as she lifted him off of her chest. He laughed, patting at her face, she focused on him calming her nerves.

"Lio likes you," Sawyer said. Hae Na just nodded her head, focusing on what was right in front of her, instead of the darkness swarming her memories and mind.

She turned when Wyatt walked up next to her. "Have you eaten yet? I was going to make some lunch."

"Wait, isn't today Friday? You guys don't have school?" she asked

"No, we graduate next week. We have to go in for a few more things but we're pretty much done," Wyatt told her.

"Right, seniors always finish earlier, it hasn't even been that long since I got out and it feels like forever," Hae Na said more to herself than anyone else.

"Yeah like what, two years?"

"Two years can feel like a lifetime," she told him.

"So can a month," Sawyer added. Still typing on his computer, he looked up when Wyatt threw a soft colorful cube at his head. Sawyer glared at him before focusing back on his screen. Hae Na smiled at the kids, Wyatt was adorable with his crush. She turned back to Sawyer, maybe it wasn't a crush anymore. Would Sawyer's parents let him stay if they knew they were together?

"You guys can play while I make lunch," Wyatt said.

Hae Na turned her attention back to Sawyer. She was careful when she stood up, dropping herself onto the couch. "So you and Wyatt," she started, her attention on Carter as she ran out of the room, yelling about getting games. Lio had found another toy to crawl after.

"Me and Wyatt," Sawyer replied. Hae Na leaned over, looking at the expansive spreadsheet. "It's my life for the next four years," Sawyer said. "Maybe." he added, his eyes skimming over a few things before switching to another spreadsheet, not nearly as large. "This one is Wyatt's, we're still debating colleges so I don't really know where to go with it from here."

"Wow, you guys move fast. How long have you guys been together as a couple?"

"Um, a week? Two? I don't even know what today is, so you'd have to ask him."

She wasn't sure if he was speaking because he was distracted or because he didn't care if she knew the information. He spoke as if he wasn't paying attention.

"That seems quick," she commented, watching Sawyer carefully.

Sawyer shrugged. "If it's going to work, I want it to work. If not then," Sawyer paused. He looked over his computer to where his brother was starting to stand up using the table. He watched him another few seconds before looking down again.

"Then?" Hae Na prompted. She knew about getting too serious too fast but this wasn't her and Sam. It didn't stop her heart from pounding in fear. They seemed too young to be so committed. Had they even had any other relationships? They haven't even lived in the world yet. She took a slow breath, her focus returning to Sawyer. She willed herself to be normal, to look normal.

Sawyer clicked through a few other tabs before he answered. "Then I want to know now. I lost my parents and losing Wyatt would be just as terrible. I can't be a naive privileged kid anymore. I made a choice and I need to grow up. He's either going to do it with me or he'll find someone else." Hae Na didn't know how to process anything he just told her. Sawyer losing his parents? She had no idea. She had been ready to tease him on the crush and he completely shut her down. He shut his computer and there he was the Sawyer Losada she had known before.

"I'm starving," he groaned. "Feed me!" His yell surprised her but not as much as the smile he gave to her reply.

"Go eat a flacking shoe." Hae Na turned from Sawyer to Carter smiling as she carried a few boxes of board games, she figured she was the reason Wyatt didn't swear. Carter set the boxes on the floor. Before she could ask what she wanted to play, Carter was already opening the box for Candyland. Hae Na slid to the floor as Sawyer went to the kitchen. They started the game, they had to stop a few times to pull Lio away from the board and cards.

1:21 P.M.

Going back to the hotel alone felt desolate, she slid off the end of the bed to the floor shifting from her half-packed bag to her phone showing three new messages. A few more texts came in, she didn't move. Laying her head against the bed, she didn't attempt to wipe the tears away, even as they tickled her face. It was hours before she moved, her body stiff and sore. She had missed group, missed class, missed calls and messages. She crawled onto the bed, pulling the mess of blankets over her she went to bed.

Sunday May 26th 12:56 P.M.

Hae Na looked out her front car window at the place where Rem had told her to meet. The building was stone grey, there were two axes crossed with the name Iron Cleaver Axe Club. "Where the hell have you brought me to?" she whispered to herself.

Rem knocked on her passenger window startling her. Hae Na shut her car off, she opened her door as Rem moved to the front of the car. Hae Na got out, shutting her door, she looked back to the ax club. "The other girls are scared to come with me, but I promise it's fun." Rem was buzzing with energy next to her.

Hae Na looked at it skeptically. "What is it?" she asked. If the other girls didn't want to go then maybe she shouldn't either.

"You throw axes at targets on the wall. The building is actually split into four places with a door for each but once you're in you can get in from any place. They have axes, archery, shooting, and plates, which is also really fun. They have a bunch of stuff to throw and destruction rooms where you can just destroy everything in it. JJ and the others love those rooms but they won't do this with me," Rem explained, her voice rising with excitement.

Hae Na wasn't so sure either but she had promised to start trying new things and this was definitely new to her. "It's safe right?" she asked as Rem held the door open for her.

"Yeah, don't worry they teach you all the safety stuff before we throw them."

"Oh good, so I won't accidentally cut my hand off," Hae Na commented. Rem paused before laughing.

Rem shook her head. "No you won't cut your hand off."

"Great, no worries then," Hae Na said, though as they headed to the wooden counter where a worker was explaining the cost and time limits, her stomach was wound in anxiety.

Hae Na felt anxiety shift into excitement as she heard the thump of the axe sticking into the wooden target in front of her. She smiled, Rem lightly nudged their shoulders together.

"It's fun right?" Rem asked.

Hae Na laughed. "Yeah it is." Hae Na threw until her arms grew tired.

She watched Rem hit the center nearly every time. She wondered if this was how the Vikings had felt. Throwing axes, wielding swords, she was starting to even gain a new appreciation for sageuks. She had a newfound interest in them, in swords and history. She thought it would be an interesting mix, putting the Vikings in a political struggle between the emperors of South Korea. She shook her head at the idea and Rem's movement forward caused her to refocus on reality.

"Want to throw again?" Rem asked, yanking the axes from the wood.

Hae Na smiled, replying with a simple, "Yeah."

Hae Na loosened and tightened her grip on the ax and lifted her arm, pausing as the song changed. Her smile slipped off of her face, her arm lowering. Pain seared across her body, tears welled in her eyes. Her name seemed foreign and distant as Rem spoke it.

Memories of Sam filled her; the feeling of her warm hands, her harsh words, the pain that both of them caused. Hae Na tightened her grip, raised her arm and threw the axe. It went too far to the right and landed far from the center of the target. Hae Na took a shaky breath and walked forward, yanking it out before she threw it again and again. The song had finished but the memories were close.

Rem didn't comment, instead, she walked to the front and yanked out her axe. Hae Na took a step back and then to the side giving Rem her place.

Rem didn't start throwing, instead she stared at Hae Na. "We all have stories or we wouldn't all have met up. I can't tell you their stories but if you want, I can tell you mine," Rem offered. Rem's eyes didn't waver, they stayed clear, she didn't even blink.

"Not if you don't want to," Hae Na told her. She hadn't told any of the girls about Sam, not yet at least.

"I've been going to the meetings for a few years, I've told my story so many times." Rem paused. Looking back to the board, she set the axe in its holder and nodded to a tall table near their booth. Hae Na took the direction and took a seat. She stared at Rem as she spoke.

"I was adopted when I was seven. He started days after I moved in. I wanted to tell someone." She shrugged, sighing. "In the end, it wasnt even me who went to the police. I was eleven when my adoptive father adopted another seven year old. The golden number isn't it? She told her teacher, we were both taken out of the house and put in foster care. They split us up and I haven't seen her since. I aged out of the system. I actually didn't even know my ethnicity until I did one of those DNA tests. I looked for my family but it turned up nothing." Rem turned her attention back to the board. Standing up she grabbed the axe, still not throwing it yet.

"I was angry for a long time, confused too but mostly I was angry and I took it out on everyone around me." Rem was quick with her throw, thump. It hit right on the bullseye. "It took a lot to let go," she said before walking to the board. She pulled it out, she stepped back into place. Her last two throws were different, one went high hitting the top of the board, the last throw was low near the bottom. It took her a minute to finish her story.

"I started coming to these places when I started the group meetings. My therapist recommended it. The therapist was court ordered but it helped a lot. Got me through a lot of things and now look at me." She tilted her head back and to the side to look at Hae Na.

Hae Na turned to her and looked at her toned and tanned body and her dark black wavy hair. Rem was an athletic punk girl who demanded attention, not because she wanted it, but because she made you look. Her teeth were not perfect, her hair was a mess of waves, her clothes were baggy, she was beautiful. Hae Na had been realizing several things since she left home; she saw beauty in more than just one person, in more than just one way.

"What's with that look?" Rem asked. Hae Na looked over at where Rem had already gathered the axe from the board.

"I was just thinking about how cool you look."

"A girl after my heart, let me tell you I've been trying to get those girls to see how awesome I am for a while. And look at you stepping right into my honey trap," Rem said. Hae Na wasn't sure she understood everything she was just told. "So our time is about up, do you want to get some lunch? They have this cool restaurant in the next building over."

"Um yeah, we could do that," Hae Na said, pinching her leg. This was not a date, she told herself. This was friendship, this was what she had lost when she was with Sam.

"Great," Rem said, nodding her head in the direction of the door. Hae Na walked next to her to the exit.

Tuesday May 27th 11:49 P.M.

Hae Na opened the hotel door. JJ walked in, looking around as if she had never been to a hotel before.

"Fancy," JJ commented, dropping her bag next to the T.V.. Hae Na didn't think it was but she wasn't going to dispute her claim. JJ looked at her pile of clothes with a tilted head before spinning around to look at Hae Na. "I don't really have anything planned, is there anything you want to do?"

Hae Na shrugged, "Uh not really."

"Well, you're new to town, is there anything you wanted to see?" JJ asked, her head still tilted to the side.

Hae Na half shook her head. "I've been here a few times, my cousin lives here."

"Oh, right. Well, how about we get some lunch and go from there?"

Hae Na nodded. "Sounds good to me."

"Great." JJ picked up her bag, swinging it over her shoulder as she headed to the door, waiting as Hae Na pulled on her shoes and grabbed her own purse. JJ walked next to her, casually smiling.

Hae Na pulled her eyes away looking forward, she walked behind JJ as a man with a suitcase came down the hallway. She regained her position when he passed.

"There was enough room for you not to have done that," JJ said, she didn't turn her head, she just looked forward.

"It's fine."

"I used to think like that too," she said.

Hae Na didn't think it was a conversation starter so she let it drop. JJ led the way to her silver car, Hae Na saw it was a Ford but she wasn't a car person so she had no idea what model it was. JJ's car was the opposite of Hae Na's, Hae Na's was a wreck. It showed what she had eaten and clothes she had yet to take out. JJ's was empty and clean as if it was brand new but it looked older and worn. Hae Na pulled the handle but it was still locked. JJ reached across the console pressing the unlock button, Hae Na opened the door.

"Sorry, this used to be my brother's car and the unlock button on my side doesn't work," she told her. Hae Na thanked her and slid into the fabric covered seat. Not a crumb in sight, no lint, dust or dirt.

"Anything you're feeling for lunch?" JJ asked as she started the car, checking behind her and pulling out.

"Not really," Hae Na told her. She had been living off fast food and ramen noodles, besides the few times she had gone to an actual restaurant. She just wanted her mom's home cooked food.

"What about sushi? Some of the other girls don't like it but I love it. Or we could get poke bowls?"

"Oh yeah that sounds good."

"Perfect," JJ said. Turning up the radio a bit as she drove, Hae Na looked out the window watching as the light sunny sky was being swallowed up by the cloudy grey sky of a storm.

Saturday May 31st 3:42 P.M.

Hae Na looked around Wyatt's room. It was different from the last time she saw it, not too much though. Wyatt was never a kid that had posters on the wall, he had plain light blue walls, a clean desk still stacked with college pamphlets. She didn't know if he had even chosen a college yet. She hadn't known about anything going on with her family. Hae Na had been disconnected for too long, and she hadn't cared. Sam had been her family, Sam had been everything she needed. She heard the door open behind her, spinning around as she watched her mom step into the room. Hae Na looked at her, wanting her to pull her into a hug and say she had missed her. Instead her mom had a stormy look of anger, disappointment and confusion. Hae Na couldn't stop herself from speaking.

"Why? Why can't you just accept me? You don't have to understand. You don't even have to care but please stop pushing me away. I'm your child, you gave birth to me, why do you have to hate me?" Hae Na begged for answers. They had cut her out of their lives, her siblings and parents didn't talk to her. Wyatt was the only one who didn't cut her off.

Her mother glared at her. "We don't hate you Hae Na."

"You don't love me either, why does it matter? Who cares if I like girls? What does it change? I'm still your daughter, I'm still your child."

Her mother pointed at her, up and down as if everything was written on her. "Look what you got into after getting involved with that woman, look what you've become."

"So it would be different if a man beat me instead of a woman? It would be different if I let a man treat me like shit? I wouldn't be broken? I wouldn't be worthless?" she asked.

"Hae Na!" her mother yelled.

Hae Na took a step back, she wanted them to understand. She wanted them to be in her life and to stop judging her. "I was beaten down, I broke down. I took drugs and when my family wasn't there for me the drugs were, she was there. I hated myself for a long time, but I met some strong women who told me that I wasn't worthless. I was worth something to them, I just met the wrong person. I made bad choices but I came out on top. I'll find a woman who loves me and I want you to accept that."

"I thought you were done with that?"

Hae Na chose to ignore what she was implying, she wished she didn't have to. "I am. I quit taking drugs and I quit letting people beat me down."

Her mother didn't let it go. "You know what I mean," she hissed.

It was useless, they would never accept her, she could plead with them until she lost her voice and when she couldn't speak they would belittle her and tear her down. She wanted her family to lift her up, it was a wasted dream. She kept her voice steady as she spoke. "Do you mean the girlfriend? I'm not done with that. I never will be, that's who I am. I like girls, women, whatever. You don't have to understand. I just want you to accept me and if you can't then you're no better than the woman who beat me. You're supposed to stand by me, you're supposed to love me, support me and you're choosing not to."

"Of course we love you but the choices you're making are going to ruin your future. You've dropped out of college to become a druggie and who knows what else. You threw us away the moment you chose that *girl*."

Hae Na had never heard the word girl hissed as an insult before. Her mother had a way in her tone that could make any word sound like an insult or swear word. Hae Na had the thought of asking her to say something ridiculous like Collywobbles or widdershins. Hae Na couldn't help the smile on her face at the thought. Her mother had a fierce glare and Hae Na knew she was holding back a slap meant for her face.

"Fine you don't want me, then don't. You have other children to control you don't need me," she said. Hae Na moved away from her mother, if she stayed any longer then she would risk her sobriety and at this point, they weren't worth it.

She was angry but the hurt was crushing her spirit, the anger was just a small flame in comparison. It was a long quiet walk back to the house. The sun was shining, white puffy clouds in the sky and there was a nice breeze to offset the heat. It was a day to be cherished, a day to be spent with family, maybe some friends. The thought only brought her mood further down.

Her phone vibrated with a text, she lifted it up.

Wyatt: Would you like some candy?

She laughed, a car honked and she looked up. Wyatt had the window down. "Would you like some candy?" he asked.

Hae Na walked over to the car, leaning over the window. "It depends on what kind you have."

"Anything you want," he told her.

"How about some ice cream?" she asked.

"I think I can manage that," he said.

Hae Na smiled and slid into the passenger seat. She fiddled with the radio, leaving it on an alternative rock station and wrapped her hands around the seat belt, slumping her body down in the seat. Hae Na lifted her feet onto the glove box, ignoring Wyatt's groan. It took her awhile to figure out that they had been driving far longer than it took to get to an ice cream place. Hae Na shifted so she was sitting up again, looking out the window. "Where are we?"

"Road trip," Wyatt said, he shifted so she could see his grin.

"No really where are we going?"

"To get ice cream," Wyatt stated.

"Where? Antarctica?"

"I thought you wanted ice cream, not a snow cone."

Hae Na scoffed. "Funny."

Hae Na tapped her fingers on her knee, she kept up with the rhythm of the radio. She had been excited to see her family again, excited to show them how much she had grown as a person. All of her built-up confidence was torn down by her mother's disapproving look.

Hae Na shifted, leaning her head against the window, she closed her eyes. Tears welled up behind her eyes, she squeezed them tight, taking a shuddering breath.

"Why are they so shitty?" she asked. She didn't open her eyes, not wanting to see Wyatt's expression.

"I don't know. My parents aren't much different, I always thought I had to be better, prove myself for them to acknowledge me. After I became friends with Sawyer and I met his parents, I learned that mine are kinda shitty and it wasn't me that was the problem."

"You spent a lot of time there," Hae Na commented.

"Yeah," he told her.

Hae Na watched Wyatt, his grip was tight on the steering wheel. "And you really love them," she stated, "Sawyer and the kids."

"Yeah," he responded softly. His grip loosened, he shifted back in his seat watching the road.

"Your parents are going to flip when they find out," she said.

"They already know and I already changed my accounts so all of the money in them is actually mine now," Wyatt said, turning his grin to Hae Na when they stopped at a red light.

She laughed. "Aren't you the smartest cookie on the cookie sheet?"

"Of course, and our grandparents are paying for college."

She looked out her window. "Just don't drop out, they won't pay a second time."

"You could still finish," he told her. He was right but she didn't know if it was right for her.

She shrugged. "I don't know if I want to, I didn't even major in what I wanted. I'm happy where I am. If I go back then I do, and if not then oh well." She was already starting to feel better.

9:43 P.M.

Hae Na moved through the groups of people, enjoying the buzz it gave her. It had been quite a while since she had been at a party. She scanned the crowd finding mostly drunk guys and drunk girls who were hanging off of drunk guys. Finally giving up her search she headed back to the kitchen for a cup of anything non-alcoholic. After waiting in a queue, she slid past a few people grabbing an unopened bottle off of the counter and an unopened bottle of coke, shimmying her way back out of the room. She headed to the pool, going to the opposite side of where a guy was pushing anyone who walked by it, in.

One girl was swimming to her side of the pool, she continued to swim in her soaked jean shorts and a black t-shirt. Hae Na watched her for a while. "Hey you want some?" she asked, holding the bottle out and shaking it. The girl smiled, ducking under the water, she swam towards her. Hae Na appreciated the way her shirt rode up before her head breached the surface again.

She pulled herself out of the water and sat next to Hae Na, the water pooling around her. Hae Na didn't comment about it soaking her own shorts.

"I'm Rowan, I figure I should introduce myself before taking you up on your offer." Hae Na handed her the bottle.

"I'm Hae Na," she said. Watching Rowan impressively take a large gulp from the bottle, her face was twisted in disgust but she swallowed all of it without gagging.

She handed it back, wiping her mouth with the back of her hand. Hae Na took it, setting it next to the bottle of coke. Hae Na kicked her feet in the water, watching the way it made waves.

"So you just graduated," Hae Na commented. There wasn't much of a reason to ask since almost all of them had just graduated.

"Yeah, I was going to ask if you went to a different school," she asked, her green eyes bright from the pool lights.

She nodded. "I did go to a different school, my cousin just graduated."

"Oh really? Who's your cousin?"

"Wyatt Evans," she told her, watching her eyes open wide in surprise.

"Really? Wow, small world," Rowan said, her cheerful tone softened. She tilted her head away from Hae Na.

"You know him?" she asked, her tone gave way that he wasn't just a face in the crowd.

Rowan nodded. "Yeah, I'm friends with him and Sawyer, and the kids are so adorable."

"Oh so you know then? I wasn't sure if they were out yet." Hae Na said. She wondered if they were out to just their friends or to the whole school.

The girl's shoulders went stiff, her face wide in surprise and then shock, her voice did not match the girl of a minute ago. "Um yeah, yeah I uh, I do," she stuttered, taking the bottle off of the ground, taking another large gulp. She swallowed harshly, coughing when she finished.

"Are you ok?" Hae Na asked. Rowan nodded, wiping her mouth again. She slid down into the pool again, dropping down before coming back up. "Do you want to swim?" Rowan asked, her cheerful voice seeping back in.

"Nah but I'll watch you swim for awhile."

Rowan didn't respond, she just dropped down under the water again.

Hae Na watched her swim for a while, her focus taken by some guy helping two drunks out of the backyard. When she turned back to the pool, Rowan was no longer in it. She looked all over but in the end, she didn't find her at the party. She went back to the pool to look around, instead, she found a fierce looking brunette who looked her over before nodding.

"Can I see your phone?"

Hae Na tilted her head. "Why?" she asked.

"Please?"

Hae Na took her phone out of her back pocket and handed it to the girl. She took it and stepped back as she typed into it. She pressed the home button before she handed it back and left without an explanation.

She searched through her contacts, messages and phone calls

and found nothing different from them. Both of her bottles had disappeared from the poolside so she decided to head back home.

When she went out to find Wyatt's car she sighed. "Those assholes left me," she said, pushing a hand through her hair. She looked down the empty sidewalk and the lit light posts and started walking.

Chapter 12 Rye

Tuesday May 6th 11:37 P.M.

Rye lay his head against the table, the laptop sat in front of him, his project mocking him from the computer screen. He closed his eyes, he didn't want to waste his lunch period finishing the project that was supposed to be done in two class periods.

Rye sat up and wrote a few sentences before pushing it away and lying down to stare at it again. He tilted his head up when he heard the chair across from him slide out. Otis dropped into it, sliding forward he grabbed Rye's laptop. He heard him type a few things, Rye sat up. Otis slid it back towards him so Rye could look at it. Instead of doing his project, Otis was looking up red-headed vultures. Rye closed the search tab and went back to his project. He smiled when the section he was struggling with was complete. He grinned at Otis, Otis looked around sliding a bag of gummy bears across the table. Rye laughed quietly, meeting his hand halfway.

Friday May 30th 7:32 P.M.

Rye stared at Otis as he parked outside of the arcade. "Really?"

"It's our last day before I leave, we're going to have fun," Otis said.

Rye grinned. "I'm always ready to kick your ass at air hockey." Otis smiled at him, as he opened his door. Rye got out, walking around the car, he met Otis in the middle. Otis grabbed his hand, intertwining their fingers.

Rye laughed as he won the third round of air hockey, Otis

just smiled at him. Rye shot finger guns at him. Otis nodded. Rye moved around the table as they maneuvered around kids and teenagers. Otis slid into the shooter game before another kid, Rye laughed as they got glared at by a seven-year-old. Rye slid in next to Otis, grabbing the red gun, he pointed it at the screen. Otis lightly pushed against his shoulder as the game started.

"Shoot it!" Rye yelled, laughing as Otis pushed against him and Rye's character died, the screen giving him a timer. Rye leaned against Otis, watching him finish off his turn. When they finished, they moved to a racing game. Rye skidded off of the track too many times for him to win, he laughed when Otis slid across the finish and Rye was still half a track away.

"This is why I always drive, and you only drive in emergencies," Otis said leaning towards Rye.

Rye pushed at him as his car slid over the finish line. "Shut up, real driving is completely different."

"Sure it is," Otis said, throwing an arm over Rye's shoulders as they headed to another game.

10:47 P.M.

They bounced around games for a few hours. When they left, the sun had long gone down and the stars were covered by dark clouds.

"Ice cream?" Otis asked.

Rye smiled. "Always, also I want cheeseballs."

Otis pulled Rye into his side. "You have no idea how much I love you," he said. Rye wrapped an arm around his waist.

"As much as cheeseballs and ice cream on a late night date with your boyfriend," Rye said. Otis kissed his right temple.

11:22 P.M.

Rye leaned his seat back, turning his body to face Otis as they waited for their food to arrive. Otis sat back in his seat, his arms half out the open window. "My mom said she's going to take our phones when we land."

"Is she seriously going to do it?" Rye asked.

Otis shook his head. "I don't know, you know how she is," Otis said, his head turning towards the worker bringing their food.

Otis took it graciously, he handed Rye all of it as he paid. Rye opened the bag pulling out the fries, cheese balls, and onion rings. Rye grabbed his cheesecake shake from the cup holder. Popping the lid off he grabbed the spoon, he rolled his eyes at Otis who snatched the onion rings.

12:27 A.M.

Rye lay next to Otis on his bed, they stared at the ceiling. Rye shifted, turning on his side towards Otis. "I'm going to miss you," Rye whispered. Otis smiled at the ceiling, closing his eyes.

"Me too," he said back. Otis turned to mirror Rye's position. "I love you." Otis told him.

"I love you too, Oats," Rye replied, his smile gentle. Otis scooted forward, still leaving inches between them. Rye fell asleep staring at Otis.

Saturday May 31st 7:09 P.M.

Rye stared at his mother like she was crazy, she accepted the look and continued packing her bag. "You wanted to work."

His mouth hung open before he yelled, "You never said you were going to Hawaii!"

She smiled sweetly at him. "You never asked, I already told you I was planning something, you didn't want to listen."

Rye turned around in a circle as she moved around him. She grabbed another dress, folding it as she added it to her bag. "The last thing you planned was a 'knitting with cat hair' class."

She pushed against him, making him take a step back. "Will you get over that already? Also it's much better than having cat hair around the house."

He sat on her bed, looking around the room filled with her random projects. "We don't own a cat," he pointed out. He looked at the painting with the only cat in their house. The cat's tail was wrong, like it had been forgotten and then added at the last second. There was a shelf of other projects, knitting, sewing, and string art.

"Well not right now but you never know, we may get one in the future."

He looked at her, though she was focused on her bag. "You hate cats," he told her.

"I don't hate cats, they hate me. You see the difference? Anyway that's not the point, the point is that you need to pack, stay with your friends or wherever for the summer."

Rye stood up. "You're seriously kicking me out?"

"You're 18 now, you're an adult. You can make your own decisions, you don't need my help," she said. She zipped up her bag and stood it up right.

"Because I don't want to go to college?"

She looked up at him. "You make your own decisions, you want to be an adult and know what's best for your future then go, call your dad if you don't have any friends but I will have Betty checking to make sure you don't sneak back in and stay here."

Rye rolled his eyes, Betty was the "neighborhood watchdog." She had her eyes on everyone on the block. Rye was sure that Betty had bugged everyone's house and that's how she knew what everyone was doing. Last year, Kevin from four houses down had a heart attack, Betty had called an ambulance and saved his life. She couldn't even see his house from her own house.

He shrugged, crossing his arms over his chest. "Fine whatever, I'll just stay with Otis and have crazy gay sex all the time."

"You wish that worked on me, Otis is going to Germany. Better luck next time."

He uncrossed his arms, dropping them back to his sides. "Then we're going to elope and get married in Vegas when he comes back."

She grinned up at him. "Have fun, send a postcard."

He sat back on the bed, laying down on it. "I'm going to have animal sacrifices and give our souls to demons."

"As long as the demon chooses to go to college then he's welcome in the house."

"You're impossible," Rye said.

"Am I? I think the same of you," she said, pulling him in for a kiss to the forehead. "Now get moving."

He texted the few friends he had, earning a no from all of them. He really needed new friends. He just needed a place for a month until Otis came back from Germany. Though his friends said no, he still headed to the graduation party with them.

10:07 P.M.

When he arrived, most people were already drunk, people had probably started at graduation and hadn't stopped. No one even really noticed him, everyone was happily enjoying their new freedom. He lost his friends along the way to the back yard. He walked around before sitting on one of the chairs near the back door, a small ways from the pool. It wasn't long before Sawyer Losada dropped down next to him smelling of a mixture of liquors and cola.

"Where are you living?" Rye asked. Sawyer looked at him like he was an idiot.

"At home, where do you live?" His words were slurred and his body was swaying with the music from the house.

"Um, nowhere," Rye told him, he supposed it was true enough.

"Nowhere? Do you need somewhere to stay? Because you can stay with us," Sawyer offered. Rye almost said no, he and Sawyer had never really been friends. Not that he didn't like him, they just had different friends. Rye pulled out his phone, finding the recorder. In this life, proof was needed.

"I can stay with you?" Rye asked.

"Yes," Sawyer told him. He was drunk and normally Rye wouldn't take advantage of people but he wasn't much of a burden and he promised himself that he would help with anything.

"All summer?" Rye prompted.

Sawyer threw an arm around him and pulled him into an uncomfortable hug. "Of course, you can stay however long you want." Rye stopped the recording, shoving his phone back in his pocket.

Rye let Sawyer drunk rant about something, Rye nodded along while texting his mom that of course he had somewhere to stay for the summer.

Wyatt Evans, Sawyer's best friend, eventually found them. He pulled Sawyer away from him but he was unsteady and drunk so they toppled over. Rye sighed, helping them both up and pulled them to the side of the house and to the front yard. He searched through Wyatt's jeans pulling out his keys.

"Where are you touching?" Wyatt said, pushing his hands away. Rye grinned pressing the unlock button.

"Sawyer, he was trying to grope me," Wyatt said, hanging off of Sawyer.

"Who did it? Who touched you?" Sawyer asked, patting around Wyatt's body. Wyatt grinned before he sloppily kissed Sawyer. Rye looked away when Wyatt pushed Sawyer against someone's car. Drunk people making out was not a beautiful sight.

When he found Wyatt's car, he had to pull them apart which almost earned him a black eye. He drove them back to Sawyer's house which took longer because Sawyer didn't know where his house was in the dark. When they finally found it, Rye made sure it was the right house by checking the keys and finding pictures of

Sawyer with his family on the wall. He helped carry them both up to Sawyer's room and he was far too tired to try and find anywhere else to sleep.

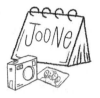

Chapter 13 Sawyer
Friday June 9th 2:07 A.M.

Sawyer was exhausted when he finally got off his late night shift. He chugged a terrible energy drink as he walked out of work to his car. Just a few months ago he had no problem staying awake until 4 in the morning for homework, video games, or even drinking with Wyatt. It was 2 am and he couldn't bear to be awake for another minute. He finished off the drink, opened the car door and put it in the empty cup holder. It was hard going back and forth between the night shift and morning shift. At this point he had no choice but to take the shifts given to him. He shook off a yawn and started the car, the roads were empty.

He tried everything to stay awake, he had to slap himself a few times to keep his eyes from shutting. He didn't even notice they had until he was opening them and had to slam the brake to keep from hitting a construction blockade. He stared at it in shock, he slowly put the gear in reverse and made his way home. He felt as if all of his exhaustion was zapped away. He pulled in the driveway, shutting off the car and he cried. His body felt as if his parents had just died.

He felt guilty like he was the one who killed them. He could have easily just ruined someone's life, he could have killed someone else's parents. He could have just killed himself. Leaving his siblings with no one to take care of them. He hit his forehead against the steering wheel as he cried. He squeezed his eyes tight as he tried in vain to breathe properly. It felt like hours before his body relaxed. He blinked at the clock, it was almost 4am. His whole body felt sore and he pulled himself out of the car and to the house. He struggled as he climbed the stairs and fell into bed.

Wyatt shifted around him, automatically throwing an arm around him. It was little comfort as he imagined his parents crash, the image burned in his mind. His eyes heated at the thought, he couldn't stop more tears from falling, a headache pounded in his head. He scooted closer to Wyatt shifting his arm to wrap his own around him. He squeezed him tightly, afraid that at any second he was going to realize that this was a dream and he was actually dead. That he didn't actually stop in time and had crashed into the wall. He wondered if his parents had seen them in the waiting room as they died. He wondered if they were watching him now or maybe they had no idea he had taken care of the kids. Maybe the dead forgot about the living the moment they died. Maybe everything was just over when you died and nothing mattered. He buried his face into Wyatt's chest, ignoring Wyatt's quiet grumbling.

11:46 A.M.

He woke up alone, he shifted so he could reach his phone off of the nightstand. He dropped the phone on the bed. It didn't feel like he had slept, his body felt as if his bones had been turned to lead. He was surprised when his door opened and Wyatt walked in with a plate of food.

"Did something happen last night?" Wyatt asked. Wyatt was always too perceptive.

"No," Sawyer answered. The lie was sour in his mouth but maybe he just needed to brush his teeth.

"Alright, I made you some lunch, the kids are down stairs with Hae Na."

"Thanks." Wyatt handed Sawyer the plate, taking a seat next to him on the bed. Sawyer leaned against his shoulder as he set the plate on his lap. He was starving but had no appetite to actually eat the turkey sandwich and chips in front of him.

"I didn't make it for it to be an art piece," Wyatt said. Sawyer turned his head so his forehead was on his shoulder. Wyatt shifted his arm so it went around Sawyer's waist.

"You had a nightmare last night," Wyatt said, tightening his arm. Sawyer remained quiet, he set the plate on the nightstand. He turned back to Wyatt wrapping his arms around his neck holding on as if he was going to be thrown off. Wyatt fell backward on the bed and slid both of his arms around Sawyer holding onto him. They lay that way for a while as Wyatt rubbed his hand comfortingly over Sawyer's back.

"I'm going to call into work tonight," Sawyer said with barely any conviction.

"Okay," Wyatt replied.

Sawyer shook his head. "I can't, we need the money."

Wyatt sighed. "You can take one day off, I'll just extend a shift."

"No, it's fine," Sawyer said, though it was slightly muffled.

"Sawyer, the world won't end if you take one day off. The money we've been slowly saving won't disappear."

"I know that but I can't even afford daycare," he said.

"We don't need it," Wyatt told him.

Sawyer lifted his head when he replied. "Actually we do."

"It's working out fine right now, we're saving some extra money and when we can afford it, we'll put them back in daycare."

Sawyer rolled his eyes. "I don't think our savings of 12 dollars a week is going to help too soon."

"It's better than 5 dollars a week," Wyatt told him. Sawyer couldn't argue.

Friday June 13th 12:04 P.M.

Sawyer paused at the edge of the hallway and turned to look at the empty place on the walls; the places that his parents had planned to fill with the memories they were going to make.

"Pictures are important, they tell the story without any words. They can remind you of something you forgot, they're like a whisper in the wind and when you really appreciate a photo then it's like a new love and I want you to have a lot of love Sawyer. So that's why I take so many photos. I want to remember you at this moment and the next moment and in twenty years I want to look back and see you right now and remember. I want to remember how I felt with you in my arms and how you laughed and the way you're looking right now. I want to remember all of it and even if I don't remember, the photo will be a reminder of the time I did forget and all the love I felt in this moment will remind me of how much I love you," his mom told him when he complained about the number of photos she made him pose for. After that, he stopped complaining.

Wyatt told him that he was with him, that they were in this together. That was a love he hadn't ever thought of especially not when he was a kid. Now he wanted it more than anything else. If his mom was ever proud of him, he wanted her to be proud of the man he chose to let in his life.

1:21 P.M.

Sawyer left the house early for work, walking into the printing store felt awkward. He went to a kiosk, loading up the photos he chose, printing them in different sizes before heading to the store to buy frames. He put the photos in the frames in the parking lot of work.

10:27 P.M.

When he got home and the house was quiet, he put up the picture with velcro backs. He smiled at the pictures. He lost a huge part of his family but slowly it was growing again. He would always miss his parents but he wouldn't let Carter and Lio feel the absence.

He crawled into bed feeling better about his choices. Wyatt lay on his stomach his head turned away from him, Sawyer slid an arm around his waist, putting his cheek against the center of his back. He wanted to shower but right now he was too content to move. Smiling, he tried to bury his face in Wyatt's shirt.

"Fuck off," Wyatt mumbled into the pillow.

Sawyer nearly laughed. "Don't want to," Sawyer whispered back. Wyatt didn't answer him, Sawyer yawned against him and rubbed his thumb on Wyatt's side until he fell asleep himself.

Saturday June 14th 8:34 A.M.

Sawyer woke up in a completely different position than how he fell asleep. Wyatt's face was pressed into his neck, his breath tickling his skin. "Wy, it's hot," Sawyer said, nudging Wyatt. Wyatt lifted his head, staring at Sawyer. Shifting up, he kissed him before pulling away.

"You didn't shower did you?" Wyatt asked.

"I will," Sawyer said.

"It's your day off right?" Wyatt asked, poking Sawyer's ribs.

"Yeah, I have a few ideas on what I want to do," Sawyer told him.

"I thought we were going to the park?"

"We are," Sawyer stated.

Wyatt narrowed his eyes. "Then what else is there?"

"Nothing," Sawyer smiled, shifting forward for another kiss. Wyatt allowed it for a few seconds before pulling away again, pushing Sawyers head away. "Go shower."

"You could shower with me," Sawyer said, reaching for Wyatt again. Wyatt leaned forward and the door opened.

"Swings! I want to play on the swings," Carter said, running into the room. She jumped onto the bed pushing herself between them.

Sawyer pulled away. "I'm going to shower," he muttered, heading into his bathroom as Wyatt started offering breakfast to Carter.

Chapter 14 Wyatt

Friday June 2nd 7:21 A.M.

Wyatt glared down at his ironed pale blue button-up shirt and perfectly fitting dress pants. He already hated this internship. His mother had bought him a whole new wardrobe for it and they didn't all fit in Sawyer's closet. He walked into the office and past the receptionist who welcomed him. He passed a few rooms and cubicles until he got to Su Yeon's desk. She was typing on the computer and looked up just as he reached her desk.

She pushed away from her desk pulling him into a hug. Pulling away, she told him, "Ji Seok, look at how handsome you are." Wyatt gave her a cocky grin that caused her to squeeze his cheek lightly before stepping away.

"You'll be down in the file room. I'm sure it'll be similar to what you did for your father."

"Great," Wyatt said, unenthusiastically.

"It won't be so bad, and you're only doing half days," she told him, her smile never changing.

"Wait seriously?" he asked. His mom hadn't given him any useful information.

"She didn't tell you?"

He shook his head. "No, she didn't tell me anything."

Su Yeon smiled. Wyatt never could understand why Su Yeon put up with his mother. He could barely do it but she was always patient and kind. The more he hung out with Rye and Hae Na, the more he started questioning everyone. Maybe his mother and Su yeon were having an illicit affair.

Her tone changed from personal to business. "You'll be working half days, you may leave at lunch. You only have to work 4 days a week and you will be getting paid."

"Do I have to wear this?" he asked, looking down at himself.

She gave him one solid nod. "Yes, it would be inappropriate if you wore anything else."

"Great," he muttered.

She smiled, a small smile. As though it was a secret, she leaned closer to him whispering, "You might want to tone down the attitude, your mother hates when you have a tone." Then just as quickly, she pulled away, leading him down to the file room.

His mind drifted back to the idea of the affair, wondering how their relationship would work if they were together. They were both married so they would have to meet somewhere else. They could stay at the office. He wondered if it was Su Yeon who would approach his mom, no it had to be his mom. She hated not being in control of anything, or maybe that's why the relationship worked. His mom wanted to lose control and she could do it with Su Yeon. Su Yeon wasn't the type to judge, she was kind and accepting. He never spent much time with her husband beyond the few seconds they spoke at family events. Su Yeon had worked for his mom for over six years, that was plenty of time for them to get together.

If they somehow were together and they decided to leave their husbands, his grandmother really would have a heart attack. The gossip within the family would skyrocket and it would never stop surrounding them. Wyatt couldn't help but grin at the thought of his mother losing her composure at such an event. Which is why it would never happen.

The file room was boring, it was exactly as the name implied. A room literally filled with files. "There are some files that need to be placed in the right cabinet and others that need to be shredded, please read the names and file numbers properly. Do not shred the files we need, if you're unsure, then set them aside and I will deal with them."

"Got it," he said, giving her a salute. She smiled at him and left through the door shutting it behind her. Only 4 hours and 49 minutes to go.

After two hours he texted Sawyer, who told him to get back to work. Wyatt ignored that and asked for pictures. He shredded three piles when his phone vibrated. He checked it, choking at the photo of Lio. Lio was caked in makeup, he had his hand to his cheek and all of the makeup was smeared on his face. Blue, purple and green eyeshadow was put on his eyelids and above his eyebrows. Pink and red lipstick was across his mouth to his cheeks making him look like a baby Joker. The caption was, *Carter's work.* Wyatt saved the photo, grinning as he shredded the next file.

11:29 A.M.

Wyatt was almost done with his files for the day when the door opened and his mom walked in. She looked as immaculate as ever, her eyes roamed over him and the pile he had left to shred.

"Your grandmother didn't like the disappearing act you so happily did."

"Seems like a personal problem," he muttered, his focus on the files in front of him.

"Ji Seok," his name was hissed like an insult. He had heard it that way a lot when he was a child so he chose to use the name his father gave him. The only people who didn't use it were his family. "She wants to send you to Korea, get you married off and going to school there."

"That's not going to happen."

"It depends on you, your uncle's 60th birthday is coming up. You will attend and you will appease your grandmother. If she decides to send you to Korea then you better pack your bags."

Wyatt grit his teeth and shoved the folders in with more force than necessary.

His mother turned and opened the door before he spoke.

"Why do we have to listen to her? Why can't I just live my life?"

"Because she's your grandmother," she said as if it was the most obvious thing in the world. He slammed the last folder on the ground. "You're too old for a tantrum. She's old, you're lucky she's only controlling a few years of your life." She shut the door behind her. Wyatt took a few breaths before picking up the last file and its scattered papers which he shoved in the machine before leaving.

Wednesday June 7th 2:36 P.M.

Wyatt took a deep breath as his mother side-eyed him. He didn't look at her, instead he stared straight ahead at the door. After another second, his mother opened the door with a smile gracing her lips. It was fake of course and he could barely muster one himself, but he did because he had to. He went to his grandmother to greet her and then to his uncle. His grandmother looked extremely pleased at this and Wyatt wanted to go home. He continued to smile until his grandmother called him aside and handed him an envelope. He didn't take it at first, and then she shoved it into his hands.

"I spoke to your mother, I think you need to go to Korea. You more than anyone need to learn more about our culture, who we are. Your eldest uncle is willing to take you in and from there you can go to university. I have also asked him to find you some matches, your mother thinks that's too old fashioned. It's tradition and so many of my kids have gone against it. I hate to see our traditions thrown away for frivolous wishes."

Wyatt tightened his grip on the envelope. He didn't open it and he didn't speak. The words he wanted to say would probably kill his grandmother.

He calmed his voice because if he went off then he would be taken to Korea despite his wishes. "Thank you," he said, taking another deep breath before continuing. "I would love to visit Korea, however I think it's best for me to continue school in the U.S. I've already been accepted and chosen a school. I also already have a girlfriend I'm very devoted to. She's a foreign exchange student from Korea, perhaps if we stay together then we could get married and move back to Korea to have children." The lie tasted sweet on his tongue, he had already told Sawyer about the lie. He would have to hire a foreign exchange student to become his girlfriend but he didn't care. He wasn't going to be shipped off and controlled.

His grandmother studied him for a second then smiled and tapped on the envelope before walking away, leaving Wyatt with an envelope he really wanted to burn. Instead, he headed to the bathroom, wanting to bang his head on the door until he found it closed. He took another breath and waited. It wasn't long before his aunt came out looking mildly surprised. She smiled politely and left down the hallway. He walked into the washroom, making sure the door locked behind him before sliding his phone out of his pocket. As it rang, he opened the envelope. He had seen similar things when Hae Na watched Korean dramas. He pulled out three photos of women, university pamphlets, and then 3 pages that looked like background checks. They had information on all three girls, what they liked, disliked, hobbies, family status. The whole thing made him sick. He set the stack on the counter when Sawyer finally picked up.

"Do you need rescuing already?"

"Yes," Wyatt hissed, making sure to keep his voice low. Sawyer didn't know Korean and he wasn't interested in getting any bruises.

Sawyer huffed, shuffling around. "What's going on?"

Wyatt moved so he was sitting on the edge of the bathtub. "I don't know if she's going to let up on me going to Korea."

"Seriously?"

"I'm not going."

Wyatt shifted so he could lean on the wall. He listened to Sawyer move around, muttering to Lio and answering Carter's questions. "I wish you were here," Wyatt said.

Wyatt heard a muffled sound and a crash before Sawyer spoke again. "What? Did you say something? Carter, hold on I'm on the phone."

"No, I'll call you when I get out of hell."

"Oo bring me a souvenir," Sawyer joked.

"Will do." Wyatt hung up before Sawyer could say goodbye. He didn't want to hear a goodbye right now. He gathered up the papers and pictures shoving them back in the envelope. He thought about shoving them down the toilet but decided against it at the thought of clogging it.

When he opened the door, he was surprised to see Hae Na's mom. She looked over him and the envelope, holding out her hand until he gave it to her.

"We're all against this," is all she said before walking away. He sagged against the doorway. It didn't mean it was official but if everyone went against it then his grandmother would most likely back down. It took him a second before he walked back towards the family, stopping in the hallway just outside of the living room. His grandmother was sitting in a chair and the rest of the adults were either standing or sitting in various spots around the room. His aunt was waving the envelope back and forth.

"This is unnecessary, you have always been harsh on him and this is enough."

His grandmother stared at her unapologetic and silent. Soon everyone voiced their agreement. Wyatt took a small step back so if his grandmother looked in his direction he would be hidden by the wall. All of them added their input; she was being harsh, she was being unreasonable, their child should go to Korea. It continued for a while until his grandmother had enough and Wyatt stepped forward.

"I will go for two weeks, after the two weeks I will come home. If you don't like that, then I won't go at all," he said. The whole of his family looked at him, he only looked at his grandmother who immediately dismissed his words. The family continued their discussions, disregarding him. He rolled his eyes, his phone vibrated in his pocket. He walked out the front door. He knew it was a mistake not to drive himself but his mom was convinced he would leave early and she was right.

He dropped down on the stairs sliding his phone out of his pocket. He opened the new picture of Lio in the bath sitting up in his little seat with a foaming glob of shampoo on top of his head. Lio was smiling, happily showing his first tooth and two more that were coming in. Another one came in of Carter with a foam beard and the last one was Sawyer, his shirt soaked in water and he was smiling. Wyatt didn't look away from the picture even when he heard the front door open and his mom's heels clicking on the porch. He saved the photos, setting his phone face down on his knee.

She sat down next to him and stared straight ahead, straightening out her legs on the steps. He pulled his phone into his lap, tightening his grip on it. "She's stubborn." He was surprised to hear her speak in English. "We've been living under her rule for so long." His mom smiled as she looked out to the street. The sky was full of grey clouds, a summer storm was coming.

"I'm not going," he told her.

"I think you should," she said. He was about to protest when she continued. "For two weeks, I think it'll be good for you. I want you to think about your future. If you like it then I want you to stay there and if you really can't stand to be that far away then come home." She said it distantly, making Wyatt want to know what she was hiding. There was a reason she never fought him when he chose to stay with Sawyer. Maybe she was having an affair with Su Yeon.

"I won't stay there even if I love it," he said. She smiled at him, it was a sad smile. He looked away from her to his phone as it vibrated with a notification. It was another picture, slightly blurry, this time they were all dressed and all sitting together. Sawyer had

Carter tucked into his left side, one of her arms hooked around his raised left arm and Lio was on his right side biting on Sawyer's finger. Sawyer was laughing.

He showed the photo to his mom. "I love them more than my future," he said. She took the phone out of his hand and scrolled down to see the caption. He tried to grab it back but she was quick, already pushing off of the stairs and standing in front of him. He glared at her, worried she would do something terrible with it.

"All the more reason to care about your future. How are you going to survive? Your savings won't last forever, that insurance money won't last forever. You can't just jump into a ready made family and hope for the best. You need a plan, you need a good job and you need to think about your future."

"Going to Korea isn't going to change that," he said. He doubted she cared about his opinion.

She looked at the photo then back to him. "No, but having family to help you may."

"I have a family." He realized how childish it sounded and looked away from her to the street.

"Don't be naive." Her words were slow and stone cold.

Wyatt glared at her, holding his hand out for his phone. She dropped the phone in his hand. "This won't be an easy road, but if you want it then fight for it." She walked up the steps past him. "Come in soon, they'll think you ran away again." He heard the front door shut. His mother had yet to make sense to him. He almost thought to ask his dad but he'd probably be just as lost as he was.

He opened the message again, the caption reading *we miss you* with a heart emoji at the end. There was no way in hell he was letting his grandmother take him away from them. Standing up, he shoved the phone back in his pocket and walked back into the house.

Chapter 15 Hae Na
Saturday June 7th 6:27 P.M.

Hae Na stood at the door, Benji opened it before Hae Na could knock. "Oh! Sorry I was going to take out the trash before you got here," Benji said, lifting up the trash bag.

"No problem, I can go with you," Hae Na said.

Benji shook her head. "Oh no you don't have to."

"It's okay, I don't mind."

"Um, sure if you're okay with it."

Hae Na smiled. Benji led the way back to the door. Hae Na tried to remember if she saw a dumpster when she parked but she hadn't looked for one so the image escaped her.

After taking out the trash, Hae Na followed her back to the apartment. Hae Na sat across from Benji who lounged in her sweatpants and baggy shirt on her queen sized bed.

"You met up with Rem already right?" Benji asked. Hae Na nodded and Benji continued. "Rem was the first person I met, she's open about her story. She's worked out how to handle it. JJ has too, I think Dana and I struggle more than they do," Benji said.

"Benji, that's not how recovery works, you can't compare yourself with them. Everyone is their own person and they heal at their own pace." Hae Na said, hoping it gave some comfort to Benji.

"I'm sorry, you're new to the program. I'm just a little jealous of them and I'm exhausted. I don't sleep a lot and my roommate has been staying at her significant others' place and I don't sleep well if no one is here. That's to say I don't sleep at all. I feel bad when I make her stay home like I'm a needy pet or something. Sorry I'm really really tired."

"You can sleep, I have a book on my phone I've been needing to read for a while."

"Are you sure?" Benji asked.

Hae Na couldn't turn down her hopeful look. "Yeah it's completely fine," she said with a smile.

"Thank you so much, I promise I'll explain as soon as I'm awake and not sounding like I'm drunk."

"Don't worry, you're good," Hae Na said.

Benji nodded, smiling as she snuggled into her pillow and was gone in no more than a second. Hae Na looked around the room, fully taking it in without looking nosy. Benji's room was messy and bare, no bookshelves. One closet with no dresser, a pile of messy clothes near it. There was no T.V., no desk, a backpack with one strap leaning on the wall near the door, a few textbooks sat near it. The bed was filled with pillows in the center of the wall. Hae Na sat on the only other thing to sit on which was a comfy worn yellow chair. Benji woke up abruptly, looking right at her before sighing and dropping back on the pillow as if she never woke up at all. Hae Na pulled out her phone, scrolling through useless things before going to the book she was planning on reading.

8:48 P.M.

Hae Na shut her mouth knowing that it was near slack as she just read her favorite character's bloody end. She wanted to scream in frustration but didn't. She looked up and saw Benji watching her.

"You're awake," Hae Na stated, surprised that she hadn't said anything.

"Yeah, good book?" Benji asked, not sounding as if she had just woken up.

"Mm depends on if you like favorite characters dying, good nap?"

Benji looked to her closet as she spoke. "Yeah, thank you and sorry." Benji looked at her, giving her a sheepish smile.

"It's okay, I got to read," Hae Na said, tilting her phone back and forth in the air.

Benji nodded, pulling herself up to sit. "My dad died when I was a baby," Benji started. Hae Na set her phone down, pushing it between the chair and her leg.

"My mom had a hard time. I have two older brothers and I was the youngest, so my uncle moved in to help and it was good for awhile. I was too young to see what was happening. My mom started spiraling, getting into different things. She was angry one minute and loving the next. She adored my brothers, praised them for everything and nothing and I was ridiculed. I would knock over a plastic cup of water and she would just yell at me and if my brothers broke a glass, 'oh they were just boys who didn't know their own strength'." Benji stopped, she pressed her thumb into her leg, continuing to do it as she continued the story.

"When my uncle came he was nice to me. After my mom yelled he would secretly treat me to candy or give me a small little present. It felt like someone was on my side, that someone actually cared about me. So I didn't understand when at night he would come into my room. Then he told me that it was love, that my mom couldn't do this, so that's why she didn't love me." Benji stopped again. She shifted a few times, she kept her face down, her messy bed head covering most of her face. "He told me that I had to do it or he wouldn't love me, that my mom would get worse and hate me more. That if I waited for him every night and let him in my bed, my mom would love me. I thought it worked." Benji took a long breath and continued.

"My mom was nicer, I got yelled at less, I didn't realise that in reality she was ignoring me. She avoided me, I was just so happy to not get yelled at. And every night I waited up and every night he came…" Her voice drifted off. Hae Na didn't prompt her to finish, she didn't even move, afraid that she might trigger something, that she might scare her. Benji snapped herself out of it, pulling the blanket tighter around herself.

"At school it was Valentine's Day and the teacher told us to draw a picture and write a story about what love was to us. That assignment changed my life. I wrote what it meant to me, and when she kept me after class to ask why there was a man in my bed in the picture. I told her, because that's what he told me love was."

"Do you know what my favorite movie is?" Benji asked. Hae Na didn't answer. "Matilda. I watched it after they took me out of my house. My teacher and her wife were foster parents, they took me in and I watched Matilda. It kind of changed my life.

"I got diagnosed with insomnia when I was eleven, my teacher would sit in my room and then I would sleep. As soon as she left, I would be awake. When they took in another foster girl, we shared the same room, and the only time I had a problem sleeping was when she had overnights with her friends or family.

"I am jealous of the others, they have an independence to their recovery but mine has never changed. I'm allergic to a surprising amount of medication, finding that out had been a nightmare all on its own." Hae Na let Benji continue, she stayed on the comfy armchair, listening.

"I tried the college thing, got a dorm, it worked out until she got a boyfriend and was never at the dorm. I went about 4 days without sleeping and I was hallucinating and I was so paranoid that everyone was my uncle and mother and let's just say I couldn't finish the school year. I went home and basically started all over again, went to therapy and now I'm here. I take a few online classes of things I like but mostly I just work and hangout," Benji said.

Hae Na waited a few minutes before speaking. "What about getting a boyfriend or girlfriend or something?" Hae Na asked.

"I don't know, I tried it and it never seems to work out, it's always me or them and I don't know," Benji said. She shrugged as she pushed out a breath of air.

"Okay," Hae Na said. This was not a problem she could fix, it wasn't something she could give advice for either. "Well if you help me find a job, I'll help you sleep," Hae Na offered.

Benji smiled. "Thank you, the others help too so you don't have to feel obligated to be my stand-in teddy bear. They're great, we had another girl with us before but she moved cities about seven months ago." Her tone dropped and she tilted her head, her hair slipping across her face. "I'm really glad you're here." Benji's voice was quiet but in the near silent room, Hae Na heard her.

"Thanks, me too. Everyone has been great," Hae Na told her. Benji nodded. It was quiet between them, not awkward quiet but not comfortable quiet either.

"Sorry, I don't have a lot to do," Benji apologized, giving her a shy smile.

"Sometimes just hanging out is underrated," Hae Na said, turning her head to the door when she heard another door shut.

"That must be my roommate," Benji said, just as her door was being pushed open and a woman was flinging herself onto the bed.

Benji scooted over giving the woman room. Hae Na couldn't see what she looked like behind wild white and grey curls.

"I see so many baked goods in my future," Benji said, relaxing against her wall.

"I got dumped by not one but both of my partners, I've already planned 12 different things I'm going to bake." Her voice was deep and bitter as she spoke.

Benji nudged her with her body. "Want to talk about it?" Benji asked.

"Not really, I'm just going to bake until I feel better."

"Well let me know if you want to talk and until then I'll eat everything you make."

The woman sat up, and Hae Na finally saw her face. It was dolled up, completely contrasting the sweatpants and baggy t-shirt she was wearing. "Oh, sorry," she said, turning to Hae Na.

Hae Na stood up. "All good, I was just going to head out. But if Benji doesn't eat everything I'm willing to take some," Hae Na said.

"I'll bring you some," Benji told her. "Thank you for coming," she added as Hae Na stepped out of the room. Hae Na waved and told her goodbye as she left.

Sunday June 8th 4:56P.M.

Hae Na nearly bit her tongue when Rowan tapped her shoulder, stepping in front of her. Her smile was bright and it made her green eyes light up. Hae Na pulled out her headphones as Rowan took the seat across from her, resting her adorable face on her fist as she leaned forward on the table. Hae Na closed her laptop, her resume and job applications forgotten.

"Have you ever heard the saying that if you meet someone accidentally three times, they're your soulmate?" Hae Na asked. Rowan tipped her head to the left side, pulling away from her hand as it dropped to the table.

"We've only met twice," Rowan said. Tapping the table twice as if to accentuate the amount.

Hae Na smirked, leaning forward herself. "Are you sure?" she asked. She had felt a strange surge of confidence when she saw Rowan, felt something she had forgotten, someone she was before. "Because I'm pretty sure I had a dream about you last night. And here you are, in front of me today. You wouldn't call that fate?" Hae Na asked, feeling just like her old self.

Rowan blushed a pretty red underneath her light makeup. She turned her face away, swallowing hard. Her hands disappeared under the table. Hae Na pulled back watching as Rowan had an internal crisis.

Hae Na reached for her muffin watching the quick flitting emotions on her face. Hae Na's eyes dropped to the shirt she was wearing; homemade and spray painted. 'Lioness pride' was written on it in orange and yellow.

Rowan took a breath, bringing Hae Na's eyes back to her face. Rowan's eyes flitted to the door when it opened, her eyes widened slightly. She raised her hand before abruptly stopping, pulling her arm down hard and smashing it against the table. She pulled in a hiss, rubbing at her elbow.

"My friend is here, I… it was nice to meet you again. And if you're right then I guess we will meet again but just in case I'll give you my number," Rowan said, holding her hand out for Hae Na's phone. Hae Na unlocked it, sliding it across the table. Rowan smiled sweetly as she typed it in.

When she finished, she slid it back across and quickly made her way to her friend. Hae Na took a bite of her muffin, nearly choking as she tried to swallow it. She packed up her laptop calmly, throwing her phone in the bag as she made her way home.

She felt panicked as she pulled in the driveway, taking harsh breaths as she opened the door and stopped when she saw the disaster of toys.

"Carter!" Sawyer yelled from the top of the stairs. "Hey Hae Na. Carter!" Carter came out of the living room, a towel wrapped around her neck like a cape.

"Sah is evil!" Carter yelled back. She ran back into the living room and saw a few of her toys getting thrown into the hall. Hae Na walked further in as Sawyer came down the stairs.

"She won't take a bath," he explained. "Wyatt isn't here," Sawyer added, sounding slightly bitter.

Hae Na was going to ask but Sawyer continued talking. "He went to go see his parents, which is good. It's just Carter hates when I give her a bath without Lio and only likes when my mom and Wyatt do it and since one of those isn't an option well I guess both of them aren't..." Hae Na realized he was exhausted, his shoulders were drooped and the bags under his eyes were darker and larger than a first time makeup tutorial.

"I can try," Hae Na offered.

"It's okay, she'll listen eventually," Sawyer said, pausing when he heard Lio start to cry. Hae Na was sure Sawyer was going to join him. "You wouldn't mind?" he asked.

"Nah, it'll be fine," she told him. He nodded, thanking her and then running up the stairs for Lio. Hae Na continued into the living room. Carter stood up looking at Hae Na and then looking at the stairs as if Sawyer was going to materialize next to her.

"How about I give you a bath and we can sing K-pop songs," Hae Na offered. Carter considered it before nodding and running past her to the stairs, already starting to sing a song Hae Na had played for her. Hae Na followed behind her, thinking she was truly the perfect distraction.

9:07 P.M.

Hae Na lay against the bed, trying not to think of the ghosts that used to sleep there. Her phone was a constant buzz against her side. When she told the girls what she had done that afternoon, the group chat had gone crazy. There was a quick light knock at her door, she sat up looking at her lit phone for the 5th time. "Come in," she said.

Wyatt looked around hesitantly before stepping in. He shut the door behind him, walking to the bed. "Thank you."

"For what?" she asked. He sat at the end of the bed, looking at the door instead of her.

She nudged him with her foot when he didn't speak. "For helping. He hasn't been sleeping well and my parents wanted to have dinner," he explained. She moved her feet as he dropped against the end of the bed. "I can't force him to sleep," he said, his focus on the ceiling.

"You care about him a lot," she commented. She never thought of how Wyatt would ever treat his boyfriend or girlfriend, never thought of him ever having one. Now here he was, officially an adult in a committed, nearly married relationship with kids.

"Of course I do," Wyatt said, sitting up.

"Have you been sleeping?" she asked. He nodded. "Good."

"No it isn't, I'm sleeping and he isn't."

"He'll sleep, look I can't tell you what to do because I have no fucking idea what I would do in your position or his, I don't even know what to do in my own. But if you want to take care of him, if you want to be there for him, you need to take care of yourself. When he's so exhausted that he falls asleep on the couch watching the kids, who feeds them lunch? You do, because you slept. Because when he trips, you're right there behind him supporting him, helping him get back up. As long as you finish the race together it doesn't matter if you walk or run. You can take a hundred water breaks. It doesn't matter how many times you trip because guess what, you're going to make it to the end and before that you'll have him by your side the entire time. You'll get to see him laugh, cry, fall, stand up, you will see the things you love and things you hate. You will see them because you'll be next to him and if he feels the same then guess what? He's going to see all that too, though I guess you'll be pushing a stroller as well," Hae Na told him.

He stood up, smiling at her. "Thanks, you're right. I just need to think about what's really important," he said. Opening her door, he left, shutting it gently behind him.

"What is important to you Kwon Hae Na?" she asked herself. She didn't know the answer but that was okay, she didn't mind running her race alone right now. She picked up her phone, smiling at all of the texts she accumulated. They were important to her. Sam had left her fearful but they had given her confidence.

It was different from the shelter where she knew she was safe just by being there but being out in the world again, being somewhere that Sam could find her, was terrifying. The others did it too, they left their comfortable safe homes everyday, went out into the world where the people who hurt them were, where other people who could hurt them resided. Being outside was a risk, there was so much unknown danger. There was also more than that, she wouldn't have met the girls if she never left the shelter. Wouldn't have reconnected with Wyatt if she never left Sam. She wouldn't sing songs with Carter, flirt with adorable girls in coffee shops and pools. She wouldn't get to see the world differently if she only worried about how it was when she was scared, cornered, and stuck.

She was going to find the important things in life and keep them close, she was going to get rid of the toxic, that was why she left Sam. She was going to live her life, she would be cautious but not afraid. It wouldn't happen right away but she had time and as long as she continued to take care of herself she could make it to a place where she could fully trust another person again.

Thursday June 12th 12:34 P.M.

Hae Na met up with the girls for lunch, she was the first one at the restaurant. She waited in her car checking her phone again to check the time and see if the girls would be late. All of them replied with an 'on my way' or 'omw' variant. She watched out the window as couples, friends, and families walked past. When she saw JJ, she pushed open her car door and stepped out.

"Hey, I was just going to text everyone," She said, her fingers already moving across her phone. She dropped it into her purse and Hae Na's phone vibrated with a text. She ignored it, walking next to JJ the few short steps to the door. The restaurant only had two small groups ahead of them.

"Five," JJ told him, turning back to the door as it opened. Rem and Benji walked in together.

"Hey," Benji said. Rem gave a nod and a yawn.

"Hey," Hae Na responded, turning back around as the host led them to a table in the far back next to a window facing the street. Hae Na pulled the chair next to JJ in the middle with Rem across from her and Benji across from JJ, leaving two seats on the end for Dana to choose from.

The girls were instantly talking; Benji started a conversation about a new show she was watching, Hae Na looked over the room, looking over everyone's little bubble of privacy. How many people listened to their conversations instead of having their own? Hae Na looked around again, there was a table across from them where a couple wasn't speaking, instead they sat quietly across from each other. They were each on their phones silently scrolling through things she could only guess.

Dana took her attention away from the couple as she walked in with a bob of black hair and white square framed glasses. Her makeup was done natural except for white eyeshadow.

"You always look so cute," Benji said as Dana took a seat next to Hae Na.

"Thanks," she said, picking up her cup of water and taking a large sip from it. "What did I miss?" she asked, setting the cup back down.

"We just sat down," Hae Na said.

"Good, so I didn't miss all the details about this new girl."

JJ sat up excitedly on the other side of Hae Na leaning over the table to look at Dana. "Nope, I was waiting for you before I asked, you have to tell us all about her," Hae Na smiled ducking her head.

"She's adorable," Hae Na said. JJ lightly nudged her side. Hae Na looked up at Rem and Benji, they both had their attention on her. "She's nice, funny, I don't know her that well yet."

"Yet," Benji said. "This is exciting." She gave a few small claps.

"Are you ready for a relationship?" Dana asked. Hae Na shrugged, it was something she hadn't thought through yet. "It's okay if you are, but It's okay if you're not," she said.

Hae Na sighed, deflating into her chair. This was going to be the rest of her life, comparing everyone to Sam, hoping that no one else hurt her, that the person actually loved her and meant the words coming out of their mouth. How could Hae Na ever be sure that someone was genuine. Sam had been nice and funny too. She had been beautiful and exciting.

"Just take it slow and don't forget that we're all here for you," Rem said.

Hae Na smiled at her. "Thanks." Rem gave her a solid nod. Their attention was soon taken away from Hae Na's potential love life to the waitress and their menus. Benji was the only one prepared and she got an appetizer while everyone looked over their menus and threw out suggestions.

Hae Na looked around again, the couple was off their phones. He made a suggestion that had her rolling her eyes. The group of three guys and one girl to the left of them were happy, laughing at something someone said, all laughing together as a group. Hae Na focused on Dana when she leaned over to talk to JJ. Hae Na leaned back giving them an unobstructed view.

"Hae Na did you decide what you wanted?" Benji asked.

"Just a burger," she responded, looking at Benji. Benji leaned forward, her hand knocking against her water glass, spilling a little over the edge. JJ had caught it from completely falling, her hand was already cleaning up the small spill and not once did she pause in her conversation. Hae Na understood why Benji had been envious of JJ, the idea that JJ wasn't constantly sure of herself or the situation she was in seemed bizarre.

"Oops, thanks," Benji said. "So Hae Na will you share your fries? I was thinking of getting fruit for a side, I'll share it."

Hae Na shrugged. "Yeah, I like fruit," she responded.

Rem sat forward, her elbow resting on the table, her hand going between Hae Na and Benji. "Well I want in on this, I want cottage cheese and fries, fruit isn't bad."

"Gross," Dana said, cutting off JJ. JJ laughed. "Why don't we just get a bunch of stuff and share everything?" Dana asked.

"Okay, I was going to get a pizza," Rem said.

"I'm getting pasta," Dana offered.

"A burger," Hae Na contributed.

"At least the burgers are huge, I'm getting wings," JJ added. It wasn't long before the waitress came back and they all gave their orders and just as she was leaving Benji's appetizer arrived smelling delicious. As a few of the girls reached for pieces, Hae Na pulled her phone out of her purse, smiling at the text from Rowan. She received a few nudges and she put her phone away, unable to hide her smile.

Hae Na reached for the last fry, she smiled as Benji and Dana fought over the last slice of pizza. JJ was already cutting it in half before either of them pulled back their forks and butter knives. Before they could take their pieces Rem lifted the plate, sandwiching both of the pieces and shoving them in her mouth, earning two loud groans of dismay.

Benji shoved three fingers into Rem's side causing her to spit parts of the food onto the table. Hae Na felt Dana's leg move next to hers and Rem slid back in her chair to glare at Dana.

"Do you always have to do that?" JJ asked. Rem shrugged. Hae Na looked between them, Rem smiled at JJ who rolled her eyes and sighed. She felt like a fifth wheel, a spare among regular tires. She picked up her drink, her eyes darting between the four of them as she sat back. They all made faces at each other, they were all comfortable with each other. They knew the things they liked, disliked, triggers, stories, and backgrounds. They were women who had seen hell and told it to fuck off. They are women who never forgot what they went through and still decided to move forward, to laugh, to make friends, to see the world in all the shades of color that it came in. Hae Na wanted to be more than a spare, she wanted to be more important.

"I'm so full," JJ commented, rubbing her small chub of a belly.

Benji leaned back patting her own stomach. "I could go for dessert," she said, Dana agreeing with her while Rem shook her head.

Friday June 15th 7:02 P.M.

Hae Na sat on the floor of the living room with Carter next to her. Hae Na wrote out one word. '아빠' "This word means dad, say Ah pah," Hae Na told her.

"Ah pah," Carter repeated.

"Perfect," Hae Na said, she looked around the empty room, she could barely hear Lio's happy squeals from the bathroom as he splashed the bath water. "That's what you can call Wyatt."

"Yaya is Yaya not dad," Carter told her.

"Okay, one more time."

"Ah pah!" Carter said excitedly.

"Okay, next one," Hae na said, writing down '아니'. "This one means no. Say Ah Knee."

"Ahhh Knee."

"You're going to pick this up so quickly, okay one more time and then we'll do another word."

Hae Na smiled as Carter went through the few words she had

been teaching her. She then moved on to a few numbers.

"Hana, dul, set," Carter said, then continued with the english counterpart. "One two three."

As Carter grew bored she started watching videos on Hae Na's phone. Hae Na grabbed a few note cards and markers and started making flash cards of the words she was learning and a few more that were easy to learn. She paused as Carter clapped enthusiastically at something. Hae Na smiled as she looked down at the cards, it reminded her of when her siblings used to help her learn Korean. They had all been so close when they were younger, now they were like strangers to her.

"Hae Na what are you writing?" Carter asked, her attention focused on her as an ad played.

"I'm making you some cards so you can keep practicing Korean."

"Yay! Then I can talk to Yaya and Sah won't know," Carter said, her excitement was contagious. Hae Na laughed as Carter went back to her video. She continued writing, finding a new passion for it.

Chapter 16 Rye
Sunday June 1st 7:58 A.M.

Rye woke up on the floor with a t-shirt on his face, he sat up looking around the room. He hadn't looked around too much last night. He mostly saw piles of laundry on the floor, a few stacks of books and paper next to a desk. He stood up, staring at the open door with a bathroom and the bed where Sawyer and Wyatt were still sleeping. He walked towards the hallway quietly, making his way downstairs. He was grateful to the builder when he found another bathroom.

The kitchen was clean, dishes in the drying rack and a table cleared of anything. He opened the fridge and searched the cabinets. He figured that neither of them would remember much from last night and even if they did, he would probably get kicked out.

Breakfast was going to be his offering. He pulled out ingredients for french toast and hoped they liked it.

He jumped when he heard Wyatt's voice. "What are you doing?"

Rye turned towards him. "Making breakfast," he said. Wyatt was unimpressed. Rye smiled, lifting the plate of french toast.

"I'm starving," Sawyer said, walking past Wyatt to the kitchen. Rye extended his arm and Sawyer grabbed the plate.

"Best drunk decision ever," Sawyer said, grabbing a fork and the syrup. Rye didn't tell him that the stack was for everyone.

Instead he watched Sawyer start scarfing it down. Wyatt sat next to Sawyer silently watching him as Rye got to work making more. When Sawyer finished he dropped the plate in the sink. "Thanks, Rye right?" Sawyer asked. He barely knew his name and he still let him into his house.

"Yeah," Rye responded.

Wyatt voiced his thoughts. "You barely know his name and you let him move in here?" Wyatt said, his tone cold.

"Just for the summer right? Also I gotta pick up the kids, bye," Sawyer said, leaving Rye alone with Wyatt. Wyatt stared at him, lifting an eyebrow.

"Uh yours are done," he said. Rye offered him a plate stacked with french toast. Wyatt stood up from the table grabbing it as Rye turned back to make a few pieces for himself.

8:42 A.M.

Rye was messing around on his phone when Sawyer got back with the kids. Carter was talking a mile a minute, Sawyer quietly listening as he held Lio and a diaper bag. Rye watched Wyatt wordlessly take Lio and Carter pulled Sawyer into the living room. She paused in her story when she saw Rye. He was glad Wyatt had told him their names after breakfast.

"Who are you?" Her hands were held tightly on her hips as she stared up at him.

He bent down. "I'm Rye."

Her eyes looked him over. She said, "I'm Carter. Are you family?"

He shook his head slowly. "No."

She looked to Sawyer then to Rye again. "Are you a friend?" she asked.

"Yes," he told her, hoping it would appease her curiosity.

"Are you Yaya's friend?" she asked.

"Who?" Rye asked, looking at Sawyer.

"Wyatt," Sawyer explained.

Rye nodded, looking back to Carter. "Yeah I guess."

He let Carter look him over again. She then nodded her approval before she went back to talking about her day to Sawyer. Rye let everyone move around him, he watched everyone interact and felt slightly left out.

Carter sighed as she finished her drawing. She looked at Rye again with interest.

"Do you want to play with me?" she asked, her face the picture of innocence.

"Sure, what do you want to play?"

"You can be the boy and I'll be the girl that saves you from the evil lambs."

"Alright," he said. Carter pulled his arm.

"Come on," she said. He let her pull him upstairs. She sat him down and gave him a doll with short hair dressed in boy clothes. "She didn't want to be a girl so he's a boy now," Carter explained, grabbing her own doll and a stuffed lamb.

"You have to sit over there with the castle, because the lamb says you can't leave." Rye followed her instructions and sat by the castle, the lamb standing in front of it like a guard dog.

"Now the girl is not a princess, she's just a girl like a normal one and she has to do lots of stuff before she can save the boy," Carter stated, grabbing a truck, a dog dish and a grey mountain made out of paper mache. "She has to climb the terrible mountain, sneak, that means so no one sees you. So she sneaks by the evil truck monster, swims through the melty mud and fights the lamb to save the boy."

Rye watched her, truly fascinated by the tale she was spinning to save this boy. She created a web of issues as she climbed the mountain. Some were a little ridiculous like the snow was too sparkly to climb or the trucks had a party so now they were sleepy, but it was still interesting.

12:09 P.M.

Sawyer eventually stood at the door, watching them before announcing that lunch was ready.

Lunch had everyone sitting at the table, Rye took the empty chair next to Carter. Grilled cheese with ham and a bowl of mixed fruit sat in the middle of the table. Wyatt made Sawyer and himself a plate, he then fed himself and helped Lio eat something that was mushy, leaving Rye to make his own. Sawyer then made Carter a plate, ignoring her protests of the cantaloupe. Carter sipped her juice from her sippy cup after each bit of cantaloupe, making a show of it each time.

Rye tried not to laugh and Sawyer sighed. Carter grinned at

him.

"Don't play into it," Sawyer said. Carter stuck her tongue out at him. Sawyer reached like he was going to give her more cantaloupe, she pulled her plate away. A few of the cantaloupe pieces rolled off of her plate and dropped to the floor. She smiled innocently at Sawyer who shook his head.

Thursday June 5th 12:49 P.M.

Rye yawned for the umpteenth time that day, the movie theater was empty. He had already cleaned the counter and floors twice. Everything was stocked and ready. Yet no one wanted to see a movie today. He yawned again, clenching his teeth to stop it.

He put on a bright smile when the doors opened and three girls walked in discussing one of the movies. He quickly sold them tickets and they headed towards the auditoriums. After a few more customers, one of the girls came back. The lobby had one other customer waiting for their popcorn and candy. He smiled at her and looked over the movie schedule again. He was surprised to see her standing in front of his counter.

"Um I... Ok, sorry. I was hoping to get your number, I know it's kind of weird or awkward but I promised to be more bold and I'm sorry this was stupid," she said. She mechanically turned her face away from him. She quickly began walking away,

"Uh, wait how old are you?" he asked, still completely stunned by the question.

"Eighteen, how old are you? Oh god, are you like 15?"

"I just turned 18."

"Oh wow, okay perfect. I mean you know like in that age sort of way," she babbled.

"Yeah," Rye shifted to see people behind her. She turned around surprised when she looked back at him.

"Oh, I'm sorry." She moved to the side and Rye continued with his work. When everyone had headed to their movies, he looked to the side to where the girl was now getting a soda and large popcorn. She smiled at him and Rye returned it. He didn't want to give her his number. He had no idea what she really wanted and he wasn't comfortable figuring it out. Otis was going to laugh at him for this, for weeks.

After a few more customers he looked around the room for the girl, he sighed when she was gone. The rest of the day slowly picked up, so he wasn't left standing around for long.

Saturday June 7th 9:52 A.M.

Rye wasn't ready the first time he saw his dad. His mom had only told him that it had been a few years and to expect change. He thought grey hair not, not this. He hadn't recognized her until she stood at his table. The cafe was busy enough to not feel deserted but not so busy that the tables next to him were full.

"You've grown a lot," she said.

Rye nodded. "That's what happens when you're gone for years," he said, unable to keep out the bitterness.

"I'm sorry." Rye played with the lid on his to-go cup. Apologies were a way to show remorse for an action caused by yourself. Sorry, sorry, sorry. Rye repeated it over and over in his head. Sorry, sorry, sorry. Rye was mad though, his dad chose to leave, chose to only call on his birthday. Rye had begun to ignore them in the last few years.

"I- I know that you're angry, and I know I made a lot of mistakes that I can't go back on but I want to make it up to you," she said.

Rye looked at her dress then her cup where lipstick stuck to the rim. "Why now?"

"I've missed out on too much and I'm tired of it. You're my child too and I want to get to know you. I don't want to miss anymore."

"That's stupid, why are you saying that now? How long has it been? I'm pretty sure you missed all of the important things."

"I don't think that's true, please let me back in your life."

Rye stared at her, stared at her long, fake lashes, stared at the makeup that made her cheekbones sharper, stared at her gold eyeshadow that made her brown eyes pop.

"I guess so," Rye responded, he never had anyone ask to be in his life, he didn't forgive his Mom? Is that what he should call her, he wasn't sure. But looking at the change it wasn't hard to see why she had left. It was actually very obvious, the proof sitting in front of him. The mannerisms, the clothing, makeup, none of it was how he remembered.

"I was thinking we could do this often?" she asked, moving her cup left and right. Rye nodded, he couldn't say no at this point. "Great, we can get to know each other again slowly." She smiled.

"Um, what about your name?" Rye asked. Mom sounded wrong.

"It's Nalani."

"That's pretty," Rye commented.

"Thank you," she said, the awkwardness setting in. They sat in silence for over two minutes, Rye counted.

Rye stood up. "I'm going to get a muffin."

She started to stand so Rye paused. "I'll get it for you, what kind?"

Rye shook his head. "Uh, it's okay."

"Please let me," she pleaded.

Rye sighed. "Poppy Seed."

"Got it." She smiled, leaning over her chair to grab her purse before going to the counter. Rye sat back down, taking a large sip from his cup.

Sunday June 8th 10:02 A.M.

The second time Rye met with Nalani, she wasn't alone. Rye watched through the window before he entered the same cafe. There was a man sitting next to her, perhaps a few years older. She fussed over his hair, then crumbs on his face. He smiled gently at her, holding her hands and talking to her. She wasn't as composed as she was the last time he saw her. Rye moved forward, pushing open the door. When she saw him, their hands separated, she stood up smiling at him. Rye's eyes flickered to the other man,

"Rye, this is Max, my husband."

Max smiled, standing as he stuck his hand out. Rye shook it. "Hi," Rye said.

"It's nice to finally meet you," Max said, letting his hand go as they all sat back down.

"I'm getting a drink," Rye said, getting up before Nalani could offer to buy him one.

Most of his thoughts were on Otis, it was strange not being able to see him everyday. He wished he had been there with him. Instead he had to do it alone, he couldn't even get a text back from Otis. He hadn't seen or talked to Otis since graduation and that was all he wanted to do. He wanted advice or to rant to him. He thought of Wyatt or Sawyer, or even just Hae Na. He texted Wyatt first.

Me: I don't know what to say to them

Wyatt: me

Rye didn't understand that, how was he supposed to talk about Wyatt? He didn't know that much about him, and he hadn't been living with them that long. He was still thinking about all the things he did know about him when he got his latte and made it back to the table.

"I have a roommate named Wyatt," he told them. They were surprised but they nodded along anyway. "And um Sawyer and Hae Na, Carter and Lio," he rambled.

"What about your mom?" Nalani asked. Rye was surprised that she didn't know she was in Hawaii. He knew they had been talking before she left.

"She's visiting family in Hawaii, so I'm staying with them."

"Well that's very nice," she commented. Rye wasn't sure if it was genuine.

"What about you?" Rye asked.

"It's just the two of us, Max works with college students and we see them from time to time…" and then silence. Rye sat back in the chair, his eyes wandered the cafe again, he sat up straighter when he saw Hae Na walk in with a girl with rainbow hair cascading down her shoulders. Hae Na turned and saw him, her eyes lighting up as she skipped over to him. The girl looked around them before coming up next to her.

Hae Na reached down grabbing Rye's drink, after taking a large drink she set it back down.

"Hot chocolate, you child," she said, setting it back down.

"It's not!" he replied. "It's like a hot chocolate latte," he muttered. She nearly cackled at that.

"Wyatt is going to love this." Hae Na was already pulling her phone out, Rye reached out to stop her.

"Don't tell him," Rye said, grabbing onto her phone.

Hae Na laughed, pulling her phone away. "Kidding," she said. Her focus shifted from Rye to his guests Rye spoke up before she could say anything embarrassing.

"This is Hae Na, my roommate and this is Nalani and her husband Max," Rye said, his hand moving out to emphasize it and knocking his drink over. Rye was done, he couldn't take anymore embarrassment. Hae Na was quicker than anyone to clean up the small spill. Rye wanted to go home, go to bed and pretend today didn't happen. Instead, the spill was cleaned, Hae Na was saying goodbye and he was left with Nalani and her husband grinning at him.

"She seems nice," Nalani commented, smiling sweetly at him.

"Yeah," he replied. Looking back at her as she stood in line, he still didn't know who she was with. "She's Wyatt's cousin," he explained. They exchanged a look that told him they were reading something wrong about the situation. He didn't try to correct them.

Max spoke up "Do you have any plans after the summer?"

Rye shrugged. "I'm not sure yet."

Max smiled, nodding. "That's okay, you don't have to know yet. You're only eighteen, there's plenty of time to decide."

"My mom wants me to go to college," Rye told them.

"But you don't want to?" Nalani asked.

"I don't know yet," Rye said, staring at his cup.

Rye looked up when Max spoke, giving him his attention. "A lot of the students I work with didn't plan on going to college but their circumstances brought them to it and it changed their lives. I'm not telling you to go to college, it's not for everyone and everyone's situation is different. I'm just saying that college is usually the plan but maybe you don't have to plan it for yourself. There are a lot of other choices you could make."

"Thanks," Rye said at a loss for any other words.

"Of course, if you need any help don't hesitate to come to us." Rye thanked him again, though he didn't think they would be his first choice to go to, it was a nice offer though. The rest of the time they talked about inconsequential things. Rye felt better when he left, the awkward atmosphere dissipated with Max's presence but he still wasn't used to them. He still wasn't used to the idea of having Nalani in his life, even though he had been texting her nearly every day. Even if they were just good morning texts, it was something more than empty silence and a birthday card.

Saturday June 21st 11:11 P.M.

Rye lay on the couch, his fingers quickly moving over his phone as he played on it. He didn't move his eyes away when he blurrily saw Sawyer standing above him with Lio over his head. "I have to take Lio in for a checkup and I forgot about this kid's birthday party that Carter was invited to. Wyatt is supposed to meet his parents for lunch so he can't take her either, so I was wondering if you could?" Sawyer asked.

Rye paused the game, dropping his phone on his chest as he looked up at the two of them upside down. Lio tilted over reaching for him, Rye lifted his hands up as Sawyer dipped him lower.

"I can but I don't have a car," Rye told him. He was sure Sawyer knew, because the two of them had been driving him around. Not to mention he always took the bus if he was alone.

"I know, Wyatt said he'd drop you off and pick you up. He needs an excuse to leave early," Sawyer told him.

Rye poked Lio's nose, tilting his head to avoid a string of drool. "Okay, I can do it."

"Thank you!" Sawyer said, lifting Lio away.

"No problem," Rye called out as Sawyer walked away.

1:38 P.M.

"I want boys team!" Carter yelled cheerfully. A boy stepped forward, blocking her way to the row of boys.

"You can't because you're a girl," he said, his face was red and scrunched up.

Carter shook her head, her long hair swept across her face from the wind. "No I'm not," she said.

The boy nodded. "Yes you are," he said loudly.

"No I'm not," Carter told him again, her own face starting to redden.

"Girls wear dresses," he said, as if it was a fact.

"I'm not a girl!" Carter yelled. Rye moved forward to calm her down.

"Yes, you are!" the boy yelled back. Another mom spoke up before he could.

"Carter, sweetie, you are a girl but it's okay, we don't need to fight about it." Her voice was nice, but Rye didn't think she should be commenting on what Carter's gender was.

"I'm not a girl," Carter said again, tears springing to her eyes. "I'm not." Rye bent down picking Carter up. "Rye, they're being mean, tell them I'm not girl," she cried.

Rye spoke up, facing the mom who had tried to comfort Carter. "Carter says she's not so why don't we let it go and let her be on the boys team," Rye reasoned.

The mom gave him a look of sympathy. "I think you should talk to her parents, it's not healthy for her to think that she's a boy."

Rye took a step back. "Why? What's wrong with it? She never

said she was a boy, she just said she wasn't a girl. Is that something you have a problem with?" he asked, turning Carter away from her.

"She'll grow up with the wrong idea," the mom explained.

"I don't think it's that difficult to understand and she can figure it out herself. Carter can be whoever she wants. Her parents respect that she understands herself more than another person's child or their parent," Rye said. Staring at the mom, he was surprised to hear Wyatt's voice.

"I think you should teach your child to be more understanding and not a little dipshit who doesn't accept people. Worry more about your kid and not mine!" Rye turned to see Wyatt with a fierce glare.

"아빠!" Carter yelled. Rye let her down as she ran to Wyatt. He lifted her up, spinning them around as he turned to leave. Rye quickly followed after them, trying to duck away from the incredulous looks and a death glare from the mom. He quickly caught up to Wyatt as they went out the side gate.

The drive was strange, Wyatt glared out the front window and Carter sat in her booster chair, with her arms crossed. Her glare was pointed towards the floor.

"Should we get ice cream? We missed out on…" Cake, Rye finished in his head as Wyatt turned his glare to him then back out the window as he switched lanes. Rye messed with the radio finding the kid station Carter listened to. He turned around to see if Carter noticed, but she was still glaring. "Carter do…" she turned her glare on him and he sat back down in his seat. Rye slid his phone out of his pocket thinking of what to text Sawyer when Wyatt's hand was held over his phone.

"I'll talk to Sawyer later," Wyatt said. His eyes flicked to him, then the road and then to Carter. "About everything."

When Carter spoke it was just loud enough to hear over the radio. "Yaya are mad I called you 아빠?" Carter asked as if she had already been scolded and she was apologizing.

"아니," Wyatt said.

Rye had picked up enough words and phrases to know that she had called him Dad and he just said no. Rye turned to look at Carter, her glare was gone but she was still looking down. Was that what she was afraid of? Not the words the kid or mom was saying but that Wyatt would be mad at her for calling him dad?

"You can call me Yaya or 아빠 or chicken head," he said, still not looking happy but his voice sounded clear enough. Carter brightened up and immediately went into singing the next verse of the song.

Wyatt turned the volume up two notches, his hands tightening and loosening on the steering wheel. Rye was curious as to why Wyatt was so bothered. Was it because Carter said she was a boy? Was it actually because Carter called him dad? Was it the mom? Was it the fight? Was it Rye?

Rye rubbed his thumb on his jeans, he looked up when Wyatt parked, surprised they were home so quick. Instead they were at the Ice Cream Bar, Carter was already excited and yelling like a banshee as she unbuckled herself and they got out of the car. Wyatt held the store door open, Carter was already inside by the time Rye reached the door. The cold air from the store hit him in the face. He had forgotten that they kept the building so cold. Wyatt pushed him through the doorway, pushing him until they reached Carter who was looking at the wall of flavors.

"Want all of them," she told them. Rye snorted. There were 50 different ice cream flavors, each flavor was set in a colorful circle with a small description below its name.

"Pick two," Wyatt said. Rye watched his eyes sweep across the flavors before landing back on Carter. Rye leaned forward to see Carter scrunching up her face as she looked at them.

"Can't read," Carter finally said, sighing in defeat of the english language.

Rye looked at the flavors himself, he hadn't eaten ice cream since Otis left. He scanned over the flavors. Each week they would choose two different flavors, sometimes they were boring, vanilla and chocolate, other times they were adventurous with cotton candy and bubblegum. Rye was feeling both adventurous and cautious. He didn't want to get sick of the ice cream but he also didn't want a plain flavor.

"There's birthday cake," Wyatt commented.

"Cake!" Carter yelled, reaching for the circles. Wyatt gently pulled her away shaking his head. Carter dropped her hands.

"What are you getting?" Wyatt asked Rye.

"Oh uh the cheesecake and mango. One scoop each," Rye said, he looked back to the wall as Wyatt stepped up the counter. Rye couldn't take his eyes away from Wyatt at the speed he told them their order. "I'll take a kids small double scoop Happy Happy Birthday with gummy worms, one scoop each of Say Cheesecake with extra bits and My Main Mango, a double scoop of Ow Hot Mama and a double scoop of Butter Me Up vanilla with Butterfinger bits," Wyatt said. His face was less angry than before but he still wasn't happy. The employee quickly put in their orders, another employee had already started on them as Wyatt paid.

"I can pay," Rye offered. Wyatt ignored him as he handed over his card. Rye wasn't going to push it so he led Carter to the end of the counter to wait for their orders. The kids order came first, though it was like a regular sized small instead of a normal kids size anywhere else. Carter made grabby hands, Rye grabbed a lid and a bright green spoon, he pressed the lid down on top. Handing both of them to Carter, she frowned down at the lid, she lifted the spoon back up to him.

"We're going home to eat it," Rye told her. She pouted, tapping his hand with the spoon. Rye had learned a few things about Carter the longer he stayed in the house. She didn't throw many fits if she didn't get what she wanted, instead she found other ways around it. Loopholes or begging, sometimes she would smile and be cute as a puppy. Her level of manipulation at the age of five terrified him.

Wyatt grabbed two more containers as they were set down. Rye grabbed his as it slid across the counter, before following them out to the car.

"Can I eat it in the car?" Carter asked.

"You can wait till we get home," Wyatt told her. Carter looked ready to argue until Wyatt cut her off. "If you spill in the car you have to clean it up, and not just the mess but the whole car," Wyatt said. Carter seemed to debate this as she looked at the car. "And Sawyer will be sad that you didn't wait for him."

That tipped the scales, she sighed in defeat as she handed him her ice cream and climbed into her seat. He handed it back when she was in with the seat belt around her. Rye took the ice cream from Wyatt, setting them on the floorboard in front of him. He carefully boxed them in with his shoes to keep them from tipping over. The ride home was less tense with Carter belting out a fourth of the actual lyrics to the songs that played. Wyatt relaxed into his seat as he drove, one hand on the wheel the other laying on his knee, his fingers tapping against the steering wheel.

8:49 P.M.

Rye was not expecting to be involved in the conversation about Carter. Wyatt had his ice cream in his lap as he sat on the floor in front of the couch with the coffee table separating them. Sawyer came down the stairs, Rye looked backwards over the couch to see him coming into the living room. Rye sat up right as Sawyer dropped onto the couch. His hair was still wet from his shower, it dripped from his hair down his face. Sawyer wiped at it absentmindedly his tired focus was on Wyatt.

"Okay, what did you want to talk about? Also just so you know, taking him to the doctor's was a nightmare. I'll talk about it later," Sawyer said, waving a hand for Wyatt to begin. Rye shifted his attention to Wyatt who had his sole focus on Sawyer. "We can talk tomorrow," Wyatt said, pushing off of the floor to stand. They had already waited through coming home, cleaning the house, dinner and the kid's bed time. Rye didn't mind waiting till tomorrow.

Sawyer shook his head. "No, let's just do it now. Then I'm going to bed," Sawyer said.

Wyatt jabbed his spoon into the ice cream and set it on the table in front of him. "I yelled at some mom at the party. Carter might not be invited to them anymore."

"Which mom?" Sawyer asked. Wyatt shrugged. Rye didn't know who she was either. "What was it about?"

"Carter. Rye, you can explain it better." Rye now understood why he was there, he hadn't even been sure of how long Wyatt had been there before he jumped in.

"The kids split up into boy-girl teams and Carter wanted to be on the boys team, and a boy told her that she was a girl so she couldn't be on their team. Carter argued with him that she was a boy. His mom or some other mom stepped in and told Carter she was a girl and I said some stuff and then Wyatt came and told her that she needed to teach her kid to be more accepting."

"Okay wait, did anyone talk to Carter about this? About if she thinks she's a boy or girl?"

"No," Wyatt said. Rye shook his head.

"Is she confused about gender or is she transgender?"

"I don't know," Rye said. Wyatt shrugged.

"Is that something I should know? Did my parents know? What am I supposed to do?"

"I - I could ask my- Nalani?" Rye offered.

"Really? You'd do that?"

"Yeah, and I think it was pretty awesome the way Wyatt stood up for her."

"I just thought you were being too nice," Wyatt said. "Look, whoever she is, whoever she wants to be, she always has me on her side," Wyatt said. Rye felt his heart flip. Sawyer made a sound and pushed off of the couch, banging his shin on the coffee table as he jumped on Wyatt.

Rye wasn't interested in watching whatever things they were about to get up to. He got off the couch, grabbing Wyatt's ice cream cup and headed into the kitchen, shoving the ice cream in the freezer. As he shut the freezer door, he heard laughing drift from the living room. He pulled his phone out, typing as he headed into his room, shutting the door quietly.

Me: I miss you. I know you won't get this until you get back, but I wanted you to know that I miss you. I thought of you so many times today, I went to a kids birthday party and I thought about when we used to go, I got ice cream and I thought of you. Of your terribly cold ice cream kisses. I have a lot to tell you but for now I'll just say I love you. Sent 9:01 P.M.

Rye plugged his phone in, hugged his pillow tight and closed his eyes, his mind swirling with thoughts of Otis. Memories from the past, Otis dragging him to meet new people, pulling him to parties where he stood in the corner or just sat quietly as Otis spoke to nearly everyone. Rye had never felt left out with Otis at his side, he always had more courage. Rye had talked to Sawyer himself, had pushed to stay in his house. Rye had done something that his mom had thought he would fail at and he had done it himself. He wanted to keep doing things he was afraid of, he wanted to go to places that he'd never been, learn things he would never have the chance to do at home, see things that are more than just a picture on a screen or in a book. He wanted to live them, he wondered how much Otis loved Germany. Maybe they would go together next time.

Rye hugged his pillow tighter wishing it was Otis.

Sunday June 22nd 10:27 A.M.

Rye yawned into his cereal, a loud thump had him looking up to a glaring Wyatt with a basket full of folded clothes. "Rye, I swear if you make me do your laundry again, I'm burning it."

"Sorry," Rye muttered.

"And clean up your room. Carter isn't this bad and she's five."

"Sorry," he repeated. "I will," he added when Wyatt continued to glare at him. The glare dropped and Wyatt headed out of the kitchen. Rye finished up his cereal and set the bowl in the sink, noticing the dishes from last night weren't washed because it had been his night to do them.

Rye stared at them long enough that he almost went back in his room to clean it up first. Instead he moved the dishes around, putting the plug in as he turned the hot water on. Rye shut the water off, heading back to his room to get headphones for music before going back to do the dishes. His mind drifted to his dad and the questions he would ask for Sawyer and Carter. He had no idea what he was supposed to ask or even how he was going to ask them. Maybe he should take Sawyer with him.

When he finished the dishes he went to the living room to find Sawyer. Instead he found Carter chopping off a chunk of her long hair. "Carter!" Rye yelled. Carter startled, dropping the scissors as she stared up at him, her body frozen. "What are you doing?" he asked. He heard someone coming down the stairs but he didn't look away from Carter, he bent down picking up the scissors and hair that she cut off.

"I don't want hair," she said. Tears began pouring down her cheeks as she ran to Wyatt's legs. Rye showed him the hair and scissors, he was as confused as Wyatt. Wyatt lifted her up, his voice quiet and gentle when he spoke, "Carter what happened?"

"I don't know," Carter said. "Mommy said I'm a girl but…" Carter trailed off.

"Okay, Carter we need to talk about this," Wyatt set her down. "Sawyer," he called out.

"What?" Sawyer called back from upstairs.

"Family meeting!" Wyatt called back. Rye wasn't really sure he needed to be in the family meeting but he decided to stay until they told him to leave. "Rye, you know about stuff like this right?" Wyatt asked him.

"What? I mean sort of not really," Rye said hesitantly. He watched Hae Na and Sawyer carrying Lio walk down the stairs. It was an easy distraction as they all got settled around the living room. Wyatt, Sawyer, Carter and Lio took the couch, Hae Na took the chair and Rye took the empty space in front of the couch, his arms resting on the coffee table.

"Carter are you a boy or girl?" Sawyer asked, his phone sat lit up on his lap.

"Both!" Carter said. "Boy now."

"Um okay, so some days you're a boy and other days you're a girl right?" she nodded at his question.

"Genderfluid," Rye said. "It means she goes back and forth, sometimes she's a girl and sometimes he's a boy, it can change every hour or every day it just depends. So Carter, some choose to go by they/them so its not only boy/girl. And some go by he/him so that's when you're a boy and She/her when you're a girl. Does that make sense?"

"Uh okay does that sound right Carter? So like now you would be he/him, is that okay?" Sawyer asked. Carter nodded again, a smile in place. "So Rye what do we do?" Sawyer looked at him.

"Uh, I don't know," Rye told him, he wanted to help but he didn't know how.

"How about we get her a haircut that can be styled both ways and buy some boy clothes," Hae Na suggested.

Rye's eyes drifted to the hair and scissors sitting on the table. "I agree," he said.

"I guess that means we're going to the mall today," Sawyer said.

"Yay!" Carter yelled, jumping off of the couch. She posed with her arm raised and her leg out behind her. "Mall!" She dropped the pose and looked at Rye and Hae Na, her fingers pointing to them. "Mall!" she yelled again.

"We're taking two cars then," Sawyer said. Rye turned his attention to him, Sawyer was typing into his phone. Wyatt was also on his phone then he turned it to Carter.

"Carter, look at these hairstyles and tell me which one you like best."

Carter spun around, bouncing on her toes as she looked at his phone. "Purple!" she yelled, "I want purple."

"Don't look at the colors, look at the style," Wyatt told her, rolling his eyes.

"Purple," Carter said again.

Wyatt looked at him. Realizing Rye was no help, he looked back to Carter. "Okay, but pick a style." Rye really didn't know how to help with that.

"Mm this one," she said. Wyatt pulled the phone away, taking a screenshot.

"I'm getting dressed, then we can head out. I have a few hours free today to go shopping," Hae Na said, pushing herself out of the chair. Rye looked down to his own clothes, he got up heading back to his room, he pushed the laundry basket with his folded clothes into his room and shut the door to change.

11:44 A.M.

Rye sat between Wyatt and Sawyer, with Hae Na sitting next to Sawyer holding Lio at the hair salon. Carter was talking animatedly with the stylist, Wyatt had shown her the picture and she smiled, it was similar to what the stylist had for her own hair.

"Do you think your parents would have agreed to this?" Rye found himself asking, regretting it the moment it came out of his mouth. He had never met Sawyer's parents, he only saw the pictures that hung on the walls. They looked like kind people, Sawyer had turned out to be amazing but you never knew who people really were until they were faced with a crisis, or with life choices for their children.

"I don't know, I could be fucking her and Lio up and I don't know. We did a lot of research last night and I think as much as I can, I'm going to let her choose who she is. Whether she's a girl or boy or both. I don't know, I've never felt like that so I can't help her. I think my parents would want what's best for her so I hope that this is right."

Sawyer said. Rye's attention was pulled away from Sawyer when Wyatt smacked his arm. "Ow what?" Rye groaned.

Wyatt nudged him with his shoulder, almost making him knock into Sawyer. "Don't ask stupid questions, and gender is not a choice Sawyer," he told him.

"You're right sorry," Sawyer commented.

Rye nodded. Wyatt wasn't wrong, it was none of his business but he was curious anyway. Rye had been thinking more about Na-lani, how much he had missed her, how much he missed his mom, but they were alive. Rye could call them and they would answer. Sawyer had lost that and he was still okay. He was an adult who was handling everything, Rye could barely muster the strength to do the dishes. How did he expect to travel around the world by himself when he could barely go to the grocery store? College was just as daunting but it held no interest to him. If he had a choice he would live in a stupid little cottage in the middle of the woods with Otis and never leave. Rye wished Otis didn't go to Germany, that instead they spent the summer together. He knew Otis would be back in a week and a half but it felt too far away. He pulled his phone out of his pocket.

Me: I'm missing you again, I wish you would steal wifi from a cafe. Though if I know your mom you probably don't even have your phone, she probably took it. I want to see all the pictures you're taking with your camera and I want to hear the stories. I love you. Sent 12:19 P.M.

Rye sent the text knowing he wouldn't receive a reply until Otis came home. Wyatt leaned into him. "A love text?" Wyatt asked. Rye hid his phone, ducking his head.

"That's adorable," Hae Na said. Rye held his phone closer to his body. He looked up to see that Hae Na was smiling brightly at him. He sat up putting his phone back in his pocket. He crossed his arms, he focused his attention back to Carter who had a pile of hair around her chair.

"Show me a picture of him," Hae Na said, reaching around Sawyer to poke him. He swatted her away. "Come on, I'm really curious." Rye sighed, pulling his phone back out he found the pho-to that they took before Otis left. He handed his phone to her.

"Oh he looks strangely familiar, you guys are so adorable, when do I get to meet him?"

Rye shrugged, his eyes drifting to the ground and back up again. "He's in Germany right now."

"When does he get back?"

"Less than two weeks."

"Oh good, I want to meet him," she said, flicking through his photos. He let her, he didn't have anything she shouldn't see in it.

They sat for another five minutes before they heard Carter's excitement. She ran over tilting her head back and forth to show off her purple hair.

"I used a temporary hair dye and I also used a purple gel. It will all wash out in the next washes or so."

"No, I want purple forever and ever," Carter said.

"Um, can we buy that stuff?" Sawyer asked.

"Yes of course," she replied. Rye shifted so Sawyer could move out of his seat without hitting him. He took his phone back from Hae Na.

"Picture picture," Carter said, trying to climb into Wyatt's lap. Wyatt pulled his phone out helping Carter into his lap. Rye turned to the camera, Hae Na made a peace sign, Carter lifted her fingers up copying her. Wyatt took a few more, Sawyer leaned into the near last one.

"Bunny fingers," Carter said. Rye and the rest of them lifted their hands. Wyatt took two more pictures before putting his phone down and gently pushing Carter out of his lap.

"Carter are you ready to go shopping?" Sawyer asked. She grabbed onto his free hand jumping and posing. "Yes!" she yelled, jumping out of her pose to pull Sawyer out of the salon. The four of them following behind them, Rye pulled out his vibrating phone.

"Hey mom," he said. Hae Na tickled his side. He shifted away from her, she laughed as she sped up handing off Lio to Wyatt and walking next to him.

His mom was around noise and then it was quiet as she spoke. "I'm checking up on you, you're not in any trouble right?"

"No, wouldn't you know if I was?"

"You're right I would, so you better not do anything that I need to kick your ass for."

He rolled his eyes. "How's Hawaii?" he asked.

"Lovely, it's really too bad you didn't want to come back with me." She said it with a huff of a laugh and Rye rolled his eyes again, she obviously didn't tell him on purpose just so she could hold it over his head.

"You didn't tell me," he told her, though she just laughed.

"Maybe you should have listened to me about the cat hair."

Rye waited outside of the children's clothing store, sitting on one of the empty benches a store away. "You're still on that? It was so stupid," he commented, mocking the tone she used when he brought it up.

"Do you miss me yet?" she asked, ignoring his complaints.

"Yeah," he said. That was probably her reasoning, that he would miss her and not leave home so soon.

"Good, think about that before you make any decisions. I'm getting old, I won't live forever."

"You're like 40."

"Exactly, so you better cherish me while I'm around."

He tilted his head back. "Maybe you should have another kid," he told her.

"Why would I do that? The one I made is perfect. How can I do that a second time?"

"What would you have done if I was like Nalani?" he asked, his mom didn't speak right away. He let the silence sit. "Never-mind," he finally said.

"Why are you asking me that?" Her tone was curious.

"Just curious," he said.

"If that's why you think I'm angry at your other mother, it's not. And I told you before that to me your perfect, any way that you are. I have to go now, I'll call you in a few days, I love you."

"Bye, love you too." Rye looked at his phone, he wasn't sure if she was lying. Would she have taken him to buy dresses? Let him grow his hair out? He didn't know. He put his phone away, getting off of the bench. He found them near the dressing room, Wyatt leaned against a small empty space on the wall between the racks of clothes. Hae Na bounced around with Lio as she flicked through clothes. Rye stood near a table with stacks of folded clothes. He heard a door open and Carter came out with a pink shirt that had pineapples on it, it was a button up and short sleeved, with dark blue shorts.

"Do you like it?" Wyatt asked. She turned looking up at him with a bright smile nodding her head. She ran back into the dressing room. It was silent between them, noise from a mother daughter pair, the daughter trying on clothes and the mom telling her that she could only pick two outfits. A pop song he didn't recognize played on the speakers above. In the corner of his eye he could see and just barely hear Hae Na swaying around and whispering the lyrics to Lio.

"Rye, you should totally wear this." He turned his attention to Hae Na, she held up a light blue shirt with a whale on it, the whale had sunglasses. He didn't understand why he needed the shirt, she continued on looking through other racks of clothes. Rye turned back to the dressing room as Carter and Sawyer came out. Sawyer had a pile of folded clothes in one hand and clothes and hangers in another.

"I think we're ready," Sawyer said. Wyatt pushed off the wall taking the folded pile from Sawyer, he walked past Rye and Hae Na. Carter trailed after him. Sawyer looked around for a return rack. He found it, hanging up the clothes on it before meeting them back in front of the changing rooms.

Chapter 17 Sawyer
Friday July 18th 3:27 P.M.

"Come on," Wyatt said. He tugged on Sawyer's arm, his grip was tight.

Sawyer tilted his head on his pillow. "Where are we going?" he asked.

Wyatt tugged again. "On a date."

Sawyer shook his head, pulling his hand back. "No."

"Sawyer." Wyatt's voice was serious, Sawyer didn't care.

"Nope, no dates," Sawyer told him.

"Fine, then we're going out for…" Wyatt paused, he took a breath. Sawyer could see he was starting to get annoyed. "Milk," he said finally.

Sawyer bit his cheek to stop from smiling. "We just bought a gallon two days ago," he told Wyatt.

Wyatt's jaw was clenched when he responded. "And? We need more, so get dressed."

"I know you're lying," Sawyer said. He smiled when Wyatt's eyes narrowed and his teeth slowly bared.

"Get dressed or I'm taking you out for milk like that," Wyatt growled.

Sawyer didn't move for a few seconds. Wyatt moved for him and Sawyer rolled across the bed away from him. "What about the kids?" Sawyer asked.

"Hae Na and Rye are watching them," Wyatt said. Wyatt was so good at handling everything. Which was why Sawyer loved when Wyatt got fired up. He was the contrast to his parents who had always been stiff and quiet when Sawyer had seen them.

"Fine, but we better not be gone long," Sawyer said. Wyatt only smirked.

Wyatt didn't confirm or deny the length, he dropped onto the bed to watch him dress. When Sawyer was in jeans and a gray t-shirt, Wyatt hauled him out the door after a quick goodbye to the kids. Sawyer huffed in the front seat, his arms crossed. "I'm really tired. I just want to stay home," Sawyer whined.

"Suck it up. You finally got the insurance money and you don't work tonight or tomorrow so try and act a bit happier," Wyatt told him, rolling his eyes at his antics.

"I don't want that money, it feels wrong," Sawyer said, watching Wyatt.

Wyatt pulled out of the driveway, squeezing and releasing the steering wheel. He didn't have a good response for him, he didn't have the same relationship with his parents as Sawyer had with his. "Stop being stupid, you need that money, you've been killing yourself with that stupid job. You can work part time, you have both of their life insurances and the money from the accident. Get student aid for college or scholarships, who cares, that gets school paid for. You can use the money for the bills, use the money for Carter and

Lio. I have the paid internship at my mom's office but even with that and Hae Na and Rye's contribution it wont go far. You need that money, your family needs that money. It's the last gift your parents are giving you, don't throw it away."

Sawyer sunk as far in his seat as he could go with the seatbelt still strapped around him. His legs were pushed under the glove box. Sawyer hid his face in his hands. Wyatt didn't say anymore as he drove, he turned the radio on to break the silence. Wyatt kept both hands on the steering wheel, his eyes on the road. He drove as carefully as he could, if they even got close to getting in an accident Sawyer would never leave the house for a date ever again.

After twenty minutes Sawyer shifted around, looking out the window and back to Wyatt before moving again. Sawyer's leg was bouncing and his fingers twitching on the door next to the window.

"You have to pee don't you?" Wyatt asked, side glancing Sawyer from his seat.

"Like really badly," Sawyer whined. His hands shifted to his legs, they were held in tight fists. Wyatt reached in the back, pulling out a baby sized water bottle.

"Fuck you, there's a gas station at the next exit."

Wyatt grinned, chucking the bottle at Sawyer's head, Sawyer glared at him after it hit his cheek. Wyatt got into the right lane and headed onto the off-ramp. Wyatt waited in the car as Sawyer went in, he checked his phone for messages. He got several wink faces from Hae Na and one from Rye that said not to worry about anything. It didn't stop his worrying anyway because he barely trusted them with the kids and he was going to leave them overnight with them. He texted Marina making sure she was going to check on them. When he got her affirmation he dropped his phone in the cup holder. A young girl held the door open for Sawyer as he came out of the store with bags of snacks and two drinks. Wyatt was going to comment that he already had a bunch in the backseat but didn't.

Sawyer got in the car struggling not to drop anything. Wyatt waited and when he was settled and buckled in, he pulled out.

"I didn't know what we were doing but if you're driving out this way then we aren't going to the movies or anything like that."

"You're right, since I knew that, didn't you think I would be prepared?"

"Uh, no?" Sawyer laughed. Turning around to look in the back seat, he picked up the bag of snacks, laughing when they almost all matched everything in the bag.

"You didn't get sour patch kids," Sawyer mocked, shaking them near Wyatt's face.

"Because I already ate them."

Sawyer dropped his hand staring suspiciously at Wyatt. "When?"

"Yesterday, when I bought the rest of the crap." Wyatt tilted his back against the headrest.

Sawyer stared at him. "How long have you been planning this?"

"Longer than you've been alive," Wyatt said, giving him a cocky smirk.

Sawyer laughed, the snacks falling all over the place, most of them dropping to his feet. "So you were conscious before you were even a sperm?"

"Exactly."

"Whatever, you're ridiculous."

Wyatt's smirk changed to a smile as he gave Sawyer his right hand. Sawyer locked their fingers together, setting their hands on the console between them. Sawyer leaned his head against the window watching the view slip past them.

Forty miles later Wyatt woke Sawyer up, he blinked awake and looked around. Wyatt was standing in the open door of the passenger side with a backpack slung over his shoulder and the snack bag in one hand. "Come on, I already checked us in."

"Checked us in for... Why are we at a hotel? And this is a nice one," Sawyer said, his eyes darting around the building.

"It's not that nice, and because we're staying here."

"What about..." Sawyer started. Wyatt cut him off, already ready with an answer.

"I already called Marina, she's going to stay at the house with Piper and Xander, it's going to be a big sleepover. It's fine, so come on," Sawyer followed him out of the car. Wyatt grabbed his hand holding onto it as he led them through the parking lot, lobby, and up to their room. Sawyer smiled at him the whole time, beaming with happiness.

"Stop smiling like that, it's creepy."

"Stop making me smile then," Sawyer retorted, pushing into the room when Wyatt unlocked it. "You got two doubles? I'm surprised. And here I thought we would be sharing a bed." Sawyer looked at the beds perfectly made, he didn't turn when the door clicked shut behind him.

Wyatt dropped the bags near the closet sliding up behind Sawyer. "We are, this one was cheaper, doesn't come with a view but I figure we don't have time for it anyway," Wyatt said, close to Sawyer's ear.

Saturday July 19th 9:21 A.M.

The next morning, Sawyer tiredly pulled himself out of bed to shower first. When he was dressed, he headed down to breakfast, loading up a plate for them to share in the room. When he got back to the room, Wyatt was in the shower. He set the plate on the desk, and dropped into the chair, biting into the blueberry muffin. He looked through a few small travel brochures they had. He looked up when Wyatt walked out of the bathroom wrapped in a towel. Sawyer pointedly looked away focusing back on the brochures.

"Don't want to see your handiwork?" Wyatt laughed, moving behind Sawyer to snatch up a piece of bacon.

"Shut up, like yours is any better," Sawyer said, tugging his shirt collar up to cover the hickies littering his chest and neck.

"Best work of art I've created so far." Sawyer snorted at Wyatt's comment. Sawyer lifted his eyes to watch Wyatt get dressed in the mirror. He looked away when Wyatt finished and looked up catching him. Wyatt had a satisfied smirk on his face when he packed up their clothes and snacks. The look didn't leave when they left the hotel or drove three miles to a street fair. When they got out of the car, Wyatt grabbed Sawyer's hand and dragged him towards the fruit stands at the beginning of the street.

"Your face is going to get stuck like that," Sawyer said, his tone was light and teasing. Wyatt's face broke into a grin, tightening his grip as they weaved through people. Wyatt slowed down into a slow walk when they got further in, Sawyer looked around. There were several couples and families walking around admiring various shops, food stands, and pop up tents.

Several stalls held art from paintings to glass art. They passed all of the jewelry stands without a long glance, topped for lemonade, and walked past a milk drive. Wyatt stopped Sawyer from continuing as he looked around at all the women and children, there were some husbands and other men talking.

"What is this?" Wyatt asked. The grin told Sawyer that he knew exactly what it was. How could you not when several women were breastfeeding openly. He remembered how his mom had done the same thing, how some people would stare and judge her. Sawyer didn't understand why anyone would judge a woman for feeding her baby.

"Are you thirsty for milk now?" Sawyer asked. Wyatt burst out laughing several of the moms and bystanders who also heard started laughing. Sawyer tried pulling his hand away from Wyatt but he held on tightly.

"I think I drank enough last night but I told you we were going out for milk." Wyatt swept his hand across the scene in front of them. "You can't tell me that I ever lied about it, so here's your milk."

Sawyer stared at him in shock for three seconds. "You're a terrible person, you know that right?"

"I always keep my promises though," Wyatt said triumphantly. Sawyer couldn't believe Wyatt could be so preposterous.

"You're so sick, come on," Sawyer muttered. He pulled him away from the whispers and laughter that followed them. He didn't slow his pace until they were mostly down the block and people had crowded their view of the milk drive's tent.

They walked around the fair another hour, getting a late lunch and then heading back to the car and home. The ride home was more comfortable than the drive up, Sawyer shifted in the passenger seat to watch Wyatt. Wyatt reached over, flicking his nose. Sawyer pulled back out of his reach as he rubbed his nose.

"Talk if you want to talk," Wyatt said. turning the radio down on the steering wheel, he put his blinker on checking the other lane before shifting into it.

"I want to, I just don't know what to say," Sawyer said. He tapped his fingers against the center console before shifting, unbuckling his seatbelt and reaching into the back seat for a bag of chips and a bottle of water. He buckled the seatbelt as soon as he was back in the seat and opened the bag offering some to Wyatt who shook his head. Sawyer munched on the chips, staring out at the darkening landscape brightened by headlights and every so often gas stations or rest stops. When they got closer to town the city, lights flooded the darkness.

7:46 P.M.

They were at the stop sign near the house when Wyatt rolled up to it and the street was empty. Sawyer stopped him from driving. "Wait," he said, his focus on Wyatt as he sat sideways in his seat.

Wyatt spoke up before Sawyer could. "We had about an hour drive and now were two minutes from home at a stop sign and now you want to talk."

"Shut up, also there's no one around. I just wanted to thank you."

Wyatt rolled his eyes. "Don't."

"Too late, also I love you, even with your terrible terrible milk joke."

Wyatt laughed. Sawyer knew that was going to be a long standing joke between them. He would probably never think of milk the same way, definitely not if Wyatt was the one giving it to him.

Wyatt put the car in park and turned to look at Sawyer, a playful smirk on his lips. "I disagree, it was the perfect delivery. If you don't know I love you by now I would kick your ass," Wyatt said, regaining the smirk when he stopped talking.

Sawyer scoffed. "You could try."

Wyatt turned back to the road when he saw lights coming up behind him, putting the car back into drive. "I would win," he commented, checking the streets again before going through the stop sign.

He pulled up at the house. "At least it's still standing," Wyatt said, parking and shutting the car off. Sawyer pulled him back into a kiss before letting him go and climbing out of the car. Wyatt followed after grabbing the bags from the back, the front door left open when he reached it. He shut the door, dropping the bag by the stairs and walked in to Carter already wrapped up in Sawyer's arms, babbling about all of the stuff she did last night. Sawyer turned to Wyatt, Carter squealed in Sawyer's ear.

"Yaya I had a sleepover last night Piper sleep here," she said, happily making grabby hands for him. He took her out of Sawyer's arms trading her for the snack bag. Sawyer took it to the kitchen.

"When the kid goes to bed I want details," Hae Na said. "Not like *details* details but you know," she clarified, wrinkling her nose as she looked over Wyatt. "Cause that's gross, anyway, it's time for bed, Carter."

"I wanna talk to Yaya and Sah," she pouted, crossing her arms as she turned away from Hae Na.

"I'm off duty, I don't care what you do," Hae Na said, smiling at Carter who dropped the pout and smiled back.

"It is time for bed, come on I'll read you a story," Sawyer said, walking back into the room.

"No, I want Yaya to read it." Sawyer rolled his eyes, looking at Wyatt who nodded.

Sawyer watched Wyatt take her upstairs before he dropped down on the couch next to Hae Na.

"Rye is in his room, let me get him before you give the details." Hae Na hopped off the couch, heading to Rye's room. Sawyer leaned into the couch and stared out at the disaster of a half torn down fort and toys scattered everywhere with pillows and sheets strewn around. He felt another cleaning day coming soon, his parents used to have them all the time. They were obsessed with everything being clean and orderly. The only ones that did not apply to the rule were Carter and Lio. He supposed Carter was going to have to start doing small stuff. After a year of being friends with Wyatt, he was no longer considered a guest, he was family. His parents had accepted him and then he was forced to help on their cleaning days. The house had never in the whole time he had lived with his parents, looked like this.

Sawyer pushed himself off of the couch and gathered up the sheets, folding them and setting them in a neat pile. He put the pillows on top of the sheet pile.

"Come on, you're so slow, you can finish your stupid game later," Hae Na said, coming back into the room. Sawyer continued cleaning, Hae Na dropped back onto the couch, Rye helped pick up the toys.

"So spill, did you have sex loud enough to get complaints?" she asked.

"Hae Na!" Rye warned.

Hae Na rolled her eyes. "Rye stop being so naive."

"I'm not naive, it's just not our business," he hissed. Sawyer watched both of them. He learned Rye hated when anyone thought he was too young or innocent to understand something and Hae Na had a knack for poking at other people's insecurities. She had done it a lot when they were younger and they had all hung out.

Hae Na tilted her head to look around Rye to where Sawyer was standing. "You don't care, do you cousin-in law? It's not like he's going to tell me anything he doesn't want me to know."

"Yes we did," Wyatt said, coming down the stairs. Hae Na's mouth dropped in shock before her lips spread into a large grin and she whooped. Rye whipped around as if to complain about Wyatt sharing his personal business then realised that it was none of his business to say anything. Rye shoved the rest of the toys in the box before walking over and dropping himself in the chair. Hae Na was giving him a satisfied smile, taunting him with it. Rye flipped her off.

"What else did you do?" she asked, tilting her head when Sawyer spoke up.

"Wyatt found a new appreciation for breastfeeding," Sawyer said. Hae Na cracked up, Wyatt shushed her. She quietly apologized. Sawyer dropped down on the couch and looked around the room with a smile, his eyes landing on Wyatt who finished the cleaning and took his seat next to Sawyer.

Hae Na jumped off the couch. "I never asked but you haven't done it on the couch right?"

"No, my parents have though," Sawyer said, laughing when Wyatt stiffened next to him. Sawyer pushed him over, Wyatt scrambled off the couch, Sawyer lay his legs across the whole of the couch.

"You're a liar," Hae Na started, pulling his legs off.

"You'll never know." When Hae Na sat down, Sawyer continued. "That's where my dad's naked ass was." Hae Na cringed, jumping off the couch again. Sawyer laughed, putting his legs back where they were.

"Okay I'm done, I'm going to my room," she said, heading out of the living room to the stairs. Rye left seconds after her. Wyatt stood above him, blocking the light from his face. "You are lying."

"Of course, otherwise I would have burned this thing. Also I never want to think about them having sex. I would be traumatized if I knew something like that," Sawyer told him. He reached out for him, Sawyer shifted to fit Wyatt next to him. "Honestly this is like the best thing my parents have ever bought."

Wyatt hummed his agreement burying his face into Sawyer's collarbone. Sawyer huffed out a laugh. "We are not having sex on this couch," Sawyer commented. He moved his arm so he could reach Wyatt's hair, it was just long enough to run his fingers through.

"Maybe not today," Wyatt whispered. Sawyer didn't like his tone but ignored it for now.

"Not while I live in this house," Hae Na said, pulling out her phone and taking a picture of the two. "You guys are so adorable, I'm putting this in a scrapbook."

"You scrapbook?" Sawyer asked, surprise evident in his voice.

"Yeah, I put all of the photos online and it does it for me. Super easy with no mess."

Wyatt sat up, Sawyer's hand dropping from his hair. "Why are you down here?" Wyatt asked, glaring at her.

"I saw the snacks you brought in, I'm raiding it," she said, skipping off to the kitchen with a wave of her hand. Wyatt watched her go before dropping back down to Sawyer.

Sawyer put his hand back in his hair, threading through it softly. Wyatt let his eyes fall shut, letting Sawyer's heartbeat lull him to sleep.

Chapter 18 Wyatt
Friday July 11th 6:00 P.M.

Wyatt stared down at the text, Sawyer leaned over his shoulder. "You should go."

Wyatt shrugged. He leaned forward away from him and set his phone face down on the coffee table.

"I want to go!" Carter said, marching into the living room. She had one of Hae Na's shirts on, tied up in a way that made it look like a dress. Her hair was clipped back with silver glitter clips, with a light dusting of white eyeshadow on her eyelids.

"You don't want to hang out with a bunch of gross boys," Sawyer told her.

"Yaya not gross," Carter said, stamping her feet. Sawyer rolled his eyes, muttering about how Carter had no idea how gross boys actually were. "Yaya please can I go?" she asked, blinking up at him.

"I don't think I'm going," he told her, shoving his phone in his pocket.

"You're going, Rye doesn't work tonight, he wants to play board games or do some craft- thing. No idea but it's the perfect time for you to go hang out with them. I have to work anyway, just go. I know you miss them," Sawyer told him. Wyatt stared at him.

"I don't, but fine I'll go."

Carter clung to Wyatt's shorts. "I want to! please, please," Carter begged.

Wyatt's brows pulled together. "Then you'll miss out on hanging out with Rye, you can go next time."

Carter shook her head. "No now!" she yelled.

"Carter, we don't talk to people like that," Sawyer said. Carter glared, crossing her arms. Sawyer sighed.

Wyatt bent down to Carter. "Don't worry, I promise you can go next time."

"Pinkie?" Carter asked, sticking her pinkie out of her crossed arms. He smiled, closing his pinking around hers.

"Pinkie," he told her. She uncrossed her arms, smiling.

7:58 P.M.

Wyatt watched a few of his friends bounce a soccer ball back and forth on their heads, each taking a drink of the beer in their hands when it passed between them. If you caused the ball to drop you had to take a shot if it dropped three times you were out. Wyatt sat on Hunter's ratty couch in the garage where they had spent far too many nights getting wasted after a win. Zeke sat next to him, it looked as if he was engrossed in the game. A small smile on his lips, his eyes didn't shift though, they stayed on Hunter. Hunter turned when Can had to take his third shot and was out of the game. He smiled encouragingly, Hunter nearly missed the ball, he quickly got back in the game. Zeke's smile faded, his head dropping to look at the floor.

"You could just tell him," Wyatt said.

"What?" Zeke asked, his head lifting.

"Hunter, you've been crushing-"

"Shut up," Zeke hissed, pushing Wyatt. He looked around to see if anyone was listening, instead everyone else was drunk or high, too busy eating or laughing to care about what they were doing or saying.

"Can! Canson! Dude, don't pee in the plant!" Hunter yelled. Wyatt looked over, it was too late though because Can was already peeing. "Fuck you, Can, stop peeing. My mom got pissed last time." Everyone else cracked up at his statement, Wyatt shook his head.

"So are you going to tell him?" Wyatt asked. Zeke shook his head. "Why?"

"He had a girlfriend," Zeke said, his voice quiet even though no one was paying attention.

Wyatt stared at the idiots pushing each other around. "And? You had one two months ago."

"For prom and now she's dating Katie Fields," Zeke muttered.

"And the one before that?" Wyatt asked, looking at Zeke.

"I'm bi, so..." Zeke shrugged, his attention was solely focused on Hunter.

"So, maybe he is too."

Zeke shook his head. "But he's only dated girls."

Wyattt snorted. "And how many guys have you dated?"

"Not everyone is gay." Zeke's shoulders dropped and he gave a defeated sigh.

Wyatt lightly smacked Zeke's chest. "And? You don't know his preferences."

"I know, but-" Zeke didn't finish his sentence.

Wyatt sighed. "Aren't you going to the same college?"

"Yeah, so? I got a soccer scholarship."

Wyatt sat forward. "And isn't he the smartest kid in school? With a shit ton of community service and extracurriculars?" Wyatt asked. Zeke nodded. "And his parents are outright pissed that he isn't going to Yale or Harvard?"

"I get it," Zeke said.

"You don't. I mean Stanford is a great school but it's not on the east coast," Wyatt told him, his hand moving in a circular motion.

"Yeah," Zeke muttered.

"I thought his dream school was MIT," Wyatt said. He didn't think Zeke got it.

"I said I got it," Zeke said, leaning towards Wyatt. "It doesn't mean he likes me, it just means he changed his dream."

Wyatt wanted to knock some sense into him. Hunter did change his dream but it probably included Zeke.

"And if you're wrong? If he hates me and we never talk again?" Zeke asked. He got far too close and Wyatt was going to tell him to fuck off but he knew that had been his fear. If Sawyer saw him differently, if he started to hate him, Wyatt would have been heartbroken. Wyatt didn't know what to tell him, Sawyer wasn't Hunter. Hunter had only ever shown interest in girls but most guys their age did, they would never know unless Hunter said something.

"You-" Wyatt's voice was cut off. Zeke leaned in brushing his lips against Wyatt's. Wyatt immediately leaned back, his eyes wide as he stared at the guilty face of Zeke.

Wyatt stood, he ignored his friends' howls of laughter and cat-calls. He saw Hunter's shocked face frozen as he passed him and left out the door. He pulled his keys out and drove home, shock and confusion had him replaying the scene in his mind. He had no idea how that happened, he made it home before he realized it. He leaned his head against the steering wheel. He pulled his phone out, ignoring several calls and texts from Zeke. He texted Sawyer.

Me: Zeke kissed me.

Wyatt did not move until fifteen minutes later when Sawyer responded.

Sawyer: ???? That's kind of funny? I think? Thought you said he liked Hunter???

Me: Call me if you're on break

It was only a few seconds later that he got another call, he ignored it and then Sawyer called him.

"Hey, are you okay?" Sawyer asked.

Wyatt leaned his head against the steering wheel. "Yeah, I'm fine. Why are you asking like that?"

"I don't know, tell me what happened. Did he like, grab you? Or hurt you? Did you make out with him? Did you punch him? Do you hate him?" Sawyer's questions were quick as he asked.

Wyatt lifted his head, setting his chin on the top of the steering wheel. "I thought you wanted me to tell you what happened," Wyatt said. He was already feeling better listening to Sawyer.

"Sorry, sorry, I'm just really curious."

"It's not even that exciting, I was talking to him about Hunter and he just kissed me, it was like half a second long."

"Why?"

"I don't know why he did it." Wyatt sat up, dropping back against the seat.

Sawyer laughed. "No I mean why was it so short?"

Wyatt's face scrunched in confusion. "Because I moved away from him, that is not a normal question. You should be mad or something."

"But you said he likes Hunter, was Hunter there?"

"Yeah, half of the guys were," Wyatt said, running a hand

through his hair.

Sawyer hummed before responding. "So he probably did it to see Hunter's reaction."

"I'm going to kill him," Wyatt muttered.

"Are you mad he attacked you or used you? Maybe this will help. They'll get together and I can have this memory for the rest of my life."

"Both, also you just want something to torment me with," Wyatt said.

"Well yeah, pretty much." Sawyer laughed. Wyatt smiled at the sound.

"Dick."

Sawyer huffed. "Don't even think about it, you want what from me? After where your mouth has been? I don't think so." Sawyer laughed, dropping the dramatics.

"Shut the fuck up," Wyatt breathed out.

"Well I have to go, I'm not technically on break."

"I love you," Wyatt told him.

"Love you too, see you tonight. And brush your teeth. Also I would kick his ass if you wanted me too."

"He'd squash you, and I'm planning on it, bye."

"Bye!" Wyatt shook his head, taking a breath he smiled. His smile dimmed as his phone vibrated again, this time he answered.

Zeke spoke before Wyatt could even say hello. Wyatt was starting to get really sick of his lack of manners. "I'm so sorry, so sorry. I have no idea what I was thinking. I'm so sorry, please don't hate me, please," Zeke begged.

Wyatt rolled his eyes. "Shut up, I don't hate you but if you ever do that again I'll sever your Achilles' heel."

Zeke let out a sigh. "I promise I won't! I'm so sorry. I just, I don't even have an excuse."

"How about you're an idiot?" Wyatt said.

"Okay, and I'm so sorry. I left right after you did. I don't even know where I'm going."

Wyatt stared at the house. "I'll send you an address."

Zeke went quiet before he spoke up. "Is it going to be like a meat factory?"

Wyatt's face scrunched up at the question. "No, what the fuck?"

"Okay, I'm terrified of those places."

"I'm hanging up." Wyatt didn't wait for a response. Sending him their address, he got out of the car.

He could hear Rye cackling from the doorway. Wyatt shut the door making it to the hallway.

"Yaya! Rye being mean! I want to win," Carter whined.

"Rye, let her win," Wyatt said.

"No no don't let me, I want to win," Carter said, her face showing her frustration.

"If you want to win then win, play until you're better than Rye and can beat him," Wyatt told her.

"It's Candyland, there's no playing until you win. It's the luck of the draw! I'm not even trying to win," Rye explained.

"Then cheat to lose," Wyatt said.

Carter shook her hand at him. "That's bad Yaya."

Wyatt shrugged. "Whatever, I'll play. I haven't been winning anything today so you can beat me."

"Yay!" Carter yelled.

8:58 P.M.

Carter, Rye, and Wyatt were silent as Wyatt moved his piece into the winning spot. Carter glared at him as he won. Wyatt looked away, pretending not to see it. He jumped up when he heard a few knocks on the door.

"No fair! I want to win!" Carter howled as he opened the door. Zeke looked at him, he shoved a box of cookies at him.

"They're apology cookies," Zeke explained.

"Cheap apology cookies."

"They were four dollars!" Wyatt moved to the side letting him in, he led him into the living room.

"Should have bought two, these will last five minutes."

"Cookies!" Carter yelled, her body vibrating with excitement.

"Carter no yelling."

"Cookies!" she yell-whispered. Wyatt rolled his eyes, lifting the cookies as she tried to jump for them. He looked down to Rye.

"What about dinner?"

"I made spaghetti. Hae Na left like two hours ago, said she wasn't coming home tonight. Lio's sleeping upstairs. He was pretty tired, sorry he might wake up early. Sawyer gets off at 11 right?"

"Yeah, okay one more game and one cookie and then it's bedtime," Wyatt told Carter.

"Okay but who that?" Carter pointed at Zeke.

"A friend, his name is Zeke."

Carter inspected him, he smiled down at her but she ignored it. "Keke," she said, nodding with satisfaction as she took her place back at the table on her green chair. She lifted up the green piece and declared, "Let's play." She slammed her piece down her hand knocking into the cards Rye had stacked spilling them across the table and board. "Oops."

"It's okay," Rye said, quickly sweeping them up into a pile as Wyatt and Zeke sat down. Wyatt tapped on the board a few times, getting Rye's attention. Wyatt tipped his head towards Carter. Rye nodded, smiling as he stacked the deck.

"Okay since I won, I get to go first," Rye declared. Wyatt sat back against the couch. His phone vibrated as Rye flipped out a red square. Sawyer was calling him.

"Hey Yaya won," Carter said but dutifully flipped over her own card as she started dancing in her chair.

Wyatt flipped over a double purple when Carter finished. He listened as Sawyer spoke. "Hey, so I fucked up at work and just got fired," Sawyer said.

Wyatt stopped moving his piece on a red, knocking over Rye's person. "What? What happened?" Wyatt dropped the little pawn, Rye put them in the right spots.

"Well, this stupid lady lied and said that I was fucking around. Like I dropped this jar of sauce and I turned around for one fucking second and this lady was walking right in it and fell. On the fucking glass, she was bitching and complaining and fuck I needed this job."

Wyatt held his stomach as he laughed.

"Are you fucking laughing? I swear Wyatt. I will fucking murder you. I will smother you with my pillow and when you die I'm going to sleep a beautiful night sleep on that pillow."

Wyatt took a deep breath, a grin on his face. "I'm not laughing."

"Liar! I'm so fucking pissed. We better have ice cream."

Wyatt looked to the gift Zeke brought. "We have cookies."

"Who made cookies?"

"Zeke bought some." Zeke looked at him, Wyatt waved him off.

"Zeke? Why?"

"Cause he felt bad, when are you going to get here?"

"Fifteen minutes, should I pick anything up?"

Wyatt flipped another card when Carter taped on his arm. "Nah, the kids already ate, unless you want dinner."

"Are there leftovers?" Sawyer asked.

Wyatt looked up, Rye nodded. "Yeah."

"Then I'll have that. What am I going to do?"

"The insur-" Wyatt started, not even surprised when Sawyer bulldozed over him.

"No, I already told you I'm not using that."

"We'll figure it out."

"Not everything works out, Wyatt. What if they take them away?"

Wyatt stood up. "Play for me," he told them, though he hoped with Carter being so close to the end that she would win soon. He headed outside, not knowing how long it would take and wanting to see Sawyer as soon as possible. "You aren't going to lose them, I promise. We aren't going to lose them, if you never trust me again just trust me on this."

"No because if it fucks up then what? Then I'll never trust you again? Don't be stupid, I just have to find another job. I'll find a job and everything will be okay. The bills will be paid on time, Carter starts school next year and I only need daycare for one right?"

"Yes, are you feeling better?"

"No, I mean I'm still pissed. Because interviews are awful but yeah I guess I'm fine. Yeah I'm fine. I really want to get drunk."

"Maybe tomorrow, when we can find someone to watch the kids."

"No that's shitty, I'm not going to find someone to watch them because I want to get drunk." He listened to Sawyer sigh and groan. "You never explained about Zeke."

"Nice change of subject, I don't really know. I'll explain when you get here."

"Like ten minutes away, I'm gonna hang up."

"Okay."

Wyatt stayed out there for five minutes before Carter opened the front door. "I won!"

He turned to her, giving her a smile. "Good job, can you go brush your teeth and get your jammies on? Pick out a book too."

"Okay," she said, turning around, shutting the door behind her.

Another few minutes passed before Sawyer pulled into the driveway. Wyatt made his way over to the car, Sawyer met him less than halfway. Wyatt wrapped his arm around Sawyer's waist, his other hand sliding against his neck, his fingers tangling in hair as he pulled him close. Sawyer ducked his head, tilting it to the side as he buried his face under Wyatt's chin. "Can we just go to bed early?"

"Yeah."

"Oh wait, you said Zeke was here right?" Sawyer asked.

"What are you going to do?" Sawyer pulled away with a shrug. Wyatt followed behind Sawyer as they walked into the house. Sawyer went right to the living room. Wyatt saw them cleaning up the game, Zeke looked over first.

"You dare try to kiss my husband again and I'll slice your micropenis off with paper." He moved quickly swinging for Zeke's face. Zeke held up his arms, scrunching his face in preparation. Sawyer patted his head. "I'm joking, I thought it was weird because don't you like Hunter?"

"Does everyone know?" Zeke looked at them with wide confused eyes.

"Yeah," Rye added at the same time as Wyatt said, "Everyone except Hunter." Zeke groaned again, hiding his face in his hands.

"Well we're going to bed after we read Carter a story. Rye lock up after Zeke leaves."

"Okay."

Wyatt said goodbye to Zeke before leading Sawyer up the

stairs to Carter's room. After three stories she was sleeping. Sawyer tugged Wyatt into their room. Wyatt stopped when they got
to the bathroom, he leaned on the doorway watching as Sawyer
pulled out both of their toothbrushes. Wyatt took the one handed
to him, a glob of toothpaste already on it. He brushed slowly as he
watched how diligently Sawyer brushed, watching him until Sawyer looked at him, his eyes squinting.

"You better - guh-" Sawyer stopped talking, foam rolling down
his chin. Wyatt brushed properly as Sawyer cleaned his face off.
Sawyer waited for him to finish before kissing him, their mouths
slid from the water on both of their faces. Sawyer smiled. "Better
than Zeke?"

"Well…" Wyatt looked away trailing off.

Sawyer smacked his abdomen. "Asshole," Sawyer muttered.

"Maybe you need more practice. Don't worry, I'm here to help
you."

"Shut up." Sawyer pushed him into the counter, Wyatt clung
onto his back. It was a short walk to the bed. They shuffled around
under the blankets until Sawyer faced his window, his back against
Wyatt's chest. Wyatt's fingers slowly stepped up Sawyer's stomach
to his chest under his shirt.

Wyatt scooted closer, his lips next to Sawyer's ear. "I love
you," he whispered. Sawyer shifted, causing Wyatt to pull his hand
away as Sawyer flipped around to look at him.

Sawyer lightly flicked his nose. "I love you too." It was quiet
between them as they took in each other's faces, as if memorizing
them. "Would you have told me if this didn't happen?" Sawyer
asked.

"In a text as I was heading off to college," Wyatt told him.

Sawyer looked away. "That's terrible."

"I couldn't tell Zeke to tell Hunter," Wyatt admitted.

Sawyer nodded. "That's up to them, maybe Hunter will tell Zeke," Sawyer said.

"Maybe."

Sawyer nudged his shoulder. "So after you send the text then what? I tell you that I like you too and we're miles and miles apart."

"I transfer schools."

Sawyer shook his head. "Your parents would kill you."

"Hmm, what about you?"

Sawyer shrugged. "I don't know. My mom would probably tell me that I should tell you, my dad would… I don't know what he would say."

"What would you want him to say?" Wyatt asked, leaning closer to Sawyer.

"That I shouldn't follow some boy who was too afraid to tell me his feelings before he left. That I could find a way nicer boy who was closer to home."

Wyatt pulled away. "Like who? Rye?"

Sawyer rolled his eyes. "Wyatt, I feel guilty."

"Why? Because you like Rye?" Wyatt asked.

"No, stupid. I just… I feel happy, right now, with you. But I feel like I shouldn't be, why do I get to be happy? I lost my parents and I…" Sawyer took a shuddering breath, closing his eyes. "I shouldn't be happy." Wyatt wiped away a stray tear with his thumb, cupping Sawyer's face.

Wyatt soothingly rubbed his thumb on Sawyer's cheek. They lay in silence, Wyatt pulled his hand back when Sawyer fell asleep. He shuffled closer pulling Sawyer in tight, pressing their foreheads together. Wyatt brushed their noses together, then pulled back enough to see Sawyer's face before closing his eyes.

Saturday July 12th 4:57 A.M.

Wyatt stared at the ceiling, sitting up he headed closer to the crying. He pushed Lio's door fully open, Lio's legs shook as he held onto the bars around his crib. Wyatt scooped him up, he made faces at him as he changed his diaper. Lio squirmed, trying to flip around as he cleaned his butt. "I think it's too early for you to be so energetic," Wyatt told him. Lio didn't listen to him as he continued to shift and move. With the final tug and push, the diaper was on and Lio was crawling away. Wyatt scooped him up, carrying him downstairs.

"What to eat for breakfast? Hmm, maybe a banana and oatmeal?" he asked. Lio squirmed around until Wyatt set him down on the kitchen floor. Lio went to his knees as he crawled around, Wyatt watched him for a few seconds before grabbing a pan and the oatmeal. He checked on Lio every now and again.

As the water was set to boil, Wyatt cut up a few bananas and apples. Lio grabbed onto his ankle, Wyatt winced as his nails dug into his leg as he crawled up into standing position. "We need to cut your nails little man." Lio smiled up at him, laughing as he slapped his hands on Wyatt's leg. He nearly jumped when he looked up to see Zeke standing in the kitchen doorway.

"Hey," he said.

Lio blinked. He turned around and started walking to Zeke before he stopped, dropped to his butt, and started to cry.

"Shit, I'm sorry." Zeke moved faster than Wyatt, swinging Lio as he made cooing sounds. Lio sniffled and watched him, Zeke smiled brightly, tickling Lio's stomach. "You, sir, are adorable," Zeke said.

Wyatt rolled his eyes, focusing back on the fruit. "What are you still doing here?" Wyatt asked.

"I got into a competition with Rye and it got late so I stayed on the couch."

Wyatt nodded, adding the fruit to a bowl. He checked on the water, glaring as it barely bubbled. "Are you hungry?" Wyatt asked him.

Zeke came up next to him. "Starving, what are you making?"

"Oatmeal, I can make something else, the others won't be up for a while."

Zeke smiled. "Oatmeal is fine, my mom used to make it for us all the time. You have brown sugar, right?"

Wyatt looked at the counter to the clear jars where flour and two sugar jars sat half full. "Yeah," he responded, but Zeke was more interested in making Lio laugh.

"My siblings weren't as cute as you," Zeke praised. "Isn't he adorable?" Wyatt made a face at him. "Sorry, I love kids and you know my siblings are all over seven. Well I love babies, not so much kids," Zeke clarified

Wyatt nodded along with a quarter of his attention. With the water now boiling, he poured in enough oatmeal and stirred.

"Are you going to tell me about your relationship with Sawyer?" Zeke asked.

Wyatt lifted an eyebrow. "Why would I do that?"

"I don't know, you don't have to. Was just curious," Zeke grumbled.

Wyatt shrugged. "It's complicated."

"I suppose it would be, but dude you live in his house, you're cooking breakfast at five in the morning and you're taking care of his year-old brother."

"He's ten months."

"Same thing. I'm not dumb, that's love. It's fine if you don't tell me anything, I know we haven't been close lately but we used to be and it took a bulldozer to get you out of bed and now? Dude the sun isn't even up yet," Zeke said. Wyatt rolled his eyes at Zeke. Of course he loved Sawyer, he never tried to hide that.

"People change," Wyatt told him. If Zeke wanted to believe he discovered something no one else had, then he wasn't going to tell him any different.

"Hmm, maybe, but if they do then it's for a reason. Self improvement, someone forces them or maybe just love. You have an ego and there's no chain on your ankle so maybe the third option is your option."

Wyatt turned the burner off scooping the oatmeal into one of Lio's bowls and a second bowl for himself. He set it on the table as he took Lio from Zeke, looking at him he said, "I never said I didn't love Sawyer. You're trying to get philosophical when you don't have to. I do love him, and the kids, and I would throw away my family and future for him if he asked. He would never do that because he's smarter than me."

"You're already drowning," Zeke said. Wyatt placed Lio in his chair, grabbing the bowl of fruit, he separated some bananas placing them on the tray in front of him.

He didn't look at Zeke when he spoke again. "I jumped off the deep end, I'll learn to swim or die trying."

"Now look who's getting philosophical. I'm totally taking a psych class," Zeke said, proud of himself.

Wyatt watched Lio smash the banana in his fist before shoving his hand in his mouth. "You do realise you have to pass college classes right?" Wyatt asked, smirking at Zeke's annoyed face.

"I'm not an idiot."

"Debatable," Wyatt muttered. He grabbed Lio's bowl and blew on it as he stirred. He set it back on the table as Lio smeared banana on his face while trying to eat it and grabbed for another piece.

Zeke spooned in brown sugar. "So harsh, fine whatever. I don't really care anyway," Zeke finished. He took the chair closest to the stove on the opposite side of the table of Wyatt and next to Lio. Wyatt blew on the oatmeal a few more times before testing it on his finger. When it was warm but not hot, he sat down, feeding Lio who opened his mouth.

"I thought you didn't like kids? You always complained about going to my house because of my siblings," Zeke said, staring at him.

"I don't like kids," Wyatt told him. He continued to slowly feed Lio, scooping up some of the food as it slid below his lip and down his chin.

"What's that saying about actions being louder than words?" Zeke asked, pointing his spoon at him.

"You sound dumb when you say shit like that, just say the quote."

"Always so mean, why does Sawyer even like you?"

"Because I'm amazing," Wyatt stated.

"He's right," Sawyer spoke up. They both turned to Sawyer in the doorway, his hair was in disarray and he still had dried drool in the corner of his mouth. Wyatt smiled gently, Lio made a noise for attention that pulled Wyatt to continue feeding him.

He turned to Wyatt and then Zeke as he spoke. "Why are you up so early and why are you still here?" Sawyer asked, his tone lighter than his words.

"Rye," Wyatt said at the same time as Zeke. "Board games."

Sawyer yawned as he nodded, he took the seat next to Wyatt,

dropping his head onto his shoulder. Wyatt lifted his shoulder the tiniest bit. "Go back to bed."

Sawyer shook his head. "Had to pee, now I'm hungry."

"I forgot you didn't eat last night, what do you want?"

"Pancakes. No, biscuits and gravy," Sawyer said, yawning again.

"You can have french toast and oatmeal."

"I'll take it," Sawyer said. Wyatt shifted, kissing his forehead as he lifted it and pushed his chair back. "I'll feed Lio," Sawyer offered, taking over the spoon and Wyatt's vacant seat. Wyatt leaned against the counter watching them. Lio made grabbing hands for him. "After you eat," Sawyer said, lifting the spoon for Lio who knocked it over.

Sawyer blinked at the mess, scooping up another spoon full, Sawyer dodged his hands making Lio laugh. Sawyer carefully pushed the spoon into Lio's mouth, Lio pushed half of it out as he grabbed for more bananas. Wyatt turned around grabbing the bread and the rest of the items and started on Sawyer's and his own breakfast. He wasn't going to attempt to wake Carter up. He could make more later for her if she wanted some; otherwise she could have oatmeal.

"I heard that you lost your job. Wyatt didn't tell me, I heard you over the call," Zeke said.

"Yeah, It was bullshit," Sawyer muttered, anger still evident in his tone.

"Well I work at this factory where my dad is the supervisor.

If you don't mind standing at a conveyor belt being bored as fuck then I could probably get you a job there. The pay isn't terrible and if you work long enough you get benefits."

"Seriously?"

"Yeah, you could probably start next week or the week after. I'd have to see how many they need for hire but I'm quitting soon for college anyway so you can just take my place."

"That would be great. I totally and completely forgive you for kissing Wyatt. You can kiss me if I can get that job."

Wyatt hit the back of Zeke's head when he paused too long in responding. "Uh, I think Wyatt would kill me, but thanks for the offer."

Sawyer smiled at him, Wyatt rolled his eyes. Wyatt paused in turning around when a banana piece flew at Sawyer's face. It hit his nose, his eyes going wide as he turned to a laughing Lio. Wyatt grinned, turning back to the french toast that was just slightly on the wrong side of burnt. He quickly flipped them, focusing more on the food instead of the people at the table.

Chapter 19 Hae Na

Tuesday July 1st 9:00 P.M.

JJ leaned in close to Hae Na and reached out a hand. She held a piece of her hair between her index finger and thumb. She let it go sitting back away from her. "I could tell you my story in 3 easy words, they're not pretty words, they're really nasty and painful words." JJ picked at her nails as she paused. Hae Na had never seen her look so unsure, so hurt. "It's not always someone's story that's important but how they overcome the things done to them. I still dream that I didn't go through it. Still wish I could be naive to these things. No one deserves to go through these things. I wonder who I would have been had these things not happened. I still wish to be that person, I think we all do. Benji would sleep alone at night. Dana could enjoy dressing up instead of using it as a way to hide. Rem would be able to look at a child without having a meltdown. And you, Hae Na, would know what real love is. You wouldn't compare every woman you meet to Sam."

"I don't do that," Hae Na protested but as soon as she said it, she knew it was a lie.

JJ didn't call her out she just continued. "And I, I could think about sex without wanting to throw up. I could let a man touch me without pulling away and having my first thought be how to get away and where to hit him first, nose or balls." She sat forward. "And you know what people do? They numb themselves with drugs." Hae Na swallowed, she had. "I can't, not after seeing what it does to people, what it did to my parents…" She broke off again, her eyes not leaving Hae Na's. She took a sip of water, then continued. "It's almost funny that they were better when they were high on something. It was when they were coming down, when they didn't have the money to buy more. I found a way out, at least I thought I did. I was wrong. I think I was too desperate. I was too eager to get out. I took the first option. It's always good in the beginning, isn't it? I could have suffered though for a while longer at least. If I were to tell myself that now I think I would slap myself until I knew he wasn't what I needed. That all I needed was myself."

"He raped me. I've never been into sex. I've never understood everyone's desire. I thought I wasn't normal. One night, I couldn't, I just, I couldn't do it, then he did it anyway. It got worse. He started to like when I said no, he thought it made him a stronger man. I thought that was the worst of it. The man I thought I loved brought his friends. They joined him. I couldn't stay anymore, I think I would have died, by them or myself. I've been here ever since."

Hae Na felt how she always did when she heard their stories. She was angry at the ones who hurt her. Sad that it happened to her. The feelings wrapped together in a bundle, tight in her gut, and it spread to her heart.

JJ smiled, tilting her head and pressing her index finger between her eyebrows. "I really appreciate you listening. You don't have to make that face though. It's been four years, I will never forgive him, I will never forget what he made me learn. And we each have our own burdens, don't take on mine."

"I…" Hae Na didn't have any words though. JJ had been right.

"It's easier to solve someone else's problems instead of your own. This is no different," JJ said.

Hae Na nodded, falling a bit in love with her.

Thursday July 3rd 10:04 A.M.

Hae Na stared at the utter destruction Carter had caused, her eyeshadows and lipsticks had been completely ruined. Carter had used them as paint and markers. Hae Na had nearly snapped at her when she caught her painting, even as Carter smiled brightly. Hae Na simmered in anger. She nearly felt sick with how much anger she felt. She backed away from Carter and the scene she made. Hae Na took a few deep breaths, makeup could be replaced but fear couldn't be. It was only makeup, she didn't even wear all of it.

Hae Na went back into Carter's room just as she finished her page. "Carter, did you ask to use my makeup?" she asked, her tone level.

Carter tilted her head. "No," she said.

"You should ask to use things if it's not yours," Hae Na told her carefully, keeping her tone strict but gentle.

"I'm sorry," Carter replied, biting her lip.

"It's okay, next time just ask okay?" Hae Na asked. She hoped it wouldn't happen again but she also knew Carter was just a kid and kids made messes.

"Okay, I'm really sorry," Carter told her, ducking her head as she frowned.

"Good, because if not then I'm going to turn into a monster and get you." Hae Na reached for Carter, Carter hopped up, laughing as she ran around Hae Na to escape. Hae Na went after her, slowing down on the stairs. When Carter reached the bottom she yelled for Rye. Hae Na chased after her, letting her make it into Rye's room.

Hae Na waited outside of Rye's room. Hanger was nearly gone

but when she thought of the money it cost her, she became angry at herself. How selfish was she? It was all material stuff that could be replaced. When the door opened and Carter came out, Hae Na snatched her up. Her teeth clenched, she was going to be a better person. Anger wouldn't rule her life. She carried Carter back up the stairs to her room. Looking over the mess again, Hae Na set Carter down. Getting two new sheets of paper from Carter's stack, Hae Na began to paint her own picture with her makeup.

The more she did, the less she felt it was a waste, it was simply a different canvas than her face.

When they finished she hung the three photos on the fridge. Hae Na's was a simple monochromatic sunset of reds, oranges, and yellows. Carter's first picture was of everyone in the house, her next picture had been her parents surrounded by pink clouds and green cotton candy as told by Carter herself.

Tuesday July 8th 2:11 P.M.

Hae Na's eyes shifted to Dana as Rowan walked towards them. Dana looked over her shoulder, a quick look back to Hae Na, then she turned her full attention to Rowan.

"It's Rowan," Hae Na quickly explained. Hae Na stepped forward so she was standing shoulder to shoulder with Dana. Rowan had a smile on her face, her eyes zipped over Dana. They stayed on Hae Na when she got closer.

She spoke up before Hae Na could. "I think this makes it fate," she said. Hae Na smiled at that, that Rowan remembered. Hae Na saw a few of her friends behind her, grouped together talking.

"I guess it does," Hae Na said. "This is my friend Dana," she added.

"Hey, I'm Rowan."

"Nice to meet you, I have to go to the bathroom," Dana said, quickly escaping. Hae Na gave Rowan her full attention. Rowan looked down then back up, smiling brightly with Hae Na's attention. "You're hanging out with your friends?" she asked.

"Yeah, most of them are leaving soon so they wanted to do a group thing."

"Sounds exciting," Hae Na told her. Rowan shrugged.

"What are you doing?"

"Same as you, only not in a group."

"That's great," Rowan said. Hae Na nodded. She could feel the awkwardness like a heavy jacket in summer. "We should hangout, sometime," Rowan said, the same feeling obviously not affecting her."I mean not right now but some time in the future, near future."

"Okay," Hae Na agreed.

"Really?"

"Yeah."

"Great! Um, I'll text you."

"Sounds good," Hae Na told her.

Rowan grinned, waving as she spun around and caught back up to her friends. Hae Na nodded a few times, unsure of what really just happened. She turned to see Dana with a frown, walking back towards her.

"The brighter the smile the darker it is on the inside," Dana told her. Hae Na didn't agree. Rowan was the epitome of innocence. Darkness hadn't touched her. Dana must have read her face because she continued. "You may not believe it, but everyone wears a mask and the scariest of all is a kind smile." She headed for the doors exiting the mall. Hae Na tripped in her step as she tried to catch up to her.

7:58 P.M.

Hae Na lay in bed, Rowan's text was open on her phone. If Dana was right then what secret darkness did Rowan have? Was she going to question everyone who smiled at her? What about Wyatt? Or Sawyer? They smiled brightly with no darkness, or was that also hidden? Hae Na sat up. Sawyer was smiling brightly, but he had to be grieving. Wyatt had to deal with the same family she did. Maybe there was merit to what Dana had said. She looked at the text. Sawyer and Wyatt knew her. They would know if something was wrong with her. Hae Na crawled off the bed, she looked in all the rooms upstairs before heading downstairs and finding half of the family in the living room.

Sawyer was lifting Lio in the air, turning him one way and then the other. Lio giggled and drooled above him.

"Hey Sawyer, tell me about your friend Rowan."

Sawyer lowered Lio, bouncing him on his leg as Sawyer gave his attention to her.

"Like what?" he asked, his face scrunched into confusion.

Hae Na shrugged. "I don't know, anything."

"Her grades were average."

Hae Na sighed. "Not shit like that."

"What do you want to know?"

"Is she aggressive?"

"Rowan? No. She was always the first one out in dodgeball if that gives you an idea of how non-aggressive she is. Rowan is the sweetest person in the world. She won some award at school because she constantly helped people."

"No criminal past?"

"I don't think so, though there was one time she found a penny and then told the whole class she stole it and apologized to everyone."

"Perfect, thanks," Hae Na told her, she turned and ran up the stairs and into her room. Snatching the phone off the bed she texted back, enjoying the feeling of nervous anticipation.

Wednesday July 16th 12:08 P.M.

Hae Na stood outside of her car. She looked up at the grey cloudy sky, a small raindrop slapped against her forehead. When she looked forward again, Rowan was walking towards her, her hair went past her shoulders in neat waves. Her signature smile was bright as always. "Hey," she said, her voice slightly higher than normal.

"Hey, how have you been?" Hae Na asked, she walked to the sidewalk. They walked side by side their arms dangling casually near each other but not touching.

"Good, I've been hanging out mostly. What about you?"

"The same," Hae Na responded. Rowan nodded, not offering another question. Hae Na tapped her hand on her thigh, failing to come up with a topic.

Rowan reached out first, pulling open the door to the restaurant and gesturing for Hae Na to go first. Hae Na walked into the noisy bright establishment where a small crowd of people waited ahead of them. Hae Na scanned the crowd for the hostess stand and maneuvered through the crowd to get to it. A girl with a tablet ready waited for her. "Hae Na for 2."

"It'll be ten minutes is that okay?" the woman asked. Her customer service voice was bouncy and high pitched, it was far cheerier than the subtle smile on her face.

"Yeah," Hae Na replied, the hostess tapped on her tablet and Hae Na turned to stand next to Rowan.

Hae Na let her eyes wander around the restaurant, it was one she hadn't tried yet. The design was beautiful; it had wood flooring and the ceiling was full of green vines and leaves. She stared at it wondering if they were real or fake. Undecided, she looked around the layout of the restaurant. She could just barely see the open kitchen. On her left side was a bar with high dark wooden stools, behind the bar had shelves of bottles. On her right side were floor to ceiling windows, vines crept up the outside of them. Square bamboo colored tables filled in the rest of the restaurant.

"Everything they make is organic and fresh," Rowan told her, taking her attention away from the restaurant.

"It's cool, I like it," Hae Na told her, earning a beaming smile for her compliment.

"My mom loves this place, so we come here a lot. It's really healthy and they have a lot of really good options. You have to try the hibiscus lemonade. Do you like hibiscus? You can try mine if you want."

Hae Na smiled as Rowan babbled on. Rowan didn't wait for an answer instead she stumbled on. She didn't stop until 'Hannah for 2' was called. Hae Na waited a few seconds and when no one stepped forward, she did. They were taken to a table by the window with the vines and were told a server would be with them shortly. Hae Na took the seat on her right, Rowan taking the seat across from her. When the hostess left, Rowan leaned across the table.

"Did they say the wrong name?" she asked quietly as if someone would overhear and take the table away.

"It happens all the time. Anytime I say my name, they always think it's Hannah."

"That would be annoying. At most, people just spell mine wrong."

"Oh that happens too, I have so many pictures of where it was written as Hannah in different forms or H e y n a. I don't mind, I think it's funny. The first time it happened I was like, no this isn't mine, and I waited so long the guy was like saying the name of the drink like ten times before the cashier came over and told me it was mine. From then on, even if it wasn't mine I've always taken Hannah's," Hae Na told her. She smiled as Rowan laughed, leaning back as she did.

Rowan was the kind of pretty that came more from her personality. The way she smiled, even though her teeth weren't perfect. Her green eyes were bright and curious.

"I used to hate my name, do you know how many times people would sing row row row your boat?"

"That's awful," Hae Na laughed. Rowan nodded, her hair slipping from behind her shoulder to the front.

Spending time with Rowan was easy, easier than the first time she hung out with Sam or even the girls. Rowan had an innocence that she and the others had lost. Sam was sharp where Rowan was soft, Sam was rude where Rowan was kind. The two were so opposite that it made her head spin.

Thursday, July 24th 6:41 P.M.

Hae Na stared at the pile of clean clothes on the dryer. Two of her bras were a tangled mess, another one was attached by the hooks to the lace of her favorite bra. She left the heap of clothes and turned to the doorway. She could hear someone in the kitchen. Marching forward through the doorway to the kitchen, she was ready for a fight. Sawyer was pouring apple juice in a sippy cup, Carter's favorite one. On one side it was a pastel purple with a princess and the other was a forest green and a frog.

"Who put my clothes in the dryer?" Her tone was snappy and annoyed, even to herself she thought it was harsh.

"Oh I did." He looked to the doorway then to her, his voice lowered. "Carter wet the bed last night, she's still kind of upset about it," Sawyer said. Just like that, she lost her anger.

"Okay," she responded going back to the laundry room like a wounded animal. She couldn't beat Sawyer. He was too sweet, too nice and caring. Her anger felt unjustified. She stared at her mess of intimates. Pushing the pile into a laundry basket she carried them to her room, dropping the basket on her bedroom floor. Picking up her phone, she scrolled through her contacts until she hovered over one.

She watched as the phone rang, doubt seeping into her bones until Rowan's grinning face popped up on the screen. "Hey!" Rowan greeted excitedly. Hae Na was more reserved in her reply.

"Hey, what are you doing?" Hae Na asked. She could see that she was sitting in a light purple room, with dark purple curtains behind her and that was it. The light gave Rowan a yellow tinge that made her hair seem more golden than it was.

"Marathoning reality T.V. since my life has dipped into the mundane."

Hae Na sat on the edge of the bed. She set the phone against an empty glass on the nightstand.

"I thought I would graduate and then be out of the house and be an adult but I'm still stuck here until August when I actually leave for college. I feel like no one ever talks about that, like the weird in-between time of high school and college. My parents told me to get a summer job but I really don't want to."

Hae Na knew exactly what she was talking about. She sat back as Rowan ranted about not wanting a job and how her friends were doing the same thing as she was, except the few that had already left for out-of-state colleges.

Talking to Rowan was different than the other girls, she connected with the girls on a deeper personal level she hoped to never share with Rowan. Rowan had the whole world ahead of her and she hoped Rowan never went through what she had.

"So what about you? Anything interesting going on this summer?" Hae Na refocused fully on the conversation as she was brought back into it.

Everything was interesting to her this summer since it was so different but that wasn't what she wanted to focus on, she wanted to focus on Rowan's mundane summer.

"I think it's been pretty interesting talking with you," Hae Na said, giving her a sly grin that had Rowan looking away from the screen with a smile.

Hae Na thought about their future, the possibilities in front of them,the choices they would make to be together. Rowan was going to leave for college, Hae Na wasn't going to follow her. She had created something here that made her happy, which made her feel truly empowered and she wasn't ready to give it up. Not for another girl, not again.

"Anyway, do you have any plans next week?"

"A few but there's always time for you," Hae Na replied. It was all fake, the smile on her face now was fake. She needed to end this conversation before she broke down. She heard the faint background noise of someone calling Rowan.

"I have to go, I kind of left dinner. I'll text you later about next week okay?" Rowan stood from her bed and Hae Na saw more of the room; a desk with papers scattered across it, a corkboard with pictures of her and her friends, movie and concert tickets.

"Okay, bye."

"Bye," Rowan waved like the star in a parade and the call ended.

Hae Na liked Rowan, liked the energy she gave off and her bubbly personality but they didn't have a future together and if she continued to believe that then maybe they could be friends. Hae Na couldn't ask or wish for more, she wasn't ready for it.

Monday July 28th 1:09 P.M.

Hae Na waved to Dana, her white blond hair was short in beach waves this time. Dana smiled brightly when she saw her. Her pace picking up, Hae Na moved to meet her in the middle when Dana stopped. Her smile turned horrified, she shook her head and then Hae Na felt herself being pulled backwards. She tried to fight off whoever it was. When free from the grasp, she tilted her head up to find an angry man standing above her, muttering insults and accusations. She tried desperately to find a way out because she realized the man was Dana's stalker.

Suddenly his hand was over her mouth and nose. Her heart rate spiked as she tried to take a deep breath but couldn't. Instead, she straightened her back and pushed against him, jostling him, then she stomped on his foot. It didn't do much to deter him, but she got a good angle to shove her palm into his nose, allowing her a moment to kick him in the balls and turn to run, pulling Dana with her. Hae Na grabbed her hand and they weaved through the crowd, trying to create as much distance as they could.

It wasn't as far as she was hoping for before they had to stop. She saw the bus coming and pulled Dana onto it, quickly paying for both of them and rushing to the back. There was only one seat left, so Hae Na pushed Dana into it and stood in front of her holding onto the pole.

Hae Na didn't know where they were going but it was away from him and that was enough. After five stops, she heard the stop for a museum and pulled Dana off. Dana followed easily, pliant like Play-Doh. Hae Na paid for their tickets and headed right for the movie theater, even though it wouldn't start playing for another twenty minutes. She chose a seat furthest from the screen and closest to the door, dropping into it. Dana slid into the seat beside her, already sobbing into her hands as another 12 people filed into the room and the movie started.

Hae Na held her hand, not trying to stop her tears. She took as many deep breaths as she could, fear making her body tremble. Dana dropped her forehead to Hae Na's shoulder, muffling her cries. Hae Na tightened her grip on Dana's hand before loosening it again. It was all the comfort she could manage right now.

When the movie finished, they wandered around the museum silently. Neither of them took in anything they saw, their eyes puffy and red, hands intertwined. Hae Na wished for her pills, anything to take away the fear. She had to think of Dana to keep her mind off of them. It was a fight she knew she'd have to face for the rest of her life; she just hoped she was strong enough to fight it.

July 31st Thursday 6:55 P.M.

Hae Na openly stared at Dana, her chestnut hair was up in a ponytail. She wore no colored contacts, no makeup, no wig. Her clothes were black; black shirt and long black baggy shorts with black sneakers. Hae Na wasn't the only one surprised to see her, the rest of the girls were too. Especially since this was self defense class and Dana had been strongly against it.

She stepped up next to Benji who was stretching. Benji looked frozen as she bent over touching her toes on her left side and she stared at Dana like she was her favorite actress. Dana ignored the looks, bending forward she touched her toes. When she came back up everyone continued to stare. Dana went to the teacher explaining something none of them could hear.

"We're going to have a demonstration today," the teacher announced. Hae Na moved around the other girls until the teacher and Dana stood face to face several feet away from each other. They were almost identical in height with Dana being slightly shorter, their hair was opposite, their forms perfect.

"We're going to show you and then I'll explain the techniques afterwards," the teacher explained. The teacher nodded and Dana walked forward, quickly attacking the teacher who blocked several times. Dana was fast, moving around while causing the teacher to struggle in her grips. It lasted several minutes until the teacher tired and Dana dropped her to the ground holding her down.

Dana helped the teacher up. "Can anyone tell me what went wrong?" she asked.

"You got tired," Rem said.

"Yes, and it will happen if you prolong a fight, it's better to end the fight quickly and run for help. Thank you for the demonstration." Dana nodded and headed towards the girls, standing next to Hae Na as they faced the teacher.

"Today were going to work on a bit of cardio and I'm going to show you the proper posture to run. I want you to keep the posture, we're going to try for short sprints today."

Hae Na was exhausted by the time they finished, she was lying across the bench in the locker room, her wet hair wrapped up in her towel. Her shirt was loose and she felt the breeze of the air conditioner where it rode up. She didn't move, instead her eyes were shut against peeping at the other girls. Hae Na sat up, her eyes wide when cold hands slipped under her shirt touching her abdomen. She held the wrist, looking at JJ who was grinning wildly.

"You're awfully relaxed after a self defense class," JJ said.

Hae Na rolled her eyes, she shifted away and turned to Dana who stood next to her at the end of the bench. Rem was right behind her. "Just tell me already," Rem badgered, poking Dana in the side.

"Fine, when I was younger I learned Combat Hopak and Real

Aikido. I was really good, I won tournaments. After… after him, I felt weak. I had been so strong, I had beaten men twice his size and yet I felt… You know how I felt, I was that strong and I was reduced to someone who had learned nothing. So I gave up, it didn't help me when I needed it most," Dana explained, shrugging it off as if it had been nothing. It was something, Hae Na believed that even the other girls hadn't seen Dana this open.

The girls were quiet, everyone sat waiting for Dana's explanation.

"After running into him again I realized that I wasn't weak, I just froze. Freezing doesn't make you weak. It doesn't take away my strength, I was just on pause when I should have been on play. By rejecting who I am it was letting him win. I was hiding when I should have been fighting," Dana said. Hae Na couldn't help but gape at her.

"So no more wigs?" JJ asked.

Dana hesitated. "I'm not going to get rid of them, I won't stop wearing them either. I like them, I know I've been using them to hide but now I want to enjoy them, enjoy makeup, and clothes."

Hae Na stared at Dana, she fell just a bit in love with her.

Chapter 20 Rye
Saturday July 5th 11:16 A.M.

Rye walked behind Wyatt and Sawyer, Carter held hands with Wyatt while Sawyer pushed Lio in a stroller. Hae Na was at Rye's side, their arms looped together. They walked under the large entrance sign, Kettleton City fair.

"We should do something fun," Hae Na said, looking at him. Rye looked around for an activity for the group of them.

"Soft candy!" Carter yelled, trying to tug Wyatt to the cotton candy stand. Wyatt held his pace pulling her with him. "We'll eat that after lunch," Sawyer told her.

Carter looked ready to put up a fight until she ran behind Wyatt letting go of his hand, causing Rye and Hae Na to stutter their steps. Wyatt spun, following after her. Sawyer stopped the stroller waiting for a few people to pass before following.

Hae Na and Rye stayed where they were. "Let them have a little family time," Hae Na said. "Besides I totally need a lemonade and Carter will probably make at least three of those spinning paint tiles." Sawyer looked back at them and Hae Na made a motion of a drink and pointed to a cart. Sawyer gave them a thumbs up and pointed down at the painting station. Hae Na maneuvered them through the growing morning crowd.

Rye was planning on going to the fair with Otis but as he was being ignored, his texts went unanswered, his calls went unreturned. He felt lost, he couldn't do anything else to get Otis to talk to him. He stood in line with Hae Na as she put most of her attention on her phone.

"Rowan is coming, so I'm going to ditch you after lemonade," Hae Na said, sliding her phone in the back pocket of her red shorts. "No offense or anything," she added. Rye shrugged, he was beginning to get used to being ditched by people he cared about. Rye shoved his hands in his pockets, stepping forward as the line moved. "Do you want anything? I'm buying." Rye shook his head, Hae Na leaned into his shoulder. "What's up with you? Where's all your sunshine and rainbows?"

"Just tired," he muttered.

"You did work the night shift huh?" she asked, distracted by the crowd.

"Yeah, didn't sleep much." Rye didn't lie. He didn't sleep much as he thought about why Otis started to ignore him. It could be something as easy as his mom or as complicated as him finding someone else.

"You know I'm here if you need me right?" Hae Na told him, bumping his shoulder with her own.

"Otis, I miss him."

"The boyfriend right?" Hae Na asked, he nodded. "He's coming back soon isn't he?"

Rye nodded. "How much longer?" Hae Na asked.

"Um... a week," Rye lied.

"That's not too bad, but I guess it's already been awhile, and you said before that his mom won't let them on wifi or anything. That's torture, who does that to a person? You'll just have to spend as much time as you can with him when he gets back," she said, looking at the menu for half a second before the person in front of her got their drink and moved out of line. Rye looked over her shoulder seeing Rowan scan the crowd.

Hae Na turned to Rye as she waited for the drink. "You could do all that dumb romantic stuff at the airport," she said as she grabbed the drink and nodded her thanks. "Oh, there's Rowan." Hae Na waved her hand a few times until Rowan waved, moving around a few people to reach them.

"Hey," she said. Hae Na returned the greeting.

Rye spoke up before it got awkward. "Hey, I'm going to find Wyatt and Sawyer."

Hae Na waved goodbye before he could receive a verbal one from them. He found his way back to the spin art booth. Carter was still painting one, Wyatt sat next to her adding green paint to his own. Sawyer stood a few feet behind them, feeding small snacks to Lio. Rye stepped up next to him, grabbing another soft banana cracker he handed it to Lio who wrapped his fist around it before smashing it into his mouth.

"Where's Hae Na?" Sawyer asked, looking around him.

"With Rowan," he said. Rye never had many friends. The friends he did have, they all ended up just spending time at one of their houses. They never would have gone to the fair like this.

He'd felt lonely before but never such a devastating feeling as seeing Otis with a few of his weightlifting friends and a few girls he barely recognized from school. Otis was home, he wasn't being kept at home, he had access to his friends. He was smiling, he was happy. Rye didn't stop looking until they had been lost to the crowd and Carter grabbed his hand with paint covered fingers.

"Want a pretty face picture?" she asked, tugging on his hand.

"Yeah," he told her. She beamed, tugging at his hand to follow her, they were going the opposite way of Otis and his group. Three booths down and they stood behind several children with parents around for face painting.

Carter let go of his hand and he felt alone in a place where thousands surrounded him. "I want clouds," Carter said. "You get a sun." He barely listened to her. When she spoke her voice seemed faded, as if he slowly lowered the volume on the T.V..

"Rye." She shook his hand, making his arm shake. "Did you hear me?"

"Sorry, what did you say?"

She sighed. "I said you get a sun."

"Okay," he said, smiling at her. She smiled back and then it was nearly their turn.

Rye heard a little boy speak up behind them, "Mommy I want flower." He turned to look at him.

"How about a dinosaur?" she said in a tone that was sweet but demanding.

The boy shook his head, looking up at his mom. "No, flower."

"Flowers are for girls, you like dinosaurs," she told him.

The boy sighed. "Flowers are pretty."

The mom looked at her husband and then back to the boy. "What about a skull?"

The boy crossed his arms, a frown too deep for his age appeared on his face. "Flower."

"John, talk to your son," she said quietly but it was still heard by others around her.

His focus was on his phone as he replied. "What do you want me to do?"

The mom's voice was a hiss as she spoke. "Do you want him to walk around with a flower on his face?"

John didn't look like he cared either way. "No, you deal with it," he told her.

Rye thought the mom was wrong, but he wasn't a parent and he wasn't about to say anything. When he and Carter took two seats, Wyatt took the third chair instead of the little boy.

"I want a dragon and clouds," Carter demanded.

"Um, I'll take a sun?" Rye asked.

"Make it look like a sunflower," Wyatt told the girl. "And I'll take a pink flower on my cheek, because everyone knows that any person can wear a flower and not worry about what other people think." Rye looked at him in surprise, his head turning a bit more to see the mom's cheeks stained red as she glared at him.

The boy was ecstatic, bouncing as he waited his turn before he started happily yelling, "I want a pretty flower." He stopped after shouting twice and an older woman pulled up a chair for him. He hopped into it and before his mom could say anything the artist started. Sawyer stepped up behind Wyatt, kissing the top of his head. Lio reached for Wyatt but Sawyer pulled him away. Rye jumped when the cold paintbrush touched his cheek.

"I'm sorry," the face painter said, pulling it away before starting again.

"It's okay," he told her.

"When he's done I want a purple flower," Sawyer said. "And I think Lio needs one too." The girl looked at the three of them and then looked at the little boy, she grinned. Rye had no idea what the older woman was drawing but he expected the mother to throw a fit.

When Rye's face paint was finished, he stood, the boy and Wyatt standing up too. Across the boy's forehead from ear to ear was a rainbow flower crown. The mother dragged the happy kid away with a scowl.

"Would you like me to take a picture of your group when you're all done?" Wyatt's painter asked. Sawyer took Wyatt's vacant chair, Wyatt picked up Lio taking Rye's chair.

"That would be great, thank you," Sawyer told her. Rye took a few steps to Carter, who had her fists held tightly on her thighs. When the girl pulled away telling her she was done, Carter relaxed.

She turned smiling brightly at Rye. "I want to see." He turned his head and she clapped happily. "I want to see me," she told the girl. She held up a handheld mirror for her. Carter had a crown of clouds in the same position as the boy's, she had a small green and black dragon down her neck, its tail curling above her t-shirt collar.

"I want it forever," she said, her eyes wide as she stared at it.

"Um, well maybe someone else can draw it for you after it washes off," the girl said, obviously not wanting to be the one to tell her she could get it forever, it just wasn't a great idea to try at the age of five.

"Carter, Rye, come on we're taking a photo," Sawyer said. Carter quickly ran over wanting to show off her new face paint. Rye hung back a few seconds, letting them take a photo together. He was surprised when Wyatt stepped over, pulling him into the photo.

"Idiot, what are you waiting around for," Wyatt muttered to him, making sure he turned his head to show off the flower. They took a few photos, some of them serious, some of them messing around. As they walked away, it was as if everything that happened with Otis was temporarily forgotten, until they ended up walking behind his group, his arm looped with a girl as she leaned in close to him.

Rye wasn't jealous, he was hurt and confused. He trusted Otis, he still did. Whatever was going on with him, Rye would let him work it out. He understood though, why people went crazy seeing the love of their lives with other people. He didn't know what was going on, what their relationship was. He had been in the same situation with Hae Na an hour before.

He was glad when Carter became distracted by another game, pulling him away from staring at the way Otis' broad back walked further away from him. Rye crossed his arms, walking up next to Sawyer who stood next to the stroller as Wyatt and Carter played a tossing game. "It doesn't bother you that they're the ones playing?"

Sawyer looked at him, handing him Lio. Lio grabbed onto his shirt looking up at him, Rye couldn't help the smile on his face.

"No, I don't really like the fair, I didn't like it that much when I was younger either."

"Really? I loved it," Rye said.

Sawyer looked at him, his head tilting just slightly. "And now?" Sawyer asked.

"Now? Now I could probably live without," Rye said. It didn't hold the same excitement for him as it did when he was a kid.

"Yeah, my parents took me every year so I wanted them to experience it too and Wyatt loves this stuff. I like street fairs more, you don't have to pay to get in and it's not so busy," Sawyer said, his attention was on Wyatt and Carter. Wyatt carried a medium sized stuffed banana, Carter carried with her a large black and red dragon that nearly covered her entire body. She lifted it into the stroller making sure it would stay before beaming up at Sawyer.

"I won!" she told him.

"Good job, you did great," he said, ruffling her hair earning a glare from her. Wyatt shoved the banana at Sawyer. "I got it for you."

"There was nothing better than a banana?"

Wyatt leaned in with a smirk. "I know how much you like it when I get you a banana."

Sawyer pushed him away. "Shut up. There are children around, idiot." Sawyer took the banana hitting Wyatt's head with it before smashing it into Wyatt's stomach. Wyatt grasped it and leaned in, giving Sawyer a quick peck on the lips.

"I'm hungry," Carter complained. Rye was sure Lio was too with the way he was chewing at his shirt.

"Me too, what do you want to eat?" Sawyer asked. Carter looked around but they had already passed where the food stalls were. Wyatt pointed her in the right direction, letting her take the lead through the crowd with Wyatt right behind her, then Sawyer and the stroller. Rye followed them lifting Lio in the air, earning several giggles from him. Rye lowered him to his hip, poking at his round cheeks. Rye dodged his grimy fingers and dipped in, kissing his cheek. Lio tried to grab his face, Rye kissed him a few more times as he waited next to Sawyer and Wyatt who were deciding what to eat. He let Lio hold his face while he tried to bite and kiss his cheek, leaving a gob of spit as Rye pulled away.

"That photo is going on the wall," Sawyer said. Rye looked up, seeing Sawyer show the photo to Wyatt.

"It's even better with the flower," Wyatt said, looking around several food stalls. "What does everyone want to eat?" Rye looked around himself, it was all junk fried fair food.

"I'm buying so what do you want?" Sawyer said, looking at him. Rye wanted a lot of things but food wasn't one of them. Rye must have been silent too long because Wyatt spoke up again.

"I'll just get everyone what I want," Wyatt said, taking Carter's hand to move through the crowded lines. Rye looked back down to Lio who yawned against his chest. Sawyer led them to a table as people got up to move. He quickly sat down making room for Rye and Lio.

"So you want to talk about why you've been weird the past few days?" Sawyer asked. Rye didn't look at him, it was easier to focus on Lio as he slowly fell asleep against him.

"Otis got back two weeks ago," Rye said, lightly tapping his index finger on the white plastic picnic bench. He could see Sawyer nod in the corner of his eye.

"But you haven't hung out with him yet," Sawyer said. Rye nodded. "Why?" Rye shrugged, his finger stopped. "Here let me set him down in the stroller."

Rye let Sawyer take Lio from him waking him up. He settled back down when Sawyer got him in the stroller, making sure he was comfortable before focusing more attention on Rye. Rye kept his eyes on the table, a crease forming in his forehead.

"He's ignoring me," Rye said. "He hasn't talked to me since he left and now he can talk to me and he's not and I don't know what to do."

"Wyatt would tell you to confront him and Hae Na would tell you to leave him. I don't know what to tell you. I can try and tell you that he probably has a good reason or I can tell you that he's a piece of shit who doesn't deserve you. I can be versatile, so what do you want?"

"If Wyatt left for Korea and he came back without talking to you, what would you do?"

"I.." Sawyer shrugged. "I would be terrified, probably. I would understand though because the kids aren't easy. I would be heartbroken but I wouldn't hate him," Sawyer said. Rye could tell that it was something he had already thought about, maybe something he was waiting for.

"He'd never leave you," Rye said.

Sawyer gave him a sad smile.

"Maybe, so what are you going to do?"

"I think I'm going to wait, I don't want to ambush him and I don't want to leave him. When he's ready to talk, he'll talk," Rye said. He loved Otis. They had been friends since they were kids and he knew Otis better than anyone else, he just had to believe in him.

They sat in silence, both lost in their thoughts. Rye scanned the passing crowds, unsure if he was hoping to see Otis again or dreading it. He sat up straighter when he saw Wyatt and Carter weave carefully through the crowd with their arms full of cardboard trays of food and drinks.

"Yeah, we probably should have helped them," Sawyer said standing up. He waved for them to see. Wyatt nodded his head, seeing them, Sawyer sat back down.

"Probably," Rye agreed as Wyatt struggled to set everything down.

"Oh no worries, I got it. Thanks for the help losers," Wyatt grumbled.

"Yeah losers," Carter repeated. Sawyer stuck his tongue out at her. She stuck her own tongue out, spitting a bit. Wyatt arranged the trays in a line, setting the pile of forks next to it.

"We're sharing," Wyatt said, taking a fork and spearing the chili cheese fries. Sawyer started to dig into the pulled bbq chicken. Carter took a large bite of a corn dog. Rye took a few cheese balls, dipping them in ranch before popping them in his mouth.

"Oh yum!" Hae Na said, leaning over him as she stole a few cheese balls. Rye pushed back, making her fully stand up. "So stingy, I'll see you guys later," she said, skipping away before any of them could even say hi to her.

After lunch they walked around until Carter whined for the rides and Sawyer thought it was long enough after lunch that they could go on a few without puking. Rye waited with the stoller and a still-sleeping Lio. He pulled his phone out, going to his messages with Otis. He had sent 14 messages; the few he sent while Otis was away and he had missed him, the ones he sent when Otis landed, and the ones where he realized Otis was avoiding him. He pressed call and held the phone to his ear, listening to it ring and then cut off to the voicemail. Rye dropped his phone into the empty cup holder, leaning his elbows on the handle he closed his eyes. He wanted to be right, he wanted the words he told Sawyer to be true but he had so much doubt swimming in his mind. His phone vibrated and he jumped, grabbing at it quickly his smile dropped as Nalani's name lit up the screen.

"Hello?" Rye asked, his voice subdued with disappointment. It didn't deter Nalani's cheerful voice and attitude.

"Hey! I was thinking we could meet up for lunch tomorrow? I know it's short notice but I have a surprise for you."

Rye stared up at the ride."Yeah, I don't work so it's fine," Rye responded.

"Okay great, I'll text you with the time," she said.

"Okay," Rye replied.

"Alright, I love you."

"Yeah, I love you too," Rye said, letting the phone drop back into the cupholder as he hung up. His heart rate slowed from the quick pace it took when he thought it had been Otis. He looked up in time to see the ride stop, letting the riders off. Carter was talking ecstatically to Wyatt and Sawyer. Rye unlocked his phone and took a picture of the three of them when the crowd cleared, he got one of the three of them together. It was a good picture, with everyone smiling.

Rye smiled when they arrived. "You ready to go?" Wyatt asked. "Sawyer is getting a headache."

"I told you I'm fine, we can stay," Sawyer tried to reason, though he didn't sound too convincing, at least not to Rye and apparently not to Wyatt either.

Wyatt shook his head. "I'm getting tired too." Wyatt faked a yawn, choking when Sawyer hit his stomach.

"Hae Na is getting a ride home with Rowan," Sawyer told him. Rye nodded, following along.

"Sah, I don't want to walk anymore," Carter began to whine.

Sawyer stopped the stroller, pulling out the dragon he shoved in Rye's arm and threw the banana at Wyatt. He lifted Carter into the stroller,careful not to wake Lio in the back. When she was in, Sawyer started walking again.

Rye saw Craig first, he knew Otis was in that group and they were headed straight for them. Rye held onto the stroller as he lifted the dragon, burying his face in it when they got closer. Rye peeked over the dragon, looking for Otis. They passed the group without an incident, Rye lowered the dragon looking back but Otis wasn't with them. He set his chin on the top of the dragon, he wanted to see Otis even if he wasn't talking to him.

Sunday July 27th 9:21 A.M.

Rye was accepting that in life you lose something and gain another. He was losing his boyfriend and gaining Nalani back and it was a price he wasn't ready to pay. Otis had been more constant in his life than Nalani. Sitting across from her in the cafe stirred up his bitter angry feelings. Nalani sat across from him, she wore a white and blue summer dress similar to one he had seen Hae Na wear. Her smile was bright and excited and Rye couldn't muster even an ounce of that feeling to return.

She wrapped her hands around her cup, her smile softening before she spoke. "Max and I have been talking and as a graduation gift we want to buy your first ticket out of the country." She waited with a smile to explain more. Rye watched her smile droop, her brows scrunching together.

"Why would you do that? You've been gone for how long? And you think a few meetups and a nice gift is going to change our relationship and all the years you ignored me?"

"I didn't ignore you," she stated. It was kind of true, Rye could have called and she had tried a few times. He could have answered the phone, but he didn't.

Rye bulldozed on. "If you think I'm just going to forgive you, you should know that I'm not going to. You have a new family, why are you trying to come back into mine? Just live your life. You're happy, aren't you? We were happy too. You don't have to pretend you love me," Rye finished off, his phone vibrated in his lap. He was stunned into silence just as he had done to Nalani.

Oats: I can't do this anymore, let's break up

Rye looked up, standing up quickly he clenched his phone.

"Rye, wait, we need to talk," Nalani said, standing up.

Rye shook his head. "I have to go."

She reached out, missing his hand. "Rye, please don't leave, we really need to talk."

"My boyfriend just broke up with me," Rye said, already at the door.

"Wait, boyfriend? You never told-" Rye didn't listen to the end of the sentence. He had one focus and that was Otis. Otis who had just broken off their relationship through a stupid ass text. Rye was angry as he drove to Otis' house.

The driveway was empty but Otis' car was on the street, he almost forgot it was Sunday. His family had to be at church, Rye hesitated, no Otis would never have been able to text him if he was there. Rye checked the door, pushing it open and headed right up to Otis' room. Rye pushed the door fully open, not expecting him to be half naked, pulling a shirt on. Otis didn't notice him until his shirt was fully on.

Startled, his eyes were wide as his mouth gaped half open before he spoke. "Rye, what are you doing here?"

"Are you serious? Are you fucking serious? You send this shitty ass text breaking up with me and don't expect me to come see what the fuck kind of drugs your on?" Rye yelled, he had never felt so angry with Otis before.

"I'm not on drugs," Otis told him calmly.

"Then what the fuck is wrong with you?" Rye asked. He watched Otis rise to his anger and then deflate into something closer to guilt. "What happened in Germany?" Rye asked, his voice shaky, his anger completely gone. What had happened while he was gone? Had he realized he didn't love him anymore?

"I…" Otis shook his head, taking a step back. "I'm so sorry. I got drunk and it's complicated."

"Did you meet someone else?" Rye asked. He didn't think it was true but he couldn't think of another reason for him to be so guilty.

"No! I mean, sort of," Otis said. He tugged at his hair, Rye looked away, his anger rising again when he saw the picture of them together was face down on Otis desk.

"Sort of? You cheated on me with a sort of?"

"No! Well, I think so. I went out with my cousins and they brought a few friends, and since I'm old enough to drink there we went out to the bars. We had a few beers and then his friends bought some shots and we went back to their friend's house and I don't know," Otis said, his face was scrunched up as if searching for the memories.

Rye's voice was hesitant when he spoke. "You don't know?"

Otis' shoulders dropped. Rye hadn't realised they were so tense. "I remember having a drink at the house and then I woke up and I…" Otis shrugged the last part, his eyes refusing to look at Rye.

Rye didn't believe Otis, Otis was not a lightweight when it came to drinking, he could beat out their entire year in a drinking contest and still walk away. He would be completely wasted but he would remember nearly everything that happened. "You just cheated? Like you kissed someone or you what?" Rye asked, his tone more gentle than before.

"I don't know! I just woke up and I wasn't wearing anything and I was sore okay? I'm so sorry," Otis said, defeat in his voice. He took a step back groaning in frustration.

"You don't remember it at all?" Rye asked.

"No, I think I blacked out, I don't know how strong the alcohol was but it knocked me out."

"So you don't even remember the guy?" Rye asked. Otis had never blacked out before, he couldn't always remember everything exactly but he always remembered going to bed.

"No, well I remember waking up next to him, he was a friend of theirs. I got out of there as fast as I could and went back to my aunt's house but I was pretty hungover and everything was just hazy," Otis explained, his face was back to being guilty. Rye didn't believe he was guilty of anything.

"Okay," Rye said, as matter-of-fact as he could sound. It startled Otis enough to earn a step forward from him.

Otis was wary but he was starting to smile. "Okay?"

Rye nodded. Otis didn't cheat on him. "Do you still want to be with me?"

"Of course," Otis said, staring at him like a puppy.

Rye knew that Otis would always question him if he didn't make some kind of stipulation. "I forgive you," Rye told him.

"Wait, really? You're not mad?" Otis looked for any sign he was lying. Rye looked back, he was actually pissed.

"No, I'm more pissed off you ignored me and tried to break up with me over a text." Otis was quiet, he was confused. "Oats, I love you and I trust you. What happened in Germany can stay in Germany. Let's just move on, okay?"

"I thought," Otis started, he tilted his head but didn't finish. Rye frowned, he hadn't expected this when he saw the text Otis sent him. He expected something stupid about going off to college.

Rye hesitated. "Thought I would get mad and hate you?" Otis nodded.

Rye huffed. Otis was a lovable person, he was nice, trusting, and fun to be around. Rye wasn't giving him up for something that wasn't his fault. "Well tough fucking luck, so are you with me or not?"

"Of course I am," Otis said, stepping closer as if Rye was a scared animal or maybe Otis was the scared animal.

"Good, because if you ever try to do that shit again I will beat your ass."

"I'm sorry," Otis said, his whole body sagged with exhaustion and relief.

Rye closed the distance between them. Rye pulled him into a tight hug, he dug his chin just above Otis' collarbone. Otis believed he cheated, Rye didn't.

"Otis, I know you feel guilty but I'm not mad, you got drunk and it wasn't your fault okay?"

Rye tightened his arms, his hands fisted in Otis's shirt. His voice was soft when he spoke. "Oats, please, just accept this as my understanding. If you want to talk about it we can but I'm already moving past it."

"That easily?" he asked over his shoulder.

Rye nodded. "Yeah, but only if you promise me."

Otis was sincere when he said, "I do, I will only get drunk with you or my sister to keep watch over my dumb ass."

Rye smiled. "Good, I missed you."

"I missed you too, so fucking much," Otis said. It was all Rye had wanted to hear since Otis left. Rye dragged them over to Otis's bed. Rye lay half on top of him, his cheek laying over Otis' heart. Otis dragged his fingers through his hair. Rye turned his head just slightly, biting Otis.

"Ow fuck," Otis hissed.

"Deserve it," Rye muttered.

"True."

Rye lay silent for a few minutes, enjoying being with Otis. Now how was he going to tell him that instead of college, he was going to travel around the world? Rye held onto him tighter; maybe it was the wrong choice, maybe he should go to college. Rye set his chin on Otis' chest, staring at him. Otis lifted his head, his smile was soft, Rye didn't want to be apart again.

"You missed a lot," Rye told him.

"What happened?"

"I stayed with Sawyer Losada for awhile, I'm actually still living there until my mom gets back," Rye said, smiling at Otis.

Otis's bright blue eyes widened. "Really? Where is your mom?"

"She ended up going back to Hawaii, she told me that if I want to leave home so bad I should try it for the summer and see how easy it is. It was actually pretty easy, but I kind of made some decisions."

"About what?"

"I don't want to go to college," Rye said. Otis sat up, dislodging Rye. Rye pulled back, sitting up straight to look at him. "I want to travel and then maybe go to college," Rye told him.

Otis was quiet. Rye waited for whatever Otis to finish working out whatever was going through his mind. Otis got like this when he was truly thinking about something, Rye always waited it out. Whether it was how to have the best Halloween costume, how to sneak in the house drunk or just how to ask Rye out. His ideas were not always good but they were always well thought out.

Rye reached out for Otis' hand, Otis let him hold it. This had been the longest Otis had ever thought about any of his ideas before. The last time it was nearly this long was when Otis had kissed Rye and then immediately asked him out, their first date was at school and it was horrible. Rye thought the less thought-out plan to play video games that weekend was far better.

"Is it because of what I did?" Otis asked, a pout already in place.

"No," Rye said. Otis nodded, going silent again.

And then Rye could see that Otis was starting to get to the end of his plan. Only a few more seconds passed, Otis tightened his grip on Rye's hand.

"Okay I got it, this is something you really want to do?" Rye nodded. "Then do it, this could work out a few different ways. One, you go off galavanting the world while I stay here and study my ass off. Two, I go with you galavanting the world then college later. Three, we both stay here for our AA degrees and then go galavanting around the world."

"Stop saying galavanting."

Otis waved him off. "Fine, where was I? Oh four, we travel in between breaks at school, five-"

Rye cut him off, if it was over ten he was going to find something else to distract him. "How many do you have?"

"Seven, eight," Otis said.

Rye smiled, taking Otis' other hand in his own. "Otis, I would love to travel with you but I know that your dream is in college."

Otis gave a small shrug. "Yeah, but we're only eighteen, my dream doesn't have to happen in the next second."

Rye leaned half of his body over the bed. "I don't want to stop you from doing what you want to do."

Otis tugged his hands. "You don't want me to come?"

"Of course I do," Rye said, sitting up again.

"Then let's go to community college, after we finish we'll travel for a year or two and then I'll go to university. If you want to be a travelling househusband then I'll support you."

"You really just said that, out loud."

"I did and I mean it. I want to support you, I mean fuck that sounds dumb what are we thirty?"

"I like it, we'll talk about it later, okay?" Rye asked. He didn't want to think of all of that right now, not when he just got Otis back.

"Yeah, lay down with me."

Rye grinned. Rye had missed him more than he had thought. He had been distracted by everyone in the house. Otis had been in his head the whole time though. Now Rye didn't know how he would let him go again. He was sure of one thing though; he would never let anyone hurt Otis ever again. And if he ever traveled to Germany, he was going to kill the person that did.

Rye woke up to a camera in his face and a grinning Otis. "Stop it," he whined, slapping at the phone. Otis held on tight, raising it up as Rye shifted and reached for it. Rye glared at the phone, flipping over he straddled Otis' chest, his knees caging his ribs. "Give it to me," Rye demanded, holding his hand out for the phone.

"No," Otis laughed, moving his arms around. "I missed you."

"And? That's so creepy." Rye groaned.

"But you're so cute." Rye halted his movement staring down at Otis. Otis waited for him to fake him out and grab the phone. Rye set his forehead against Otis'.

"I missed you a lot," Rye whispered, brushing his lips against Otis's. He quickly snatched the phone, pulling away in victory. Otis wrapped his arms around him, stopping him.

Rye held it out of his reach, he grinned wildly at Otis.

"That was just dirty."

"Pretty sure it was clean, not my fault you got distracted."

"It's completely your fault." Otis grinned, raising his eyebrows a few times.

"We can, after I delete these photos," Rye said. He wanted to kiss Otis a thousand times and then a thousand and one more just in case.

"Leave one of them," Otis said.

Rye swiped through them deleting all but one photo. "So creepy," he muttered as he smiled. Rye knew how he felt though, he didn't know how they were going to survive the rest of their lives. The idea that they would break up in the future nearly stopped his heart. It was a possibility though, people and relationships changed. The world would change and so would they, but would they change together or apart?

"We need to take more pictures together, so if you try to break up with me again I can burn and stab your photos."

"Pretty sure that's a pop or country song."

"Probably a thousand of them," Rye shrugged. Otis copied his shrug, mocking him.

Rye didn't think this was the only issue they would have, this was only the beginning. Right now he was going to enjoy everything he had. He was going to do what he could to stay with Otis for the rest of their lives. They would change, their lives would change, but if they continued to love each other then they would make it work and if they didn't then it was something he would deal with later.

Chapter 21 Sawyer
August 20th 7:53 A.M.

Sawyer liked to think he did quite well the first week Wyatt was gone. There were two weeks before school started, one week before Wyatt came home and one and a half weeks before Lio's first birthday. Sawyer made it down the stairs before he heard Lio crying in his crib. He trudged back upstairs and brought him down to the living room, changed his diaper, then headed into the kitchen. Flour, sugars, and spices covered the floor, stove and counter. Spilt milk puddled the counter, and a glass measuring cup lay in shards on the floor. Carter sat at the table mixing a bowl of what he could only imagine for breakfast.

Carter looked up grinning. "Making craps for Yaya."

Sawyer tried to be calm when he told her again that he was still in Korea. She pouted, pushing the bowl of batter across the table spilling half of it. Sawyer watched it spread out on the table, dripping onto the floor. "Is that where you go when you die?" she asked.

"No, it's a country and he's not dead."

"I want Yaya!" she yelled.

"He'll be back in a week," he tells her again, Lio starts crying at his side. Sawyer tiptoes around the mess putting Lio in his seat. He was content for a second before he started moving and crying to escape. Sawyer moved to the fridge and a bunch of things were knocked onto the floor. He picked them up, putting them back in the fridge. He opened the cupboard grabbing his cereal, pouring the milk into it before putting it back in the fridge. He grabbed Lio's blue spoon and fed him. He watched him get a good handle on it before he turned to Carter who was back to mixing what was left of the batter.

"Carter, I need you to help me clean up the kitchen," he told her, hoping she would finally listen. The living room also had toys scattered around, the laundry and dishes needed cleaned.

"No! I want Yaya!" Carter yelled. She glared at him as her hand stopped stirring.

Sawyer sighed, he knew this was going to be a battle until Wyatt came home. "I know but he won't be home for a week."

"NO!" she screamed, flipping the bowl before she scrambled off the table.

"Carter!" he yelled. She stopped in her tracks looking back at him with wide eyes. He lost what he wanted to say and she glared at him.

"I hate you!" she yelled before she was out of the kitchen and he could hear her climbing the stairs.

He turned to Lio sighing. "How does a five year old know what hate is?" he asked, Lio smeared milk and cereal across his face. Sawyer banged his head against the table covering his face in flour.

Sawyer carried Lio to go check on Carter. He paused in the hallway halfway to the stairs when he heard a knock on the door. He looked down at Lio who leaned away from him wanting to be set on the floor. Lio babbled as Sawyer walked to the door. He pulled open the door, nearly shutting it again. The social worker stood there as casual as she had been months ago, in jeans and a simple t-shirt.

"Hello again, I'm sorry this has been delayed. Are you ready for the house inspection?" she asked as if he could really say no, but saying no would make him look like he wasn't ready. He wasn't but she didn't know that. He moved aside, realizing he still hadn't spoken yet.

"Right, yes. Yes, we, uh, are ready," he stuttered out. The moment she stepped in she looked around. Sawyer shut the door, realizing the mess still in the kitchen.

"Did you want to see Carter?" Sawyer asked.

She turned to him smiling. "Yes, I would."

"She's upstairs playing," he told her, hoping that Carter would be less of a mess than the kitchen. She looked at him for a few seconds before nodding as she headed away from the kitchen to the stairs. As soon as she was upstairs, Sawyer ran to the kitchen. Setting Lio to crawl around the floor, he quickly grabbed a few towels from the laundry room and began wiping up the mess. Quickly throwing those in the washer, he cleaned as fast as he could, wiping, sweeping and wiping again. When it was mostly clean, he scooped up Lio and headed up the stairs.

He stepped outside of Carter's door and leaned back against the small expanse of wall. He easily heard their voices with the door open.

The questions turned towards Sawyer and Wyatt and how they were taking care of her. Carter responded happily about Wyatt and talked about different things they did and then she got onto talking about Piper and forts. Carter didn't talk about Sawyer; she told her about Rye and the games they played, talked about painting and

K-pop with Hae Na. When she took a second to breathe, the social worker brought up Sawyer.

"Sawyer is a meanie, he made me eat peas, he won't let me talk to Yaya, he won't let me wait for Yaya in the living room. He wouldn't let me go to Korea with Yaya," Carter continued her rant about the "terrible" things Sawyer made her do. Sawyer rolled his eyes, looking down at Lio who blinked at him. Lio smiled when he realized he had Sawyer's attention.

"I would like to speak with you alone, it will only take a few moments." She told him standing in the door way of Carter's room.

"Of course, Carter, why don't you go down and call Wyatt?" Sawyer said, handing her his phone.

"Okay," she said running down the stairs.

The woman spoke before he even had the chance to look away from the stairs where Carter had run down. "This isn't a situation that needs to be interfered with, you haven't had any complaints or allegations against you. I'm simply making sure that you are fit enough to take care of your siblings. After everything that has happened, it would be understandable that you are unable to do so. However, I have found no reason that you shouldn't take care of them."

"You don't want to interview me?"

"Normally, I would but in this situation I think it's unnecessary. You chose to take custody of them and I heard you've completed school with good grades. You've shown plenty of signs that you are taking this seriously and that you care about them. You don't have to worry about another visit unless a report is made."

Sawyer's whole body sagged in relief. "Thank you, thank you so much."

"I wish there were more people who cared about their families, this has been an easy job," she said. Sawyer followed her down the stairs, he held the door open for her, she smiled as he passed. He returned the gesture, he waited for her to get past the short porch before he shut the door and slumped against it.

8:00 P.M.

Sawyer waited for the call like a lifeline, he checked the time again. He knew Wyatt was awake, it was already past 9:00 A.M. for him. He jumped when the call came in, quickly answering it. Immediately he glared at Wyatt.

"What happened?" Wyatt asked. Sawyer could only see his face, neck and just the top of his bare shoulders. Sawyer didn't want to look at him from a screen. Sawyer dropped the look, his face morphing into longing.

"Thank you," Sawyer said. He meant it. Wyatt was the smart one and Sawyer was the idiot who thought that Wyatt should leave for college leaving Sawyer alone.

"For leaving? Want me to stay in Korea?"

"No, fuck no, I'd kill you. I mean for choosing to do online classes," he said. He didn't know what he'd do if Wyatt had chosen to leave for college, even though Sawyer pushed him to go.

"I can't always listen to your dumbass, you have terrible ideas." Sawyer huffed a laugh. He stared at every spot Wyatt showed him, watching the way Wyatt's eyes trailed over him as well.

Sawyer shifted further down in his bed, opening his mouth to tell Wyatt about Carter but he cut Sawyer off. "The kids are asleep?"

"Yeah, I put them to bed an hour ago."

Wyatt grinned and Sawyer narrowed his eyes. "You're thinking of something terrible."

"It's not terrible," Wyatt said, his voice lowered to just above a whisper and going husky.

Sawyer looked around as if there was anyone to catch him. "We are not having phone sex," he whispered. Wyatt laughed, and then shifted around so Sawyer couldn't see him and then he was back on the screen, the same as before. Sawyer realised he was now in Wyatt's left hand. "I'm serious."

"I didn't say anything," Wyatt said.

"Are you jacking off right now?" Sawyer asked, his eyes narrowed.

Wyatt grinned. "I thought you didn't want to have phone sex."

"Wyatt," Sawyer said as a warning.

"For a whole week I haven't heard that name, I like when you say it," Wyatt said in a seductive tone that had Sawyer rolling his eyes.

"Then I'm not saying it," Sawyer told him defiantly.

Wyatt's voice was teasing when he spoke his name. "Sawyer."

"Don't you dare," Sawyer warned.

"Sawyer," Wyatt said, breathily.

"I hate you so much right now."

"Say my name, please?" Wyatt asked, jokingly.

"So much, just stay in Korea for all I care... Wyatt," Sawyer said, dropping the phone on the bed, covering his face. He heard his name a few more times before Wyatt went quiet. It took a few minutes before Sawyer could bring himself to look at the phone. When he finally did, Wyatt was just sitting there like normal.

"Are you done?" he asked. Wyatt focused on him, grinning.

"Wouldn't you like to know."

"Ridiculous, you're completely ridiculous you know that right?" Sawyer asked, he almost forgot about Carter. "Oh, I have a story for you."

"Is it a good story?" Wyatt asked, his tone returning to a flirty tone.

"It's not that kind of story," Sawyer saide relayed the actual story and Wyatt lost the smile on his face. He was quiet for a minute afterwards.

"Do you think she needs a therapist? She seems too young to really know what's going on and she keeps asking if I died."

"I don't know, I don't know what's really normal or not. You would think child development would have prepared me for this and it has not. I told you before she was getting attached to you."

"She's five though, what kind of daycare do you have her in?" Wyatt asked.

Sawyer sighed, leaning his head back. "There's nothing wrong with her daycare," he said tilting his head to the side to look at Wyatt.

Wyatt shrugged, Sawyer was able to see the small birthmark on his shoulder. Sawyer quickly looked away, refusing to have those thoughts right now. Wyatt caught it anyway and pestered him until Sawyer finally hung up on him.

Chapter 22 Wyatt
August 13th 11:43 A.M.

Wyatt dropped his bag at his feet as he sat on the train that would take him into Seoul. He mindlessly played games as he waited for it to take off and start the hour journey. He looked at his instructions again before his phone died.

He walked up stone steps to the house. The front door opened and he was greeted by his aunt. He bowed, his glasses slipping down his nose. He couldn't wait to switch back to contacts.

"Come in come in," she said, looking him over as he stepped in. He took off his shoes putting them away in the shoe closet, taking the pre-offered slippers. "Was it hard coming?" she asked in English.

He was surprised by her English, he responded in Korean. "No, it was easy to find." They walked into the living room, it was empty of anyone else.

"Oh you speak Korean! It's very good," she complimented him with a bright smile.

"Thank you," he replied.

She gave him a tour of the house, finishing upstairs where the bedrooms were. Three of them were filled with his cousins', and his aunt's and uncle's things.

"This will be your room," she said, pushing the door further open. The room was simple, with a bed, desk, and wardrobe.

"The bathroom is down the hall, you can rest and wash up. Come down when you feel hungry," she told him.

"Thank you," he responded, bowing.

She smiled brightly at him and then he was alone. He set his bag next to the wardrobe. Sitting on the bed, he pulled out his dead phone and reached over dragging his bag to the bed. He pulled out his charger and adapter, plugging his phone in. He pulled out some clothes, pushing himself off of the bed to shower.

It was only a half hour later when he came down the stairs, she was sitting in the living room with a plate of peeled and cut fruit on the table as she laughed at the T.V. He sat down on the other side of the couch. He used the fork to grab a piece of apple. She smiled and nodded at him, he smiled back awkwardly. They watched T.V. until his cousin came home with a friend, they were both dressed in uniforms.

"Hae Won! You skipped cram school again," his aunt nagged.

"Mom," she whined. "I wanted to come home and greet our cousin," she said. "Hello," she said to him. He didn't have time to respond as she pulled her friend up stairs as she stared at him.

"Ungrateful child," her mother tsked, shaking her head before laughing at the show again.

Wyatt felt awkward as he sat there, he had left his phone upstairs and the show wasn't keeping his interest, it was a strange counseling show where they all sat on the floor with pillows as they talked to someone in the crowd. He looked around the room again. There were doors that lead out to the garden, pictures were on the walls. Even one with his own family, taken when they visited eight years ago. He heard his cousin head down with her friend, she was in casual clothes, a salmon colored t-shirt and black shorts, she headed right for the couch.

"Ji seok, want to go out with us? This is Mi Young." She said gesturing to her friend.

"Where are you going?" her mom asked, looking at her.

"Just to a cafe, he should have fun while he's here," Hae Won said, smiling innocently at her mom.

"Alright but be back for dinner, your uncles are coming," her mom told her.

"Okay." She waved for him to follow her. He got up, running up the stairs to grab his wallet and phone before following them out. They started walking down the hill when his cousin turned around, walking backwards, her friend giggled as she walked next to her.

"Ji Seok, do you have a girlfriend?" she asked. He wondered if he told her the truth how far it would go in his family. His mother would kill him if he messed this trip up.

"No," he said, truthfully. She nudged her friend who turned her face away. "But I do love someone."

She nodded. "Ah, one sided love?" she asked. She turned so she was walking next to him, her friend on the other side of her.

"Something like that," he responded in English.

"You should help me with my English homework, mom is making me take extra lessons."

"Are you still in school?" he asked. He was sure they got out mid-July but he wasn't exactly up to date on Korean school culture.

She sighed dramatically, bending her body over before standing up. "We have extra classes," she said. He saw them holding hands, they were swinging their arms back and forth. She reminded him of Hae Na, he could just imagine the destruction they could cause together. He shook his head, if they ever met he would not be at that family reunion.

"Like summer school?" he asked.

She nodded. "Yeah, Jong Hyun is working right now. He should be at dinner tonight, we're going to Norebang," she said.

His cousin chose the first song, singing as he made a choice for his own song. Singing was something he only did for the kids or when he was drunk. Sawyer was a singer, though he was nearly tone deaf. He took a few pictures on the dark red leather couch in the room as lights swirled around. He'd send them to Sawyer when he got back to the house. He stared at his phone background, it was the picture Sawyer had sent him when he was at his uncle's 60th birthday. It was his family. He quickly flipped his phone over when his cousin grabbed his arm. Handing the mic to him, he looked at the screen; it was a popular song that Hae Na and Carter had listened to quite a few times. They sang together and after the fourth song he was tired. He dropped back on the couch as they danced and took selfies with each other; he got in a few of them but for the most part they had fun together.

Mi Young excused herself. When she was gone Hae Won dropped down on the couch next to him. "She's in love with Jong

Hyun, you'll help me get them together right?"

"Why?" he asked. That was the last thing he wanted to do while he was there.

She stretched her legs out leaning back against the couch. "Help me and I won't tell mom about your boyfriend," she said. He shook his head, she was just like Hae Na. How two people could be so similar having never even met, amazed him.

Wyatt shrugged. "Tell her."

"Really?" she asked sitting up quickly, almost flying off the couch. "I was joking," she added. He shrugged again. "대박." *Amazing*, she said, the grin on her face did not ease his tension.

Mi Young came back and they finished off the time they had left. Wyatt wanted to text Sawyer that he wanted to come home. He followed the girls home and he was met with a completely different situation in the house. He could smell the food as soon as they walked in the door.

"We're home!" Hae Won yelled, dropping her shoes at the door. Mi Young picked them up putting them away along with her own. Wyatt put his away following them in, a few of his uncles were in the living room watching a soccer game. They all greeted him when he came in, he greeted them and continued to the kitchen where his aunts were cooking. It had completely transformed. There were so many dishes, some he didn't even recognize. There was a whole fish, sweet and sour pork, perilla leaves marinated in soy sauce and red pepper flakes, water kimchi, cucumber kimchi, and that was only half of it. They all greeted him with smiles. One aunt pulled him aside asking about the U.S. and all of his other family that never visited South Korea. He didn't point out that they didn't visit either. He smiled and took their small abuse as they tugged at his hair and squished his cheeks. He finally escaped to the living room where he was only asked a few questions before they all focused on the soccer game.

They all gathered around the table for dinner, Jong Hyun came home after everyone was settled, and quickly dropped in next to him. He bumped his shoulder in greeting and immediately started to eat. Wyatt bowed his head, the aunts continued to fill his bowl with pieces of fish and chicken.

Wyatt wasn't expecting at their first dinner, with most of his family sitting at the large table, laughing and moving around each other, that his cousin would open her mouth. She did as she promised, she was evil.

"Mom, you should see Wyatt's boyfriend. He's cute," she said. Wyatt expected silence, he expected to hear a pin drop. Instead, it was more noise of happy shrieks and attention from his aunts. His cousin snatched his phone from where it was sitting next to his rice bowl and lit it up, showing his aunt.

"Omo, 귀여워." She squealed like Carter when she was excited. He had to agree though, they were all cute. Everyone else looked at him for a second then nothing, there was no cruelty, no snide remarks, no rejection. This was not what he was expecting, this was acceptance.

His grandpa stood from the table, heading out of the room. The rest of the table remained normal. After a few minutes, Wyatt decided to check on his grandpa, finding him in his bedroom. The door was open and he was going through a box of old photos.

"할아버지," Wyatt said. At his title, his grandpa turned holding a photograph up.

"I found it," he said, holding it out for Wyatt. Wyatt carefully took it.

It was an old black and white photo; two young women stood side by side, both had beautiful smiles on their faces. Their shoulders touched, one woman had her head tilted nearly touching the other's shoulder.

"할머니?" Wyatt asked, wondering if it really was his grandmother in the photo. He placed his finger on the woman with her head bent. It was her.

"This was her…" His grandpa trailed off, instead, he just gave him a small smile. "Take this photo to her," he told him, squeezing his shoulder.

His grandpa pulled away. "She has always wanted the best for her family, she may not always choose the best methods. Everything she does is because of fear of the past, fear that her children may come across similar things," he told him, giving him a little push.

Instead of going back to the table, he went upstairs and put the photo in his bag. He dropped onto his bed, staring up at the ceiling. He closed his eyes, grinning like the Cheshire Cat. His grandfather gave him the possible key to ensuring his grandmother's blessing, meaning the rest of the family would follow suit.

He nearly couldn't stand from the amount of food he ingested. Jong Hyun pulled him upstairs to his room anyway. Jong Hyun's room wasn't too much different than the guest room he was staying in, the difference was the bit of mess of clothes, and all of his personal stuff on the desk and walls. Jong Hyun dropped onto his bed, Wyatt took his desk chair.

"What's the wifi password?" Wyatt asked in Korean. Jonghyun laughed, holding his hand out for the phone. Wyatt unlocked it, going to his wifi before handing it over. When it was connected it continued to vibrate with notifications.

"You're popular," Jong Hyun said. Wyatt waited until it stopped to look at it. Several were from Sawyer, a few from Rye, and a bunch from Hae Na. He chose Hae Na's first.

It was a video of her in a car riding passenger. "Hey loser, I want a ton of photos and talk really good about me so I can visit next time," she said. Jong Hyun stood up next to him to watch. The video ended and another one started. "If you meet any K-pop stars, take pictures and get me an autograph," she said, grinning before taking a bite of a burger and ending the video.

The next video, she was in a rest stop bathroom. "Do you see this? These stalls are tiny, I'm short and I can still see over the door. Rowan, go sit on the toilet and see if I can still see you." Hae Na shifted the camera to Rowan who rolled her eyes but went anyway. "See! I can see you pee, show me the stalls in Korea," she said, ending it with her fingers in a piece sign that turned into scissors.

The last video was of Rowan. "I was going to send it from mine but then I thought you'd never open it. Have fun Wyatt and be safe, You're still one of my best friends even if you don't think so. Bye." She waved and it ended.

"Do you have a girlfriend?" he asked in Korean. Wyatt shook his head and clicked on Rye's messages; there were several pictures of different dogs and one that told him to be safe and have fun. He didn't open Sawyer's, he wouldn't until he was alone.

"I'm supposed to show you around tomorrow," he said. "We're going to meet up with my friends."

"Alright," Wyatt pushed off of the chair "I'm going to bed."

"Really?" he asked, checking his smartwatch for the time.

"Long day," Wyatt responded in English. Heading back to his room, he dug in his bag for his headphones, pulling them out. He got into the bed watching Sawyer's videos.

Sawyer had the phone for a second before it was blurry with movement and ended. The next one had Sawyer holding the phone up. "We're trying this again, Carter knocked it out of my hand, Carter, stop, ow." The video moved to show Carter hitting his hands against him.

"I want to send a video to Yaya first!" she yelled. The video cut off and the next one had Carter holding the phone.

"Yaya, I miss you and love you and I hope you have lots of fun seeing Korea. Sah said I couldn't go with you like a meanie." She glared above the camera where he figured Sawyer was. "Next time you better take me or I'll be really…" The video cut off, Wyatt grinned at it.

Another one started. "It's my turn now." Sawyer pulled the phone away, he could still hear Carter whining in the background as Sawyer ran up the stairs. "Look at that, athletic enough to outrun a 5 year old on the stairs," he said taking deep breaths. "I'm dying," he said. The video stopped and the next one had Sawyer in the bathroom as Carter banged on the door. "I'm going to keep it short before she goes all Johnny from The Shining on me, let me know when you arrive and everything is good. Also next time we actually talk, I'm doing it when she's sleeping," he whispered the last part. The next few had Carter telling him all about her day. The last video had Sawyer alone in bed. "You haven't responded, I'm going to leave it up to the lack of wifi. I know your plane landed like 3 hours ago. Anyway have a good time, we'll somehow survive without you, maybe."

Wyatt leaned back against the wall taking a video of himself. "The plane didn't crash. I didn't get lost and I'm at my aunt and uncle's. I'll keep you somewhat posted until I get back," he said, sending it to the three of them and Rowan.

Chapter 23 Hae Na
August 13th 11:01 A.M.

Hae Na drove to Rowan's house, parking in the driveway. Rowan came running out of the house, a small blue backpack on her back.

"Hae Na!" she yelled. Hae Na got out of the car, catching her as she slammed into her.

Hae Na smashed back against the car, the air knocking out of her. "Trying to kill me?"

Rowan shrugged. "Not yet." She grinned, kissing Hae Na's cheek. "I gotta grab the rest of my bags and then we're ready to go, my parents are coming down next week with the rest of it," she said, running back towards the house. Hae Na shook her head, she would miss Rowan when she left her at the college, but this would be a good parting. Hae Na always loved road trips, her life wasn't sunshine and rainbows but it was stormy clouds and rainbows. She didn't have a clear path but she was making her own choices and choosing her own direction. She stood in the doorway to Rowan's house catching the pillow Rowan threw at her. Hae Na hugged the pillow grinning at Rowan.

"I'm leaving!" Rowan said

"Be safe, have fun," her mom yelled back.

"No goodbye hugs?" Hae Na asked.

"We already did, she doesn't want to be seen with a puffy red face, come on," Rowan pushed her out of the doorway, shutting it behind her. She pulled her duffle bag over her shoulder.

It was quiet as they drove out of town, the music on low. Hae Na tapped her fingers against the steering wheel absently.

Rowan shifted down in the passenger seat, tilting her head back as she looked at Hae Na. "Wyatt left today, right?"

Hae Na grinned, nodding before responding. "Yeah, Sawyer is going to shit a brick townhouse."

"Why?" Rowan asked, a worried crease in her brow.

Hae Na laughed. "Carter is going to drive him crazy."

"Maybe we should wait to go," Rowan offered.

"No, he can handle it," she said, turning to see Rowan's worried face. Hae Na rolled her eyes. "Really he'll be fine. Carter can be a terror but it's nothing he can't handle and Wyatt is only gone like a week."

"Two I thought," Rowan said.

"One and a half? I don't know, look he'll be fine and I'm only going to be gone a few days. If you aren't careful I might get jealous," Hae Na warned, her tone light and joking.

Rowan smiled. "No you won't."

"Why?"

"Because I like *you,*" she said. Her voice was solid, she was sure of her answer.

Hae Na's smile was broad, her focus remained on the road. "I like you too," Hae Na said.

Rowan laughed. Leaning over to Hae Na, she lay her head against her shoulder for a few seconds before pulling away.

August 14th 11:23 P.M.

Hae Na wrapped her arms around Rowan, the bed was small just like the dorm room. Rowan's things were mostly put away, in the dark the mess couldn't be seen. It was just Hae Na and Rowan. Hae Na smiled, burying her face in the back of Rowan's neck. There were no nightmares tonight, no shadows that turned into monsters. Just the warmth and comfort of someone who cared in a new uncomfortable place.

Hae Na didn't love Rowan, wasn't sure she could. Not the way that she had loved Sam before it turned to shit. She could be there when she needed to rant about her friends. She could be there to cuddle with her when she was lonely. She could hold her hand to feel connected. They could stay up late talking or eating late night snacks. Hae Na could do all that. Hae Na would be satisfied with that, she would have to be clear with Rowan about it. Even if they had talked about being in between friendship and a relationship, they hadn't figured out the details of it. Hae Na was sure of one thing though, she could love Rowan. She just didn't think she could be in love with her. Even with that she thought they would still be in each other's lives one way or another.

Chapter 24 Rye

Friday August 1st 3:02 P.M.

Rye laughed as Otis nearly tripped over the tent stake. He looked over as Otis' phone as it pinged with a message. He leaned over making sure it wasn't his mom. Not recognizing the name, he pulled back. Otis came back less than a minute later, Rye grinned at him.

"Do you feel like a real man, peeing in the woods?" Rye asked.

Otis smiled, posing as a strong man. Otis lowered his voice as he spoke. "Yes, I am now a man of the woods. Don't fear, we can survive anything."

Rye pretended to swoon. "Where have you been all my life, woodsman?"

"Waiting in the woods for you," he said, dropping down on the log next to Rye. Otis wrapped an arm around him, pulling him close. "We should probably start the fire soon."

Rye nodded. "Probably." It was a few more minutes before they moved. They built the fire, and Rye stood back as Otis lit it. After a few tries, it finally took. They took their places again, Rye watched the fire as Otis checked his phone. Rye refused to look over, he trusted Otis.

"Rye," Otis said.

Rye's focus was on the warmth of the fire and Otis at his side. "Hmm?" he responded, absently. Rye tilted his head back, looking up at the clear sky littered with stars.

Otis' voice was steady with an edge. "That guy messaged me," Otis said.

"What guy?" Rye asked. Otis stared at him, not buying his naive act. Rye stood up, shoving his hands in his pants pockets. "Okay, okay. You don't have to tell me anything," Rye said.

Otis followed him with his eyes opening the message, he held out the phone to Rye.

"I'm not going to hide anything," Otis said.

Rye didn't move. He trusted Otis but he didn't trust this guy. "Tell me what he said," Rye offered.

"Rye, read it." Otis shook the phone, waiting for him to grab it.

Rye shook his head. "No, I trust you. Whatever you tell me I'll believe," he said.

"I don't believe it," Otis' arm dropped, then lifted again for Rye to take the phone.

"What are you talking about?" Rye asked. What could he have said? Rye's curiosity was out weighing everything that held him back.

"Please?" There was something in his voice that changed, Rye took the phone. Rye scrolled through it. It wasn't just a message, there were pictures too. A few of them were Otis and the guy laying in bed, Otis seemed to be sleeping. A new one came in with a video. Rye shoved the phone in his back pocket. He looked at Otis, Otis was staring at him.

"I told my sister," Otis said, looking down at his feet.

Rye's voice was quiet when he spoke. "When?"

"A few days ago, she had me binge watch that one cop show about special victims."

Rye took a step closer, Otis reached out for him. "I'm so sorry," Rye whispered. It was nearly drowned out by the sound of bugs and creatures in the woods.

Otis shook his head. "I don't really remember, so I don't know how to feel. I know you tried to tell me before but I wasn't really listening."

Rye dropped to his knees in front of him, Otis looked away towards the woods. Rye held both of Otis's hands. Rye didn't move, he heard a clap of thunder and cursed the weather, it had been clear a minute ago. Otis didn't move, his grip held tighter. Rye looked up to the sky, he didn't notice the clouds had moved in so quickly, he was hoping it took at least until tomorrow for them to reach the campsite. Rye jumped when he felt drops fall on his head. He stood up, silently tugging Otis towards the tent. Otis willingly followed him. Rye let go of his right hand, ducking into the tent. Rye slid his shoes off in the entrance.

Rye sat on his claimed side of the tent, Otis kicked off his own shoes. "So I was raped." Otis said it so matter of factly.

Rye didn't answer, it wasn't a question and even if it was, Rye couldn't answer it. The rain hitting the tent drowned out all of the other sounds. Rye pulled his knees up in front of him, wrapping an arm around them as he stared at Otis. Otis had his eyes closed, the shadows made his light hair look dark. "What do I do now?" Otis asked.

"I don't know, is there something you want to do?"

"No, I just want to forget it, I mean I don't even remember it." Otis' voice was starting to rise. Otis sat up. "So what? He drugged me? I mean, you're right, when have I ever blacked out from drinking? So I was a target? He just handed me a drink and then what? He... he just... it's just over. He fucking took pictures and I have nothing, not a fucking memory. So I'm a victim who can't even remember the crime? Fucking convient, why the fuck would he send that? If he knew I wasn't going to remember why would he do that?" Otis waved his arms around before dropping them down his lap. "And it happens all the time, to women, men." Otis shook his head and then he looked over at Rye in horror.

"I'm so sorry Rye," Otis said. Rye was confused, didn't he already know that he didn't cheat on him?

"Why?" Rye's eyebrows furrowed as he looked at Otis.

"I made you..." Otis started.

Rye spoke up before Otis could finish. "Stop, stop you have never made me do anything," Rye said, trying to reassure Otis.

Otis shook his head. "But I pushed you." Guilt thickened his voice. Rye wanted to take it all away.

"Hey no, that's not what happened."

"You don't even like sex," Otis said.

"I never said that," Rye told him, shaking his head.

"Oh god I deserved this," Otis said, guilt on his face.

"Otis! Stop it! Listen to me. You didn't deserve that, no one does. It was horrible what happened, and if it had happened here I would tell you to report it. I don't think we can do anything since it happened in Germany and you're already home," Rye started. He wasn't finished, he could never let Otis believe he was like that man. "I love you, and yeah sex isn't the biggest thing for me, I'm asexual. We've talked about that, and you've always respected me when I say no."

"But-" Otis tried, stopping when Rye continued.

"I love you Otis and I like when we have sex. I like being with you, will I ask you for sex? No, probably not but it doesn't mean I don't want to be with you, I just would rather cuddle next to you than suck your cock. You have never made me do anything that I didn't want to do."

"You didn't want it though," Otis said as if begging Rye to tell him he was right. Otis was wrong.

"Otis, just because I'm asexual it doesn't mean I can't or don't like sex. You are not like him, you are not like men and women like him. We can do whatever you want so that you don't feel like you are." Rye never wanted Otis to feel like he forced Rye to do anything.

"Like what?" Otis asked, his eyes wide, his lip pushed up.

"I don't know. I can do something different. If I say yes then it's a yes, no is no a no. Does that work? You always ask me before we do anything anyway. Do you not realise that?" Rye asked, hoping Otis would see that he really was different.

"Well I just want to be sure you want to," Otis said.

Rye understood. "And that's what makes you different Otis. You don't take anything, you ask for it." Rye knew this wasn't going to fix it. He knew Otis was going to have to work towards asking him again. They had only had sex five times in the time that they had been going out. Rye knew they would work up to it again, but first Otis was going to have to heal. Maybe Otis didn't realise the damage that man had done, but Rye could see it. Rye held his hand out to Otis who ignored it. Instead Otis crawled towards Rye, he paused before touching him.

"Can I?" Rye asked before Otis could. Otis nodded, dropping his forehead to Rye's chest. Rye wrapped his arms around him. Germany was a lot higher on his travel list.

9:34 A.M.

Otis decided the rain wasn't going to stop their hike, Rye stared at him as if he was crazy. The rain hadn't let up a drop and when he went out to pee he came back soaked. Rye was still drying his hair when Otis announced they were still hiking.

"Shut up, no we aren't," Rye told him, throwing the wet towel at his face. Otis grabbed it, twisting it up. "I will kill you," Rye said, holding his arm out to stop him. "Oats, I swear I will."

Otis raised it up before dropping it, grinning brightly at him. "What else are we going to do all day?" he asked, and Rye stopped his retort, waiting for Otis to catch it. Rye frowned when he didn't, not even a waggle of eyebrows. "I guess we could drive some-where," Otis said, already looking up sites on his phone. "It's rain-ing pretty hard, driving might be a pain. We probably should have checked the weather."

"This wasn't my idea, it's all on you," Rye told him.

"Fine, I should have checked it," Otis said, smiling at Rye. Rye smiled back.

Monday August 4th 2:09 P.M.

Moving his things back to his house felt bittersweet. He felt as if he had just left for summer camp and just when he started feeling homesick and went home, he missed the camp. His mom opened the door as Otis parked.

She pulled him into a tight hug. "There's my baby. I missed you in Hawaii."

"You could have taken me," Rye muttered bitterly, she waved his words away with a hand behind his head.

She let go of Rye, turning her focus to Otis. "And you, how was Germany?"

"Good," Otis said.

She nodded, letting go of Rye and pulling Otis into a hug. "So are you boys hungry for some chinese?" she asked. It was just like old times.

It felt good to be home, he liked the feeling of leaving for a place and the feeling of coming back to the place he called home.

Wednesday August 8th 12:02 P.M.

Rye wiped at the counters, customers were abysmal on that Wednesday afternoon. His older coworker, Rob, was showing the newbie how to make ice burn. She poured the salt in her hand, closing her fist when he placed ice in her hand. She looked surprised for a second and thoughtful the next. Rye looked back to the front when two girls walked up, Rye smiled and they went to the counter with the tickets. Rye dropped the smile and checked if he needed to stock up on anything on the counter.

"Hey, what flag was that girl wearing?" Rob asked. Rye looked up but the girls were already gone. Mattie who had been working the tickets shrugged. "You have gay friends, shouldn't you know what it was?" Rob asked Mattie.

Mattie sighed, turning a bored look at him. "What does that have to do with anything?" She asked.

"Well shouldn't you know?" he asked. His tone leaned on the far side of accusing instead of curious.

Her hip was cocked against the counter as she stared at him. "I'm bad at memorizing things like that, they tell me them and then I forget. Why do you care?"

Rob held his hands up. "You don't have to get snappy, I was just asking."

"What color was it?" Rye asked. Rob looked at him as if he was changing his mind about Rye. Rye looked to Mattie who scrunched her forehead.

"Purple and black with white I think." Mattie said.

"Purple, grey, white and black?" Rye asked.

"Sounds good to me," she said, leaning back against the wall next to the counter. She yawned, turning her head to look at the empty lobby.

"So you know what it is then," Rob said, nudging Rye with his shoulder.

Rye hesitated to tell him but in the end he didn't think it was a big deal. "It was probably an asexual flag," Rye said. Rob laughed. Rye didn't know why it was funny but most of the time he didn't understand Rob.

"What is that? Like she can have babies by herself?"

"You are an idiot," Mattie said, emphasizing each word. Rob glared at her. Rye was already regretting telling him, now they were going to have to spend the rest of the day listening to Rob try to figure it out. Rye picked up a stray straw throwing it in the trash.

"Asexuality is the lack of sexual attraction to others, or low or absent interest in or desire for sexual activity, so basically they're a plant," Rob said in a condescending tone as he read off his phone.

"Shut up Rob," Mattie said. He did as the door opened again and a guy walked to her counter.

Rye wasn't opposed to being called a plant, there were definitely worse things. Plants were pretty, useful, dangerous, it probably depended on what plant he was being referred to.

"Its bullshit though, that's just an excuse for women to say they don't want to have sex." Rob commented.

"It's not only women," Rye said, feeling the solid ground below him get lower as he dug his own hole.

"Yeah right, what guy doesn't want sex? And any guy who says he doesn't is lying for attention or for some girl to offer it to him thinking he's a nice guy or some bullshit."

"That's not true," Rye said. The ground might have been sinking beneath him but he was going to stand on it no matter what. He wasn't going to let Rob spout off ignorant shit.

"Like you would know," Rob responded, as if the possibility was out of a fantasy.

"I'm asexual," Rye said and he felt like the hole completely dropped, leaving it so far above his head that he wouldn't even be able to climb out. He didn't look at Rob, instead he found a clean spot to clean again.

"I heard you and Mattie talking about your girlfriend the other day," Rob said, as if that made it even more impossible.

"So?" Rye asked. Right now he felt if he told him that Otis was a guy it would only get worse. He wasn't ashamed, he just wanted to avoid the confrontation. Rye was getting sick of hearing Rob talk.

"So you're telling me you don't have sex with her? Then you're not dating, that's called friendship. I bet she's cheating on you with a guy who will have sex with her." Rob laughed after his comment, as if he were a comedian who loved his own jokes.

That hit him hard, Rye clenched his fist in the rag. Mattie spoke up before he could even look to see the disgusting face of Rob.

"That's fucking bullshit, you don't have to have sex with someone to love them, you have sex with your mom? Or your sister?" she asked. He wasn't sure if family was the right way to go.

"I ain't dating them, and what about you? You don't have sex?" he asked her as if accusing her of a crime.

"Yeah, I do, but it doesn't dictate whether I'm in a relationship or not. If I want to be with someone and they love me they sure as fuck better respect whether I want to have sex with them or not. If I never want to have sex with them or anyone ever again he better respect it. That doesn't mean we become friends, he would still be my boyfriend without sex," Mattie said. She sounded annoyed and tired as she talked to Rob.

"So you're saying it's a choice, so you can have sex, then being asexual or whatever is fake. And it's not really love unless you have sex with them and if they dont isn't that rape?"

Rye stood away from the counter, dropping the rag on the floor. He was pissed and he wasn't going to let him continue being ignorant. "What the fuck is wrong with you? It's not a choice, and yes asexuals can and some do have sex. It's their choice what they do and if they have relationships where they do, it doesnt mean they're not asexual and if they have relationships where they don't, it doesn't mean that they aren't in a relationship. You don't know what the fuck you're talking about and you're making yourself sound like a fucking asshole."

"You're lucky I don't deck your fucking face," Rob said. He pushed Rye away from him. Images of Otis and the asshole in Germany swam in his head, The video he had made knowing what he did to Otis and not giving a fuck. Rye swung his fist, he was in shock as he watched Rob slip back on the floor.

12:59 P.M.

Rye sat in the driveway in stunned silence staring at his slightly pink knuckles. He jumped when he heard knocking on his window. Carter was smiling at him as she peeked inside his window. Rye shut the car off, carefully opening the door as she got out. Grateful his mom let him driver car that day for work.

"Rye come with us for candy!" she yelled, her voice deep. She raised her fists in the air as if it was a large victory.

"Uh." He looked up to Wyatt who was holding Lio, an eyebrow raised as he looked at him. "Sure, let me change first," he said.

"Hurry," Carter said, starting to push his legs to the house. He helped her by quickening his pace, he passed by Wyatt into the house and when he got to his room he realized he didn't live there anymore. Rye leaned against the doorframe.

"Long day at work? I think it's only been like an hour."

"It... I got fired, can I at least borrow a shirt?"

"You know where they are," Wyatt said, he turned away. Rye followed him to the bottom of the stairs before taking them at a run. He went to the clean basket grabbing a grey shirt of Wyatt's and Sawyer's black shorts. Rye changed quickly making it back down the stairs as Carter pouted and tapped her foot. When she saw him, she hit her wrist where a red and yellow watch sat.

"So slow," she said. Her whole body drooped as if the wait had drained her. Wyatt nudged her with a knee and she took off for the door like a rocket. As she scrambled out of the door, Wyatt looked at him. "Why did you get fired?"

"I punched a coworker," Rye said. Wyatt's face did a strange mix of emotions before he laughed. "Seriously?"

"He said some shitty stuff and I got angry."

"You got angry? The one who put on tutu's and danced ballet with Carter around the house? You, who didn't even gag when Lio puked in your mouth? You, who-"

"Okay, I get it, damn."

"If you got that angry then it must have been pretty bad."

"It wasn't that bad, it was just shitty and ignorant. I was mad about some other stuff and I kind of just took it out on him," Rye said. He got in the passenger seat. Wyatt went to the back to strap Lio in.

"Carter, Rye had a bad day so what kind of candy do you think we should get him?"

"You don't-" You don't have to was what Rye was going to say but Carter cut him off, her voice louder than him. Wyatt was already pulling his door open and sitting down as she started yelling.

"Sour candy! And sweet candy, hot and lots of candy" She clapped her hands several times. "Ice cream," she added. "Ice cream and candy."

"Has she had caffeine?" Rye asked, he looked back at Carter who bounced in her seat. She got even more excited when Wyatt turned on the music.

"She took a nap today, she had a nightmare so she didn't sleep as much last night." Rye nodded, smiling at Carter who was making faces as she sang.

The candy store was massive, Carter slipped through their legs and made a run for it.

"Carter no running," Wyatt said, handing Lio to Rye as he went after her. Lio struggled in his arms to be let down, Rye let him, following closely behind him as he giggled while he followed after Wyatt and Carter. He ran a few steps before he dropped to start crawling. Rye lifted him up, showing him the different types of candy. Lio reached out for every piece, Rye kept him at a safe distance. Rye maneuvered them around the other customers through the store. He tried to keep Lio interested enough in the things he could just barely grab, and when Lio would get frustrated they would move on. He was slowly realising how much he was going to miss them.

Monday August 11th 2:07 P.M.

Rye squished himself into the side of the couch, his legs were pulled up tight to his chest. His mom was standing next to the coffee table separating different pieces of fabric. Rye had asked her a question she had yet to answer.

She stopped sorting, setting her hand on a purple and blue floral patterned piece of fabric. "Before I tell you the answer, I want to apologize. I made a lot of mistakes. I shouldn't have kept your other mother away." She held her hand up, stopping him from protesting. "Yes, we both agreed but I brought up points that forced her hand. It was a mistake," she said. She began separating the fabrics again. He couldn't tell how she was dividing them up, or if she even knew.

She continued speaking. "I love your other mother," she added. Rye didn't miss the word love instead of loved. "I didn't leave her because she transitioned. I still wanted to be with her. She didn't want me. I was afraid you would choose her over me, you two were so close. So I pushed her to leave without you while she transitioned. I'm so sorry Rye. I thought you would go with her for the summer," she told him.

Rye looked to his left, on the wall was a photo. It was of Rye and Nalani, Rye was three in the photo. He was laughing while Nalani smiled brightly at the camera. His mom hadn't gotten rid of any of her photos. Some of Nalani's old clothes sat in a box in her closet. "I didn't want to force you, so when you told me you were staying at a friend's house, I didn't say anything. Nalani told me that your meetings were going well so I left it alone. Except your outburst, Rye how could you treat her like that?"

Rye didn't know how he felt. It was as if too many emotions were warring against each other and canceling each other out, leaving him confused and numb. His mom still loved Nalani. Nalani was a happily remarried woman. Rye was a lost and confused teenager with no clear goal for the future. Rye looked at his mom, her head ducked down towards the table. Rye choked, tears streaming hotly down his face. His mom's head shot up. He couldn't hold back a sob. He cried harder when she wrapped her arms around him. Rye clung onto her, he had missed his mom. Otis had hurt him, Nalani hadn't trusted him. Rye had felt alone, all summer. Even with everyone in the house, they had been a distraction. He thought he handled everything like an adult, he had been pretending.

Chapter 25 Sawyer
Wednesday August 27th 3:07 P.M.

Sawyer had gone to the airport too early and now he was leaning against the wall near arrivals waiting. The plane wouldn't land for another 30 minutes and he would have to pay more for parking. He looked around at the other arrivals, some greeted family, others continued on to baggage claim. He couldn't remember if Wyatt checked in a bag or not.

He scuffed his shoe on the floor, looking up when he heard a squealing sound similar to Carter's voice. Instead of a child it was a young woman. She dropped her bag, it slid towards the man who opened his arms. She jumped into them, it was very moviesque. He spun a few times before letting her down and picking up her bag. They left holding hands, he vaguely wondered why they didn't kiss. He shrugged off the idea and thought of how Wyatt would react if he tried to jump into his arms. He didn't doubt Wyatt could hold his weight, he was more interested in his reaction. They hadn't done more than hold hands in public and he never thought to ask him how he felt about PDA. The only time they had really gone on a date was when they went out of town. Doubt swirled in his mind.

He was surprised when his phone started vibrating. "Hello?" His voice expressed his surprise.

"Did you forget to pick me up?" Wyatt asked.

"No, why would you think that?"

"Your voice, also we just landed," Wyatt answered. Sawyer could hear the background noise of passengers grabbing luggage and shuffling around.

"You're early and I'm here," Sawyer told him.

"Only by five minutes, I'm hanging up now."

"Wait, I have a question," Sawyer said, though it took Wyatt's prompting for him to ask. "How do you feel about PDA?" Sawyer asked, picking at a hold in the bottom of his shirt.

"Are you asking me about having sex somewhere or asking if you can kiss me when I get off the plane?" Wyatt asked, loud enough that Sawyer was sure everyone on the plane heard.

"Look around, do you see those looks on their faces?" Sawyer asked.

Sawyer could imagine Wyatt's defiant face. "I don't care about their faces, I only care about your's," Wyatt said.

Sawyer ignored the warm feeling. "So how do you feel about it?" he asked again.

"It depends on what you mean."

"The kissing," Sawyer explained.

"Then I'm fine with it," Wyatt told him, causing Sawyer to smile.

"Just fine?" Sawyer asked, he needed to be sure.

"I'd be disappointed if you didn't," he said. Sawyer grinned when the phone hung up before he could answer him.

Sawyer pushed away from the wall, now eagerly awaiting Wyatt. A few people had shifted around when another plane landed and people continued to pour out from the escalators. Sawyer rocked on his heels, his eyes scanning the crowd. More people moved, there were more conversations and cries of joy as people were reunited. Then Sawyer saw him; he only had a backpack on, his own eyes were scanning the crowd. Sawyer waited until they landed on him before he smiled. Sawyer took several steps back, away from the growing crowd as Wyatt weaved through people exiting the escalator. Wyatt was surprised when Sawyer began running. Wyatt froze and braced for impact, Sawyer laughed in his arms. Wyatt quickly slid his arms under him to keep him in place and walked to the wall, pushing him against it.

"I missed you, kids are at Marina's," Sawyer said, giving him a butterfly kiss before moving in for a real kiss. Wyatt obliged, pushing him further into the wall. Thoughts disappeared when Wyatt closed the distance between them and pressed his lips to Sawyer's. Every rational and irrational thought disappeared, his only focus was the desperate and soft kiss; it was everything he had been missing and wanting since Wyatt had left. Sawyer pulled away grinning. Sawyer wrapped his arms around his shoulders holding him in a tight hug. "We are not having sex here, let me down," Sawyer demanded, even though he never wanted Wyatt to let go.

"*I don't want to,*" Wyatt responded in Korean. Sawyer pulled out of the hug setting his forehead against Wyatt's, he rolled his eyes.

"You think I don't know what that means, but I do. With you, Hae Na and now Carter speaking it, I catch onto things."

"사랑해" Wyatt continued in Korean.

"I love you too," Sawyer responded in English. Wyatt smiled, letting Sawyer's legs drop to the ground.

Sawyer rolled his eyes. "You better not leave again."

Wyatt lifted an eyebrow. "Who was the idiot who wanted me to go off to college? You can barely last two weeks, also did you gain weight? Have you been stress eating?"

"Shut up, you sanitized rag," Sawyer muttered.

Wyatt laughed. "I think we need to work on your insults."

"I like them, you dirty balloon animal," Sawyer said, smiling.

Wyatt knocked his shoulder into Sawyer's. "Soggy pillow," Wyatt said.

"Cracked remote," Sawyer shot back. They continued back and forth until they got to the car.

Wyatt leaned in towards Sawyer as they walked. "Crusty door handle," Wyatt said.

"Sticky coaster."

"Rancid spoon," Sawyer responded back.

"Loose socket."

Chapter 26 Wyatt

Wednesday August 27th 7:34 P.M.

"I never thought a play date sleepover was a thing, but now I think it's the absolute best thing in the world, also don't tell Carter you got home today, she thinks you're getting back tomorrow," Sawyer said, tipping the bottle to fill the shot glasses. He pulled it back, sliding one to Wyatt. They both threw the shots back, Wyatt watched Sawyer grimace at the burn, his body gave a shiver.

Wyatt did a quick drum roll on Sawyer's left leg. "I know, so T.V. marathon or dance party?" he asked.

Sawyer watched his hands before looking up at him. "First food, then more alcohol, then a dance party while we cook and T.V. marathon while we eat."

Wyatt squeezed his leg before slapping it, he stood up before Sawyer could retaliate. "Finally, the man has a good idea," Wyatt said.

"Dick," Sawyer said, kicking his leg out and missing Wyatt as he stepped back. Wyatt headed towards the kitchen backwards.

"Drunk already? My name is Wyatt," Wyatt called out. Sawyer got up following, he reached out trying to grab Wyatt who ducked out of his grasp.

"Shut up," Sawyer muttered.

Wyatt grinned, he dodged around like he was kicking a soccer ball. "Make me," Wyatt teased.

Sawyer shook his head. "Hmm, maybe later." Sawyer looked into the fridge and then the cupboards. "Maybe we should order something."

"Mr. Money bags wants to order food?"

"Shut up, we haven't had takeout in awhile."

"Korean sounds good," Sawyer said, turning to stare at Wyatt.

Wyatt patted his stomach. "See now you're speaking to my stomach."

Sawyer sighed. "We don't have any Korean delivery," he told him.

Wyatt shook his head. "An honest tragedy, especially since there is everything but," Wyatt said. He reached out for Sawyer, Sawyer looked from his hand to his eyes.

"So Chinese?" Sawyer offered. Wyatt nodded. "Good, we can take another shot while we wait." Sawyer took his hand, a small smile on his face as their fingers intertwined.

"Yeah," Wyatt said.

Sawyer led him back to the living room, holding tight to Wyatt's hand. Wyatt smiled brightly behind him. He never wanted to let his hand go.

9:37 P.M.

"I miss them, I miss them so much," Wyatt moved forward. "Don't leave! Please." Sawyer reached forward grabbing onto Wyatt.

"I'm pausing the movie," Wyatt said, his voice quiet and calm. Sawyer let him go, Wyatt paused the movie. He shifted to make it more comfortable for both of them. Sawyer was tucked down next to him, Wyatt's arm wrapped around him. "I should have waited. If I came with you then none of this would have happened."

"Sawyer, it's not your fault," Wyatt told him.

"Then why do I feel so guilty?" Sawyer asked, looking up at him. Wyatt didn't answer.

Sawyer grabbed Wyatt's hand after he set the bottle down. He placed his fingers in between Wyatt's. "I want to hold your hand," Sawyer stated.

"I brought you something."

"Is it candy? Oh no, ice cream. Ice cream sounds so good right now," Sawyer said dreamily, forgetting about Wyatt to his dessert fantasies.

"Not quite," Wyatt shifted. Getting off of the couch, he stopped when he was tugged back. He looked down to where he was still holding Sawyer's hand.

"Don't let go," Sawyer begged.

"My bag is upstairs," Wyatt said, Sawyer frowned. Sawyer suddenly jumped up, wobbling before he grabbed the bottle and bumped into Wyatt.

"Ow," Sawyer said, pulling back to glare at Wyatt's back. "Let's go," he lifted the bottle up as if going into battle. Wyatt took the bottle grinning stupidly at Sawyer as they climbed and tripped and slipped down the stairs. They both lay awkwardly against the stairs, Wyatt's stomach burning from laughter. Sawyer had yet to let go of his hand.

"Wyatt, come on." Sawyer tried and failed to pull Wyatt up the stairs. Wyatt tugged Sawyer further down. Wyatt kissed Sawyer's chin, Sawyer slid further down, making Wyatt kiss his nose and then his forehead. Wyatt stared down at Sawyer who stared up at him. "You're really cute," Sawyer said.

"Shut up," Wyatt said.

"So cute, like uh…" Sawyer stuck his tongue out a bit before pulling it back in. "A bunny," he finally finished.

Wyatt pushed at him. "You're drunk."

"On your love," Sawyer replied, giggling as he did.

"Oh god," Wyatt said, tilting his head back on the stairs.

"No, I'm Sawyer," Sawyer said, laughing as he started climbing up a stair to meet Wyatt.

Wyatt flicked his forehead, then rubbing his thumb over it. "Shut up," he said softly.

"I love you," Sawyer said.

Wyatt moved his hand to cup Sawyer's face. "Yeah me too,"

he said, leaning and pulling Sawyer closer to him. Sawyer's grin slowly faded before it disappeared with a kiss from Wyatt. Wyatt pulled away, "Come on, I'm not making out with you on the stairs."

"Why not?" Sawyer whined. Sawyer kissed him again, and a third time. He pulled away Sawyer's hands wandering under Wyatt's shirt.

"Because you have a bed," Wyatt told him.

Sawyer paused with his mouth open. "Oh yeah," he said. Sawyer crawled after Wyatt up the stairs, then proceeded to fall onto his bed. "Nice bed, no don't let go," Sawyer said as Wyatt tiredly walked away.

Wyatt looked at him. "Do you want your gift?" he asked.

"I want your hand." Sawyer's smile was lopsided as he reached for him again.

"Should we go back to the kitchen for a knife?" Wyatt asked.

Sawyer's face scrunched up. "A knife?" he asked.

Wyatt shook his wrist. "So you can have my hand."

Sawyer shook his head, his voice sappy as he spoke, "No, don't hurt yourself, I love you."

"Yeah, yeah I know," Wyatt's smile was broad.

"I love you, I love you I looooove you," Sawyer sang out. Wyatt had never felt happier.

"I love you too, so do you want it or not?" Wyatt asked.

Sawyer bobbed his head yes, reaching his arms out. "Yes, I want it, gimmie."

Wyatt hesitated staring at the happiness on Sawyer's face. And then he reached in his backpack and pulled out an ouija board. Sawyer stared at it. "Are we actually going to use it?"

"Do you want to?" Wyatt asked, hesitating.

Sawyer shrugged. "Yeah, let's do it, wait, we need, like, a candle or something."

"No, we'll end up with the house burning down around us. I already got a candle app, so we're fine," Wyatt said, shutting the light off and turning on the app for his phone and Sawyer's lamp before grabbing his bag.

"A candle app?" Sawyer asked, shaking his head. Wyatt set the board on the bed, sitting down across from Sawyer.

"Yeah and here's the planchette," Wyatt said, setting the wooden magnifying glass on the board.

Sawer smiled at him, his body tilting to the side. "Fancy, you even know the name for it."

"I do, put your fingers on it," Sawyer did as instructed, Wyatt putting his own fingers on it. "Ask it something," Wyatt said, Sawyer looked at him. Wyatt nodded his head forward.

"Like what?" Sawyer asked.

Wyatt shrugged. "Anything."

Sawyer looked back down at the board. "Hmm." Sawyer stared at the board, shifting around the planchette.. "Am I going to puke tonight?" He slid it to yes and laughed. Wyatt let him ask dumb questions and moved it around the board to answer them. Sawyer lost his smile and Wyatt nearly missed the next question. "Are you proud of me?" Sawyer didn't move it, Wyatt slowly slid it to yes. Sawyer surged forward wrapping his arms around Wyatt, knocking them both off of the bed. Wyatt tried to breathe, he didn't push Sawyer off of him. Instead they lay on the floor until they both fell asleep.

5:07 A.M.

Wyatt woke up with pressure on his chest. Sawyer was still laying on him, Wyatt wriggled his way out from under him. He grabbed Sawyer, pulling him onto the bed. Sawyer barely fought him and when he was on the bed he snuggled into his pillow. Wyatt pulled off his drool covered shirt, throwing it at Sawyer's face. He stretched out, grabbing the ouija board off of the bed. He dropped it on the floor, pulling the blanket over Sawyer before heading downstairs for food.

He finally understood what family was. Family stood at his back, protecting him. Family stood in front of him, guiding him. Family stood next to him, accepting him. Wyatt may have been naive, his mother may have been right. But he had learned that family was important and he loved them more than anything.

Chapter 27 Hae Na
Thursday August 21st 6:14 P.M.

Hae Na stared at the shoe-streaked white speckled tile floor thinking of all the people who had come here before her. Their footprints were swept away each day, some shoe prints returned and others didn't. Today was her turn to tell her story, to share the darkest part of her life. To share everything that made her into the person she was, to show the cause of her move, the loss of her degree, the disconnect with her family, the loss of the person she thought loved her.

Hae Na looked up, she saw the faces of people who knew her pain, who understood her. There was no judgment in this room, no rejection or misunderstandings.

"My name is Hae Na, I've sat here for weeks listening to everyone's story. I've related to a few of them and others in my head I was like why didn't you leave? Why didn't you just take your things and leave? And then I realised that I didn't either. I let my girlfriend abuse me, I let her hit me when she was angry. I let that happen because I thought that it was okay. I thought that if she loved me then it was okay. The bruises would heal and she wouldn't be angry forever. I was wrong."

"I left because she shoved pills down my throat. That was my breaking point, that was when I thought, no this is enough. I did try and leave her but I went back. I chose her, I chose her over my family. I couldn't be wrong, because that would mean I lost the love of my life and my family. Then what am I left with? Myself. My mother couldn't understand why I would choose a woman. She thinks it's a choice, with everything going on in the world she still thinks that sexuality is a choice. Like the worst thing I could do to her is bring a girl home and never have a child. There are people starving, people dying of incurable diseases but this is the worst thing I've done.

"It's not my whole family, not everyone knows. My cousin's parents don't care, my cousin doesn't care. When I left home, I thought I had the world. I had someone who I loved and who loved me, I was going to college, I was independent and free. Then she closed me off, I was losing friends, I was skipping classes to hide bruises. This wasn't the carefree life I thought I was going to live.

"When I left I had nowhere to go, my home wasn't an option so I turned to someone who offered me kindness. She offered me a card, a safe haven. I met amazingly strong women and I realized that leaving wasn't always an option. Everyone has different circumstances, being alive is better than being dead. I realized that when I nearly overdosed on pills and alcohol.

"Some women can't leave if they want to survive and some can't stay if they want to live. Society forces us to judge actions we don't understand. A woman who stays in an abusive relationship because of a child, a woman who can't leave because it's easier to see your enemy face to face instead of constantly looking over your shoulder. I met a lot of women after leaving and each one has a different story, a different monster in their bed. But I learned that we're all the same, we all have a monster. People who aren't in this room have a monster; abuse, mental illness, addiction, depression, grief, fear, stress. We all have a monster and we all cope differently. Ice cream after a breakup, frozen peas on a black eye, a nap when the world is too much to cope with.

"I'm sorry, I'm preaching at this point. What I want to say is that everyone has strength even if it doesn't feel like it. Even if you're hiding under the blanket hoping that the darkness surrounding you is really just the dark and not a monster lurking close. Whether it takes one day, one month, ten years, whether we stay away or whether we go back. One day we'll all be free and have the strength to make it happen." Hae Na finished her story, realizing she never really told her story like the others. She didn't tell them that Sam had first hit her when they had both been drinking at a bar. A girl had bumped into her and spilled her drink, Sam had walked over when the woman was wiping down the front of Hae Na's shirt. The woman had been so drunk that the moment she turned away from Hae Na, the spilled shirt was out of her mind and she was grabbing onto some guy's arm she probably didn't know.

Sam had gripped her wrist so hard Hae Na was sure it would snap in her hand. She was yanked outside, Sam dragged her all the way home and pushed her so hard into the wall it left a dent.

She didn't tell her story the same way because they all had gone through similar things, they knew what abuse was, she didn't need to tell them. Instead, she wanted to tell them how far she had come, the person she had now become. How much she had grown, she wasn't done yet. She had a new goal, she was going to be like Henny and help young women like herself.

Chapter 28 Rye
Saturday August 23rd 12:07 P.M.

His hair and clothes were still damp from the rain outside, the hot latte in front of him helped keep his hands and insides warm. Rye sat across from Max, while Nalani sat across from his mom who sat at his side. They had been talking like old friends for nearly an hour. He and Max gave each other small smiles every time they happened to look at each other. Most of the time Rye went through random things on his phone, it was starting to get really old now.

Max leaned forward. "Have you decided on where your first destination will be?" he asked. Rye was surprised by the question, he set his phone down looking up at him. He hadn't thought about it but he knew anyway. Germany had been his first thought after hearing Otis' story but really that's not where he wanted to go. He wasn't ready to confront that. Instead, he wanted to follow Wyatt, he had two destinations in mind. South Korea and Japan.

"I think I want to go to South Korea and Japan."

"Any reason or just have an interest?"

"Hae Na and Wyatt are Korean. Wyatt just got back from visiting his family in South Korea and it looked amazing. I also thought of Japan since it's so close and there's so much to see there."

Max nodded, his smile gentle. "That sounds like a great plan, How long do you plan to stay?"

"Uh, that I don't know," Rye told him, picking at his cheese danish. He didn't really know much.

"You could always buy a one-way ticket," Max told him, his comment stopped the conversation next to them.

Rye smiled at him. "Yeah, I could do that."

"It gives you a bit more freedom with time. You can tell me when you're ready to come home and we'll buy your ticket back."

"You don't have to do that," Rye told him.

"We want to. We would also like you to visit and stay with us sometime," Max said. Max had a gentle voice when he spoke. "If you want to," he added.

"I- Yeah I do," Rye told them, pushing his mom off as she wrapped her arms around him, pulling him into a tight hug.

Rye didn't have a plan for the future, but he did have people around him who loved him. He had people who would be around if he asked for help, not only his family but the one he had created at Sawyer's. He had people behind him so he was more confident in walking forward, even if Otis wasn't by his side at that moment. Otis would be there when he reached out to him.

Chapter 29 Charley and Marco Losada
Friday April 4th 6:31 P.M.

Charley leaned across the dinner table, her eyes looking around as if there were people spying on them. Her husband humored her antics by slowly leaning forward.

"Why do you think Sawyer really offered us the night off?" she asked. She didn't move away, instead, her soft gaze stayed on her husband's dark brown eyes.

"Wyatt will probably be over," he said.

She grinned as if that was the answer she was waiting for. She pulled away, excitement clear on her face. "I think he's going to confess," she said.

Her husband rolled his eyes but smiled at her anyway. "He won't," Marco told her. She pouted, reaching for her drink. She held it before her mouth, setting it back on the table.

"It won't be long before they go off to college, it has to be soon or it may not happen at all."

"They're kids, does it really need to happen?" he asked.

"No, I suppose it really doesn't but I think they would be great together. Wyatt has been around for years, you've seen how much happier he is with Sawyer."

"It may not be the same when they go to college. They may find other people," he told her, always the voice of reason to her small dramatics.

"You're right, but-"

"Darling, if you want him to tell Wyatt then you're going to have to tell him you know about his crush. How do you think he's going to feel about that?" he asked. She mock glared at him.

"I can push without being obvious, they should see if it works, if not then it doesn't." She shrugged as if she wasn't interested but he knew she was.

"And if they stop being friends?" he asked. She drooped down at his question and sighed, sitting back in her chair. She didn't answer his question. He sat forward. "I do think they could last long term, but pushing them before they're ready to say something, won't help them."

"Fine fine, I'm just so proud of the two of them. I want them to be happy."

He smiled at her, reaching across the table for her hand. She set her hand in his. "So do I," he told her.

"And you know if they ever stopped being friends Carter would be devastated not to have her Yaya around. Oh no, she's going to be a nightmare when he leaves for college."

"She won't care when Sawyer leaves but the moment Wyatt is gone, that's when the fits will start," Marco told her with a smirk.

"She's been so good until now," Charley sighed, before laughing at the thought.

Marco looked at his watch and then back to his wife. "We may have left too early for dinner."

"What about we drive around and get some dessert?"

"I think that is a lovely idea from my beautiful scheming wife," he told her. She smiled back, as pretty as the day he met her. He never wanted to live a day without her.

CPSIA information can be obtained
at www.ICGtesting.com
Printed in the USA
BVHW031705120121
597662BV00001B/44

9 781735 864808